Flying at Night

Center Point
Large Print

**This Large Print Book carries the
Seal of Approval of N.A.V.H.**

Flying at Night

REBECCA L. BROWN

CENTER POINT LARGE PRINT
THORNDIKE, MAINE

The text of this Large Print edition is unabridged.
In other aspects, this book may vary
from the original edition.
Printed in the United States of America
on permanent paper.
Set in 16-point Times New Roman type.

ISBN: 978-1-68324-911-5

Library of Congress Cataloging-in-Publication Data

Names: Brown, Rebecca L. (Rebecca Lynn), 1976- author.
Title: Flying at night / Rebecca L. Brown.
Description: Center Point Large Print edition. | Thorndike, Maine :
    Center Point Large Print, 2018.
Identifiers: LCCN 2018024544 | ISBN 9781683249115
    (hardcover : alk. paper)
Subjects: LCSH: Housewives—Fiction. | Mothers of children with
    disabilities—Fiction. | Autistic children—Family relationships—
    Fiction. | Air pilots—Fiction. | Grandparent and child—Fiction. |
    Domestic fiction. | Psychological fiction. | Large type books.
Classification: LCC PS3602.R722694 F59 2018 | DDC 813/.6—dc23
LC record available at https://lccn.loc.gov/2018024544

For Tom, who will always be home to me

Author's Note

When my son was in fifth grade, he had a difficult year. He was kind and thoughtful, but didn't make connections with other kids easily. He was smart, but couldn't focus in school or understand body language and nonverbal cues. He was floundering. He was evaluated by a pediatric neuropsychologist and, much as with Fred in *Flying at Night*, the diagnosis came back as high-functioning autism spectrum disorder.

To say that I was shocked would be putting it lightly. As Fred's mother, Piper, says, I fell into "the black hole of his diagnosis." Not only was I sure it was my fault. I was certain I should have caught it sooner. It took me a good deal of time to come to terms with what my son's diagnosis meant for his life. I felt like a horrible mother. Everyone kept telling me that he was still the same kid, but why didn't I feel that way?

With time comes a good deal of perspective and knowledge, and when I wrote *Flying at Night*, I had a great deal more of both. My son was doing well, making his way through life in his own quirky way: happy and successful. Pure of heart and amazingly self-aware, he gave me his blessing to talk about his journey, because he wanted the world to know what people labeled with autism spectrum disorder could achieve.

I knew what I needed to write wasn't a manual on dealing with autism, nor did I want to hold up my family's experience with autism as a shining example of success. What I wished I had during my own darkest days was some reassurance that this multitude of confusing emotions was *okay*. There is a side to parenting that we don't share on Facebook and Instagram: the gritty, ugly, hard things about loving so deeply and so purely.

Flying at Night is an ode to mothers who fight impossible battles for their children every day without blinking, go to sleep and get up and do the same again. We never know the hidden struggles that others are waging unless we bring our own pain and heartache out of the darkness and share it. We share it for one reason: so others know they are not alone. Thank you, dear reader, for opening your heart.

Rebecca L. Brown

Flying at Night

I *Autumn*

Piper

You would think that a woman named after a plane, the daughter of the briefly famous emergency-landing pilot "the Silver Eagle," would feel at home in the sky. At least she'd be comfortable with the idea of flight. Rather, I've spent my entire life close to the ground, not trusting that steel tube to stay aloft so far above land, or maybe not trusting the man flying it. My stubborn reluctance to fly was further evidence to my father of my status as second-rate adventurer and thus second-rate child. This battle over flight raged for my entire childhood, but airplanes never played as prominent a role in my life as they did from the fourth birthday of my son, Fred, until three months before his fifth. For those nine months, I lived and breathed jets, helicopters and fighter planes. I called my son Orville at his demand. I stalked appliance stores for refrigerator boxes that could stand in for crude, wobbly airplanes—cardboard boxes that Fred ate in, played in and slept in when I was simply too worn-out to fight him.

As you can imagine, my father, Captain Lance "the Silver Eagle" Whitman, was thrilled with my son's obsession. For those nine months, I was elevated to the first-class status I had craved my entire life. My father saw me. And, more important, he saw my son. He did everything he could to feed Fred's obsession. He sent us links to Web sites that categorized every aircraft that flew before 1965 and troubling GIFs of planes crashing, which I dragged right to the trash. My father bought Fred subscriptions to somewhat obscure magazines with bikini-clad models lazing on the noses of jets, which Fred never batted an eye at. Whenever the Silver Eagle wasn't actively flying and Fred was awake, he wanted to meet us at the airport, where we could sit by the windows that overlooked the runway and he could answer Fred's questions about elevation and capacity, while Fred expertly removed each sprinkle from a doughnut to eat individually. Fred was the apple of my father's eye and I was lucky enough to bask in the cast-off glow as the person responsible for shepherding Fred to and from my father.

And then it was over. The morning Fred woke up and renounced his seven a.m. viewing of *Planes and How They Fly!* I was immediately transported back to my ten-year-old self, the one who had refused to step onto Daddy's plane, knowing she'd pay the price—his silence—for days. Airplanes faded from Fred's mind as quickly as they had rooted themselves there nine months earlier. He no longer called me Piper, and

I became Mommy once again. Fred's miniature metal airplanes lay grounded in their basket in his room for a week before I had the courage to return my father's calls and politely decline his invitation to join him at the airport.

"What do you mean he doesn't want to go to the airport? It's been over a week."

"I asked him, Dad; he doesn't want to go. He's drawing race cars right now."

"Let me talk to him, Pipe."

I turned to hand Fred the phone, but he met my look with a steely gaze. His feelings were clear. "So, Dad? I don't think Fred's into planes anymore."

"Of course he is. It's not something you just forget about one day."

"I think it is for Fred." Fred was oblivious to my conversation, oblivious to the amount of courage it took for me to let down my father.

The Silver Eagle didn't go down without a fight. "I'll give it a day."

When after three tries the answer from Fred was the same, my father gave up. Gave up on me, gave up on Fred, gave up on us. The light that had shone in his eyes when he'd discussed Cessnas with Fred was gone.

Fred never showed any sign that he mourned the loss of his grandfather's attention; it was all too obvious to me that I had a much larger stake in our interdependent relationship. The Silver

15

Eagle had been a conduit for information, and when Fred's need for information died, so too did his interest in my father. I cringed to think that maybe they weren't so different after all. Fred moved on to race cars and we immersed ourselves in the world of Formula One, learning the names of drivers and sponsors as if they were the letters of the alphabet. After his interest in that was worn-out, he moved on, oddly, to arachnids, and so did I. We spent hours outside searching for spiders to trap and hold in plastic containers until they died and Fred wept for them. During that time, he requested that I call him Charlotte, which was awkward for me in social situations, but as usual Fred was oblivious to his own strangeness.

After he tired of spiders, it was on to the mechanics and wonders of the human body. His passion for how things worked knew no limits. In the evening, after Fred tossed and turned his way to eventual sleep, I watched videos of the inside of the throat during a hiccup so the next day I was ready to give an answer to the question that had stumped me earlier. Fred was well versed in the details of sex education long before most children, and, embarrassingly, he educated several members of his kindergarten class.

And the questions . . . . There was a relentless surge from his mouth every moment he was awake. Questions in the car that had no answers:

"Mom, why is this a car seat?" Questions I couldn't escape. My therapist told me that no one's brain can handle so much stimulation and I should just inform my son when I'd had enough that I would take a break from listening for five minutes and he shouldn't expect an answer. He began directing his questions to whatever inanimate object he happened to see out the window. While the chatter didn't stop, my responsibilities lessened for minutes at a time.

My husband, Isaac, preferred to make up answers. His gentle playfulness was mostly well received, but I grew tired of the silliness and wondered why he felt it was acceptable to tell our son things such as "The water in the lake only looks blue, Freddy. It's actually more of a persimmon paisley sort of thing." Isaac swung him up into the air and Fred begged to be let go, then immediately asked to be swung again. When I asked Isaac if it was really a good idea to lie to our son, he said, "Life's short. He'll find out the real, boring answers soon enough. Let's let him be silly and just be a kid." I don't know if it was the fatigue of his punishing work schedule or his genetic and unending optimism, but I felt in that moment that perhaps he didn't really know our son at all.

If I could go back to those days of Fred's early boyhood, the days I'll remember as wrapped in spiderwebs and discussions of why baby teeth fall out, I would in a heartbeat. I've become a walking stereotype: I'm the doting stay-at-home mother who gave up her own once-successful career as a watercolor artist for textbooks rather than trust the care of her child to another woman. Mourning each day lost, holding on too tightly to a boy running toward manhood. I knew other mothers who abandoned careers to stay home and raise children, but the difference was that the second their last babies climbed aboard the bus to kindergarten, they packed themselves into out-of-style interview suits and returned to the real world. My son had boarded that bus years before and still I was home.

There should have been others, other babies for me to pour my love into, but it wasn't, as they say, in the cards for Isaac and me. Isaac was nothing if not supportive, his default position, but somehow we never got around to filling out all those adoption applications. My excuse was that Isaac was never around to help me fill them out, perhaps over a glass of wine, laughing together as we tried to paint the rosiest picture possible of two less-than-fertile adults who wanted another chance. Isaac was busy saving the world, and the truth was that I grew comfortable with just Fred. We became a couple of sorts, and I couldn't bear to take that away from him, replace my undivided attention with a screaming purple-faced baby plopped in his lap from time to time.

Anyway, Fred was suspicious of babies, never a child to volunteer to entertain an infant or hold a squirming cousin for a photo. At those moments, seeing him eye toddlers nervously from across the gravel pit at the playground, desperately trying to protect his legion of sand turtles from clumsy feet, I knew in my heart of hearts that Fred would be my only one.

These days I suspected Fred was having more trouble fitting in at school, although my only clue was his answer to my daily question: "Who did you play with today?"

It was always a few seconds of deep thought before he answered, "My own self, Mommy," with a shrug. Then he was back to studying the elaborate illustration of a medieval battering ram. He became frustrated with homework in first grade. He could do it, but he didn't want to. He wanted to do only things that he chose. For years, we fought nightly battles over homework. I didn't blame Fred for fighting back; I felt strongly that education had moved in a decidedly horrible direction toward standardized tests and rote learning and briefly considered homeschooling.

For once, Isaac didn't back me up. He was adamant that Fred needed the social interactions that school provided. He fell asleep easily the night we discussed it, but I was up for hours rolling my silent response around in my head: "What social interactions?" I could categorize in my mind every instance of Fred's ambivalence toward kids his own age: every ignored advance made by children at the play area in the public library, the hopeful smiles they laid upon him only to have him look right through them, the greetings of "Hi, Fred" when he walked into a room. As I watched him run around, up and down the climbing structures at the Castle Park playground with his hot pink cape flowing behind him, I could tell he was completely unaware of the small cadre of children who had enrolled themselves in his play and chased around after him.

On occasion, he would stop, turn around and seem genuinely surprised to find that he was playing with other kids. He'd toss off a stern direction: "The dragon was last seen heading west toward the mountain!" And they'd all be off again. I counted myself lucky that he wasn't antisocial or a bully or the kind of child who stepped on ants on purpose. He was kind and thoughtful, mostly with adults and with the children he knew very, very well, such as Antonio, the older and very patient boy next door. Otherwise he was polite and cautious, if a little distant.

We pegged him as shy and encouraged play-dates. There were children in the neighborhood who were always eager to share in the fruit of his only-child status and immerse themselves in piles of Lego bricks. With each report card and conference, I waited for a comment, however veiled, about Fred's quirkiness, but that comment never came.

I mourned his younger days. While his obsessions continued, the objects of them took a darker turn. Fred had little interest in playing war, but it was suddenly all he wanted to talk and read about. When he was eight, I decided, after reading a wide variety of parenting books on raising boys, that I would not forbid Fred from reading about and talking about weapons and armies and war. We would learn about these things in their historical contexts. I steered him toward the catapults and battering rams of medieval England, the weapons that were the most unlike the modern weapons that made me cringe. Fred had other interests, though, as deep down I knew he would. After discovering that there was a war christened "the war to end all wars," and then further discovering that it, indeed, hadn't, Fred became fixated on the world wars. Of all the socially uncomfortable situations Fred had put me in during his lifetime, I've never experienced as much disgust from other adults as I did when he became enamored of the weapons of war.

On Saturday mornings, we made our weekly trek downtown while Isaac was at the office working with law students on whatever

21

exoneration case they were throwing themselves into. I don't want to give the impression that I was immune to the plight of the wrongly imprisoned, but after ten years, one case of mistaken identity sounded like another to me, with only the changing details of where and when and what color skin. On an early fall day when summer was still laying claim to the temperature, we rode the bus downtown to the grassy square around the Capitol building. We stood outside the glass doors, waiting for the Wisconsin Veterans Museum to open; this was the only place at that time that I felt like I could truly relax and breathe. My mind could uncoil from its crouched position, ready to pounce and explain away Fred's often tactless fascination with the mechanics of war. He could wander around the displays of weapons and uniforms, flags, photos and other relics, keeping up his endless stream of one-sided dialogue. (He directed the conversation, but I was expected to listen intently and add *hmm*s and *I see*s at the appropriate times.) Visitors didn't recognize my son as anything other than a cute little boy with a respectful interest in Wisconsin's battle history— at least that's what I told myself.

Fred's favorite video, the one he would watch until I stopped him, featured a soldier recalling the day his platoon was ambushed in the jungles of Vietnam and he lost all the men in his unit. Fred watched it raptly, waiting for the black-and-white photo of a soldier standing amid vines and mud, cigarette hanging out of his mouth, phone receiver in one hand. There were three things that fascinated Fred about this four-minute clip. First, he couldn't believe that a man as powerful and shrewd as a platoon leader would smoke, especially after Fred had learned, when he was obsessed with the human body, what smoking did to a person's lungs. Second, he recalled that the first cordless phone was made available to the U.S. public in 1986, so the presence of a cordless phone in the remote jungles of Vietnam in the 1970s enthralled him. Last, Fred learned from the video that the fuzzy photo was taken just minutes before the man was killed in the ambush.

I felt the quiet awe come over Fred when the photo flashed on the screen, and I would be lying if I said it didn't bother me. I watched his small face in profile, his disheveled mop of hair, the way his blue eyes flashed when he took in the details, the way after several months he could whisper the soldier's monologue along with the video. He stood, leaning against the short podium that encased the television screen, his little hand, dirty fingernails, poised over the worn silver button, ready to push again as soon as the brief credits rolled. I can only describe what I felt during those times as a slow, steady panic. But then, just before he pushed the button to start the video again, he would turn and search me out, and I could see the sadness on his face, intermingled with fascination and, thankfully, a small amount of fear.

"Mama, isn't it horrible? They all died. The enemy just bombed them all and they all died, all except just one, just Don Weaver. Do you think they had kids at home in America?" he asked, not really expecting an answer, just wanting to let me know he recognized Don Weaver's pain and felt sadness in his awareness. I sank back into my wooden bench and the panic would disperse because I had solid proof that my sweet Fred was not a monster.

It was difficult to get Fred out of the veterans museum, but we eventually left with a small whispered bribe of a chocolate whoopee pie from the café inside the library, though I felt ashamed to be bribing my son with chocolate in the face of so much loss and devastation. With Fred's face smeared with chocolate cake and buttercream, we headed down to the Children's area in the basement of the library, once a crumbling example of midcentury modern architecture, now a sterile new series of right angles with fluorescent lighting and midcentury modern decor. We chose a mammoth stack of nonfiction on the world wars. Fred politely handed the round-faced, pink-haired librarian his library card, well used already though its owner was only eight. She smiled down at this caramel-haired little imp, making her lip ring rise. When I pushed the stack of books toward her, that lip ring dropped back down as a look of concern rose quickly.

"These books aren't really meant for kids, ma'am," she said calmly, as if perhaps I had run through the library randomly grabbing books, in some sort of Grocery Cart Shopping Challenge, paying no heed to the age of my actual child.

"They were over there." I pointed to the shelves nestled among the bright plastic miniature Eames-like furniture that littered the Children's area.

"That's the Young Adult section." She was quiet, waiting for me to admit defeat.

"Yes."

She slowly scanned each one with the bar-code reader; with each beep I could see her working up what she was going to say. Finally, after silently scanning all ten, she pushed them toward me and said, "I mean, if it was my kid, I wouldn't let him read this stuff. Violence begets violence. I mean, that's just me." She stared another beat so I would be sure to understand the line I was crossing into the land of irresponsible parenting, along with the clueless fathers playing Call of Duty with their five-year-olds and the young couples bringing their toddlers to R-rated films laden with both breasts and bombs.

I grabbed our stack of books, muttered a quick

thanks and hurried Fred off to the elevator. Though I was used to adjustments for Fred's quirks, I had been raised to prize politeness above all else, so I always slunk away with my tail between my legs instead of marching out with my middle finger raised in salute to all the assholes who judged my son and me.

Fred

World War II had the most deaths in all of the wars of history. Seventy million people died. Pretty much all the places in the world were in it, even the United States of America. It started a very long time ago and went about six years. Even though the United States of America was a big fighter in it, there wasn't any wars that took place at America. There were a lot of battles that happened in World War II, even one called the Battle of the Bulge that I like, because it makes me think of a big fat tummy. One time Mom asked me why I liked to think about wars. That is a hard thing to answer. Wars have a lot of machines and I like to think about how they work. Wars are history and I like to think about things that happened before. Wars are full of facts and I like to know facts. At wars people feel really sad or really angry or really happy. Don Weaver was a guy at the Vietnam War that was not as long ago as World War II. At the museum I can watch a movie about him and he talks in it and says that all his guys got bombed by the enemy. His face is very sad and his voice is very sad. He doesn't cry. I wonder why he doesn't cry. Mom said it happened a long time ago and maybe he is used to talking about it. I think he talked about those guys so much the crying is used up.

When I was at the Wisconsin Veterans Museum one time there was a bigger boy with yellow hair and a green John Deere shirt and blue jeans with a hole in the right knee and he was pressing all the buttons on the screen that Don Weaver plays on. He was pushing them all at once with both hands and the screen was glitching. I don't think that people should try to make things glitch on purpose. Things are supposed to be right and not glitch. I was worried about Don Weaver and his video so I told the boy to stop. He looked at me and said who do you think you are? And I said I was Fredrick Whitman-Hart and that he shouldn't mistreat the machines because the Wisconsin Veterans Museum is a nonprofit entity and if someone breaks the Don Weaver video they have to use donations to fix it and there might not be enough because I have seen that most people don't put money in the clear box on the wall by the exit and only some people put in dollars or fives and one twenty. He stared at me and then he said shut up you asshole. I don't think he cared about nonprofit entities or Don Weaver. When he left with a dad and a sister they did not put any money in the clear box on the wall by the exit.

I like to draw pictures of things to show more facts. I drew a picture of a gun from World War II called a Vickers. I like to call it the Walking Bird Gun, though, because it looks like that.

The Silver Eagle

So, I'm flying out of San Diego last week, and as I'm greeting passengers from the cockpit with Dave Huang, this new Oriental copilot I got, this good-looking athletic guy takes one look at me and says, "Captain, I'd like to shake your hand." Now, I'm a pretty outgoing son of a bitch, but you can bet I didn't know this guy from Adam. So I say, "Well, all right, but if I owe you money or booze, we'll pretend this never happened." We had a good laugh and then he says, "You're the Silver Eagle! I'd recognize you anywhere." Turns out, he worked the control tower at Kennedy '93 to '99.

The Silver Eagle. I always liked that. After the emergency landing I made of that 747 back in '95, the press got wind of my middle name, Eagle, and dubbed me "the Silver Eagle." It was all over the national press, even got a note from my cousin Vanessa in Great Britain. Now, it wasn't something any of my cohorts wouldn't have done; it's a pilot's duty to keep his crew and passengers safe, and that's all I did. My job. It was just pure luck that it made the news like it did. *The Today Show, Good Morning America*, a short piece on *60 Minutes*. A tribute from that old crank Andy Rooney on true patriots. You might have seen me in the credit union commercials that played for a few years afterward. I played a few rounds with Barry Alvarez. The celebrity died down after a while, which was for the best, but I can't say I didn't enjoy it while it lasted.

Now, if your father was doing interviews on the goddamn *Today Show* or showing his handsome mug in commercials, I'd like to think most kids would think that was pretty damn cool. Every appearance we made in public as a family, I had to practically slap the smiles on their faces, they were so unmoved by the whole thing. If the greatest football coach in the history of the Wisconsin Badgers asks your happy family to appear in a promo for a celebrity golf tournament, you're sure as shit going to drag the whole damn family to the clubhouse in their Sunday best whether they like it or not. It's not like there wasn't anything in it for them—there were credit union car blankets and as many Wisconsin Badgers T-shirts as they could get their goddamn hands on. My daughter, Piper, was particularly bad-tempered, some sort of unusually large bug up her ass. I'm driving the Buick and the car is just filled with this silence that's just begging for a laugh to break the ice, so I say, "So Pete from maintenance says to me, 'My wife died yesterday and I'm trying to cry, but the tears just won't come out.' And I say, 'No problem, Pete. Just imagine she came back.' " I thought that was a goddamn gem, but I got nothing, not a chuckle, so I go for the old standby.

"Piper!" I say to get her attention because she's staring out the car window again, looking like some sort of depressed corpse. I finally catch her eye in the rearview mirror.

"Knock-knock!"

She waits a long time before she finally says, "Who's there?" with a level of enthusiasm that perfectly matches her damn personality.

I shout, "Polish burglar!"

This goddamn family doesn't know how lucky they are. We got to the clubhouse and it seemed I got my signals crossed, because the promo was just for me and the coach after all. Judy told me later that Piper was supposed to help set up for some art show over at the high school, but hey, she should be pretty damn happy she shook Barry Alvarez's hand.

Piper

By the time Fred's fourth-grade fall conference arrived along with the drab, damp leftovers of all the once-gorgeous fallen leaves, I was satisfied that although Fred didn't love school, he was succeeding. He did math homework without complaint, detested spelling because the words were too easy for him. He was constantly trying to make the dreaded direction "Rewrite each word three times" more interesting by using multiple types of script, erasing certain letters and then challenging himself to fill in the missing letters. As a result, his homework took twice as long as it should have. Bedtime had become a series of battles fought over the exactness of routines and timing, battles I most often fought alone, as Isaac had taken on the case of a young Latino man who had been falsely imprisoned. Pro bono. His work on the Innocence Project was far and away his favorite part of his job at the university. Teaching law to an equal balance of eager do-gooders and money-focused frat boys paid the bills but took up his days. The Innocence Project had to fill in the cracks. Fred and I were constantly searching for a crack of our own, however small, that we might sneak into. Isaac was always quick to point out how many school concerts and elementary school gallery nights he'd attended over the years. If Fred played soccer I know Isaac would have stood on the sidelines of every game. It was the constant stuff, the never-ending cycle of meals and baths and bedtimes, that I forged through alone.

Bedtime had to begin at seven p.m. We read exactly three books, no matter their length or topic. The first battle was generally a struggle between me trying to choose three books of a reasonable length, and Fred trying to choose his three favorite books (sometimes nonfiction tomes with hundreds of pages). When we finally agreed on what to read, we took turns reading while Fred had a snack, ordinarily a small plastic bowl of twenty-two Frosted Mini-Wheats, only the flavor changing depending on his mood. Next was toothbrushing, during which Fred insisted on brushing his teeth for a minute on each the top and the bottom, since he'd seen detailed views of plaque under a microscope in a book on dental health and hygiene when he was five. Then I was required to lie with him on top of the leopard-print fleece blanket he called "Fuzzy," for a minimum of seven minutes. During that time, we looked at the digital clock and made up math facts based on the numbers displayed. Although I kissed him good night and typically staggered out into the light of the hallway by eight p.m., Fred would still be tossing around, tangling up his sheets until ten o'clock many nights, his insomnia as much a part of the routine as the Mini-Wheats and the singing of "I've Been Working on the Railroad." I usually went to bed shortly after that, though I never really rested well until I knew Isaac was home; my anxiety was constantly in flux, never knowing when he would turn in. I preferred to be well asleep before he climbed into the bed with a loud, self-satisfied sigh, because if I was awake or gave the impression of being awake, he would want to discuss my day, Fred's day, his day.

As I lay there and struggled to keep my fake sleep breathing deep and even, Isaac would climb beneath the covers, toss his arms over his head and promptly fall asleep. My own insomnia, though nothing like it was in college, visited most often on these nights that I faked my own restful sleep, perhaps a sort of instant karma. I looked at his profile in the light that crept in from the crack under the door. His sharp features were visible even in the darkest of nights: long, straight nose, prominent brow and defined chin. His dark brown hair curled over his forehead and he slept with his mouth open, breathing as if he owned the air. It was during these minutes that could easily stretch to hours that I examined my life, regretting leaving my career behind, wondering at my satisfaction level.

I also waited for Fred to wake. He had, in the

last year, begun sleepwalking, awakening in the middle of the night and getting dressed for school, sometimes turning on the shower in the bathroom, occasionally even peeing onto the floor inside the bathroom door, mistaking the empty space for a toilet bowl. I waited for the moment I heard him bang around his room and then gently guided him back to bed, retucked him in and took a few quiet minutes to study his sleeping form and pray to the universe that he was okay.

All these late nights and interrupted sleep led Fred to be generally fatigued, and he reported that he was falling asleep in class. I assumed his fourth-grade teacher, Mrs. Tieman, would inform us during the conference that Fred was tired in class and needed more sleep. I arranged to meet Isaac in front of the main door of the old Tudor building with Fred in tow. Fred had been promised my iPhone in the hall while his father and I talked to his teacher. Isaac assured me that he wouldn't be late, but I was prepared to be angry with him at his tardiness when Fred and I walked up the sidewalk, trudging through wet, decaying leaves, once bright, now hard to distinguish from the cement itself.

"Dad!" Fred shouted, running ahead to greet his father. He was surprised to see him, shocked that this meeting with his teacher merited a midday sighting of his elusive but much-loved father.

I was surprised too, surprised that I'd have to pack my disappointment away for another day. "Wow, I wasn't sure you'd make it," I said as neutrally as I could.

"Of course I made it, Pipe. This is important. I've got to hear what the teacher has to say about my little genius. Right, Freddy?" He offered Fred a high five, which Fred accepted before running ahead to the door and turning to wait for us. As we picked our way through mud puddles that would soon be covered with a layer of black ice, with those decaying leaves trapped until the spring melt, I watched my husband as he looked all around him, taking in the world. He was grinning in a subdued way, not giddy, but pleased with what he saw.

When we met in college, it was one of the first things I noticed about him as I stood behind a counter in a campus coffee shop, making subpar lattes for grad students who didn't really care as long as the brew was caffeinated. He was in law school and spent hours studying at a back booth. It didn't seem to matter how many hours he sat poring over law books, how late at night or early in the morning, how muggy the September or how painfully frigid the January; he was always cheerful. He smiled, made small talk, was polite and gracious. I was in the midst of my senior project for art school and spending every hour I wasn't working in the coffee shop holed up in a studio. His generally upbeat worldview was a balm for my solitary, lonely life. Even when he talked to me about law cases that sounded depressingly soul crushing, he spoke of loopholes and strategies that might just maybe work.

He wasn't good-looking in the sense that most women would consider him a catch when they first saw him. It was after they talked to him, I noticed them sidling up to me at barbecues and neighborhood birthday parties. They nudged me and whispered, as if my husband were a great secret, "He's a real catch," congratulating me on being chosen by him. And he was: kind, thoughtful, intelligent but not a know-it-all; funny but never offensive. I had been caught or I had caught him; though the language changed, I was still considered the lucky one either way.

After the receptionist buzzed us in, Fred led us through the maze of halls, all identical to me, with bright blue lockers and glass display cases with papier-mâché sculptures, always representative of another culture, some multicultural experience. Fred pointed out his own sculpture, which looked suspiciously like a cannon.

"Mr. Burke usually says no weapons, but since they were supposed to be sculptures about slavery and the Civil War was about slavery, I could make a cannon. But not a gun," Fred said before moving on and leading us to Room 15, where Mrs. Tieman was finishing up with another set of parents. There was a lanky, shaggy-haired boy slouched in a chair in the hall, an iPad held up close to his face. We approached and he looked over the top. His eyes brightened when he saw Fred.

"Hey, Fred," he said with a smile.

Fred was busy studying the game options on my iPhone and ignored the boy.

"Fred," I said. "Fred."

"Huh?" he finally replied.

"Someone said hello to you," I said through my pasted-on smile.

"He said 'hey,' " Fred said, squinting up at me.

"Yeah, but 'hey' is like saying hello." I tried desperately to speak quietly to Fred and make the whole exchange seem as natural as possible. The boy watched Fred over his iPad with a blank face.

Now Isaac swooped in. "Hey, buddy, what's your name?"

"Jackson," he said.

"What game you got there, Jackson?" Isaac sat down in the small chair next to Jackson while the boy animatedly discussed which version of Angry Birds he was mastering.

After several minutes of Isaac carrying on a conversation with Fred's classmate while Fred scrolled through apps on my iPhone, the door opened and Jackson's parents emerged. I recognized them from a variety of school events over the past five years, but I had never formally met them. I found that Fred's lack of interest in socializing with other children had limited my own socialization with other parents. If your child has no friends, then in the social circles of elementary school, neither do you. At countless concerts and class plays, I had observed mothers finding one another in crowds to set up playdates and fathers shaking hands and discussing neighborhood barbecues, but no one approached me no matter how I smiled and tried to look like my son and I fit in. Here in the hallway, we parents all nodded politely to one another and smiled. Isaac patted Jackson on the back and Fred took up Jackson's slouch in the chair outside the door. I knocked lightly on the doorframe and poked my head in.

"Hello?" I said.

"Oh, come in!" Mrs. Tieman gestured from her chair. Isaac and I entered and sat across from her in child-sized chairs. I immediately felt the power balance calibrate to favor Mrs. Tieman, in the only adult-sized chair in the room. I sat a whole head below her, close enough to the scratched-up laminate tabletop to see that at some point LT hated PM and thought it prudent to scratch the tiny letters into the edge of the tabletop with something sharp—an unfolded paper clip, perhaps. I ran my fingers over the script, barely discernible among the other scratches of general wear. LT had spent a lot of time at this table, hating PM.

"Let's get started—shall we?" Mrs. Tieman asked as she pulled out a plain manila folder with Fred's name at the top. "I've got his assessment scores right here; you can look them over to see if you have any questions, but you'll also take them with you." She presented us with a slim packet of papers covered with horizontal bar graphs and percentages on the first page and what seemed to be the same set of numbers represented with a line graph. I was pleased to see that the third page contained no pie charts or Venn diagrams, just paragraphs of text. I realized that I was hoarding the packet and Isaac couldn't see, so I pushed it over to him and he nodded and scanned the pages as I had, looking for percentages.

"As you can see from his assessment scores, Fred is doing just fine academically."

"Great! So, we're done here, right?" Isaac joked.

Mrs. Tieman laughed inelegantly and cleared her throat. "I have some other concerns about Fred; I'd like to talk to you about them."

I must have gasped because Isaac looked at me and firmly grabbed my hand under the table and gave it a light squeeze.

"So, I'm finding that Fred has a hard time focusing in class. When I give instructions, or talk at the front of the class, he seems to be daydreaming. Often if I ask him what was said, he's not able to tell me."

"Well, are you lecturing?" I asked, maybe a little too fiercely. "He doesn't learn well by being talked at." Isaac squeezed my hand tighter. I shook my hand loose of his and folded my hands on the tabletop.

Mrs. Tieman was calm. "There are going to be times, more and more as Fred gets older, when he's going to have to listen to an adult talking for some amount of time. I do try to keep those times to a minimum, but they will happen." She looked back and forth from Isaac to me.

"When we had our recent district assessments, Fred insisted on sharpening his pencil repeatedly, and it was very distracting to have him up and down so much, not to mention it made it hard for him to focus."

"He likes a sharp pencil; he likes things to be just right," I replied, and felt Isaac's hand on my upper back.

Mrs. Tieman looked down at her notes and cleared her throat. "Fred uses the bathroom much more often than other children. Sometimes even soon after he's already gone."

"He has a small bladder!" I knew in that moment that I hated Mrs. Tieman. I hated this woman in the embroidered apple cardigan, with the coarse gray hairs sprouting wildly through her thick black hair, cut unflatteringly close to her face. I hated this woman whose slanted penmanship graced my son's work in bold red. I hated this woman who knew nothing about daydreams and the importance of a sharp point on your pencil and had never experienced the annoyance of a small, anxious bladder.

"Mr. and Mrs. Hart," she began.

"It's Whitman. Mr. Hart and Mrs. Whitman," I said louder than I intended to. I felt Isaac stiffen beside me.

"Excuse me. I'm not quite sure how to say this, but what I'm trying to say is that I think Fred may have some psychological . . . issues."

"I'm sorry? What?" asked Isaac.

"Look, there are a few things that concern me. If you'll just let me show you . . ."

She continued, but I sat frozen; suddenly the schoolhouse clock ticked more loudly on the wall, and the hard plastic of my small chair cut into my back. I was sweating but shivering at the same time and I couldn't say anything. She misunderstood our silence as assent and continued. "Look, this is a nice class, a really nice group of kids, and Fred hasn't really bonded with any of them. He's polite and can be friendly but doesn't go out of his way to interact with anyone."

"Fred has friends, a friend in the neighborhood. And friends from past classes. I asked that he be placed in the same class with Roland because it's hard for Fred to make friends, but the principal didn't do it. I asked for that and *you* didn't do it." I spoke quickly and heard the tremble in my voice.

"Okay, well, I didn't say anything about this when it happened, but last week we had a drum corps come for a concert in the gym. Everyone else handled it just fine, but Fred became very agitated and covered his ears with his hands. He started to cry, so an aide took him to the library for the rest of the concert. It was very strange for a nine-year-old." She shifted in her chair and somehow a waft of her perfume found me and I felt myself gag.

"He doesn't like loud things," I heard myself say, but I could sense the fight leaving my voice. I sounded weak and defensive.

"And then there's this," Mrs. Tieman said as she opened up a classic black-and-white-speckled composition notebook with Fred's name on the front. "This is his journal and, well, I find Fred's troubling." She pushed it across the table to us and I looked down to see pages filled with Fred's neat penmanship. I was certain I already knew what he was writing about, the only thing he ever talked about, read about. The margins were littered with nine-year-old-boy illustrations of a huge variety of World War II weapons, some I recognized from our reading. I felt proud for a second—he was a good artist with an eye for detail and perspective—but quickly remembered that Mrs. Tieman's goal was not parental pride; it was concern.

"He's interested in history, Mrs. Tieman. I don't see what's wrong with that," Isaac said as he protectively placed his hand on the journal.

"He's just much too absorbed in this world of weapons and war. A nine-year-old should have a wide variety of interests, and some of the kids in the class have become uncomfortable with his focus. A little scared, you could say."

Scared? Of my Fred? I wanted to meet them, each child who was scared, and personally reassure them that Fred was no one to fear. He slept with a stuffed hedgehog, rubbed bald from love. He cried when we came across dried-up worms on the sidewalk, tenderly carried them to the dirt and buried them. He was scared to watch all the Disney movies that his peers had been raised on. When he was four he worried about the Little Engine That Could. ("Mom, what if he can't this time?") My boy was no threat.

"I think we should talk about an evaluation with the special education team," Mrs. Tieman said.

The rest of the conference was fuzzy for me. I suddenly felt so tired. I heard Isaac and Mrs. Tieman discussing plans, but I sat there mute, entirely sure that this must be a nightmare, *the* nightmare, and I would soon wake up to Isaac's gentle snores and the sound of Fred mistakenly peeing on the bathroom floor. When she was done, Isaac took my elbow and helped me up, shook Mrs. Tieman's hand and steered me toward the door. When I saw Fred slouched in the chair outside the door, the only thing in the world I wanted was to scoop him up and run.

Fred

In London in World War II there was a horrible bombing. They called it the Blitz. During that bombing one kid out of ten died trying to escape. Kids couldn't escape very well because they were little and not strong like grown-ups. Some grown-ups even forgot about kids and left them behind. I saw pictures of kids and they were crying. I wonder what it feels like to be that sad. That sad because all the grown-ups ran away without you and left you to get bombed.

Jackson called me "teeny weeny" once.

Mrs. Tieman smells like Finish dishwasher detergent, and when she comes by me and bends down her breath is too hot and smells like sausage. The colors in her hair are strange, the white ones don't fit in with the black ones, and I know that her sweaters are scratchy because I have felt that kind of sweater at the store and it scratched my skin.

When she talks to us about adding three-digit numbers or photosynthesis she stands in front of a cupboard with glass windows. The light shines on the diamond shapes and makes her outline fuzzy for me. Things should be clear and not fuzzy. There are sixteen diamond shapes inside every rectangle and at least two of them are cracked in each rectangle, which means that one-eighth of them are broken. At first I felt really bad about that and wondered how she could stand it. I was thinking about the broken glass a lot. Like, how did it get broken? When did it get broken? Did anyone get hurt when it got broken? One time Mrs. Tieman said Fred I am trying to tell you about photosynthesis. Are you listening? I said okay Mrs. Tieman but there are approximately twenty-six broken diamonds behind you. She sighed a very small sigh and said Fred this school is very old and things get broken sometimes when they are very old. It doesn't have anything to do with photosynthesis. I agreed with her there. The broken diamonds do not have anything to do with photosynthesis, but that doesn't mean they are not important.

Also, when your parents are having a conference about their kid they should close the door all the way. Because a kid can hear pretty well. It's not like the distance from the classroom to the hall is very far.

The Silver Eagle

The only damn reason I play squash is the steam afterward. Real sports should be played outside on grass, cement or clay if absolutely necessary, but not in a glass room with a cappuccino machine down the hall and jazz piped into the locker room. The steam room is the only place a man can feel like he's been involved in any kind of real sporting experience in some converted warehouse on the west side of town. I wouldn't even have been here if Bob hadn't told Judy that she ought to encourage me to get out more. Then my wife went out and got me a membership to a squash club, just because that son of a bitch Bob Willson needed a squash partner. So I have to use the damn thing, or it would be over a thousand bucks a year down the tubes. Bob is a surgeon, orthopedics, and heads over to his office around seven, either there or the golf course if he's not due for surgery. So I told him, "You got me into this damn thing—the least you can do is meet me for a match after I get in from a red-eye, Bob." Well, I got him there, so we have a standing court time of five a.m. twice a week, depending on my flight schedule.

Tell you the truth, after six months of this

bull crap, it's starting to grow on me. The steam shower more than the squash. A man's closer to his manhood when he's sweating his balls off with another man. I'm a baseball man myself. Cubbies. Have been since I was growing up in Chicago. Baseball, now, that's a real sport. Wide-open grassy field, groundskeepers crisscrossing, big blue sky overhead, cold beer and sausages. I grew up hearing the horror story of game seven of the 1945 World Series. I can still hear Harry Caray's voice calling out strikes when I close my eyes. Summer nights sitting on the porch with my father and the radio, the sounds of crickets and baseball in the dark. That's what sports should be. I was an Ernie Banks fan as a boy, determined to grow up and beat his record myself. The lucky bastard I am, I was at his last game in 1969 after sixteen seasons. Took the whole family in '88 when they turned on the lights for the first time at Wrigley, though my damn kids didn't grasp how important it was.

Squash is a whole different ball game, pardon my pun. No tense moments with the bases loaded. You got eye protection instead of nut protection and you've got some damn rubber ball and a miniature racquet. I try my best to keep that little rubber ball between the lines on the wall, but I gotta be honest with you: I'm a strong man. Always have been. I was all-city in baseball and football in high school. Played ball in college before I tore my knee up and had to switch to track. I was fast, too. Hurdles, long jump. I did it all.

When I started flying I started jogging. Every city I landed in had sidewalks; every hotel had a treadmill or two if the weather wasn't conducive to running outdoors. I run five miles a day every damn day of the week with my dog even if I'm playing squash with Bob. Playing squash with Bob is more like running around the playground with my grandson than any real type of workout. Bob's put on a few over the last twenty years. He's no runner. While he puts up a good fight every week, it'll be a cold day in hell before Bob Willson beats me in a damn game of squash.

This week I get in on the red-eye from Kennedy at four and bust my ass over to the club so I can meet Bob by five. He's waiting for me when I come in.

"Eagle! You're late, my man," Bob yells between thwacks of the ball against the backboard.

"Just a minute or two, you cranky old bastard. I'll be right there," I shout over my shoulder on my way to the locker room. Actually, the sign on the door says, "Men's Lounge." That should tell you just how much real work is happening here at the squash club. A man uses a locker room to change, shower, put on deodorant, run a comb through his hair and clothe himself. I tell myself the next time I see some young guy lounging around the locker room in a velvet armchair with a cappuccino I'll slap the bastard upside the head with his *New York Times*. I change into my sweats, take a quick piss and wash my hands. I look in the mirror as I scrub. I'm still a good-looking son of a bitch.

Bob's waiting for me on court three, though there are openings on all the courts that early on a Tuesday morning. He prefers court three and I figure I have to let the guy have his small victories. He's had a hell of a year. He lost his wife to breast cancer back in the winter and he's got a son who's on parole for some check-writing fraud. Bob is hanging on, though.

From the first point, I can tell Bob is here to win and I play my heart out for once.

"What's going on today, Bob? You wearing your big-girl panties?" I bark at him between points.

"Nah, you bastard. I've been practicing; wouldn't hurt you either, I gotta say," he says he slams the ball back at me again.

Now this guy has me running around the court like a damn chicken with its head cut off. Either he's gotten a lot better over the last week or I'm losing my touch. By the time the game's over my heart's racing. I beat him, again, but just barely. Bob's panting hard but smiling big.

"I'm taking a steam," I say, and wipe my

dripping brow with my towel and pocket the ball.

"I'll be there shortly. I gotta tell Smith at the desk that I got within five of you today, Eagle." Bob's proud of himself and rightly so; he played a fine game even if it is just goddamn squash.

The Men's Lounge is almost empty; there's a young guy lacing up his Nikes. He looks up and gives me a curt nod. Young people now, so cold. They just don't know how you make contacts in this world. You gotta be friendly, be the guy who says good morning, offers a wink. It's those guys who get things done.

"Hey there! Good morning to you. It's going to be a great one," I say, and clap him on the back as I walk past. He shoots up from the bench, like I goosed him or something. People just aren't used to friendly.

I strip down and wrap one of those tiny towels around my waist, barely covering up my ass. I crank up the steam and help myself to a glass of some sort of cucumber mint spa water. Not even plain old water is good enough anymore. As I open the door that delicious heat floods over my body and I know the last hour's been worth it. A man's got to earn the right to sweat like this. I find my usual spot—second row, corner—and lean back into the cool of the wood and fill my lungs with steam . . .

Piper

My father died on a Tuesday morning after a particularly vigorous game of squash with his friend Bob. He was found by Bob at 6:13 a.m., lying on the floor of the steam room, his towel in a small heap next to him. I've always noted the irony of that, how my father would have hated dying naked, as the one lasting tenet of his lapsed Catholic sensibilities had been physical modesty. Bob took a pulse, listened for breath, yelled for the desk clerk to call 911 and started CPR. It was unknown how long my father had been lying there alone, no oxygen to his brain, steaming like a lobster. The paramedics arrived at 6:20 a.m. and took up the fight. I imagined EMTs scrambling around his limp, wrinkled body, desperately trying to revive him. It was 6:38 a.m. when they were finally able to restart his heart with a lucky pulse of electricity.

Bob called my mom at 6:40 a.m. as the ambulance pulled out of the parking lot of the squash club, a warehouse I always thought looked like it could have been a machining shop or a porn studio. My mom called me at 6:42 a.m., as I was trying to prod Fred along through the tortuous morning routine, made more difficult by Fred's insomnia and my own.

"Your father had a heart attack. At the squash club," Mom said flatly.

"What? I mean . . . is he . . ."

"No. Bob started CPR and the paramedics were able to restart his heart," she said.

There was a brief silence as both of us felt the weight of this. "So . . . he's okay?" I asked as I tried to stuff acceptable lunch food into Fred's *Star Wars* lunch box.

"Well, they don't know how long he went without oxygen. They don't know what kind of damage there might be. They don't know if his heart can continue on its own. He's going to University Hospital," Mom said.

"After I get Fred on the bus I'll come over there," I said.

"That's fine. Can you call Curtiss? I guess we should let your brother know," she said, and hung up.

I called Curtiss, who after floating around working at a number of art galleries was finally getting his doctorate in art history at the University of Chicago. I relayed Mom's call and waited for his reaction. "I have midterms to proctor, but I can come up on Thursday."

Our family's collective nonpanic at my father's condition might have been shocking and even disturbing to many. The Silver Eagle, true patriot,

54

lies at death's door and his wife and offspring will get to it when they get to it. There's a history here, one carefully covered and silenced. There's a facade, curated over years, smoothed out by endless practice pretending everything is all right. As children, my brother and I learned that it was best to just avoid our father. If avoidance wasn't possible, one could hope that he was in one of his shining moods. His everything-is-dandy-let's-go-get-an-ice-cream-cone-and-toss-the-ball-around moods. Though these moods were shiny and glistening at first glance, it took very little to tarnish them: a drip of melted ice cream on the upholstery in the backseat, an easy grounder missed, unexpected traffic from a funeral procession. With each glitch notched in my father's plans, the golden light of his good mood slipped away exponentially so that a trip that started not twenty minutes earlier with a smile, a whistled tune and a warm feeling was at next glance a disappointment to all involved. My brother silently weeping after my father threw a baseball glove at him after one too many missed fly balls. Me, scared to move wrong, catching ice-cream drips before they even formed, protecting the seat and in turn myself. My father driving us home, silent in voice, but his aura red with rage.

When I was older, I learned that my mother was facing much worse than my father doled out to his children. Where our childhood missteps drew an irrational amount of anger from our father, our mother never knew where or when or how the emotional and verbal abuse would strike. He alternated between bellowing about the toughness of the pork roast and days of silence after a surprise afternoon pop-in from my mother's childhood friend. When I became aware that there were ways to massage my father's moods and ego, I became an understudy for my mother. I learned to make peas with mint and scallions. I woke early to get my weekend chores done, since my father despised laziness. Even when he was away on a trip, there was no rest. His spirit had the fantastical ability to be in two places at once; the chores were still done early, the peas still perfectly prepared, in case he should magically appear at the front door by some sort of time-space hiccup. We were ready. My mother and I were ready. Curtiss was never interested in bending his will to my father's person, neither absent nor present. Curtiss did his own thing, and though I tried to make him understand the importance of obedience, he refused to abide by the rules, however wobbly, that kept the peace.

This, of course, was the secret history of my family. The public history documents a gregarious, popular man, a shy, supportive wife and two bright children, one ambitious and one slightly rebellious but with good intentions. During the period immediately following my father's famous emergency landing, the period of his brief celebrity, he was at his most tolerable. A multitude of interviews and public appearances forced him to play the role of good-natured, compassionate hero so often that he would sometimes bring it home with him. I felt during that time what it might have been like to have a real father. He spoke publicly about his pride in his children, saying things that I had never heard within the confines of our normal life. He praised my intelligence and artwork, artwork that he had just months earlier described as lacking passion and a waste of my high school career. He spoke kindly of my brother's idiosyncrasies, calling him a freethinker and acknowledging that he had a bright future ahead of him, when he had previously knocked the wind out of Curtiss with pounding criticisms. He spoke of my mother with love and respect and never once let on that he had punished her with a weeklong silence when she expressed her desire to take a twice-weekly water aerobics class at the YMCA with friends whom my father didn't appreciate, friends of my mother's who treated him like an equal.

The question always asked of me and the same one that I had asked over and over since I was young enough to understand its weight was "Why did she stay?" I cursed her and wished she could have been someone she wasn't. I vividly recall an argument with her when I was fourteen.

I can still see myself standing before her with my hands on my hips and I can still hear the sharp edge in my voice.

"What is wrong with you, Mom? You just let him walk all over you! Can't you stand up for yourself for once?" I yelled at her and immediately regretted it, as it felt for a second as if I were channeling the very man I railed against.

She faced me head-on, her eyes filled with tears, but gave me no response other than "Go to your room, Piper. I don't want to see you right now."

I begged and pleaded and tried to convince. I reasoned far more than my lifetime of therapists have recommended. I inserted myself into my parents' marriage for the sole purpose of saving my mother. And yet, after thirty-eight years, she was still there. Still cooking pork roast just right, still finely grating the Parmesan for the peas, still putting off visits to her only sister until the timing was right.

I came up with several reasons their marriage lived on, some changing with the seasons of life and others enduring. When I lived at home and was completely surrounded by the dysfunction, I felt like my mother thought that she was doing my brother and me a favor by not divorcing my father. A lot of research at the time sternly warned parents of the detriment to children of divorce. I always wondered if the children were consulted for this research; the idea of living apart from the daily stress and tension of my parents' marriage delighted me, and I think even now what a different person I might have become if I'd had the chance to live outside that black hole of repressed rage before the freedom of college.

My mother had also, once, in a fit of truth telling when I was a freshman in high school, expressed to me her desire not to share custody of Curtiss and me with our father. The scene was burned into my memory because of her shocking honesty. She and I walked out of the McDonald's to our car and found that the car parked next to us was the location of the stereotypical shared-custody hand-off of children from one parent to the other. After we got in the car, she turned the key and stared out the front window.

"Mom?" I said, eager to get home and on with my very important life.

She shook her head and stared. Then she spoke so quietly I strained to make out her words. "I couldn't do it. I couldn't leave you with him. Not alone." Then she rubbed her eyes and backed the car out and we drove home in an uneasy silence. In that moment, I had my first deep understanding of how much she was protecting us from his moods.

Perhaps the thing that "saved" my parents' marriage was the thing that destroyed the marriages of many men in my father's career: his job. He was gone for days at a time, flying around the world and leaving us behind, where we were finally able to breathe in his absence. The fact that he was a somewhat absent father was his best attribute. My mother was a slightly more relaxed version of herself when he was gone. I followed her lead and tried to sleep in, maybe skipped vacuuming between the couch cushions just this time. Curtiss went about whatever he was doing without criticism, disappearing for hours and returning with a private smile and a ragged notebook clutched to his chest.

There was rarely a time when my father came home early, flights not typically getting in before they were due. We were often granted hours of extra freedom when he would call to tell my mother he was stuck in bad weather in Cincinnati and wouldn't be flying out until morning. This freedom, though, was tricky because we never knew just how long it would last; our guards were always up well before his arrival because we knew that his mood would be dire after spending a night at the Holiday Inn at the airport.

After Curtiss and I left home, my parents were alone. I set about making my way in the small-time art world, frequently finding my work in demand for waiting rooms and motels, not what I'd dreamed of in art school, but I was making a living. Then I set about making myself a new family, all the things I had always wanted a family to be; in other words, the things I did not have. I set aside my artistic ambitions and found a niche in freelance work for children's nonfiction texts, though the work ebbed and flowed with the economy and I often found myself without work for months at a time. I volunteered for lunchroom duty at Fred's school. Curtiss drifted around the country, working at art galleries and museums and generally not sharing much about his life with us. He had settled in Chicago a few years ago, and though he was only hours away, I still saw him only at holidays, when he refused the turkey and gave out gifts of gorgeously wrapped coffee table books on Kandinsky and Manet.

I carried a private hope that as we left home and my father aged, he would mellow and soften and become easier to live with. He got a dog, and I saw a side of him for the first time that showed a kind of compassion and gentleness that I had not known. He had on occasion found reason to treat Fred with that same kindness, but I noted that it was always on his terms. At this point, my only guess as to why my mother stayed even after we were gone was that it had become a habit. The way it was. It was easier now to carry on with the status quo than to rock the marital boat and see who drowned and who survived. I can only imagine that a call from Bob Willson that my father had had a heart attack in the steam shower at the squash club was the exact call my mother always secretly hoped to get.

Fred

Today was the day that I had to have a meeting with Mrs. Bach. Mrs. Bach is a psychologist at Wendell Elementary School. She said that means she talks to kids about their problems. I said that I didn't have any problems except my penis was itching me. She looked surprised and then she told me that it wasn't appropriate to talk about our private parts with just anyone. We should only talk to our parents or a doctor or nurse about our private parts. I said that she was the one who wanted to know about my problems and I saw in the school directory that she is actually a doctor. It says "Dr. Bach." She was quiet and made some notes in her binder. I folded an origami rose out of shiny silver paper that Uncle Curtiss got for me from the art museum gift shop in Chicago. The price tag said fifty sheets for $5.99, which means they cost about twelve cents each, which I think of whenever I fold something.

Mrs. Bach started asking me questions and I answered them and then she gave me a packet with more questions. I asked her if it was really necessary to answer more questions. She said that yes, they were trying to find out how to help me in school. I don't need help in school. I need help with my itchy penis I said. She wrote something else down in her binder and passed me the packet and a pencil that was just barely sharp. I asked her if I could sharpen it before I answered her questions but she said it was sharp enough. I did not agree with her and said I couldn't go on until she let me sharpen my pencil. She got up from the little rainbow-shaped table and clicked her high heels over to her desk and opened a drawer and found a pencil sharpener. I relaxed. She made notes in her binder. I answered her questions with my sharp pencil. They were easy, except the one about who are your friends. First I wrote no one, but then I remembered that Mrs. Tieman says that we are all friends in this class, so I erased that and wrote everyone. But then I remembered that I do not want to be friends with Jackson because he told me that the word "vagina" isn't in the dictionary and it certainly is because I checked myself and wrote down the definition for him and he laughed. I crossed off everyone and I was trying to think of how to write everyone except Jackson without being unkind because you shouldn't be unkind, but Mrs. Bach took away my packet and my pencil.

I handed her the origami rose that I had in my pocket and I told her that it was for her. She said thank you and smiled at me, but I wondered if she would really keep it. I told her the paper cost twelve cents and had come all the way from China by way of Chicago. She wrinkled her eyebrows and said all right you can go Fred.

I had to go back to my class then and learn more about comprehension strategies for non-fiction texts. On the way I had to stop at the display case with my Civil War cannon in it. At the veterans museum you can see a cannon and you can touch a cannon, but it is disrespectful to sit on the cannon. Some kids do it anyway and their parents just let them. There are a lot of Civil War weapons and uniforms and flags and pictures at the veterans museum. There is a picture of a prisoner of war. A guy from the South was captured by the North and they didn't kill him, which I thought was nice. He is sitting on a chair and all his bones show through his skin. He does not look happy, but he doesn't look sad either.

When we made our papier-mâché statues in art class to represent the Civil War experience, I wanted to make a statue of the prisoner of war. Mr. Burke shook his head no, no, no when I tried to explain to him that a person who was in a war could still be alive but so, so close to dead you almost couldn't tell. He told me that was the sort of thing that would be scary to some kids. I said but it's history Mr. Burke. He finally let me make a cannon but no cannonballs. That was strange to me because a cannon without cannonballs is useless in battle. He said this isn't a battle Fred, it's a display case. I did make some tiny cannonballs out of clay and I put them in my pocket but I forgot to take them out and they went through the wash so my cannon was useless after all.

Piper

After I got off the phone with my mother, called Curtiss and got Fred onto the bus, I called Isaac, who was already at work. He expressed more surprise and sadness than any of the rest of us had. My father afforded Isaac many of the same kindnesses that he afforded perfect strangers, so Isaac regarded many of the stories of my childhood as the exaggerated remembrances of a sensitive child. He often gently accused me of overreacting, unable to believe that the good-natured, joking man he knew could present an entirely different face to his family. A somewhat vengeful part of me longed for a day when my father's rage was pointed decidedly at Isaac, but some part of me knew it was unlikely.

"But he's not that old. He's in such good shape. All that running, all that squash. Shit," Isaac said.

"Yeah. It happens," I said.

"Did you want me to come over to the hospital? I have classes this morning and a brief due for the Sanchez case by five, but maybe I could . . ." He trailed off, waiting for me to let him off the hook. I knew he was in the middle of a case that had received some small level of national attention.

"How about I text you after I see him and I

know more?" I said. Isaac and I performed this charade over and over: he acted like he could get out of work if I needed him and I reassured him I did not. Both of us were lying to each other and had been for so long that pretending had become our main method of communication. I had always known that my husband had a passion for justice but had always held out hope that I could ignite in him an equal or greater passion for a family life. I found that so far I could not, but we played at a happy marriage the way two small children play blocks side by side and never interact. It was a situation that I learned to live with, a situation that I always told myself I would deal with when the time was right. But the rightness of time had a curious way of always sitting just beyond the horizon and I had become resigned to that. I wasn't sure what Isaac would even be able to offer me: a back rub? Hugs that didn't stop until I wrenched myself from them? Isaac had always been infinitely fonder of physical contact, while I found it often uncomfortable and awkward. He came from a family of huggers and kissers, a Scandinavian family who believed that every hello and good-bye deserved an overabundance of touch.

I took my time getting to the hospital; I stopped at a gas station and picked up a Diet Coke and a package of Peppermint Patties. I got my mom a box of Good & Plenty, her favorite, or at least I assumed so, since she always ate them from our trick-or-treat haul, set aside in the pile of things children don't actually want to eat, along with nut rolls and peanut butter chews. I got her a tall cup of strong coffee and a selection of celebrity gossip magazines, her guilty pleasure.

The University Hospital complex was an enormous compound of misfit buildings ranging from the boxy brick of the 1950s to the steel-girded constant construction of the current day. The main building was a monolith in concrete, with narrow windows, similar to those I saw on prisons off the highway. There was valet parking, but my father had taught me that you never trust the valet, and despite my best efforts to cast off as much of my father as I could, I drove past their eager-looking faces. I found a spot in a lot called H and made my way through a maze of stairwells and corridors before they opened up into a large atrium, bustling with the sick and the well. At the information desk, I gave my name and my father's name, and an elderly volunteer with a frizz of white hair and a drooping name tag on her chest immediately came around the desk and comforted me all the way to the ER. I was handed off to a stern nurse who silently led me by the elbow to my father's curtained cubicle. My mother sat in a mauve vinyl chair next to him. She looked up at me from her crocheting and said, "Piper."

In quick strides, I reached her and wrapped my arms around her. She had always been plump but had lost weight in the last year, since she started going to yoga and a Zumba class at her gym. When my father was home he pouted when she left for the gym, but I liked to picture her tossing her yoga-mat bag over her shoulder, pulling on her comfortable-looking sandals and walking out without looking back. She wept onto my shoulder, which surprised me, and I held her for a long time. She was shorter than I was and I found my face buried in her hair, a sandy blond that I knew she kept up with monthly visits to the salon. Her hair smelled like the perfume she had worn since I was a child and I was thrown back to my childhood, being comforted by her, her soft body and sparkling tops pressing into my cheek. When she finally pulled away, I saw that her mascara had run down her face and a quick glance at my shoulder told me that it had also run onto my T-shirt. I grabbed a tissue and she blew her nose and carefully wiped her eyes. She had worn mascara every day of my life; I couldn't remember a time seeing her eyes not rimmed in black, her lips not painted a soft pearly pink.

"Well?" I asked. I stood next to my father's bed. He was barely recognizable as "the Silver Eagle" at all. We could easily have been weeping at the bedside of the wrong silver-haired asshole without knowing it. His face was a strange greenish gray color and mostly covered by a mask and tubes. His bare chest was covered with electrical nodes and I noticed for the first time that my father's body had aged. His barrel chest was now home to sagging pectorals and I could detect a thin layer of pudge around his middle.

"His heart is beating on its own, but he can't breathe on his own. There's been no response from him at all. They suspect it's highly possible that there's been brain damage, but they don't know how much. After they're sure his heart is stable, they'll start the tests and scans and whatever else they need to do to tell us if he's in there. One of the nurses said that the doctor would be back in ten minutes, which really means an hour," my mom said. We were all unwillingly influenced by my father's rage over the tardiness of those providing a service: clerks, waiters, dentists, doctors. Never mind that as a pilot he was a member of the tardiest industry of all.

"So, I guess we just wait, then, right?" I pulled a wooden folding chair off a peg on the wall and prepared to wait. I sipped my soda and ate my Peppermint Patties while I read *Us Weekly* and tried to lose myself in the world of celebrities doing sometimes awful and sometimes completely ordinary things. My mom crocheted with great speed and concentration.

Forty-five minutes later a young Asian man entered the room with clipboard in hand. I was always surprised to see doctors who were younger than I was; I immediately felt dissatisfaction with my life, a feeling of having accomplished so little in the time I could have been becoming a doctor. I'm sure that my father, had he been alert and more alive, would have seconded that notion without hesitation.

"Mrs. Whitman? And?" He turned to me.

"I'm his daughter, Piper," I said, and stood. My mom also stood, all of us standing for no reason except it was something to do.

"Nice to meet you, Piper. I'm Dr. Wong. I've been assigned to your father's case while he's in the ER." He quickly nodded at me and went on. "We do know that your father has had a major heart attack and lost oxygen to his brain for some time. The timeline is questionable. Witnesses say he went into the locker room at about 6:05 a.m. and wasn't found until 6:13. We don't know exactly when the heart attack event took place. His friend Dr. Willson started CPR right away, but the paramedics didn't get his heart restarted until—"

My mother interrupted. "I'm sorry, Dr. Wong, but we know all this already. What does it mean?"

"Oh, yes, sorry. What it means is that in any case his brain went without oxygen for a time. The amount of time is critical here—it could mean anything from irreparable brain damage to moderate brain damage. We will know when we start the battery of tests, but we need to wait until his heart is stable."

"So, we don't know anything yet? That's what you're saying, right?" my mother said. It was rare to see her assert herself in this way; she was always overly patient, to make up for my father's impatience.

"I understand your concern and distress, but we don't have anything concrete yet," Dr. Wong said. He promised to be back again in an hour. I assumed that the right time to start testing my father's brain would be when the numbers in green and red and the different tones of beeps and blips of the machines aligned to mark something significant.

My mother and I sat together in a suitable silence. We listened to the hospital conversations around us: the whirring of machines keeping my father alive competing with the beeping of another machine constantly measuring that aliveness. There were muffled voices from surrounding spaces; sometimes a woman cried a pitiful low cry and was quickly silenced by kind, soft voices.

I was relieved when a nurse came and said that my father would be moved to the ICU. I was being driven mad obsessing over this stranger's repressed cries. Meanwhile, I had not shed a tear over my own father. I told myself it was because there were too many unknowns, but that was only because the truth was impolite—I was not grieving. When we were escorted to the waiting room so they could transport my father to another floor, I couldn't stop myself from peeking into the curtained space next to our own. It was not a woman after all, but an elderly man holding the hand of a shriveled white-haired woman lying like my father, covered with mask and tubes, wires crossing her bare, flat chest.

While my mother and I milled around the cafeteria searching out the enormous chocolate chip cookies that were recommended by the nurse staffing the waiting room desk, my father went into cardiac arrest. We were wandering back up to the ICU with our cookies already half-eaten when we saw a crowd of medical personnel surrounding my father, a feeling of general panic in the air. My mother dropped her cookie and ran toward the throng, somehow knowing it was her husband at its center. By the time she reached his bedside he had been stabilized and had averted death yet again.

Dr. Wong, with sweat on his brow, explained, "The transport caused your husband to have a major seizure, which shocked him into cardiac arrest again. We were able to stop the seizure and stabilize his heart, but this raises questions about what we can expect in the future. I'm going to get a neurologist down here right away to talk about our options."

When the neurologist joined Dr. Wong beside my father's bed, my mother and I were asked to step outside the sliding-glass door of his new room in the intensive care unit. Their voices were a low hum; sometimes one or the both of them would gesture to a clipboard or brightly lit machine. The neurologist performed what appeared to be a very brief examination on my father's limp body.

My father only lay in the hazy semidark, with no movement or change. The neurologist slid the glass door open and invited my mother in. He subtly but clearly did not invite me in before the glass door slid closed again. I took the opportunity to walk down the hall and call Isaac. I pulled my phone out of the depths of my purse and noticed I had a message. It was from the psychologist at Fred's school; she had done a preliminary survey on Fred and had a referral for a neuropsychologist she wanted us to see. I didn't remember agreeing to any preliminary surveys, but the time immediately after Mrs. Tieman's declaration of Fred's psychological problems at the conference remained hazy. It was also possible that Isaac had signed something while I was engulfed in my fog of disbelief. I played the message a second time and made a note of the name of the doctor and the number that Virginia Bach had left. I called the office and was surprised to find that a recent cancellation meant that Fred could get in that week.

As soon as I wrote down the date, time and directions to the clinic, I remembered that I was standing in the waiting room of the ICU because my father was hovering on the edge of life. The strangeness of my actions wasn't lost on me. A normal response might have been "Gee, my father's in a coma right now; we'll have to wait to schedule that appointment until he's either dead or not." I didn't even give it a second's consideration: if I had to choose between my father and Fred, there was no weighing of choices, no pros and cons, no hard deliberation. It would be Fred every time.

The neurologist performed his battery of tests on my father the next morning. Dr. Wong had stabilized my father's heart to an acceptable state. My mom described procedures and surgeries I paid little attention to, as my mind was on the looming appointment for Fred. The results from the CT scan, the MRI and a barrage of other tests identified only by a series of letters were conclusive; my father showed only basic brain-stem activity. He was a vegetable. My mother received the results from the neurology team with a look of steely resolve, firm nods and no tears. She was resigned to the facts, accepted the truth of science. The team suspected she was deep in shock and they pulled me aside and gravely instructed me to care for my mother in her fragile state for the next few days. I knew the truth, though; I knew what was behind those blank eyes and stiff gestures. My mother was only playing at grief, acting the part of the soon-to-be widow. The emotion that ran through her veins, as thick and life sustaining as blood, was relief. While my father hovered near death, my mother wished only to prod him along, because that, too, was the light at the end of her tunnel.

During those long, quiet hours I sometimes forced myself to dig through my memory for something from my childhood that I could hang on to, some nugget of goodness that my father had once shared with me. I came up with a handful of fairly benign but overall positive snapshots in time: the Washington, DC, art show I was awarded a spot in when I was twelve, when he seemed genuinely proud to introduce himself as my father; getting the Christmas tree one year when he must have been in a particularly high mood and wore a Santa Claus hat; his grave nod and wink at me as I took the graduation podium as salutatorian of my high school. I held on to these memories with clenched fists, sure that I would be required in the coming days to share those and more as we worked our way toward a funeral and the freedom beyond, the possibility of a life without "the Silver Eagle."

Fred

Mom met me at Wendell Elementary School today instead of at the bus stop. She was waiting by the fence outside exit B. I did not have to take the black-dot bus home today. We went in the Subaru Outback to the Chocolate Shoppe ice-cream store where they have four freezer cases of ice cream and eight flavor barrels in each case. At the Chocolate Shoppe ice-cream store you can have samples on tiny white plastic spoons if you cannot decide what kind of ice cream you want. I sampled Blue Moon, Superman, Zanzibar Chocolate and Orange Sherbet and then Mom said I needed to make a choice so I chose vanilla. The reason that we had to go to the Chocolate Shoppe ice-cream store today instead of home on the black-dot bus was that Grandpa is going to be dead soon. He is dead in his brain, but machines can make him breathe. His brain was shriveled up a bit because he had a heart attack at Madison Squash Club on Tuesday.

Mom said that he decided a long time ago that he didn't want to be a person who had a shriveled-up brain and machines to help him breathe, so he wrote it down in a legal document that was notarized. I know about notarizing things because Dad is a notary public with a stamp, but it isn't for fun, it's only for very serious matters. They are going to unplug all the machines that are keeping him alive and then he will not be able to live because of his shriveled brain so he will die then. After he dies we will burn up his body because it also says that in the legal document too.

She asked me if I wanted to talk about Grandpa's shriveled-up brain and unplugging the machines and burning up his body. I did not want to talk about that, but I was very interested in the history of ice cream in World War II. She asked me if I had feelings about Grandpa. These were my feelings:

A little bit sad because Grandpa was a person who knew a lot about some things and does anyone else know those things?

A little bit glad that Grandpa did not have to die in any wars because then it doesn't really matter what the legal documents say about dying. You do not have a choice about unplugging machines. You are just bombed or machine-gunned or crashed from the sky.

When you are a person who is going to die is that something that you know about? It does not seem fair to be in the shower and then dead without a warning in between.

Even though I know a lot of information about dying because of all the guys that died in wars that I know about, I don't have any information about when a person that you know dies. Will it feel different to be Fred without a grandpa?

She said that on Friday we would go say good-bye to Grandpa before he was all the way dead. She said also on Friday I had an appointment with another doctor. I asked her if it was for my itchy penis, which was my biggest problem. She said no, it was a talking doctor and she would call Dr. Goldman about my itchy-penis problem. She hugged me, which was a little nice but also a little too close. Then we ate our ice-cream cones and didn't talk about anything.

Piper

It was decided that Friday would be the day to take my father off life support. His heart was able to beat on its own, but he was prone to sudden, violent seizures. He was breathing with the aid of a machine and there was scant evidence that he could have done it on his own. His limbs remained mostly nonresponsive to stimulus, with only an occasional twitchy movement that the doctors and nurses believed was just coincidence rather than anything purposeful. All but one of the specialists summoned to his bedside described a situation with no hope (extremely limited brain activity, the likelihood of a severe amount of brain damage, with paralysis a strong possibility). The fifth doctor, a neurologist from a neighboring hospital who had been called in, felt certain he saw something, a small spark of possibility. A white spot of hope that everyone else wrote off as a machine malfunction. The medical version of a fly on the lens.

My father's medical power of attorney clearly stated that in the case that he should become essentially brain-dead, his wife would have the power to decide his future, knowing full well what future my father had in mind for himself. My father was not a subtle man, not an indecisive, quiet man. The future he had always imagined for himself would be exactly the same as his present or, now I should say, his recent past. He had planned to fly for as long as the airline would let him and then retire to travel the globe with my mother, never mind that her only desire was to see the spring cherry blossoms in Washington, DC. His vision of himself was one of hardiness, strength and vitality. I was as certain as my mother that he would have had no interest in a life half-lived.

The dimly lit cubicle, curtains closed to the lake view to keep stimulus down, was almost always filled to capacity as crowds of visitors took turns surrounding his inert body, wanting their chance to say good-bye to "the Silver Eagle." My mother and I spent good parts of the day in the family waiting room while an endless trail of people went in with get-well cards and came out shaking their heads over the tragedy of it all.

My mother's sister, Jeanne, drove from Saint Paul on Thursday afternoon, her Toyota Prius packed with various bags of knitting and reading materials, frozen casseroles and sugarless gum. I imagined her humming along to the radio gleefully the entire four-hour drive. Jeanne held her sister's hand, diverted some of the curious well-wishers from their constant badgering questions and generally did all she could to make the experience as smooth as she could for my mother. At the time I was soothed by my aunt's presence. It was lovely to see my mother reunited with her sister, as their time together was often limited by my father's demands and foul moods. It gave me a taste of what my mother had been like as a girl, just a glimpse here and there of the bond between little sister Judy and big sister Jeanne. It brought me to tears to see my aunt wordlessly hand my mother exactly the item she seemed to be searching for before she asked. I had always wished for a sister, and my older brother, Curtiss, and I shared none of the sibling closeness I envied. We were two people who had nothing in common except our roots, and once the tree was cut down and hauled away we were left with only the shared remembering of holidays and vacations.

Curtiss was still unable to get away from his teaching responsibilities in Chicago, he said. My mother and I didn't push the issue, knowing my brother's history with my father was fraught with anger and amounts of pain that even I, his sister, did not understand. He was certain he could get away for a funeral but didn't feel the need to say good-bye to my father's lifeless body. I wasn't even sure what kind of good-bye Curtiss would have said.

Thursday dawned gray and windy, small

crystals of precipitation floating down from the sky, too small to be called snow and too hard to be rain. We should have seen the confusion of the clouds as an early omen of what was on the horizon. I decided to keep Fred home so that he might say good-bye to his grandfather. I was skeptical that it would be a moment that Fred would cherish, but all the parenting guidance I read strongly advised a proper good-bye, so as not to confuse the child. I found it unlikely that my father's death would confuse Fred; he had been asking questions and formulating theories about death from an early age. His interest in World War II had now brought the complexity of his questions to an alarming maturity as he quoted mortality rates and causes for soldiers and civilians for both the Allied and Axis troops. I was fairly certain that if Fred understood the critical role antibiotics played to prevent widespread disease in war-torn regions, he understood that his grandfather wasn't coming back.

As a college student, I had witnessed the death of my grandmother from lung cancer. I had stood next to her bed with several of my cousins and my aunt Jeanne and watched her take each deliberate, soft breath until one of them, without announcement, had been her last. It was peaceful and quiet, an afternoon in June in the den at my aunt's house. The sun shining through the dusty windows, creating a kind of halo around my grandma so that my memory of that event is wrapped in a sort of magical haze.

We were told there was a possibility that this could be violent, even frightening. Though the morphine would help, there could be seizures, strange heart activity, pneumonia from the extended length of CPR, and even an appearance of aliveness. Dr. Wong assured us that any eye opening or small movements of any kind could be attributed to basic brain-stem activity and nothing more. I was ready to steel my mother, hold her up if things got difficult, pull the plug myself if she was unable to. Looking back, I can see now that my anger at my father had frozen into a sort of solemn pragmatism, trying to move as smoothly and steadily through the steps of his death as I could, trying to get to the denouement.

My mother would give them the okay to turn off the breathing machine and monitors and discontinue the various medications my father received intravenously at seven thirty a.m. The medical staff had assured us that he would continue to receive a hefty dosage of morphine so that he wasn't in any pain as he drifted toward death. Quickly, they believed; dead by sundown was their prediction. My mother asked me if I could be in the room, so Isaac and Fred spent a morning together at home, sleeping late and eating chocolate chip pancakes, I imagined as I made the trek from section two of the parking ramp to the ICU.

At 7:20 a.m. I met my mother outside my father's glass-doored room. For a few minutes, we both stood and looked in at him through the glass.

"He's all alone," she said. "Your father hates to be alone. He wouldn't even let me go to the grocery store by myself." She leaned into me, and sobs that had built up fought their way free of her resolve and my mother cried.

I put my arms around her and held her. "I know, I know."

"He would hate to see what he looks like now—he's so vain." She let a laugh sneak through her tears. "Sorry. I shouldn't say things like that."

"Say whatever you need to."

"Did you know that his father was an air force pilot who had another family in California?"

"No, no one ever told me about the second family."

"Your father didn't like to talk about his childhood; it was very painful," she said. "When your father misbehaved, your grandfather made him kneel in the corner with his nose to the wall for hours at a time. Your grandmother just stood by and let it happen because she would get smacked if she tried to intervene. She never knew how to behave with your father, her son. She had to decide almost daily if she was going to rescue her son or herself." My mother had straightened up and no longer required being held. "His sister died when he was in high school, drowned fooling around with some kids at a quarry lake. Your father was there. I'm not sure his family knew how to deal with her death, if they ever really dealt with it."

"He had a hard life, Dad," I said. For a moment, I was lost in the realization that my father had once been a small boy—a small boy with a cold and demanding father and an angry and overwhelmed mother. I allowed myself to follow the trail of an idea that who he was was perhaps not his fault. It was an uncomfortable idea for me; I had felt a lot of things for my father during my life, but I could not remember this feeling of uneasy compassion.

My mother stood up taller, smoothed her wine-colored cardigan sweater, picked a stray hair off the right cuff and then ran her hands over her blond bob. There was a period of silence between us as we stood watching the green and red lights take turns flashing. The beeps coming from another machine would be mostly regular, but occasionally erratic, as if trying to convey a sudden urgent message.

She turned to face me, her face changed from sadness to the same steely resolve it had had all week. "Piper, he did have a hard life, but he didn't need to take it out on us. We were the ones who could have made him better. We could have if he would have trusted us to, but instead he took it out on us. On you. And me and Curtiss. Oh God, how awful he was to Curtiss. Every day I regret not putting myself between him and your brother. That poor boy. I wonder sometimes . . ." She trailed off and was quiet for a moment, but I wasn't sure she was done. "The only thing that man treated with any kindness was that dog. That fucking dog. He'd walk to the ends of the earth for that dog." She shook her head. "In all my life, I never thought I'd be second to a dog."

She paused, then said, "All right, let's go." She grabbed my hand and marched us straight to my father's bedside. We stood together, watching his chest rise and fall. After a few moments, a sober-looking Dr. Wong and a nurse I didn't recognize slid open the glass door and joined us. I was glad that my mother's face still bore the trace of tears from earlier. I hated to think that there would be any question about my mother's motives. Dr. Wong spoke in a hushed voice to my mother, reviewing what would happen next, double-checking that this was indeed my father's wish; she signed forms without reading them.

Then the nurse began unplugging IV lines, all but one. She disconnected nodes and turned off monitors and removed an oxygen mask from my father's face, until the only sound in the once noisy room was the sound of our own breathing and shuffling. Outside, the precipitation continued to be unsure of itself, leaning toward snow but looking as if a change of just a few degrees could thaw it to a cold gray rain.

I wish that I could say that my father died peacefully just minutes after his life support was removed, but by the time Fred came to say good-bye at ten a.m., he was still experiencing minor twitching movements and some larger seizure activity. His eyes fluttered several times and his right hand seemed to grasp at something. All normal, we were assured. I was concerned that when Fred visited he might have to endure something scary or confusing or, maybe even worse, something that would be mesmerizing to him. Marla, the nurse, wrote her name on the whiteboard in a cheerful, loopy handwriting and then assured me that the morphine levels were high enough that Fred would be safe from anything more traumatic than his grandfather's inert body in a hospital.

Isaac and Fred joined me in my father's room. Isaac always believed the best of people and was genuinely sad over the loss of my father. Fred seemed mostly curious, with a wrinkled brow that I recognized as his apprehensive but contemplative look.

"When will Grandpa die?" he asked.

"Well, buddy, we don't exactly know that yet.

The doctors and nurses don't think that he's able to breathe on his own very well, so soon he'll just stop breathing. His heart isn't very strong either. Remember when I told you about his brain?" I crouched down to squat next to Fred and hoped my mere closeness could allay his fears.

"Yes, he suffered brain damage and his brain isn't operating the rest of his body anymore," Fred replied. "But what if it isn't?"

"What if it isn't what?" asked Isaac.

"What if it's not shriveled up? What if it's just kind of resting? What if he just starts breathing again?" Fred delivered his litany of questions with a serious eye toward medical curiosity, but I also sensed a hint of sadness.

I scooped him onto my bended knee, where he sat stiffly but didn't push away. "Aw, honey, Fred, love. I know it's sad that Grandpa isn't going to be with us anymore, but the doctors all agree that his body and brain aren't strong enough to keep going without a lot of help from the machines, and Grandpa didn't want that, remember?"

"Almost all the doctors agree," Isaac said in a near whisper. I didn't know if he meant to question our decision, my mother's decision, or if he merely felt his lawyerly need to cite specificities. Either way I turned around and glared at him.

I turned back to Fred. "Would you like to go,

or do you want to say anything to Grandpa?" I stood and stepped back.

He stepped right up beside the bed. He stood and looked over his grandfather's body. Isaac came and stood next to me and began rubbing circles onto my back through my sweater. I flinched at his touch. After several minutes, Fred stepped back and turned to me.

"Are you done, honey?" I asked.

He nodded, but I could tell he wanted to say something more. He looked thoughtful for a few seconds before he finally said, "He smells funny."

Fred

When you are in a war and you die, nobody gets to say good-bye to you. You are there fighting in the war and then all of a sudden you are dead. Your mom and dad or your wife or something doesn't even know they didn't get to say good-bye until someone tells them. A soldier in a uniform comes to the door of their house and says I am sorry but your person is dead.

I told Mom this before and she said that is why when soldiers go off to war everyone in their family is very sad because they are saying good-bye just in case. I asked Mom what happens to your body if you die in a war. Mom said that there is a special airplane that brings home the bodies of the dead guys. But what if you are in a bomb? I asked her.

She said if you are in a bomb then they collect the most things they can of yours to send to your family on that airplane. Like your shoes or your dog tags or helmet, or maybe a piece of your uniform. I wish very hard that I am never in a bomb because it would be sad for Mom to only get my helmet and shoe.

I said good-bye to Grandpa today. He looked like Grandpa, but not. Grandpa liked to comb his hair and he never had dry, dry lips. He smelled like something else, not himself. He was breathing, but very slow and wheezy-like.

There is something else. I didn't tell Mom because she said it wasn't possible. Maybe I did not see it after all, but I'm pretty sure I did. Grandpa smiled at me.

Piper

I had nearly forgotten about the neuropsych appointment scheduled for that afternoon. Had it not been for the call from the disjointed feminine computer voice, I easily would have missed it. The anxiety I had in anticipation of this date had been lurking below the pile of mixed emotions I had been sifting through the last few days. Now that the day was upon me, my nerves felt like frayed electrical cords, ready to spark at any moment. Fred and I went from the hospital to the McDonald's down the street, a congregating spot for both hungover college students and the homeless that we rarely frequented despite its proximity to home. Fred insisted that before we went to the doctor's appointment he needed chicken nuggets and sweet-and-sour sauce, his usual (more often than I ever would have admitted to any of my cohort, who favored organic produce and spelt breads). After Fred had methodically eaten every French fry and chicken nugget and turned up his nose at the browning prewrapped apples and opened and broken the toy, he declared he was ready to go. We screwed the top on the chocolate milk, though I knew saving it was a fruitless action, as it would most likely sit in the cup holder of his booster seat for a few days and then be gingerly plucked from the car and taken directly to the outdoor trash can, no chance for recycling.

The neuropsychologist was someone we had not met before, in a slowly decaying office park off the highway. When we walked in I was struck by how, in my experience, the offices of mental health professionals were similarly found in basements and old office buildings and places where other doctors wouldn't ever think of conducting their more important business. The smell of mildew was strong in the lobby and I immediately had a bad feeling about the whole visit. Isaac had begged off coming because of a court appointment regarding some decision about a long-ignored DNA test kit, rotting away in some basement, a crucial piece of evidence in a high-profile case. I was fine with it; I was used to handling all things Fred on my own anyway. In the waiting room, there was a pile of ragged Golden Books, year-old magazines on golf and copies of *Southern Living* and numerous copies of a magazine put out by some pharmaceutical company, one giant advertisement for a new drug for high blood pressure masquerading as a news source. Fred reluctantly sat in the chair next to mine. He sat back slowly and tried to keep his body still.

"What's up, Fred?" I asked. I picked up the

August 2012 *Southern Living* just so my hands were occupied.

"Tweed," he replied. "Smelly." One of Fred's idiosyncrasies was his particular feelings about both texture and smell. I could see that he was in a sensual hell.

"Sorry, bud. Hopefully it won't be long." I opened my magazine randomly to an article on the many possibilities of black-eyed peas.

"What's going to happen in there, Mom?" Fred asked quietly.

"I think the doctor is going to ask you a lot of questions. She's probably going to ask me some too."

"What's her name?"

"Dr. Suzuki," I replied.

"Japanese?"

"I don't know, Fred. Her first name is Helen. I didn't ask what ethnicity she was."

"Half-Japanese, maybe." He thought for a moment. "Did you know that the Japanese were put in prison camps in the world war? In California. I read about it. I wonder if Helen Suzuki knows anyone who was in a prison camp in World War II. I think I'll ask her."

I did not respond.

"Mom, I think I'll ask her. Okay?" he asked, and waited for my reply. Fred was perfectly sociable and conversational as long as the subject was one he had chosen. He required me not just to listen, but also to participate minimally in whatever monologue he might be engaged in. The conversations at our house were typically pretty one-sided, with a heavy emphasis on Fred's interests.

"Okay. Just be polite, all right?" I said. I looked at his profile, with its wrinkled, worried brow and slightly dirty face, and had the sudden urge to grab my son. I pulled him into my lap, wrapped my arms around him, though he squirmed, and buried my nose in the soft skin of his neck.

"Fred?" A young Asian woman approached us. She was wearing a pants suit and wore her long black hair in a shining plank down her back. Fred disentangled himself from my embrace. She smiled broadly at Fred and shook my hand. "My name is Helen."

"Suzuki?" Fred asked.

"Yes. Let's go have a talk." She led us up a half set of stairs and down a winding hall with wood-paneled walls and macramé artwork. The mildew smell persisted and I hoped the seating wouldn't be tweed. Her office was at the end of a long hall with windows that gave a full view of the highway. She had a leather couch and a large crate of grubby plastic building blocks, the kind that Fred had outgrown by the time he was three, when he had moved on to real Lego bricks. She gestured for us to sit on the worn couch and we sank into its cracked leather as she sat primly in a wooden desk chair across from us.

She started asking questions about what Fred liked to do and what our life was like. I caught myself answering for Fred a few times when he didn't answer right away and I thought I could see her make a mental note of Fred's overbearing mother. I sat back and tried to become an observer. Fred answered her questions politely but gave little detail.

"Fred, who are your friends?" she asked.

"I have two friends on my street. They are a brother and a sister and they live at 2388 West Elm Avenue and are named Antonio and Gabby."

"What about at school, Fred? Do you have any friends at school?" Helen asked.

Fred looked troubled for a moment. "School is really for learning and not for socializing."

Helen Suzuki looked thoughtful and jotted something down on her legal pad. "Oh, I see. Do you have any kids you spend more time with at school than others?"

"My table pod is Jacob, Maya, Sara and Hiram," Fred answered.

The questions continued, and every once in a while the doctor paused to write something down.

"What did you do today, Fred?" she asked. A tiny wave of panic arose in me.

Fred answered without pause. "I went to the

third floor of the hospital to say good-bye to my grandpa whose brain is dead; then I went to lunch and then I came here."

Helen looked at me, her pen in midair.

"Um, yes. My father is in the hospital and he's . . . not doing well. We thought it would be best if Fred said good-bye before he came, in case, you know . . ." I trailed off.

Helen nodded at me, madly started writing again and then turned to Fred. "So, you went to the hospital and then lunch? Where did you eat lunch?"

"McDonald's," Fred answered.

"Oh, McDonald's?" Helen said.

"Yes. It's a popular fast-food restaurant," Fred explained.

Helen stopped writing and looked up at him. "Fred, I have a questionnaire I'd like you to fill out. Do you know what that means?" She dug through a manila folder on the desk next to her and pulled out a packet of forms.

"Yes, a questionnaire is just a lot of questions that you answer."

"You're right, Fred. There's a little desk down the hall, a drinking fountain and a little refrigerator with juice boxes. I'll show you." She stood up and put out her hand to Fred on the off chance that he felt compelled to take it. He stood but ignored the hand.

"Can I have a quite sharp pencil?" he asked as

they exited the room. A minute later she returned, closed the door and sat back down in her chair across from me.

"He's a sweet boy. So polite," she said.

I felt like this was my chance to fill in the cracks that the survey was sure to have. "Yes, he's so kind. He's nice to everyone and he feels things so deeply and he really wants to make sure that no one's feelings are hurt and he's always asking me about how I feel and—"

"Piper, you don't have to sell me on Fred; I can see he's a great little boy. I do have some questions for you, though." She opened up her folder again and pulled out another form. "Does he usually avert his eyes?"

"What?" I was confused.

"He wouldn't make eye contact with me. Is that normal for him?" she asked blankly.

In that second I could see Fred's eyes, the light blue color that had garnered compliments since his birth. I could close my eyes and picture how those eyes changed depending on what he was talking about or what I was saying or what he was seeing. I felt like I could describe to Helen Suzuki the entire catalog of Fred's expressions.

"No. That's not normal. He makes eye contact fine. He just doesn't know you. He has to know someone for a while, that's all," I said.

"Okay." She wrote something on her pad and

without looking up from her form she asked, "What about his speech patterns?"

"I'm sorry. What do you mean?" I stumbled.

"Well, he described McDonald's as a popular fast-food restaurant when I restated what he had said, as if he didn't think I knew what McDonald's was," she said.

I paused. "He likes details. He likes people to know details about things. He just wanted to give you more information about McDonald's. He's smart. He's really smart." I could feel a tremble growing in my voice.

"Piper, I don't doubt that he's smart. Have you noticed, though, that his speech patterns aren't typical for his age?"

I didn't know what to say because I didn't have many opportunities to observe him in conversation with his peers. The bubble of apprehension deep in my gut began to expand as if I had mistakenly turned down a road I had glimpsed but never walked. "He likes to be specific," I said.

Helen continued to ask me questions about Fred's early childhood: when he started to talk, when he walked and a lot of questions that I had previously viewed as neutral and without the weight I could feel them now gaining.

"Has he ever been more interested in the physical toy than actually playing with it? A singular object or objects that he seemed to be interested in?" she asked.

"He's never been obsessed with objects, but he has topics that he's interested in pretty deeply."

"To the extent that he's not interested in anything else?" she asked, pen poised.

I knew the answer to that question—it was an easy one. I was further along the road than I was comfortable being. Somewhere in the recesses of my mind, the darkest corners, which I avoided, I had the feeling that I had been waiting a long time for someone to ask me these very questions.

"He's not autistic, if that's what you're getting at," I said.

Helen was imperturbably calm. "Piper, I'm not getting at anything; I'm just asking questions to gain a fuller picture of Fred." She stared at me for a moment and then opened her folder again. "I do have some questionnaires for you and Fred's father and also his teacher, if you don't mind. I've included a self-addressed stamped envelope for his teacher so she can just send it back to me. I'm going to go get Fred now, and then he and I will have a few moments together while you wait in the waiting area." She stood and opened the door. I wished more than anything that I could toss her questionnaires back into her face, grab Fred and run. I followed her out and we weaved our way back to the main hallway, where I found Fred with a small pile of empty juice boxes.

"Fred!" I said.

"The water tasted like pennies, Mom," he said

Fred

Helen Suzuki asked me a lot of questions but she did not look at the questionnaire. I said some of the things you are asking me are in the questionnaire. She said let's have a conversation. I said okay and she asked me what I liked. I said I like World War II and she looked surprised. I said I don't actually like it but I like to learn about it. Did you know that seventy million people died and it lasted six years and lots of countries were involved in it? She said yes Fred I knew all of those things. I learned about World War II in high school and college. What else do you like to talk about? I tried to think about that because I really, really like to talk about World War II. Then I said World War I. She wrote something down on a piece of paper.

She said let's talk about school Fred. I said okay. She asked me about my teacher. I said Mrs. Sandra Tieman taught fourth grade. She asked me if I liked Mrs. Tieman. I said Mrs. Tieman is hard to understand because she uses her eyebrows to talk a lot. Helen Suzuki asked me what I meant. I said that when she talked her eyebrows moved around too much. Then it was hard to concentrate on equations. She wrote something else on her paper. We talked some more. She asked me about my grandpa. I said he is dying at the hospital on the third floor and they unplugged the machines and his brain is shriveled but Dad thinks maybe it isn't and I don't know because he smiled at me. She looked surprised again. It was easy to surprise Helen Suzuki.

Then I said Helen Suzuki can I ask you something too. She said sure Fred. I asked her if she knew about the Japanese camps during World War II. She said yes. I said well I just want to say that I am sorry that the United States of America did that. I said sometimes when people are scared they do things that aren't really okay.

She said thank you Fred. That's very kind of you.

Piper

Night fell and still my father lived on. In retrospect, I can see that he was a little more alive than he had been that morning, less dead than expected. The nurses encouraged my mother to go home, get some rest; Marla insisted that she would call right away if his condition changed. I could count on one hand the nights I had fallen asleep with my father at my side. My father had not been one to sit beside my bed and read to me from the leather-bound book of Grimms' fairy tales we kept in the living room with the encyclopedias, but I suddenly felt a nauseating panic well up in my chest when I thought about him lying in that hospital bed, on his way to death in an empty room. I still don't know if my panic was a result of really, truly not wanting my father to die alone or wanting more than anything to make sure that he was dead. I sent my mother home and requested extra bedding so I could sleep on the vinyl-upholstered sofa next to his bed.

It was a difficult night. He was twitchy, and gurgling noises escaped from his throat periodically, always just as I drifted off. I had been assured that these were normal parts of the process of dying. Finally, I got up off the cramped bed and stood next to his bed. A soft halo of light shone over him from a dim fluorescent bulb. His eyes opened and closed rapidly and occasionally his right hand weakly squeezed the air. I pictured him lying in the shower, dead. I imagined his last squash game with Bob, not knowing it was his last, and I felt a funny kind of sadness. The kind of sadness that reflects what could have been instead of what really was. I know now that much of the sadness I experienced at that time was a mourning for the father I never had and, once he died, would be guaranteed to never know.

My father and I had a brief collective history with squash. Last fall, my father insisted I join him for squash when Fred was at school. He assumed that since I had been a passable tennis player in high school I would be a natural at squash and offer him the level of competition that Bob did not. He was quickly disappointed, as I consistently hit the ball too hard and missed my target, though the space between the lines painted on the concrete wall was wide enough that it should have been easier.

"Damn it, Piper. It's not that tough. Just don't hit so damn hard." He seethed at me from across the court. He took a deep breath and reset himself as a fellow squash player knocked on the glass door and waved.

"Hey, Johnny. Let's grab a match next week!"

my father said, even as he turned to glare at me once more. Years of therapy were supposed to have taught me to let behavior like this roll off my back. My father, the self-absorbed narcissist, gave the best of himself to the world. We, his family, got the emotional dregs of his difficult childhood. The years of therapy, though covered by a generous insurance policy through the university, provided me with lots of theoretical but little practical support. I felt tears spring to my eyes. I knew at that instant that I would be the world's worst squash player; otherwise, I risked the possibility of my father believing that he could "whip me into shape." I was right; he never asked me to join him in the dim warehouse for a game of squash again. I cringed the day he told Fred that when he was ten he would teach him to play squash. I was determined that Fred would never be trapped inside that glass box with my father's critical eye and sharp words. As I stood there over my father I thanked some unseen godlike being that my father would never get the chance to teach Fred squash.

The palliative care specialist had said that some people believed that speaking to a comatose person could help aid the person in his or her journey to death. There were plenty of things I would have liked to say to my father, but I didn't imagine that was what the palliative care specialist meant.

I took a deep breath. "Remember when I had the chicken pox and Mom got it too and you had to take care of me? You sat with me on the couch and watched *Looney Tunes* with me all day. You only called it crap once and I even caught you laughing at the one with Bugs Bunny as the Barber of Seville." My voice sounded strangely loud in such a quiet, still space. My father's eyes blinked at me.

"Um . . . And then there was the time that you took me to see *Return of the Jedi* in the theater because Mom and Curtiss didn't want to go. We shared popcorn and you bought Junior Mints and I ate them just because you seemed so happy to share them with me." I put my hand down on his, a strange sensation. I hadn't held my father's hand in at least thirty years. "Remember how you asked the usher at the door on the way out if the Ewoks were midgets in bear costumes?" I laughed and felt a small, almost undetectable twitch under my hand. I pulled my hand back and my father moaned. I looked around and found, of course, that no one had witnessed it.

I had to know if I'd imagined that flutter of movement. "Do you want to hold my hand?" I asked my father. He moaned softly and his eyes fluttered open and closed and then settled closed again.

I put my hand inside his. It was warmer than I expected and dry. I was transported to the roller rink in second grade, desperately trying to make it around the rink with my ankles knocking together, madly scrambling to hold on to the edge, when out of nowhere came my father, no roller skates on, grabbing my hand and leading me around the outside of the loop, not saying anything, just making sure I didn't fall. He had come to pick me up from Shannon Fowler's birthday party and seen me struggling. I felt a well of emotion overcome me, sadness over the mostly shitty father he had been, more sadness over the few moments of true love he'd ever shown me. A tear dripped down the end of my nose and my father opened his eyes and smiled at me.

Early in the morning a nurse came in to check my father's stats and his morphine levels. She was so quiet that I woke up only as she slid the glass door closed on her way out.

"Wait," I cried out, and sat up. She turned around.

"Can I help you with something?" she asked with none of Marla's gentle cheerfulness.

"Last night. I was holding my father's hand and he . . . he opened his eyes and he looked at me."

"It probably just looked like he was looking at you. It's very common near the end for a patient's eyes to open and close and roam around the room but not really focus on anything," she answered, still with her hand on the door.

"No, I think he looked at me."

She sighed.

"Because then he smiled at me."

She stepped away from the door, toward me. She looked at me with pity. "Oh, honey, smiling is a basic brain-stem activity. Newborn babies look like they're smiling too. It's one of the easiest actions a brain can perform."

"Oh. I see," I said, and lay back down. She left and I was there alone with my father again. I stood and went back to his side, but his eyes were shut, all movement stopped, no twitching. No moaning, just the slow rise and fall of his chest.

My mother arrived at the hospital accompanied by my aunt Jeanne. I had to get Fred to school but told my mother I would come back. I wasn't sure if I should tell her about the smile, wasn't sure what the point in telling her would be. I didn't tell her then; I wouldn't know until later how important it would become.

I rushed home and took over for Isaac, who was running late for a court date, shoved a barely toasted toaster waffle into Fred's hand and ran him to the bus stop just as the bus pulled up. I jumped in the shower, letting the water rush over my body, and felt the warmth down into my bones. I turned off the water, stepped out and wrapped up in my bathrobe. I went into Fred's room and fell across his twin bed. The sheets were rumpled; stuffed animals lined the wall, arranged in a specific order I still didn't grasp. I turned my face into his pillow and inhaled. The smell of his baby shampoo, which we still used because he was afraid to get soap in his eyes, the smell of the fabric softener and, most potent, the smell of his dried drool. I breathed it all in and fell into a deep sleep.

The phone woke me two hours later. My robe had fallen open and I was shivering. I ran for the phone and answered just after the machine picked up. I had to wait for the message to stop playing and then interrupted. "Hello?"

"Piper, you have to come right away. Something's happening."

I found my mother sitting on the hospital room's vinyl couch with Jeanne huddled close with her arm protectively around her.

"What's going on?" I threw my purse onto a chair and approached my father. He looked exactly as he had the night before: eyes fluttering, right hand twitching, and occasionally a faint moan passed through his unmoving lips. "What?" I asked my mother.

"He looked at me. He smiled at me, I think," she said, her voice shaking.

"Oh, that," I said with relief. "The nurse told me this morning that's just basic brain-stem activity. It doesn't mean anything, Mom. Babies do it too." I didn't mention that he had smiled at me and I'd felt something stir in me, a quiet panic that maybe there had been some level of recognition in that smile.

"She told me that too." She stood and came over to me, taking my elbow and leaning in close to my ear. "I felt something, though. He's in there."

"Mom, they said that there's no chance he's in there. You saw the brain scans all the doctors showed us." Even as I said it, I knew I was lying to her by omitting the rogue doctor's opinion. I turned to Jeanne. "Auntie Jeanne, would you take Mom for a cup of coffee down in the basement, maybe a cookie, if it's not too early?"

"Sure, Pipe. A cookie sounds good to me, too." She gathered up her large quilted purse and her knitting bag and another reusable grocery bag full of reading materials.

After they left, I was alone with my father again. I leaned over him and whispered, "What are you doing?" I felt his stale, warm breath on my face. His eyes flickered and then opened. He looked at me, right into my eyes. We held each other's gaze for longer than I could ever remember. His hand rose inches off the bed as if he was his usual self, gesturing to make a point. This was not supposed to be the way it went. There was a trajectory and this was certainly not on it. I had used up my curious sadness and felt my anger flare again.

"What the fuck are you doing?" I asked again, so quietly I wasn't even sure I had spoken aloud. I must have, though. For the first time in my life I said exactly what I wanted to my father, no fear of retaliation. I spoke my mind with no hesitation, no worry for what my mother would endure because of my disrespect. I said loudly this time, "Dad, what the fuck are you doing?"

And he answered, "Chuck Yeager."

Fred

Charles Elwood Yeager was born in 1923. That was between World War I and World War II. That was his name but everyone called him Chuck. He was a kind of general called a brigadier general and he was in two wars, and one of them was World War II but he was only a private then. The thing that is most special about Charles Elwood Yeager is that he was the first pilot that could fly faster than sound. He is still alive and he lives in California with a different wife because the first one is dead.

My grandpa taught me about Chuck Yeager because he is an important man. My grandpa loved Chuck Yeager so much that he named his dog Chuck Yeager. Chuck Yeager is a kind of dog called a border collie. He is only medium big, but very furry. He has black and white spots and one totally black ear and two totally black feet; that means one-half of his ears and one-half of his feet are both black. That is a coincidence. This is what else I know about Chuck Yeager the dog:

His name is Chuck Yeager. Not Chuck and not Yeager. If you say Chuck he will look at you, but he will not come.

He is four years old, but his exact birthday is a question mark because someone dumped out a box of puppies on the side of the road and that was Chuck Yeager and his brothers and sisters.

His tongue is out pretty much all the time. And he pants like he is hot, even when it is winter. Grandpa said it is because he is so curious; I tried it one day and Mom said I looked ridiculous.

He stares at me.

He has a toy that is rubber and shaped like the letter L. Grandpa put treats in it that smell very bad to me but very good to Chuck Yeager. He learned how to use his mouth to throw the toy into the air and when it bounced on the ground the treats would come out and he would eat them. Chuck Yeager is a very smart dog.

Sometimes he can be a very dumb dog. He does not like to come back when you call him. Grandpa has to yell Chuck Yeager you son of a bitch come here! Then he comes back.

When you walk Chuck Yeager he poops on the sidewalk and you have to pick it up with a plastic bag and carry it around. I think Chuck Yeager looks embarrassed when he is pooping and I try not to watch.

Grandma is not Chuck Yeager's biggest fan, but she takes care of him anyway.

Mom asked for a dog for every birthday and

every Christmas for her whole life and the answer was always NO. Mom is not a big fan of Chuck Yeager either. I asked her why and she said it was just on principle.

Piper

My father died and then lived, and then, as he was supposed to be proceeding toward his permanent death, he stopped, turned around and headed back the other way. It was not how things were supposed to work, not what was supposed to happen. I cannot explain the surreal feeling of carrying on a stunted, but actual, conversation with my dead father. After he spoke I pushed myself back from his bedside and breathed frantically, convinced that I had imagined the whole thing. And then he turned his head, just enough that his wobbly gaze could find me again, and he repeated himself.

"Chuck Yeager?"

His voice was thick with morphine and raspy from having a breathing tube jammed down his throat for the better part of a week, but there was no doubt that he had spoken actual words. To anyone else these two words could easily have been dismissed as the ramblings of a man just inches from death, a morphine-induced, meaningless declaration that was just one more sign that the end was near. Not for my father, though. He had inquired twice as to the whereabouts of his dog.

Chuck Yeager was a fine dog, if you were the type of person who happened to notice the thickness and coloration of a dog's coat or the shape or placement of its ears. I had grown up yearning for a dog, any kind really, and I had a long itemized list of what I was looking for in a canine companion. I read books on dog breeds and used limited allowance funds to buy *Dog Fancy* magazine. I dreamed of dogs, and a puppy was at the top of every Christmas list I ever wrote. I never got one. Then, three years ago, my father came home with a fat, fluffy ball of black and white and I saw a tenderness in my father that I had never seen before. A tenderness I had observed in other grandparents for their grandbabies.

My mother remained polite toward the dog but determinedly unbonded. When my father was away on trips, she walked the dog dutifully, fed him on the schedule that the dog had established and tossed the tennis ball to him from the recliner in the family room, until she was weary of it and she finally put it up on the top of the refrigerator where Chuck Yeager would whine at it until something more interesting came along. Chuck Yeager ate organic dog food and had a crate of dog toys, both rubber and fleecy, a rope for tug-of-war that only my father was allowed to get out, and a glass jar of freeze-dried liver on the kitchen counter. When my father was home they ran five miles, enough to tire the dog out for most of the day.

I had once taken care of Chuck Yeager, when my parents attended my father's cousin's funeral in Michigan. He was still in his adolescent stage, I was told, matter-of-factly, by my father, an instant excuse for any bad behavior. I found him to be unnerving rather than naughty. He often sat and stared at me, tongue lolling out one side of his mouth or the other. Every once in a while, he emitted a quiet, high-pitched whine, to gently remind you of his discontent.

I was concerned about how he would do with Fred. Fred had never been a big fan of dogs and regarded them with the same indifference with which he regarded other children. They were of no interest to him. Fred, however, was of great interest to Chuck Yeager, and the dog followed him through the house and dropped his toys at Fred's feet. Isaac thought it was adorable, but I remained suspicious of the dog's motives, secretly fearing that I would find him savagely ripping Fred apart in the night, just to have something to do. I would tie on my often-neglected running shoes and run with him, but the physical activity that was supposed to exhaust him seemed to further energize him, and his mind never tired out. Fred continued to ignore Chuck Yeager for the most part, perhaps making him all the more desirable to the dog, who was not used to being ignored. I always thought he saw Fred as a living puzzle he needed to figure out, like his treat-filled rubber tube but bigger and smelling vaguely of urine and chocolate. I was not eager to dog-sit again. Luckily, my parents rarely traveled together, so I had not been called upon to do it more than once, so far.

And so I sat in the hospital that day, my father's unlikely words echoing in my head, wondering what my next move should be. Smothering my father with a pillow briefly occurred to me, but I was certain I would be caught and my mind disappeared down the rabbit hole of life in prison, no mother for Fred, and on and on. I breathed short, panicked breaths and steadied myself by grasping the rail on my father's bed. His left hand moved toward mine, which caused me to quickly let go and step back again.

"Shit. Shit. Shit," I said. Then the tears started; my frustration with my father for not just giving the hell up and dying was immense. It clogged my chest and racked me with sobs. I sat down n the vinyl couch and buried my head in my arms, my body shaking. What was I going to tell my mother? Maybe, I thought, I could get away with nothing at all; maybe another heart attack would surreptitiously strike and the past few minutes would never have to be spoken of at all. I thought of my father, lying there with limited brain capacity, worrying about his dog, and I felt the tight anger between my shoulder blades loosen just a bit. Seeing him lie there and knowing the first thought of his new lease on life was one of love softened my rage at him. For years I'd heard from a variety of people, including a therapist and my own husband, that I had to be exaggerating my father's flaws—he couldn't be that bad. I staunchly defended myself, citing years of critical silence and verbal abuse. But there were these moments, unexplainable moments, when the innate love a child has for a parent seeps through the hard shell of indifference.

It was then that my mysterious and often absent brother appeared, having driven from Chicago in the early morning, expecting a funeral to be imminent, steeling himself, I imagined, for a good-bye he was only too eager to say.

"Pipe?" he said from the doorway.

I looked up. "Curtiss." My brother was standing there, as handsome and pained as always. A very expensive wool coat was draped over his arm and a bright red scarf wound several times around his neck. He was tall like my father, but with none of the muscle that made up the Silver Eagle's bulk. Curtiss had always been slight, with long, thin hair and brooding eyes. My father had come at him with a scissors to cut his hair when he was fourteen and Curtiss had fled to his room and blocked the door with his dresser. My father had responded by taking the door off the hinges, a nightmare for any boy going through puberty. Soon after, weary of the battle, my brother gave up any words at all. He seemed to disappear within himself when my father was around and disappear out into the world when he wasn't. I had always felt that I stopped knowing my brother when I was fourteen and he was sixteen, and I regretted the times before that when I could have known him but hadn't taken the time.

We shared holidays and e-mails now, but he remained a stranger to me in many ways. His partner, Daniel, was vivacious and loving toward Fred but continuously busy with his career as a foot doctor to the Chicago elite. His work hours and travel to international conferences made him unable to attend the few family gatherings that Curtiss did, we were told. I wished that just once Curtiss would stand up to my father, bring Daniel and introduce him as the lover and partner he was, instead of as an old friend. Then we could all avoid the awkward questions my father peppered Curtiss with about his timeline for marriage and why he had not yet found the right girl. I was never certain if my father knew my brother was gay and was torturing him or honestly couldn't conceive of the possibility. But it wasn't my battle to fight.

It would have been nice to believe that now that my brother was present, I would have a partner in the decision making, a cohort in grief. Perhaps I could even hand the reins over to someone stronger and braver than I. That wouldn't be the case, though; Curtiss had always struggled with his feelings about my father. Their relationship was fraught with tension from the time my father could tell that not only would Curtiss never play on an all-star Little League team, but he would never even pick up a bat.

"Where's Daniel?" I asked. My father lay still, eyes closed, the perfect picture of a quietly dying man.

"He's at a conference in Orlando, on laser foot surgery. He'll come up right before the visitation." Curtiss sat down beside me. I knew I had to tell him. He had to help me figure out what the hell I was supposed to do with our undead father. As a child, I had looked up to him, considered him the solution to every problem, followed him around until he grew so sick of me he biked off with friends and left me breathlessly trying to chase him down on foot.

"Curtiss, I'm not sure there's going to be a visitation. Or a funeral." I paused, not for dramatic effect, but just because the words were so unbelievable. "Dad just talked to me."

"What? No. You told me on the phone he was brain-dead. You said you took him off the life support," he said. Curtiss shook his head. He was unwinding his cashmere scarf from his throat like it was a boa constrictor releasing its prey. He bunched it up in his lap and settled his long thin hands on top. I noticed that his nails were smoother and shinier than my own and wondered again about the life my brother led, which I might never be privy to.

"That is what they said, all but one of them. We took him off life support yesterday, but he didn't die. Not yet. They said it could take a while or happen quickly, no promises either way, of course. But he isn't dead; he just talked. He asked for his dog, twice."

"His dog? He asked for his dog?" Curtiss said. He sat back into the couch. I wished, not for the first time, that I could lean into him for comfort. "What did you tell Mom?"

"Nothing yet. It just happened. What am I going to tell her? Shit."

"Maybe we should talk to a doctor first, let them figure out what's going on. Maybe this is just a fluke? A last-words-before-death kind of thing?"

"Mom's just downstairs in the cafeteria. She'll be back any minute. You always have to wait at least half an hour to get a doctor when you need one. Unless you're in cardiac arrest or dying or something."

"She's obviously going to find out, Piper. Do you think it's better to tell her, or just let her see for herself?" Curtiss asked. He stood now and looked down at my father, his forehead knitted into worried lines. My father did not speak to him, I noticed. He did not open his eyes to him, or move his hands.

Curtiss and I stood in silence, waiting for my father to wake up and speak to us again. I sneaked a glance at my brother's profile and I was instantly thrown back in time. I was eight and Curtiss was ten and we stood in front of my father, waiting for his silence to turn to rage. I glanced nervously at my brother, who, although disheveled and sweaty, looked calm.

"Curtiss, Piper. Who's going to be the one to tell me what went on here?" my father asked. He looked up at the ceiling, where a large brown stain shaped like a cloud had blossomed in the plaster.

I had promised that I wouldn't tell. I had promised Curtiss that I wouldn't tell that he was the one who had shaken up the two-liter bottle of Dr Pepper so hard that when he opened it, a geyser of soda sprayed onto the ceiling.

My father stared at us, looking from one of us to the other, waiting for one of us to either confess or turn in the other. But I had promised Curtiss I wouldn't tell.

After minutes of my father's stony silence, he finally said, "I can't even begin to describe the level of disappointment I have in how you two assholes have turned out."

That was it for me. "Curtiss. Curtiss did it."

• • •

"Curtiss!" my mother said from the open door. She practically ran into the room and enveloped my brother in her embrace. "I'm so glad you're here. We have to make plans." She released him from her hug and held his hands and looked him over. "You look wonderful, dear; I'm so sorry Daniel couldn't be here. Orlando, right? How's the dissertation going?" she asked. It seemed that my mother was a bigger part of my brother's life than I thought. I felt a twinge of jealousy, as I had always imagined that the teams should line up as the kids versus the parents.

She turned to my father. She did not reach out her hand, did not even speak to him, just stood next to the railing of his bed, willing him to give up, I imagined. He would not.

Then my father raised his right hand again, a bigger movement now. He reached for my mother's hand and almost caught it. My mother gasped and pulled her hand away. Both Curtiss and I moved up, flanking her. My father reached up again and my mother tentatively offered her hand. His eyes opened and bounced around the room before his focus found my mother's face.

"The pills," he rasped. My mother's eyes widened.

"What pills, Dad?" I asked, and leaned in closer.

"Chuck Yeager," he said, and his eyes rolled back into his head.

My mother and Curtiss and I stood silent for a long time. My mother took deep, gulping breaths with her eyes closed. She clenched my hand on one side and Curtiss's on the other. My brother and I both waited for her to speak first.

"The dog," she said. Still, we waited. "The dog's pills. He wants me to remember to give the dog his pills." She shook her head with disbelief. She didn't seem angry. My mother, my father's bride, married almost forty years, and she had doted on him every one of those. And still, he asked about the dog.

"Mom?" Curtiss asked.

"The dog has epilepsy. He has seizures, so he takes pills," she said. Her voice was flat and devoid of emotion. Her eyes stared straight ahead. "I've never forgotten to give that dog his pills. You have to hide it in his food, cover it with meat paste from a can. Sometimes he even eats around it. Then you have to open his mouth and stick the pill way down in the back of his throat. Then you hold his muzzle closed and rub his throat so he has to swallow. That's what I do. Twice a day," she said. I wondered if this was what the staff had warned me about, if this was what shock looked like, what it sounded like: describing in detail how to give a dog a pill, when your husband lies in front of you, miraculously undead.

Later that morning the doctors reconvened and reported back to us that yes, it was possible that they had missed something in the multiple scans; perhaps one of the fuzzy shadows meant something after all. It was possible that they had turned off the life support just a bit too soon, though this sort of thing was rare. It was possible that they were wrong; these things happened. They were always careful to include qualifiers like "possible" and "might" and "rarely." The fifth doctor looked smug and I imagined that he was desperately trying not to say "I told you so" every chance he got. There was a new urgency in the room, the medical staff rushing around the small space, checking stats, testing reflexes. The kind of urgency normally reserved for those at the edge of unexpected death was now being exercised in the case of unexpected life. The doctors immediately started treating my father for pneumonia, since now that he was a living person again, it was unethical not to. His morphine dosage was reduced to see just how alive he really was.

My mother was led into a small conference room just down the hall from my father with a team of specialists to discuss the next step. The door was definitively shut behind her, leaving my brother, Jeanne, and me out in the hall, alone with our disbelief. I paced up and down that hall for the better part of an hour, running through the events of the past twenty-four hours. I counted tan and burgundy floor tiles, windowpanes, light fixtures and anything else I could locate so I didn't have to consider the very real possibility that my father wasn't going to die.

They say even children who have been horribly abused or neglected still feel a connection, a tie to their abusive or neglectful parent, that same tentative tie I had felt just hours before. If I ever found that Fred had wished me away the way I wished my father gone, I would be heartbroken. But still, the only coherent thought I had as I paced that hall and waited to get word from the team of experts who had almost guaranteed my father's passing was: *No. This cannot be. The Silver Eagle must go.*

For that brief period of time I had felt his death was imminent, I felt a freedom from judgment, not just in that moment, but for the rest of my life. I felt able to breathe; the weight that had been pinning me down since my birth had lifted and the feeling of emancipation was exhilarating. As I strode up and down the hall, my shoes squeaking with each step, I fought back the panic. I have occasional panic attacks now, enough to know the telltale signs of their beginning. I felt the place where my stomach was supposed to reside become a vast, empty space, as though I was full of nothing. I began to get thirsty, wanted to drink gallons of water, an instinct to wash away the panic. It would be over quickly, but the feeling of failure to cope and the attendant shame could last for hours.

I'd had many of these panic attacks when I was young and lived at home with my parents; when my father was home it could be almost daily. Every panic attack seemed to be accompanied by an overwhelming feeling of self-loathing, which adolescents are prone to anyway. When I went away to college, they all but disappeared, returning when I was home for as little time as a weekend. An early therapist easily pinpointed their cause: fear. Fear of disappointment, fear of anger, fear of punitive silence.

When I was pregnant with Fred, my anxiety was crushing, culminating with a day early in my second trimester when I called a terrified Isaac home to find me huddled in the corner of our bedroom, sobbing, bereft with anxiety about the life I was growing inside me. Since Fred's birth the panic attacks had decreased, but on occasion when I arrived at my parents' house, pulled up in front of the gray colonial I had grown up in, I could feel the emptiness in my gut attempt to suck me in. With Fred still buckled in the car I would indulge in cleansing breaths and repeat my mantra under my breath.

"I am fine. He cannot hurt me," I said quietly as I walked, the cadence of my steps measured out to match the words, my mantra.

Curtiss had gone back to the room and was sitting quietly beside my father. He was hunched over the side rail of our father's bed. His body was softly lurching, and as he looked up from his arms, I could see his face was wet with tears— wet, but frozen in a mask of rage. I had witnessed Curtiss cry plenty in our early childhood; he had been an emotional and dramatic child who wailed over every paper cut and was often convinced that a fall off of his bike required a visit to the emergency room for a broken hip. The last time I saw Curtiss cry was when he was eleven. He had been accidently hit in the nose with a soccer ball at the park and ran to my parents with a bloody nose. My father had said, "What's the point of even having a son?" and walked away from us. I watched my father's impressive figure recede as he crossed the grass to the car, and with it I saw Curtiss shrink and fold up into himself.

The door down the hall opened and my mother stepped out, the team of doctors following her. If it was possible for her to be further in shock, she was there, hovering on the edge of sanity. There was a wild look in her eyes and she was clenching her purse to her chest as if she might be ordered to hand it over. I gently took her arm and led her to the family waiting room, her steps slow and plodding. Curtiss saw us and leapt up, wiped his eyes with his cashmere scarf, and rushed out to join us.

I closed the door behind us and sat next to my mother on the tweed love seat across from Curtiss. We waited. After a few minutes of watching my mother stare absently into the air in front of her with a wounded expression, I reached out to hold her hand, but she pulled it away.

"Mom? What did they say?" I asked.

She did not reply, but closed her eyes and began weakly rocking back and forth.

"Mom? What did the doctors say?" Curtiss asked.

She suddenly turned to look at him, as if she had just realized that she was not seated in this room alone. She sighed.

"He's not brain-dead. The fact that he can talk means that he's not brain-dead. He's making sense. It's not just crazy rambling. They have to treat him now, for the pneumonia and anything else they find. There's going to be lots of tests, lots of acronyms, CTs and MRIs and what was the other one?" she said and then paused to think. "Yes, PET scan. The other one is a PET test. I can't believe I forgot because when they told me I thought: pet, just like Lance asked about. His pet. Isn't that funny?" my mother said with an eerie lack of feeling, stilted and cold, the female voice on an answering machine, with the inflection and tone of her speech not quite human.

She continued. "They'll do these tests and other ones, too, as soon as they can, and then repeat them as the days go by, but he's not brain-dead; he's just not."

"But they told you he was," Curtiss said.

She nodded slightly, almost imperceptibly. She was staring above Curtiss's head at a heinous oil painting of sailboats, meant to calm. "They made a mistake. They read the images wrong. They were wrong." She shrugged. "Sometimes it happens."

"But he didn't have oxygen to his brain. They don't know how long he lay there without oxygen," I said.

She stared into space and nodded again. She stopped suddenly and grabbed my hand roughly and looked into my eyes in such an unsettling way that I was terrified for my mother's mental health. "A miracle."

"That's what they said?" Curtiss asked, his skepticism thick.

"Oh, no. No. They said sometimes it happens and we don't know why. Isn't that what a miracle is?"

I put my arm around my mother and pulled her into me. Her body was stiff and unyielding. She stared down at her hands for a few seconds and then sat up straight.

"I think I'd like to go home now," she said. "Where's Jeanne? I need to go home and walk the dog."

As the day wore on and my father fought his

way free from the morphine fog in which he had been buried, he looked around more. He found my face and Curtiss's face and seemed to focus for seconds at a time. When he moved his hand the gesture was still slow and jerky, but the doctors seemed to strongly believe that he was not paralyzed based on the movements he was initiating and also the results of the heat, cold and pain tests they conducted on his legs. He spoke little, mumbled mostly, and did not ask again about his dog. I wondered if he could somehow sense that my mother had gone home to walk Chuck Yeager and felt more at peace. I was unsure at that point how much was going on in his mind. We were uncertain how much of his capacities in cognition and language he would have. I did get to speak to one of the doctors; they were interchangeable in my mind. When they were sure he was woken from the drug haze, they would start a battery of tests and I was promised there would be more answers. I wasn't sure I wanted their answers. The one answer I wanted now seemed to be an impossibility.

Fred

My grandpa is not dead after all. I said good-bye to him, but it was a mistake. This is a hard thing for me to think about because it makes me think about soldiers. If there is a war and you are very badly hurt, someone might say that you are dead. They might throw you into a hole with other dead people or they might put you in a box. But what if they are wrong? What if your brain is trying very hard to wake up but they do not have time to wait for it? I did not really know that this could happen.

But now I know it can happen. The doctors said Grandpa was dead but then he wasn't. Mom said that there will be lots of tests soon and we will know what exactly happened to Grandpa's brain. We will find out what kind of person he will be. Like a fully working person or maybe a half-working person. After Mom told me about the tests and Grandpa's sleeping brain, I made her promise that she would not think that I was dead in the nighttime. Sometimes my brain sleeps very hard and is hard to wake up.

Dad came in my room after he got home from working on cases. He knew what happened and I told him what I thought about it. He said Fred do you know what I think? And I said no what do you think Dad?

Dad said he thought it was a miracle. An act of God that brought Grandpa back after he was supposed to be dead. I had to think about that for kind of a long time because God is something I am just not sure about. Mom says no and Dad says yes and that is very confusing. Dad talks to me sometimes about God and once I asked him if God was like Santa. Dad said no Fred don't say that. I did not know why that was bad because Santa is also someone you can't see that does nice things for people. I told Mom about it and she laughed. I did not mean for it to be funny.

Mom said tomorrow I can see Grandpa again. I hope that I can. I hope that my brain keeps waking up.

Piper

After the medical team was sure that my father's awakening was no fluke, they moved him to a new, larger room in the cardiac rehab wing, though my father's heart hardly even seemed like an issue anymore. The series of tests showed a heart that was nearly fully recovered and a brain that was essentially waking up. My father gained new skills each day, sometimes physical, sometimes cognitive or verbal. There were a few days where he gained nothing and spent the entire day either in a jerky, fitful sleep or vacantly staring out the window, responding to little. The doctors explained these days away as time that his brain was growing, synapses reconnecting, connections building, almost like a child's brain does as he or she sleeps. Those reconnections and the relearning of simple skills came with a burdensome amount of confusion, initially for us, and, as the weeks slowly crawled by, also for my father.

He walked the day after his awakening and within a few days he was able to use the restroom on his own, speak and answer questions, use both hands, write his name, and remember the date. The list of things my father was capable of grew rapidly, but he often blurred the line between reality and fantasy, confusing what happened and what he invented. Often, I felt like I was spending time with a preschooler, rich with imagination, obstinate and full of questions.

"Piper, can we go to the island again?" he asked me a week after his awakening as the sun shone in the window and frost covered the tree branches.

"What island, Dad? I don't know what you're talking about."

"The island with the monkeys. There are monkeys and you can take a boat over and sleep in a tent."

"I've never been to an island like that, Dad," I said.

"Yes, you have. We go every year. The children don't have to wash their hair," he answered, and was suddenly deep in thought.

The next day he would want to discuss something else completely different but equally fabricated, and would have no memory of our multiple conversations about Monkey Island. He was most confused about how he had ended up in this situation to begin with.

"Dad. You had a heart attack. Bob found you unconscious in the steam room and started CPR. They don't really know how long you were out. You had some brain damage," I explained yet again, my patience worn thin. He just shook his head in disbelief.

He fervently declared that he had been in a plane crash and implored anyone who visited to listen to his story.

"The plane was going, was going down. I had to turn the nose up. Get that nose up. Don't want to crash that baby," he said convincingly in his halting, raspy voice, using his shaking hand to demonstrate his imagined rocky landing.

When the visitor reminded him that he had not actually been injured trying to land a faulty airplane, he scoffed at their ignorance and anxiously grabbed the sleeve of the next aide or janitorial staff member who wandered close enough to his bed. Countless hospital workers unfamiliar with his case asked about the specifics of his plane crash, and I disappointed many of them when I revealed the true story of his hospitalization. Eventually I gave up and nodded along with my father as he detailed his heroics in stilted words, so many of them difficult to pull from the recesses of his brain. His brain remained a mystery, not only to me, but to the hospital staff as well. The likeliest explanation they mustered from their tens of thousands of dollars of tests and scans was that he was lucky. Luck saved my father; that and the fact that he had played a vigorous game of squash. His blood was superoxygenated and even though he wasn't breathing in oxygen on his own, his superior blood was making enough to hold off brain damage.

Fred came to visit him often; his school was just under a mile from the hospital. I left in the midafternoon and fetched Fred from school to visit with his grandfather. I hovered near as Fred sat with my father, never quite trusting that he wouldn't suddenly return to his real, true self and find the sharp words that I believed were hidden somewhere in his mind. He regarded Fred with a great deal of curiosity, as if he was completely unfamiliar with the concept of a child. He bombarded Fred with questions that Fred patiently answered.

"You're small. Why are you small?" he asked Fred one day as he studied his large hand next to Fred's small one.

"I am only nine, Grandpa. I am also on the small side. I am only in the fifteenth percentile for height and the eighth for weight," Fred said.

My father nodded gravely, as if he understood the vital importance of these concepts to a nine-year-old boy.

"I'm not small. I was in an airplane crash," he said. Fred listened patiently while my father regaled him with his fabricated anecdote, until it became so vivid and disturbing that I cut him off and shepherded Fred out the door. My father lay back in his bed, tears in his eyes.

The Silver Eagle

It was a fuel leak. Fuel starvation. Very rare. It wouldn't steer. The sounds of metal ripping, the flight attendants' voices ("Brace, brace, brace!"), then so much silence. Woke up to screaming. Some weeping. Trying to break out of the buckle. Wouldn't unbuckle. Finally, free, a wall of fire between the cockpit and the cabin. I have to push through, tear off my clothes, get rid of the fire. The smell of jet fuel and the smell of the bodies burning. The heat of the fire. The air is gray, full of dust, hard to see. I have to move through the dust. There are people still in the seats. A woman is praying. I put my hand on her shoulder and her body tips forward. She is dead.

I can see daylight in front of me and I go toward it. There are people around me, but most of them are dead. I can see now parts of the plane have just disappeared. Dust. I move to the light. I am moving so slowly, underwater. My lungs are full of water and I cough. It is dust. I can see the light ahead, but the air is gray; the sun is gone. There is paper everywhere, dancing in the air. I get closer and see it is money. I come to the edge of the hull of the plane. I look down and I see people moving, some lying still, some running away. Bloody people. A child crying from the ground. I look down. It's twenty feet. I look back up to the sky and behind the swirling dust and smoldering ash floating in the air I can see the yellow ball of the sun and I know I have to jump.

I jumped and hit my head. I woke up in the hospital. Here, at home. They told me I have a brain injury. I have pneumonia, from the ash. Breathing in the smoke. They didn't know about the crash. They said no, no, no. Heart attack. But I was there. I saw the dead woman praying. I saw the money floating through the air. I saw the yellow ball of the sun.

They didn't want to know about it. It hurt them too much to hear.

I think the boy was there. The boy jumped with me. He took my hand, my dusty, bloody hand and said jump.

Fred

I am confused. It is hard to understand brains. My grandpa had a heart attack and now his brain is making him forget what is real. He told me yesterday that he was flying a plane and it crashed. He was telling me all about it when Mom made him stop and made me go home. She is worried that it will make me scared. I told her that there are so many things in the world to be scared about and this is just one. That did not make her feel better. I used the Google to look up plane crashes when Mom and Dad were having a disagreement about who would take me to the doctor about my itchy penis because it still itches. If you use the Google to find out about plane crashes, you will see some pictures that might make you worry. I think you shouldn't do that. It might give you bad dreams and then you wouldn't want to fall asleep because in your dreams you would see the pictures of the planes torn apart and the people lying in the grass and some of them might even be dead.

After I saw those pictures I had to tell myself the names of biplane fighters used in World War II so that I didn't think about bodies on fire. I said them over and over until Mom yelled Fred are you in bed yet?

Piper

Curtiss stayed only a few days, holed up in a hotel near the stadium, visiting our father once a day for never more than one hour. I thought it might have been helpful for me to be present for these visits, but after the first few minutes I decided that the tension and awkwardness were more than I could manage and I disappeared for that hour. Curtiss came for dinner several times, causing me to scramble around for a suitable vegetarian meal, which was tricky, as Fred loathed all vegetables and happily declared himself a carnivore. After dinner, I cleared up while Isaac and Curtiss sat and discussed Isaac's caseload through the Innocence Project. Those evenings were strange because they represented the most time I had spent with my brother over the last twenty years, and the most family meals in a row that Isaac had ever made it to. Curtiss was happy to ask all the questions that I had long grown weary of. Seeing my husband's eyes light up in conversation with someone else should have made me jealous, but I felt only relief that I was free to come and go as I pleased.

"So, you're saying that the evidence against Sanchez is purely circumstantial, right?" Curtiss asked.

"Exactly, and yet the case was declared open-and-shut. Sent him right to death row," Isaac said, gesturing wildly with his beer bottle.

"Explain to me how that could happen," Curtiss said, and Isaac gladly obliged, discussing gruesome details that caused Fred's eyes to widen until I hauled him off to bed.

The conversation rarely turned toward our father, until I found Curtiss standing beside our father as he napped on the morning Curtiss was due to leave Madison for home. Since he'd woken up, our father had regarded Curtiss with a level of suspicion one usually reserved for the strange man loitering on the edge of a playground full of children, which certainly didn't endear him to Curtiss.

"So?" I asked as I walked up next to him. I gripped the cool metal bar that protected my father from falling out of bed.

"I'm heading out, Piper. In just a bit," Curtiss said. "I'm going to try to get home before the rush-hour traffic hits I-90."

"Just like that? You're out of here?" I asked, and crossed my arms on my chest.

"What do you mean? I've hung out here for four days. What more would you like me to do?"

"What're we going to do with him, Curtiss? What are we going to do with Mom? She's going to lose it."

"I'm sorry, but I can't make it my problem," he

said, and reached up and smoothed his hair down and tucked one side behind his ear.

"But it is your problem, our problem. It's our parents," I said, desperate not to be left holding the responsibility for keeping my mother sane.

"Piper, years ago I came to terms with the fact that my father, *our* father, is a fucking asshole, and I don't waste any emotional energy on him anymore. Mom is going to be fine. She's been fine for almost forty years. What's she going to do? Suddenly realize she wants to divorce him? Right," Curtiss said, and returned to Chicago with no qualms.

Isaac visited my father during lunch breaks and between classes. We seemed to be on alternate schedules, though I felt like I was always at my father's side and found it difficult to believe we missed each other every time. I was fine with that, though; it would have been difficult for me to sit by my husband's side as he pored over my father's every move and word and further reminded me that he found it difficult to take time out of his busy schedule for me or his son. My mother was in the hospital room every day with my father, arriving after she walked Chuck Yeager and leaving again in the midafternoon to walk him again. Every day she brought something for my father from home: a favorite casserole, his favorite mesquite BBQ potato chips (though the cardiac nurses tut-tutted those).

She dutifully brought him sweatpants, T-shirts, socks and underwear and then carted it all home to wash before bringing it back again. She sat next to him as he slept, as he watched whatever football game was on the small television that hung from the ceiling in the corner. She baked him his favorite Boston cream pie on more than one occasion, though I knew from my childhood that the process was lengthy and involved and most of the cake went to my father's visitors. I had always loved Boston cream pie but knew even as a child that the work that went into it was always greater than the appreciation my mother received. By the time I was a teenager she had all but stopped making it altogether, which resulted in my father pouting every time a dessert appeared on his plate that wasn't Boston cream pie.

The visitors flowed in regularly, so many that one full wall of my father's room was covered with get-well cards, the sort of thing my father just a few weeks earlier would have dismissed as sentimental crap. But he said not one negative thing, just smiled a stiff, crooked smile and nodded wearily as another one was taped to the wall, overlapping someone else's. After two weeks, the hospital staff grew weary of the stream of people and began to limit visits to fifteen minutes and allowed only two people at a time to enter. My mother was a constant; she was virtually silent and blended in with the furniture if a particularly unsympathetic nurse happened to be on duty. She kept a small notebook that she wrote in diligently when she received the daily reports from the medical team: the neurologist, the cardiologist and the internist.

My mother brought him the daily newspaper and read him the sports pages aloud, until the week before Thanksgiving we walked into the room to find my father tearing through the paper himself. He looked up at us with panic in his blue eyes and his brow furrowed. "I can't find the article—the article about the crash. Why didn't the papers pick it up?" He tossed the papers to the floor and my mother bent slowly to retrieve them while I sat and tried once again to explain to my father that there had been no plane crash, but rather a heart attack. His eyes were wet, something I had never seen before, and he leaned his head back onto the pillow and sighed.

"No crash?" he asked.

"No crash, Dad. No crash."

My father began physical and occupational therapy the week of Thanksgiving; he was on a stringent schedule, which left much less room in his day for visitors. His doctors warned us that he would start to become very fatigued, as the work he did with the therapists taxed him both physically and mentally.

Thanksgiving Day dawned bitterly cold, but

clear. The view from my father's hospital room was stunning: the university campus, full of regal old buildings, two lakes and the trees and nature of the arboretum surrounding it all. My father, however, did not notice any of it. He refused to look out the window at all. He was in what Patty, our favorite nurse, called "a funk."

"Lance, why don't you try some of the sweet potatoes?" my mother said as she attempted yet again to fill my father's plate with the meal she had prepared. She had insisted on bringing a complete Thanksgiving dinner to the hospital, where my mother and father and Isaac, Fred and I could eat together with our paper plates on our laps. Curtiss spent Thanksgiving with Daniel's mother in Racine, not that we had any expectation of his presence after so many years of absences. There were mountains of food—and the sheer amount was stressful to me—and I waited for the yearly argument to arise between my parents about her overcooking. My father paid no attention to the food and hardly even looked at the pictures and videos of Chuck Yeager on my mother's phone. They found a fan in Fred, though, who watched a video of Chuck Yeager running in circles around my parents' backyard on a loop until Isaac took it away from him and Fred was left to watch football on TV or push food around on his plate.

Over his uneaten banana cream pie, my father

finally spoke. "Rick from the airline stopped by yesterday. I asked about the crash investigation and he said there was no investigation because there was no crash. He said I had a heart attack and I said, 'Well, that's the first I've heard of that.'"

We sat in silence, each waiting for someone else to speak. Isaac cleared his throat and said, "Well, Lance, that's true. You did have a heart attack, at the squash club. Your heart's doing pretty well now."

"Why didn't anyone tell me?" my father asked. He didn't wait for an answer and went on. "What about the crash?" He looked around at each of us.

"Dad, there wasn't a crash. There was no crash. I'm not sure what I can do to prove it to you. You had a heart attack. Just a heart attack. Your heart stopped and then they started it again. Okay?"

My father looked at me blankly. "My heart feels fine. I have ash in my lungs, though, don't I?" He looked to my mother.

"Lance, you have pneumonia from the CPR. When the EMTs gave you CPR, you got fluid in your lungs. It will go away. You got bruised ribs from the CPR, too. You have been saying your chest hurts."

"Not from the crash?"

We all shook our heads.

"Why the hell am I here, then?" he asked, and violently pushed the plate of pie to the floor. I reached down to clean it up and felt tears prick my eyes and my chest tighten. I was certain I couldn't live with my father in this condition much longer, but the doctors were unsure to what degree his memory would return.

My mother took his hand. "Lance, you had a traumatic brain injury. Your brain didn't have oxygen for a few minutes. There was some damage to your brain. You have to stay in the hospital and do some more rehabilitation before you can leave."

My father processed this, shaking his head. "No. No, I just don't see it. I feel fine. I am fine. I read the paper today. I talked to Rick yesterday and I asked him when I was going to be back on the schedule. There's not a damn thing wrong with me," he said. Today marked the first time since his heart attack that I had heard my father raise his voice and curse.

"Dad, you're going to be here a bit longer. There's still more work to do. You're not ready to go home yet. What did Rick say about flying, Dad?" I asked.

" 'All in good time,' he said."

"We'll have to see what the doctors have to say about it, Dad," I said. We all knew he would never fly again. We had agreed that we wouldn't break the news of his early retirement until just the right time. I was still unclear about when that might be, but I was hopeful that my mother possessed the answer, though the thought of leaving her to do the deed made me uneasy.

That night Isaac and I put Fred to bed together and then to my surprise Isaac didn't crack open his laptop or reply to the slew of e-mails that always awaited him at day's end. My life, firmly centered within the four walls of our home, made it difficult for me to understand his constantly filling mailbox, his correspondences with hundreds of people. I had a handful of e-mails a day and most of them were related to furniture sales or fifty percent–off shoes. I had intended to read in bed, but Isaac joined me and it seemed obvious as I sat with my book open on my lap and him lying idly beside me that he expected a discussion.

"How are you feeling? About Curtiss going home?" he asked, lying next to me, his head propped up by his hand.

"Fine."

"Come on, you've got to be feeling something. Do you think he's coming back?" he asked.

I thought for a moment. "No, I don't think he is."

"I just don't get it. I mean, I know you say that your dad was a difficult man to live with, but to leave him like this. To just walk away. I just don't get it."

I had to think carefully about my reply; it was late and I didn't want to become embroiled in a conflict that would need to be unraveled and smoothed over tonight. "I know, Isaac. Your family life was nothing like ours; your dad is the kindest, gentlest man I've ever met. I don't think there's a mean bone in his body. You'll never really get it," I said. I wanted to change the subject and I knew the clearest and quickest way to do so.

"Where are you at with the illegal search-and-seizure strategy?" I asked, and Isaac was off, regaling me again with his unending quest for justice, his hands flying around in the air as he mapped out tactics and options, his eyes bright and sparkling with his one true passion.

Piper

By mid-December my father's condition had improved enough that the conversation turned to releasing him from the hospital and managing his transition to home. I still spent the hours each day that he wasn't in therapy beside him, cataloging his daily improvements. He consistently recognized me and Fred, too. When I entered his room each morning bearing a token of some kind—the newspaper, a doughy scone from the cart in the hospital lobby, a clean pair of sweatpants—his face glowed with a kind of childish joy that wasn't familiar to me because Fred had always been a serious child. When Fred was an infant, Isaac and I said that he looked like a cantankerous old man as he slept, his hair a fuzzy blond doughnut around the crown of his head, a receding hairline already at one month old. Though Fred was often happy, every moment of elation was accompanied by an underlying look of worry. Even as he performed his "happy seat dance" as he ate his favorite foods, his face was a mask of concern, smeared with chocolate pudding or sweet-corn butter.

For my entire life my father had worn a look of grave displeasure around his family and masks that ranged from confident hero to gregarious social butterfly around the rest of the world. Now my father had a face that emoted constantly; whether he was exhausted, depressed or over the moon about a fumble snatched up and run downfield for a touchdown, his feelings were unmistakable.

It was a few days before I noticed that my mother hadn't arrived after Chuck Yeager's morning walk. I asked her on a Tuesday, the first solid snowfall of the season, why she hadn't come to the hospital the day before.

"I was working on preparations. Getting ready for your father to leave the hospital," she replied quickly, but I sensed a slight waver in her voice, a tripping up. I assumed that the stress of the entire situation had gotten to her. I had no idea what preparations might be needed, what the rehab team might be telling her in the closed-door meetings. From what I could gather, the next step was a daily rehab program, communication with speech therapists, social workers, psychologists and internists. Beyond those clues, I knew nothing about what lay in store for my father.

It was that Wednesday that Isaac and I were scheduled to return to Helen Suzuki's office for the report extracted from a second appointment with Fred, two hours of neuropsychological testing. It was easy to ignore the date on the calendar as I busied myself with my father. I felt, however, an undercurrent of anxiety that flowed through my body at every moment, flavoring my morning coffee, making sleep slow to come and bringing me to the edge of a panic attack on more than one occasion. I did my best to push it away, replace it with the simple idea that if there was anything wrong with Fred I would have already noticed. *Someone* would have already noticed. It was easy to go on playing this game and I could continue to play it convincingly until someone intervened to explain that I didn't get to make up the rules.

Isaac requested an early appointment so he could return to his work grading exams after we received the news that our son was just fine. We took turns reinforcing our conviction in the car on the way to the office.

"Maybe he's just got such a high IQ that he's bound to be a little different."

"Sure, I bet that's it. Have you picked up the dry cleaning? I need my gray pinstripe for a court date on Friday."

"I'll do it right after I drop you at the office."

It was easy to focus on the whereabouts of a gray pinstripe, when in truth, deep in my gut, I knew something was about to change.

Helen Suzuki greeted us warmly and led us not to her office overlooking the parking lot but to an interior room lit by table lamps instead of harsh fluorescents. There were plants on wicker plant stands, an intimate table and four chairs. There was a bulging file folder placed in the middle of the table. In my memory, that file folder, resting innocently on the laminate-topped table, glowed with a sinister light. I stopped in the doorway. I felt my body sway, and Isaac stepped behind me, hand on my lower back, knowing just what I needed. I walked into the room and pulled out a chair across from Helen, hardly aware that my body was moving, aware only of the thickness of that folder.

Isaac sat next to me and pulled my hand into his lap and squeezed it, and for once didn't let go; his grip, which sometimes felt stifling and constrictive to me, was warm, firm and grounding.

"Well?" he said, directing his sharp, level gaze at the doctor.

"First, I want to say that meeting Fred and spending time with him was a truly wonderful experience. He's a very special little boy." Helen smiled her quiet smile and nodded to herself as if to reassure herself that this was indeed true.

"Okay, but what did you figure out?" Isaac asked. His normally cool demeanor was thawing; I could see a bead of sweat moving its way down from his hairline, tracing the sharp angles of his cheekbone. I shook my head, tried to focus.

"Let's start by going over these test results," the doctor said, and flipped open her file folder.

"His IQ is high, 155; you'll see it's in the range of superior intelligence. He scored very well on all the math and spatial tests that I conducted." She flipped quickly from test to test but fanned them out in front of us like evidence. I tried desperately to scan the results of one test while still trying to comprehend the next set of results that Helen had begun to describe.

"As you probably know, Fred's verbal intellectual ability is above average. But I did find he scored significantly lower on the tests I conducted of nonverbal intellectual ability."

"I'm sorry. What does that mean?"

"It means that he has some weaknesses in respect to visual scanning, visual-motor functioning, and fine-motor coordination. Maybe you've noticed that he has some weaknesses with his large-motor skills too."

I pictured Fred running through the park; his legs and arms seemed unsure what to do, just following the lead of his trunk. I pictured Fred on the soccer field at five, when Isaac and I had insisted that he try soccer. The few attempts he made at all to make contact with the ball ended with him on his butt in the grass, tears staining his cheeks. I felt my own face warm up, the red creeping across my cheeks. Helen Suzuki went on, presenting pages of graphs and charts, percentages with Fred's score highlighted, sometimes at the top of a range, other times at the bottom. It all made little sense to me.

Helen took a deep breath and adjusted her posture, her long plank of shiny black hair swishing gently across her shoulders. "Piper? Isaac? I had some thoughts about the social communication questionnaire I asked you both to fill out. You see, a lot of this data is pointing to something quite specific, but the questionnaire you filled out was a bit of a puzzle. Your answers were, well, quite contradictory at times, and I wondered if we might fill it out again with the two of you together." Helen pulled out a fresh questionnaire and poised her pencil above it, ready for our consent.

A tear formed in the corner of my eye, and before I could wipe it away undetected, Helen Suzuki looked up at me. Her expression softened. She set down her pencil and pulled a box of tissues from a nearby shelf. "Piper, sometimes we answer these questions about our children and we aren't completely honest with ourselves. Perhaps we underreport what we've seen or experienced. It's human nature. We have a strong tendency to see the good over the bad when we're talking about our children." She handed me a tissue and picked up her pencil again, but waited for me to consent. I nodded.

She began to ask us questions, questions about Fred's early childhood, his interests, moods, social skills. Did he ever show a compulsion for a certain toy? Did he ever show sensitivities to light or noise? Did he suffer from insomnia? Sleepwalking? Anxiety?

With Isaac sitting beside me, the truth poured out of me. Did Fred show obsessive interests? Yes, since he was two years old. Did Fred ever show any interest in other children? No, never. Does Fred use gestures? No, not really. The questions went on and on, and as each answer left my lips, a tiny piece of my hope that all was well died. I knew what the outcome would be; every answer I gave to every question cemented the diagnosis, but until the expert said those words, they were waiting just outside the door, poised to come in the second she invited them.

She took a moment to tabulate results on a legal pad, while Isaac and I waited in silence. He pulled my forehead to his lips and softly kissed me. Helen opened the fat folder and pulled out a few pages stapled together. The top of the first page was titled "Symptom Criteria for Autism Spectrum Disorders."

"The tests I've conducted and the results of the questionnaires that you and the teacher have filled out, as well as the one Fred filled out on himself, point to autism spectrum disorder. To be sure, we have to go over this checklist to see if he meets the number of specific criteria in a few different areas," Helen said.

With my hand tightly wrapped around Isaac's,

I struggled under the weight of more questions, gave more examples, and dug the truth out from under the immensity of my love. At the end of the third page, Helen circled "Level One."

"Fred has autism spectrum disorder but is high functioning, which makes him a level one, meaning he will require support, but not substantial support." She opened the file folder and handed over a stack of pamphlets and handouts, all emblazoned across the top with the words "Autism Spectrum Disorder." I sat with the pile in front of me, overwhelmed by the strange sense of loss I felt.

"I don't understand how I missed this," I said. As I thought of the level of negligence I must have been wallowing in, I gasped and clasped a hand over my mouth, shocked at my own inattention to my son's development. I wept into Isaac's shoulder and he held me, buried me in his tweed sport coat.

"Piper, there wasn't anything you could have done differently; this is not your fault. Fred is high functioning and nobody blames you for not coming in sooner," Helen said, and she again handed me the box of tissues.

"But how come no one else noticed? Why didn't his school figure it out? He's nine, for God's sake!" I sobbed into my tissue.

"It doesn't really matter now, does it? I mean, now we know what we need to do for him, we

163

just have to do it," Isaac said soothingly into my hair.

I pulled away and turned to look at him, so sure there must have been someone else sitting beside me, not the father of my child. "What do you mean, it doesn't matter now?" I asked him.

Isaac said, "I just mean, we just have to keep moving forward. We've gathered our evidence; now we need to plead our case to his school and—"

I interrupted. "This isn't a court case, Isaac. This is our child. This is Fred."

"Of course, I know that, Piper. But it's Fred. It's still Fred. This doesn't change anything. He's still our Fred," he said.

Helen Suzuki sat still and gazed down at the file folder on the table and quietly organized the large pile of papers, the evidence that Fred was not *just* Fred, not *still* Fred. Fred was now a child with a label. A child with problems, a disability. I did not understand how Isaac could believe that this didn't change anything. Helen described the next steps in the process, how to go about getting Fred an educational diagnosis, because the label she gave him was considered a medical diagnosis and wasn't enough to get Fred help at school. I didn't understand what kind of help Fred would get at school; academically he was doing fine. Did they have someone who could teach him to make friends? Someone to let him know when he was talking like an uptight adult? I felt certain in that moment that Fred was doomed to a lonely life.

Helen volunteered to speak to Fred about his diagnosis if we wanted, when we felt like he was ready for it. I couldn't imagine having that conversation with him and thanked her and said we would be in touch.

When we got out to the car, I collapsed into my seat and sobbed; a howling, screaming sadness poured out of me. Isaac sat quietly next to me in the driver's seat and rubbed my neck as my body shook with grief and rage. He didn't speak, which I was thankful for. I was unsure how to explain to him or anyone else how terrified I was for Fred. For me. I had pictured a life for Fred. After he grew out of this awkward, quirky stage, I pictured him with friends and someday a girlfriend, college, a marriage, children of his own. Suddenly, all these plans I had made for him, the life I had fantasized for him, were in jeopardy. If he never learned how to make friends, how would he ever make connections in the world? Would he even leave home? As my mind reviewed all the possibilities lost, the plans upset, my breath heaved from my tightened chest. Isaac did not make a move to start the car. He didn't take his hand off of my neck. It was minutes that we sat there before I was wrung dry of my tears. The windshield was covered with patchy snowflakes, few enough in number that I could make out individual flakes on the glass, sitting still and perfect before they finally melted into one another and became water droplets, meandering down the windshield in tiny rivers. I gathered my breaths into some sort of rhythmic, organized breathing.

Isaac reached into his pocket and pulled out his phone. I was certain that he was checking his messages, of which there were always plenty. His fingers moved across the touch screen and he held the phone to his ear. He spoke into the phone. "Rachel, I'm going to need to take the rest of the day. Can you let Miranda know I'll be in tomorrow?" He paused and listened. "No. I'm not checking my messages."

Isaac took me home. He made me toast with cinnamon sugar and tea with honey and lemon, something I had done for him during law school. He walked me up to our bed and wrapped me up in our down duvet, and I laid my head on his shoulder. He stroked my hair and listened to my fears, my doubts, my worries. He listened without judgment. It was one of those moments that had become fewer and fewer as the years went by, a moment when I felt sure I was with the exact right person. We fell asleep like that, wrapped around each other, like we had done when we were young and new to each other. We awoke shortly after noon when my phone rang.

"Mom?"

"Piper, I need you to come down to the hospital. We're talking about your father's next steps," she said, her voice cutting in and out as if she was calling me from a parking garage.

"Mom, it's been a difficult morning. Can you just fill me in later?" I was hesitant to leave the warmth and safety of Isaac's arms for more discussion about therapists and discharge notes. My grief was still thick around my heart, but I felt like I had a partner in slaying it.

"Piper, honey." Her voice was quiet, hard to hear over the intermittent static. "You have to come. There's, well, there's some things you're going to need to know about." Her voice cut out and I was left holding my own phone in my hand, wondering why she had sounded so guilty.

"I have to go in to the hospital. My mom wants me to be there," I said.

"I'll come with you. You know, in case you need a lawyer present," Isaac said, and smiled. He kissed me and wrapped his arms around me. "You know, Pipe, we're going to get through this. This thing with Fred is going to just be a blip on the radar screen of our life."

I didn't want to argue, so I nodded. I played along.

We reached the hospital by midafternoon and entered my father's room, expecting to be late for a meeting with his team. We found the room empty and an aide told us that my father was at an occupational therapy appointment. I wondered aloud at where my mother was.

"Oh, she's down the hall in the family meeting room with another lady. They've been sitting down there for a long time now," the aide said, and pushed her cart on to the next room.

Isaac and I knocked on the door of the family waiting room and my aunt Jeanne answered the door. "Oh! Jeanne, I didn't know you were here. I thought you went home," I said, and moved in for a hug. Jeanne hugged me awkwardly, letting me go earlier than was normal for her.

"Isaac! This is a treat." Jeanne hugged him and then squeezed her large, round body past my mother's chair to sit on the opposite side of the table, next to her. My mother stared down at her hands. The air suddenly felt thick, too warm, and a slightly sour smell seemed to emanate from the striped wallpaper.

"What's going on?" I asked my mother. She didn't look up.

"Have a seat, Piper. Isaac," Jeanne said. She put her hand on my mother's back. My mother suddenly came alive, as if just realizing that someone had even entered the room.

"Piper," she said. "Your father's team has told me that he'll be ready to leave the hospital by the end of the week. He's improved enough so that he can just use outpatient services."

"So, he's going home?" I said.

"Well, no," she said. A heavy silence settled over the table like a dense fog. I waited for my mother to break through it and explain what the hell was happening.

"Your mother thinks it would be better if your father didn't come home," Jeanne said.

"Where's he going to go?" Isaac asked.

"A nursing home. A lovely one," Jeanne said.

"Jeanne, I'd really like to have my mom tell me all this," I said to Jeanne, without taking my eyes off my mother.

"I can't do it, Piper," she said so quietly I almost missed it.

"Can't do what? Take care of him? Can't you hire a nurse?" I asked.

"No. Not that. I can't live with him anymore," she said. Now she looked up at me and any hesitation in her voice vanished. "I gave that man almost forty years of my life. Forty years. I can't live with him anymore. I can't fold his socks and walk his dog. I can't. I just can't live with him yelling. The yelling and then the silence. I don't want to. I'm done. I thought he was dead and done but then he wasn't," she babbled on, but then took a deep breath and centered herself. "But I am. I have to be. I can't do it anymore," she said.

I was confused, despite all those times I had hoped she'd walk away. "But, Mom, he's different now. He's not yelling or angry. He's broken. How can you leave him?" I asked, my words slow and stumbling, unsure of their place in reality.

"It doesn't matter. I can't give up any more of my life for him. I know that you and Curtiss didn't have a pleasant childhood and I'm sorry for that. So very sorry for that. I should have taken you and left. That's what I should have done, but I didn't. I stayed because he told me he needed me. He did need me; he couldn't have functioned without me. He didn't know how to start the washing machine. He didn't know how to cook. He was like a child sometimes. But when he was angry, well, I tried to insulate you and your brother from the worst. I'm tired. I can't pretend anymore."

"You don't have to love him; you just have to let him get better. Can't you wait until he's better? I don't understand why you think you have to do this now."

Jeanne piped in. "It's a natural transition."

I turned to her. "What exactly do you have to do with this?" I still wasn't angry, just slow with perplexity and limited in my ability to believe that it was real. None of the divorce fantasies I had for my mother involved my father sitting on a hospital bed, trying to relearn how to tie his shoes.

"Your mother is going to come back to Saint

Paul and stay with me for a while," Jeanne said.

"What? You're not even going to be around? You're leaving the state?" My anger was building. "Who's going to be his advocate? You aren't even going to be involved? You're his medical power of attorney."

"Actually, Piper, I'd like to sign that job over to you. Your father is considered unable to make that decision right now, so I can choose someone else and I'd like you to do it. You'll just have to check him into the nursing home and help him get settled and then all his care will be in their hands," my mother said to me, her eyes searching my face for an easy agreement. She pushed a few pieces of paper across the table to me. Isaac reached for them right away and scanned them quickly.

"You're sure about this, Judith?" he asked. "You could just go home and visit him, rebuild your relationship while he heals."

" 'Rebuild my relationship'?" My mother stood and her eyes filled with fury and tears. "You don't know the first thing about my relationship. You don't know that man like I do. No one does," she shouted. She turned to me and said, "Do you remember when I told you I walked into a door and got that bruise on my cheek? I know you remember; you were in high school and certain that your father had hit me. I worked so hard to convince you. I lied and lied for so many years.

He hit me, Piper. It was just that one time, but he did. The rest was words. Just his horrible words. Nothing was ever good enough for him. When he was gone, I could breathe; I could see the sun. He was supposed to die. He should have died. Damn Bob had to walk in and give him CPR. Why did he have to do that? When I thought he was going to die, I felt like I had another chance at my life. But then there was this miracle, this fucking miracle, and here we are!"

"Judith, I'm not sure you should be saying these things," Isaac said calmly.

"I don't care what you think. I'm tired of lying. I don't care what happens to him next. I'm done caring. I didn't want to give you this responsibility, Piper, but I'm just done," she said, and sat down hard in her chair. She sobbed into her folded arms, head down on the table.

I sat for what felt like a long time. It was not a responsibility that I would ever have wished for, but the alternative was what? He became a ward of the state? He withered away in a home with no one monitoring his care? It felt like a fate not even my father deserved. Finally, I slid the papers toward me and opened to the page that had been marked for my signature. Jeanne reached into her large handbag and pulled out a pen and handed it to me. I signed the paper and pushed it back toward my mother.

"You have to do something for me. You have to

say good-bye to him. You don't just get to walk away," I said, surprised at how authoritative I sounded, as if I had any business demanding she do anything.

"Fine," she said.

The Silver Eagle

Judy is wife. Judy is mother. Judy is coffee in the morning and tea at bedtime. Judy is soft and round and small. Judy is the smell of chicken noodle soup and apple pie and laundry detergent. Judy is spray starch and tape measures. Judy is tulips and lilies of the valley. Judy is Christmas and Judy is a New Year's kiss. Judy is next to and behind and in front of and near. But sometimes she is also far, outside and far.

When I lie down Judy is next to me. Sometimes she is far and the next to me is empty. When I drive Judy is next to me. Judy doesn't like to drive. Judy likes bird feeders and finches. Judy likes cardinals and wrens. Judy doesn't like the squirrels. Judy can hum but not sing. Judy scratches backs and trims hair. Judy is everywhere unless she is gone.

Once Judy was hello. Judy was love. Judy was flying. Judy was a navy blue suit and a brown leather suitcase. Judy was winks and shiny lips and curled hair. Judy was large and round and then holding babies and then walking children to the bus and then packing lunches. Judy was sad. Judy is sad. Judy is silent behind her smile. Judy is nods and tears and shaking hands. Judy is sorry sorry sorry. Judy is driving away. Now Judy is good-bye.

Piper

My mother left that evening; she didn't waste time considering other options, wondering what would happen in her absence. She dropped Chuck Yeager off at our house, handed me a bag of dog food, a bottle of pills and an envelope filled with cash for his care. He looked confused at the end of his Day-Glo orange leash. She assured me again that all the arrangements had been made. This was what she had been doing for all those weeks, when I believed that she was meeting with therapists and specialists to discuss home care. She was securing a pet-friendly room for my father in a nursing home with a good reputation. She reached out to hug me, but halfway there backed away, understanding that my stiffness meant "No, thank you."

"Piper, I do love you. I love you very much. I hope someday you can understand why I had to do this," she said, and turned around and walked back to Jeanne and the warm car, packed for Saint Paul.

I looked down at Chuck Yeager, who watched his mistress walk away and gave out a soft whine. "Come on, buddy," I said, and pulled him away from the door. I unclipped his leash and he tore off to investigate the house. I shut the door. I hadn't even told my mom about Fred's diagnosis. I probably could have found an appropriate moment, but I didn't share it with her. Part of me didn't want to let her that far into my world. The other part of me wanted to tell her and show her that people deal with pain. You grab it and hold on to it and wrestle with it if need be, but you don't throw the towel in before the fight. Even if I wouldn't have admitted it to her in that moment, I knew she had been fighting, harder and longer than I knew, and for that reason, I couldn't hate her as much as I wanted to for leaving me to hold everything together when I was amid my own crisis.

"Mom!" Fred called from the living room.

"Yes, Fred?" I called back.

"Chuck Yeager peed on the back of the couch!"

That night Isaac was adamant that Chuck Yeager wasn't sleeping in our bedroom, though I knew he slept on a dog bed on the floor of my parents' bedroom. I led him to the couch and pointed to it. "Lie down," I said. He looked up at me with his deep brown eyes and raised an eyebrow at me, still sitting primly in front of the couch.

"I know it's not what you are used to, or whatever. I'm sorry. We're both going to have to get used to a lot of different shit now."

He panted and his extra-long tongue hung out

the side of his mouth as he considered what I had said.

"Mama!" Fred yelled from upstairs in his room. It was well past ten o'clock and he should have been asleep hours before. I sighed and started up the stairs to lie with him again. I pushed open his door.

"You brought Chuck Yeager!" he cried.

I turned to see that indeed, Chuck Yeager had silently padded up the stairs behind me and now sat next to me, panting in Fred's doorway. Chuck Yeager pushed past me, leapt up onto Fred's bed, turned around three times and plopped down in a semicircle at the end of the bed. He looked at me as if to say, "This will do." I started to pull him down by his airplane-covered collar when Fred said, "It's okay, Mom. He can stay."

I stood in the doorway a few moments longer and watched Fred huddle down under his covers, working his feet around Chuck Yeager. They both sighed. I was mostly certain that Chuck Yeager's intentions were good but flipped on the baby monitor on my way out, just to be sure.

The hospital decided to release my father on Saturday. I planned to leave Fred home with Isaac, but at the last moment Isaac received a prison call from a client who swore up and down that he had a tip from another inmate that there was evidence in his grandma's basement that could help prove his innocence. I might have felt worse about yelling at Isaac if he didn't get phone calls just like this at least once a month. The closeness that I had felt with him right after Fred's diagnosis had evaporated to a memory as we returned to our old patterns.

"It's okay, Mom," Fred said. "I can go with you to check Grandpa into his new nursing home room where they allow pets." Fred was sitting on the floor next to Chuck Yeager, who was busily chewing the leg off one of Fred's old stuffed animals, one I'd tried to throw out many times over the last few years. Fred always noticed its disappearance just as I thought I was safe and the raggedy, old stained giraffe was out of my life forever.

So, Fred, Chuck Yeager and I rode to the hospital in the Subaru, Chuck Yeager steaming up the rearview window with his constant panting and increasing my anxiety with his manic pacing. When we arrived at the hospital, we put the windows down a little and left Chuck Yeager while we went to collect my father so we could deliver him to the Manchester. Fred busied himself taking down all my father's get-well cards and the many photographs that people had given him, almost all of them showing my father grinning broadly in his pilot's cap, arms slung around some buddy or other. There were no pictures of my family, and in light of how things proceeded I wondered if visitors had found it strange. I wondered if everyone else had seen my mother's departure coming, sensed that the facade of this family was just that—a flimsy cardboard caricature of togetherness.

My father was quiet. "Dad, I have Chuck Yeager in the car," I said.

He looked at me strangely. "Who?" He was knitting his hands together in his lap, a nervous act that made him look like a frightened old lady.

"Your dog, Dad. Chuck Yeager is the name of your dog," I said.

He nodded, but his face betrayed his confusion. My father's first words when he rose from his deathbed were now just a string of meaningless letters.

"We're going to move you into your new place."

"I've got all your pictures and cards, Grandpa," said Fred.

My father turned stiffly to look at Fred. "Okay." He looked at me and said, "So, I'm going home?"

I paused. Fred said, "Grandpa, you have to go to a different place to keep getting better. Grandma is in Saint Paul and you can go to the nursing home and Chuck Yeager can come with you. They said so." Fred bent down and tied my father's Reeboks. He watched Fred, astonished, as if Fred were performing a magic trick.

"How do you make your fingers do that?" he asked Fred.

"I can teach you, Grandpa. It just takes practice. But practice doesn't make perfect; it just makes better. Mom told me that and don't forget it."

My father nodded at Fred some more. There were days when he talked the ear off of anyone who happened to pass by the room, and then there were days like today when he didn't seem able to pull the words he wanted from the recesses of his brain. As we were saying good-bye to the staff, I realized that we should have brought them something, done something for them, marked his release somehow and thanked them for making it possible. I promised myself I'd send a fruit basket, knowing as I noted it that it would never happen.

We walked out to the car, my father shuffling along and Fred holding his hand, pointing out some slippery spots on the pavement. I had only the things my father had worn in the hospital, so he was shivering inside his sweatshirt, his Cubs cap pulled down low over his forehead, but his ears sticking out, red with cold. We arrived at the car and I opened the trunk so my father could say hello to Chuck Yeager. The dog was wildly throwing himself around the trunk, crashing around the small space in his excitement. My father sat on the back bumper and Chuck Yeager crawled into his lap, a wiggling ball of black-

and-white fur, covering my father's face with his large tongue over and over. His tail wagged in almost a full circle. My father put his face down into the deep, full fur on Chuck Yeager's neck, the softest part of his coat.

He looked up at me as Chuck Yeager panted away in dog ecstasy. "You have a very nice dog," he said to me.

"But, Dad, that's your—"

Fred interrupted. "Thank you."

We pulled under the covered front entrance of the Manchester just a short time after leaving the hospital. I thought it would be best to leave Chuck Yeager in the car until we had my father settled in his room. I pictured the dog tearing around, unplugging IV lines and jumping on the terminally ill. My father was slow to get out of the car. Fred held out his hand to my father and my father took it. I felt a tug of jealousy in my stomach as I tried to think of the last time Fred had initiated holding my hand. I followed behind them.

"So, this is home? It doesn't look like I remember it," I overheard my father say to Fred.

"Just for now, Grandpa, until you get better," Fred replied.

The front desk was inside a main lobby with a cathedral ceiling and a huge crystal chandelier looking over everything. There were shabby chairs set up in groupings, only a few occupied by elderly residents and some by their awkward visitors. I had always sworn up and down that I would never put my mother in a place like this; I had never even considered my father.

The panel on the front desk was fake wood and the corner of one side was peeling off. The woman behind the desk was dressed as if she worked in a hotel. I wondered how many people were actually fooled into thinking this was a posh resort—more tenants than visitors, I expected.

"Welcome to the Manchester. Can I help you?" the woman asked in a bored voice. Up close I could see that she was younger than I thought, with a tiny tattoo of a teardrop on her right cheek. Her hair was greasy and black and strained to stay inside the pins that kept it clipped off her heart-shaped face. She placed her hands on the counter in front of us and I saw her chipped blue polish and another tattoo of a ring around her wedding-ring finger. I would have thought she was too young to have ever been married, but I knew very little about the type of woman who might have a face tattoo.

"I'm here to check my father in," I said. "Lance Whitman."

"We don't usually take new tenants on the weekends," she replied, drumming her fingers on the desk, in no particular rhythm, a free-style-jazz type of nervous tic.

"We came over from University Hospital." I

started to dig into my purse to pull out the name of the social worker whom I had spoken to on the phone the day before. She had been so sorry for my situation and very obviously wished I would give her some hint that it was okay to disparage my mother.

"I can't help you with that, anyway. You have to go up to the nurses' station on the third floor, in the east tower," she said.

"Which is where?" I asked, and in response she pointed vaguely to her left, where I expected there might be an elevator. "Thanks so much," I said, unable to keep the sarcasm out of my voice. She had already moved on to digging through the desk drawer and didn't even notice me leave. I didn't find my father and Fred where I'd left them. I quickly scanned all the wingback chairs, every cluster, every love seat, upholstered with threadbare maroon, mauve and forest green stripes. The carpet, too, I noticed, was threadbare, some spots worn down to the subfloor underneath. I had to remind myself that I had done some research after my mother's news to make myself feel better and the Manchester was supposed to be one of the nicer nursing homes in the city, and I had trusted my mother.

"Fred?" I called, quietly at first. But then realized I wasn't really bothering anyone because most of the residents were hard of hearing and the visiting relatives were only too glad to have something else to focus on. "Fred?" I called louder. I made my way down to the end of the hall, past all the chairs and love seats, finding neither my father nor my son. I knocked on the men's bathroom door and when no one answered, I pushed the door open cautiously. No Fred. I raced back to the front desk. "I can't find my son. Or my father. Have you seen them?"

The girl looked up at me. "Did you check the game room?"

"You have a game room in a nursing home?" I asked.

"I know, right?" she said, and pointed me in the direction of the east tower elevators. There next to the elevators was a beat-up door with a scratched gold plaque above it that read "Game Room."

I pushed the door open and the room was empty except for my father and Fred. My father was sitting down in some sort of cockpit-type seat, gripping a steering wheel with one hand and shifting some sort of lever with another. "Fred!" I called.

Fred turned to me. "Mom, he thinks he's flying, but we didn't put any money in so it keeps just showing us the introduction graphics again and again. It's World War II planes, Mom. I asked him if I could have a turn, but he said no," Fred said.

During a brief pause where the screen went

black I was finally able to pull my father away from the game console, and I retrieved his suitcase from where he had dropped it by the door. We found the elevator and rode up to the third floor.

"It smells in here, Mom. It smells like meat with gravy mixed with strawberry Jell-O," Fred said, sniffing the air. He was right, but I was trying to keep this positive.

"Smells like lunch!" I said, and smiled at my father. He seemed lost in thought. "Dad? Are you okay?"

He shook his head and muttered, "I couldn't get that plane up in the air. Kept driving around the runway. Wastes fuel."

The doors opened to the third floor and as much as the first-floor lobby had tried to look like a hotel, the third floor was trying to look like a hospital. More accurately, a hospital in the midst of a natural disaster. Wheelchairs were parked up and down the halls; in a small commons area a TV was blaring CNBC, but the only person in front of it was dozing on the vinyl couch. The entire area had the vague smell of disinfectant and elderly body odor. I turned to find the nurses' station and walked up, keeping a hand on my father's shoulder.

"This is Lance Whitman. He's supposed to check in today," I said to the nurse sitting behind the tall counter.

She didn't even look up. "We don't do intakes on weekends," she said as she scrolled through a computer chart.

"No, you see, all the arrangements have been made and they released him from the hospital and you agreed to take him when they released him. I have the name here . . ." I dug into my purse and came up with the social worker's card. "Peggy," I said. "Peggy set it all up with my mother."

"Peggy should know better," the nurse said. She finally looked up at me and saw my father staring down at her.

"Your name is Rhonda," my father said with sudden joy. "Help me, Rhonda, help, help me, Rhonda," he began to sing at the top of his lungs. He took Fred's hands and danced him around as he sang. I remembered him singing along to it on family car trips. It was always his choice for music, alternating between the Beach Boys and sports radio, never allowing anyone else in the car to choose.

"Okay, okay," she said with a faint smile on her face. "Let me see what I can do." She got up and walked away. We looked around the commons area. The walls were painted a seafoam green that did nothing but accent the harshness of the fluorescent lights above. One of them flickered and buzzed. I had been standing there for less than two minutes and the spot above my right eye where my migraines started was twitching. There was a crooked Christmas tree in one corner, a fake one with flocking. It was sparsely decorated, but the lights were flashing in a pattern that changed every ten seconds or so. I could hear someone wailing from down the hall.

Fred grabbed my hand and squeezed it. I was prepared to come up with an excuse for the lights and the smells and even the moaning. "Mom, I don't see any dogs," he said.

Rhonda returned and said, "Well, I don't know who Peggy worked it out with, but there's a room for your father and it's ready for him." Rhonda seemed perturbed that Peggy had gotten something past her.

"It's a pet room, right?" I asked.

She looked at me blankly, one eyebrow raised.

"My father has a dog and Peggy was supposed to make sure that there was a room for him that allowed dogs."

Rhonda seemed smugly satisfied and said, "Peggy didn't do that. The companion animal rooms are on the fourth floor."

"Can he have one of those rooms? He needs to have his dog with him."

"What dog?" I heard my father ask Fred.

"The rooms on the fourth floor have a waiting list. Do you want him to get on that waiting list?" Rhonda asked.

"Sure. Then we'll move him again when one of those rooms opens up?"

Rhonda chuckled to herself. "No, ma'am. You don't get to have a spot on the waiting list and a room on the third floor. It's one or the other."

I made a quick decision to take the room on the third floor and forget the waiting list, as my father had already forgotten about his dog.

Rhonda led us down the hall to Room 325. She knocked lightly on the door and then pushed it open. There was a man asleep in the bed closest to the door. His face was covered with liver spots and white hairs sprouted out of his nose, ears and cheeks. He was sleeping with his mouth open and a loud gurgling noise came from his throat. I stepped into the room, determined to ignore his noises. The smell was overpowering: urine. The man had obviously urinated in the bed.

"Rhonda, do you smell something?" I asked, curious what she would make of it.

"Oh, sure. Mr. Howard's wet himself. I'll call an aide." She yanked on a call string that hung by his bed and disappeared down the hall.

My father took a few tentative steps and sat down on the edge of the bed. "I can see the lake," he said.

Fred hopped up beside him and began to point out all the other things that he could see out the window while my father silently nodded along. My eyes were watering at the unbearable smell coming from Mr. Howard. After a few minutes, a burly aide walked into the room.

"What?" she asked.

"Rhonda called you. I guess Mr. Howard needs to be changed," I said, feeling as though it should have been obvious as soon as she lumbered into the room.

"Damn, Rhonda," she said under her breath. "I changed him this morning. He's been sleeping all afternoon and if you wake him up, he's a bear." She was a large woman and began manhandling Mr. Howard. She talked to him loudly the whole time. Finally, feeling that Mr. Howard's privacy had been invaded in too many ways, I pulled the curtain around my father's bed shut and the three of us sat on his bed. As if we were hiding, we were silent, unmoving, waiting for the aide to finish with Mr. Howard and for the smell to leave with her. At last we heard the shuffling end and heard her loud footsteps plod out into the hall. I opened the curtain, but the smell remained. I could see from my vantage point on my father's bed that she had taken the soaking adult diaper that Mr. Howard had been wearing and dumped it into the small open-topped trash can next to his bed.

I turned to my father and said, "Dad, you're not staying here." I don't know where those words came from at that moment. My heart pounded in my chest because I knew I was bypassing the easiest course of action. I could have been rid of my father at that moment. I could have walked away from the man who had called me a bitch at thirteen when I didn't pick up my laundry fast enough. The man who had called me lazy when my teenage self wanted to sleep in on weekends. I could have left behind the man who had given me the silent treatment for an entire month because I had the gall to go to the prom. I didn't walk away. As I looked at him sitting there, on the edge of the hospital bed, clutching my son's hand and staring out the window, that man was already gone.

"Dad, we're going," I said.

"This isn't home?" he asked, surprised.

"No, Dad, this isn't home."

Fred

Today was the day that we tried to take my grandpa to live at a new place. I thought that place smelled pretty bad in a lot of different ways. When we walked in I could tell that it was not going to be a good place for him. The only best part was that there was a game room and my grandpa could pretend to fly a plane. I do not know for sure if he knew he was pretending or if he was really flying in his mind. The plane was supposed to be a World War II bomber but the guys who made the game got lots of the details wrong. Like the name of the plane was spelled wrong and the colors on the wing stripes were just all wrong. It is disappointing when people make mistakes when they could just look it up or ask someone like me.

My grandpa couldn't stay there. It made him sad. He thinks my grandma is coming to get him soon, but I don't think she is coming back. I think she has gone away from him to Saint Paul. In 1945 a mother in Chicago named Mrs. Frank Benes asked the government of America to let her keep her son at home. That was because two of her other sons were already dead in the war. I read about this on the Google. It didn't

192

say if the American government let her do that. I couldn't find an answer. I am still looking for an answer because a question without an answer is not comfortable for me. It hurts my brain and it hurts me in my heart when I don't know what happened to Mrs. Frank.

Grandpa and Chuck Yeager are going to come back to our house. Grandpa is going to live in Mom's office. It is different from his home, but it doesn't smell like gravy and pee. I hope that this room doesn't make Grandpa so sad. I hope that he remembers Chuck Yeager is his dog because Chuck Yeager is lonely for him, I can tell. He takes big sighs, looks at the door and then lays his head down on his paws. Grandpa is lonely too, but I can't tell what for. Maybe he is lonely like I am and he doesn't know why.

Piper

We returned to the car, where an overjoyed Chuck Yeager met us with eager panting and drooling and proceeded to spray his saliva all over the trunk of the Subaru as he spun himself in circles chasing his tail. My father looked at him blankly and then at me. "Wild dog," he said.

I sighed. "That's your dog, Dad. That's Chuck Yeager." I started the car and added with no small amount of spite, "You trained him."

"Well, I don't know how to train a dog," he said, and turned back to face the windshield, directing his gaze to the concrete pillar in front of us.

We drove quietly home. The trip was short, but it was held up slightly by a large amount of traffic from some university sporting event I had no doubt known about and then forgotten.

"Hockey game today," my father said.

"How can you remember that, but you don't recognize your own dog? Seriously, Dad, this dog was the love of your life." I was irritated, but the source of my irritation wasn't obvious to me. Perhaps my decision had begun to rest its full weight on my psyche.

"Impossible. Judy is the love of my life. I am

194

going home to her." He crossed his arms across his chest to demonstrate the finality of his statement.

"Dad, we're actually going to my house. We're going to look for a different place for you to stay while you recover."

"From the plane crash," he stated, but I could see a flash in his eye, a twinkle of uncertainty—the first inkling that maybe things were not as he thought.

"No, from the heart attack," I replied, my nerves unraveling like the stray thread on a sweater that eventually causes the whole thing to fall apart.

"I had a heart attack? Why didn't anyone tell me?" he demanded.

"Grandpa, we do tell you. You just forget because your brain got kind of damaged," Fred piped up from the backseat.

I waited for my father to yell, to curse at Fred, call him a liar.

He was quiet for a moment and then visibly straightened his shoulders and adjusted his posture. "Thank you, boy. You're the only one who I can trust to tell me what's going on around here."

Stuck in traffic, I dropped my head down to the steering wheel and rested it there, afraid of what would come out of my mouth if I dared look at my father.

"Mom, you have to be patient because his brain is kind of damaged," Fred said knowingly.

I picked my head up and tried to steady my breathing. I looked at Fred in the rearview mirror. He sat in his booster seat, with Chuck Yeager's head resting on his shoulder from the trunk. I gave Fred the biggest smile I could muster. I felt a flash of shame that my nine-year-old son was calmer and more in control than I was. I rolled my shoulders and cracked my neck and loosened my death grip on the steering wheel. I flipped the radio on to the station that I usually listened to because I liked the male and female DJs.

My father listened to a song by U2 for a moment and then said, "Is this all there is?" Even in his brain-damaged state he would still control the radio. I scanned until I found the local oldies station and immediately the car was filled with the silky alto of Karen Carpenter. The tension in my father's shoulders released; he leaned his forehead against the cool of the window and watched the scenery fly past as we drove home.

We arrived home and unloaded Chuck Yeager first; he ran straight to the backyard, where he immediately treed a squirrel and commenced barking and whining at it. I took the five cleansing breaths recommended by my therapist, rolled my neck around, latched the gate and went back to the car to get my father. He and Fred were already on their way down the sidewalk. I jogged to catch up to them, slipping and sliding a bit on the thin coat of ice on the sidewalk.

"Hey, guys! We're going home," I called after them.

Fred turned back to me. "We're looking at the Christmas lights. Grandpa wanted to see the Christmas decorations on our street."

"It's the middle of the afternoon; it's not dark yet." It didn't make sense and the pointlessness of it caused the knot of stress in my neck to tighten.

"I know, but it makes him seem kind of like happy," Fred said. I stayed some steps behind and watched them. They stopped in front of each house and Fred described what the house looked like in the dark, my father entranced. I imagined this couldn't last long; a protracted verbal narrative of Christmas lights seemed like something my father would detest, as he loathed Christmas in general, with all its jolly sentimentality. They walked for ten minutes, then turned around and headed back toward me. My father had a peaceful look on his face and took hold of Fred's hand.

"I'm ready to see Judy," he proclaimed.

Fred looked at me and a dark haze of worry flooded his previously sunny mood. I shrugged as if to say, "What can we do?" and we walked back home. Chuck Yeager was obsessively circling

197

the tree where the squirrel chattered down at him with anxiety.

I opened the front door and we crossed the threshold into the warmth; when Isaac wasn't home I turned the thermostat up, and then turned it down right before he returned. My father's glasses fogged up and he delicately removed them to wipe on his sleeve.

"Judy!" he shouted as he wiped his glasses.

"Dad, this is my house. Mom isn't here. She's with Jeanne in Saint Paul," I said quietly.

He ignored me and moved into the foyer and peeked his head up the stairs. "Judy? You up there?" We all waited silently for the reply that I knew wouldn't come.

"Dad?" I tried to put my hand on his arm, but he pushed it away.

"Judy!" he shouted again, his voice tinged with panic, something I couldn't remember hearing before. I was familiar with angry, disappointed and gregarious, but not panicked. He always seemed to be in control.

He started up the stairs, stomping loudly as he went and shouting my mother's name.

"Should we go up there, Mom?" Fred asked quietly.

"No. I think we should just let him see for himself," I said. Suddenly, the gravity of the whole situation took my breath away and I was aware that I was sharing it with my nine-year-old son. I knelt down to him and tried to take his hands. He wiggled away, just far enough that he was out of my grasp.

"Fred, I'm so sorry that you have to see Grandpa this way. Why don't you go outside with Chuck Yeager until Grandpa calms down a little?"

He shook his head. "That's okay, Mom. I'm the only one who tells him the truth, so I better be here."

"You know that's not true, right? I'm not lying to your grandpa, Fred." I could handle my father's incredulity, but not my son's.

"Well, I know that and you know that, but Grandpa believes that you are a dirty liar, so it's true to him," Fred said. We leaned against the hallway wall and listened to my father's heavy footsteps traverse the second floor.

There was a shrieking cry from upstairs and a loud thud. I bolted up the stairs, tossing my hat and scarf off as I climbed. I followed the sounds of howling and sobbing to the bathroom, where my father was crouched down on the floor next to the bathtub. The zinnia-covered shower curtain was puddled on the floor around him with the rod lying across his back. His face was wrenched with pain and he gasped through his sobs. Fred's face was frozen in a look of fear and worry, and I deeply questioned my rash decision. I stood rooted to my spot in the doorway, unable to go toward him. This was not my father; this weeping mess was not the man who had raised me. I would know what to do if this was Fred. I would scoop him into my arms and rock away all the sadness and pain. I might even know what to do if this was Isaac, but the man lying in front of me, curled into a ball, was something I could not handle. He was not a touchy-feely person. He was not someone who reached out to squeeze a shoulder or hugged for any reason other than duty. He was not a person to proclaim love or support or even anything more than indifference aloud. I couldn't now find the words or the actions that would repair this man. I had already failed my job as caretaker. I wanted nothing more than to telephone my mother and beg her to return.

Fred squeezed past me and knelt beside my father. "Grandpa, the shower curtain rod is on your back. I don't think you want it there. I will pick it up for you," Fred said. He hoisted the silver rod up and into the bathtub and sat down next to my father, hugging his knees to his chest, his body just barely brushing against his grandpa's. He sat that way for much longer than I was comfortable with. The air grew thick with my impatience, my desire for everyone to get up off the floor of the bathroom and just move on. But they continued to sit. My father's sobs quieted until they were nothing more than a series of deep breaths. I sat still, with my back against the doorjamb, waiting it out. I could hear the two of them breathing, Fred taking deep, cleansing inhales until my father's panicked gulps matched Fred's calm breaths. Fred was rocking lightly, his shoes tapping against the tile floor every now and then. I heard my father's body shift and turned to see over my shoulder that he had sat up and was leaning against the bathtub. He looked like a shell in that moment, deflated of his confidence, knowledge and past successes.

"She's not here," he said.

"No, Grandpa. Grandma Judy isn't here. She is on a break in Saint Paul, Minnesota," Fred said.

"Why? Why does she need a break? Is something hard?" my father asked.

"You are hard, Grandpa. She is on a break because you are hard."

My father was quiet for a moment, and then he said, "I am hard."

"It's okay, Grandpa Lance. Sometimes I am hard too." They were silent again. I peered over my shoulder, tears ran from my eyes and I saw that Fred was holding my father's hand.

Lance

The office of my daughter's house is my new home. I sleep on something called a futon. I can sleep comfortably enough. When I wake up in the morning and the light is coming in the window, the painting that she made of koi fish in a pond looks like it is golden and shining. When I lie down on my futon bed in the afternoon or the evening, the gold and shine are gone. Sometimes something looks one way for a time and then becomes another thing. The fish are flat and orange, black and white. The painting doesn't have anything to say. Above my futon is a crack in the ceiling, a big long crack. I lie here in the dark, but I can still see the crack. It frightens me because it means something is broken.

Judy is on a break because I am hard. I am a hard person. I do not remember to hang up my wet towels and I don't like to eat cold sandwiches. Sometimes I want to watch TV when there is a sport on and I don't listen to the people talking to me. I snore at night. I think I might take all the sheets in the nighttime and leave Judy with none. I think these are the reasons I am hard. I did not know that I was hard enough to make her leave. I think that I will just try to do better. I will concentrate on picking up my wet towels. I think there's someplace special that you hang them. The boy would know that. I'm going to learn to eat any sandwich that someone gives me and share the sheets.

There's a dog here, a beautiful dog named Chuck Yeager. My daughter and the boy keep telling me that it is my dog and the dog seems to try to tell me the same thing with his eyes. He stares at me and whines and cries like there is something he wants from me but I don't know what it is. My daughter tells me to go into the yard and throw the ball for him. I try that, but he stands next to me and watches and then we both watch the ball fall from the sky and roll under a bush and neither one of us wants to go and get it.

My daughter takes me to therapists. She takes me to the doctors for my heart and for my brain. Lisa is trying to teach me to make patterns with different-colored shapes. Paul is helping me learn to tie my shoes. Renee is helping me practice conversation. They are all a bunch of assholes.

II *Winter*

Piper

Though Curtiss probably wished we could return to our comfortable routine of minimal contact and polite pleasantries, I was not about to let that happen. I called him weekly and left messages on his voice mail when he didn't answer.

"Just wanted you to have an update for the week, Curtiss. Dad is refusing to learn to tie his shoes and won't see a therapist to deal with his emotional issues from the brain damage. That's about it. Same as last week. Same shit, different day! Call me!"

When Curtiss would finally get around to calling me back, our conversations had taken on a new tension-filled routine.

"I'm not sure what you want, Piper. Do you want me to send money? Would that help?" Curtiss asked.

"He's not like an abandoned pet, Curtiss. God! He's your father and you could come up and help me out. That would be helpful." I was angry with him. I felt like once again he had walked away from me and left me at a critical time.

When I was a junior in high school, Curtiss went away to college and left me alone to navigate life with my father, and for those two years I held a vicious grudge. Curtiss left me alone to battle my father's moods, alone to absorb Curtiss's portion of his criticisms, alone to protect my mother from his cruel tone and even crueler periods of silence. Curtiss visited home rarely, but when he did I made sure that he could feel my wrath underneath my layers of friendly conversation. Finally, when he returned for my own high school graduation, he addressed my years of quiet fury.

"Piper, you just don't know how it is. It's not like this in other families. It's different when you get out into the world." Curtiss interrupted our silent drive to the post office for our mother.

"You think I don't know that, Curtiss? I've been living with it, alone, for the last two years." I seethed, arms crossed.

"Pipe, what was I supposed to do? Never leave home? Live there forever? I didn't do it to hurt you. I had to get out. I had to get away from him."

"What about me and Mom? What about us, Curtiss?"

"I don't know what to say, Piper. I just know that as soon as you leave this house you'll understand why I left. Why I left you behind. I did it because I had to and you'll do the same thing."

Though my anger still simmered that day,

the second I was dropped off at my dorm room with a pile of plastic crates and a floor lamp, I immediately felt what Curtiss promised me I would. Pure, unequivocal freedom. I was, for the first time in my life, a person separate from my father. I was a being in complete control of my actions, my thoughts unblemished by his stern consternation. Whether I did good things or bad, those things were mine. When I slept late and skipped Geology 101, I didn't have him pounding on my door and ranting about his lazy daughter. When I got a C on my first chemistry test, there was no one waiting when I walked in the door, no one asking why I didn't study harder or better.

The first month of my college experience was like one long vacation, interrupted by tiny pockets of responsibility. I ate the marshmallows out of Lucky Charms cereal and drank orange Tang by the quart. I did it because I could; there was no one telling me I was consuming a "disgusting" amount of sugar and destined to become a fat slob. As I neared the end of that first month, a tiny voice began poking its nose into my business. As the days went on, the voice become louder and more persistent, until its tone and volume were remarkably similar to my father's. I enjoyed a good solid month free from his voice before I discovered that it lived within me too. I started studying harder, waking up early to run and lift weights, and gave up my marshmallow habit. I found by October that I was chained to his opinions, his beliefs and his strong distaste for imperfection. I spent the next several years exorcising him from my subconscious. By the time I entered adulthood through marriage and then child-rearing, I had mostly learned how to expel his intrusion into my subconscious life.

The exception to that was when I went home and visited my parents on school breaks. I avoided going home until Thanksgiving of my freshman year, which was no easy feat, given that there was a bus that traveled between Madison and Chicago several times every weekend. I couldn't avoid Thanksgiving, though my anxiety started eating away at me days before I climbed aboard the bus with my Discman and duffel bag. My anxiety owned me for the next four days, causing sleeplessness, intestinal distress and frequent panic attacks. As I stepped back onto that bus at the end of the weekend, carrying a paper bag with a pumpkin pie in it, I could feel the anxiety disappear along with the exhaust from the bus.

I found fewer and fewer reasons to return home, acquiring friends to spend minor holidays with, insisting on taking summer courses and living on campus, dragging my to-be-shelved cart around the library I worked at as many weekends as I could bear. It was pure irony, then, that as soon as Isaac started looking for a job post–law school, the University of Wisconsin was at the top of his list. I put up only a minor fuss, still worried that a woman who spoke her true feelings might feel the sting of her husband's silent rage. I figured as an adult I could remain free from my father's interference in my life.

The university job ended up being a dream come true for Isaac and the perfect fit, academically and professionally. I was three months pregnant when we moved back to my hometown. The anxiety and stress at that time of my life raged and threatened my sanity and health. I was unsure how to exist in the same city as my father and not let him control me. So many of those feelings of doubt disappeared the second I held the sweet, crying Fred in my arms in the delivery room. I took an emotional sledgehammer to the angst and reassembled the intensity of it into the purest, sturdiest love the world had ever seen.

Fred became the center of my world. My father, his opinions, and his general rage fell to the bottom of the list of things to worry about. We could spend time with him if pressed, but were able to quickly pick up and go if I felt like his wrath was beginning to reach its long sticky fingers around Fred or me. I found having a child the perfect excuse for disappointing my father. We couldn't eat at the right places, or participate in the activities he wished to do; we couldn't dine late in the evening or skip breakfast in order to eat a large lunch. I continued to feel a relative level of freedom that I hadn't found when I lived with him. The only hiccup in my purposeful ignorance of his wants and needs was the fact that my mother still lived and breathed by them. Though I could walk away whenever Fred got fussy or plead soccer practice to get out of a dinner invitation, her life remained the same. I tried to convince myself that it couldn't possibly be worse than it was when Curtiss and I lived at home. No kids meant less stress, I reasoned, never mind that she was the only warm body left to soak up his tyranny.

When Fred was a year old, she gave me a check to pay for swimming lessons for my boy, who hated having water poured over his head in the bath. For not asking his permission, she was punished by my father with his derogatory comments and sharp moods for a month. I entered therapy, where I had to make peace with the fact that I could not rescue my mother. She had to rescue herself. As bad as it got, I didn't see her taking that leap. She was trying to see clearly through vision clouded with endless justifications and absolutions. I had given up, and then . . . and then my father went and had a heart attack. He almost granted her freedom with no price paid. Almost. I knew exactly why my mother walked away. I understood the alternative was unthinkable for her. I knew why my mother left the Silver Eagle behind, walked forward without looking back. What I didn't know and still don't is why I couldn't do the same thing.

I was spending more time with my father than I ever had before. I transported him daily to a wide array of therapists and specialists: speech therapy, occupational therapy, physical therapy, a cardiologist, a neurologist and a general practitioner. My father was like a sulking lump as I carted him from one appointment to another, and then home and then sometimes out again. His face betrayed no emotion; in fact, he rarely spoke to me. I suspected he was deeply depressed. The list of specialists involved in my father's care was long and complicated, but the one doctor he refused to see was a psychiatrist. The books I read on caring for victims of traumatic brain injury clearly stated that though this recovery would be grueling for the victim and caregivers, it could be alleviated a bit by regular visits to a mental health professional.

My father would pick at his dinner and then leave his spot at the table, plate still laden with food I was trying to get him to eat, his chair pushed back from the table as if he might return at any minute.

Isaac was particularly concerned with his mental state, which I had to admit shamefully bothered me because I felt like my own mental state was precarious many days. Taking my father in had been a nonissue with Isaac; in fact, I think he said something about repairing my relationship with my father or something similar that I tuned out because it was exactly what he would say.

"Piper, I think you need to try again, try to get him in to see a therapist," Isaac said matter-of-factly between bites of pork tenderloin and quinoa.

"He's a grown man and I can't force him into the clinic. I can't physically get him in the door. The last time I just made an appointment without telling him and then pulled up to the clinic, it was like he knew immediately where we were. I don't know how. He wouldn't get out of the car and I can't force him."

"There's got to be something you can do, Piper. He's just not right. Too sad," Isaac said. Isaac came from a family of stout optimists. The glass was always at least half-full; there was never reason to be anything other than fine, and people just cheered the hell up.

Fred, who had been quietly alternating eating grains of quinoa and single peas, finally spoke. "Do you want me to talk to him, Mom?"

My heart ached, the ache of the knowledge that we might all have been in over our heads. But I decided to try again the next day.

"Don't need it," my father said as we drove home from an appointment with an occupational therapist who was still attempting to reteach my father how to tie his shoes. It was difficult to do because my father refused to participate in the lesson. I could sense Paul's frustration hovering just below his expertly calm surface. I mouthed my apologies to Paul as I steered my father out of the waiting room and to the car. I knew that simmering frustration well because I found myself drowning in it with almost every interaction with my father.

"Dad, you do need it. You had a major injury to your brain. You're going to need to talk to someone."

"I'm fine, Piper."

"Dad, you're not fine. You're refusing to learn how to tie your shoes," I said, carefully controlling both my tone and volume because I knew the potential for explosion was close.

"I know how to tie my shoes," he said, looking out the window with his arms crossed tight across his down coat.

His false confidence put me over the edge. "Then why don't you just tie the damn things and be done with it?"

He shrugged but didn't answer.

"Dad, you're acting like a willful child. Just tie the fucking shoes and move on!" I shouted, slamming my hand on the steering wheel, resulting in a sharp horn blast that startled him more than my increased intensity did.

He looked at me a beat too long and then turned away. He was silent for close to a minute before he turned back to face the window and said quietly, "It's too hard. My brain tells my fingers what to do but they won't do it." This from my father, who had once flown huge planes full of hundreds of trusting passengers and whose quick thinking had once prevented the deaths of all those innocents.

Immediately I felt guilty, ashamed. I had forgotten that confident pilot was long gone. I inhaled deeply and forced myself to dig into my rapidly diminishing well of compassion. I reached for my father's hand, which was resting on his thigh; I paused but then took it. I held it the rest of the way home. I held it like I'm sure he must have once held mine; though I couldn't recall any specific instances, the feeling was just familiar enough.

As my father continued to struggle with his new reality, I also struggled with my own. Isaac soundly avowed again and again that Fred's diagnosis was for the best.

"Piper, it's a necessary evil; it's the way we're going to get him the help he needs to succeed in life, now and later," Isaac said one night as I folded laundry and he matched up a variety of sizes of white sweat socks. I found that since my father had moved in, Isaac was around more in the evenings and on the weekends, spending a good deal of that extra time sitting with my father and trying to talk him into completing brain teasers or reading aloud to him from the *New York Times* until my father wandered off.

"It's a label, Isaac. What if people find out, like other kids, and they're mean to him? What if he never learns how to have a normal social interaction and never has any friends?"

"He's still our Fred, Piper. He hasn't changed," Isaac said.

I lost count of how many times Isaac tried to mollify my anxiety, my sadness, even my anger, with that statement in the early days of Fred's label. As if his simply declaring his beliefs strongly enough would make them so. I think that Isaac figured if it worked in the courtroom it would work in all areas of life. Eventually, I tired of trying to argue my position against the attorney I shared my bed with. The invisible gulf between Isaac and me, which he would have said I dug myself, grew. I nodded. I smiled. I grew gifted at presenting the very face of mollification. Inside, though, I knew my truth. This was not our Fred; this was my child who had been branded as different, lesser, lacking. This was the fruit of all my love and labors, marked with a scarlet *A* for autism.

I'm so ashamed of where my early thoughts went that it hurts me now to revisit them. This boy I grew, nurtured, and then presented to the world was sent back defective. I watched him when he was unaware and felt myself tense up with a sort of disgust at what I saw. His idiosyncrasies went from being quirky to being the mark of a person who wasn't normal. He could merely be sitting with one hand on Chuck Yeager's back, watching TV, clicking his tongue every five seconds without even knowing it and I had to clench my fists to keep from lashing out.

I hated myself in those early days; I hated the shameful, unexplained anger I felt toward my own child. I'd leave the room, eyes wet, and try to process where my rage had originated as I sat on the back stoop, punishing myself in the cold December air. I pinched myself, fingernails sometimes leaving bloody welts. I knew a mother shouldn't feel this way and I feared it would become obvious to other people, Isaac, Fred. I was terrified my reprehensible thoughts would show up in thought bubbles over my head and I would be revealed for what I really was: a horrible mother.

The origin of my complete disappointment in Fred came to me in bits and pieces over several days' time. As I prepared dinner one evening just before Christmas, I looked over the raised countertop and saw my father sitting at the dining room table, staring into space, the newspaper spread out in front of him. The flashback came at me with a force that startled me. I was taken back to my junior year of high school.

"What's this?" my dad asked as I handed him an envelope that I had brought home from school that day. He set the paper down on the dining room table, opened to the sports page.

"Report card," I replied.

He peeled open the envelope, lifted the delicate onionskin paper from the envelope and shook it. His eyes scanned over the letters and numbers and finally the bottom where it stated that I had again made the High Honor Roll.

"Hm," he said, and I waited for him to continue with a hearty congratulations. How could he not be proud of a child who had brought home seven As and one A−? "What happened in math?" he said, and handed me the paper and turned back to the sports page. I stood before him and waited, just in case. Finally, he turned to look at me over the top of his glasses. "Did you need something else?" he asked.

One afternoon I came into the dining room from the basement with yet another basket of laundry and found Fred and my father with the chessboard. I dropped the laundry basket on the floor, spilling out Isaac's boxer shorts and my own undergarments. I recalled sitting at the coffee table as a twelve-year-old, playing chess with Curtiss. We were both new to the game and had gotten ourselves into a position where we were both left with two pieces: a queen and a king. My father walked by, stopped and said, "What the hell happened here? It's like two retards playing chess." And then continued on his way.

These instances built up in my memory, became a mental file folder overflowing with every time I was reminded that this family didn't do imperfection. As I dissected my rage and more and more frequently found its root in my childhood, my anger at my father bloomed into an all-consuming fire. I found myself scarcely able to speak to him without my emotions violently splitting open my calm caretaker's voice. I began to speak to him as little as possible, sometimes going whole afternoons and evenings without speaking to him directly. He sat in silence often. His recovery may have suffered as a consequence of my reticence, but at the time I cared about nothing but directing my vicious rage away from Fred. My father never called attention to my silence, but Fred did.

On Christmas Eve, he and I lay side by side in his bed as I worked through the steps of his bedtime routine. He was flanked by stuffies and covered up with his fuzzy blanket. Chuck Yeager lay at the foot of the bed, pinning the covers to Fred so movement was difficult.

"Chuck Yeager, get down. Down," I said to him, and directed him toward the floor. He looked at me and then looked at my finger and sighed.

"Get. Down. Now."

This time he looked at Fred, imploring him to make the final decision.

"It's okay, Mom. He's okay there. I like to feel tight in my bed; it's quite relaxing for me," Fred said. "Okay, Chuck Yeager. Okay." The dog stood, stretched, turned around in three circles and plopped down in what seemed to be the exact same place. He yawned and placed his head on the lump of Fred's legs and raised an eyebrow at me. He was truly the smuggest dog I had ever known.

"Mom, Jackson said that there is no such thing as Santa Claus and I told him that that was certainly not true because Santa came to my house every year and left me toys without price tags."

Fred's conversational awkwardness and inability to let a comment go unanswered was beginning to become a social boon. I truly believed that Fred would argue the existence of Santa to his grave unless he had defining proof of another explanation for the pile of toys under the tree. I gently tried to urge him toward an understanding that would not destroy him or embarrass him. I introduced the possibility of another explanation. Fred listened intently, answered my questions but didn't show emotion one way or another. I took his silence as processing my wisdom and felt nearly as smug as Chuck Yeager as I lay with my head nuzzled into my son's shoulder.

"Mom?"

"Yes, baby?" I said softly into his ear, his wisps of hair tickling my lips.

"I hope Santa brings me a World War II Lego set from the Internet."

He had not taken my words to heart after all.

"But for Christmas I also want you to stop being quiet mad at Grandpa. It makes him sad," Fred whispered in my ear, creating a warm, wet heat in my ear canal.

"Oh, I'm not mad at Grandpa, honey."

"When you are in the living room and he is in the living room, you don't have any conversations and your eyebrows are bent and your mouth is tight and sometimes you look at him and your eyes squinch up."

I didn't say anything for what felt like a lengthy amount of time, but Fred just lay still and breathed his warmth on me. Finally, I said, "Fred, things are hard right now. It's hard for me to have Grandpa here sometimes. It's a lot of work and sometimes Grandpa and I don't think the same way about things."

"Like what?" he asked.

I couldn't expose Fred to the world of my family. I couldn't toss him in there and expect him to emerge undamaged. It was a road that he

222

never needed to travel; I had been determined to make his childhood different from my own in every possible way. "I'm sorry, Freddy. I'll try harder. Hey, how about you tell me something? What makes Grandpa happy?"

"Planes. The newspaper. Watching sports on the TV. Seeing the Christmas lights with me. Teaching me chess. Thinking about Judy. Ironing. Looking at the big black atlas," Fred listed.

I was amazed; I had seen my father partake in these activities and had not noticed an even minute change in his stoic and sometimes blank presence. "How do you know he's happy, Fred?"

Fred thought. Then he said, "When Grandpa is happy, his eyes crinkle at the corners and they get a little flash of light in them. Like you, Mom."

Fred

Mom told me about Santa Claus at bedtime. She told me that some people think that Santa is real and some people think that he is not real. She said Fred can you think of another way that those presents would get under the Christmas tree? I said I could not think of another way unless Santa has an elf that does it for him. She said Fred do we usually let strangers come into our house and walk around and maybe go by the Christmas tree? I said that I couldn't really think of any strangers that we let come in our house except the man that has to come sometimes and fix the Internet. I asked her if she thought he was the one who brought the presents. She was quiet for a little bit of time, like half a minute, and she looked like she was thinking about something very hard. Fred, she said, what about your parents? Could they be bringing the presents? I had to think about that because in some ways it made a good amount of sense. Since they live there, they would not be strangers. But Mom I said we don't have enough money to have double presents. That is not in the budget. I know that because when I want to buy a Lego set I see on the computer Mom always says that we do not have money in the budget this month to buy more Legos, Fred, unless you don't want to eat food. I do think I would rather eat food than Legos.

Mom started to explain about the myth of Santa Claus and how it's been a story and a tradition that's been passed down by people to each other for a long time, say five hundred years I think. Lots of cultures do it she said because it's fun. I didn't think it sounded healthy to lie to kids for that many years, but I didn't say that out loud. It was confusing. None of the evidence really matched up. Dad would say that it wasn't an open-and-shut case. I think that Mom was trying to tell me that there might not be a Santa; it might be her and Dad. She said that's what lots of kids believe and they still have a fun Christmas. She said maybe I shouldn't talk about Santa Claus at school so much. I just said okay Mom that sounds good. But inside, my brain was swirling around with ideas. I guess that Santa Claus is maybe not real after all.

But just in case he is, I'm going to believe for just one more night.

Lance

At Christmastime Judy and I have a tall tree, a tree that goes all the way up to the ceiling in the living room, and I put the star on the top from the top rung of the ladder. I always liked to have a tall tree. When we go to get it at the Christmas tree lot I always ask the gentleman to show me the tallest trees they have. I don't tie it on the roof because those needles will scratch your paint. It rides in the car with us, the tree trunk between Judy and me and the kids holding it in the backseat and the tip out the back window. The kids complain about being crowded and poked, but once we get that tree up in the house, everyone has fun decorating it. We can't decorate it right away. First the tree has to rest overnight in the garage so any loose needles fall out. Then I set it up in the living room in the tree stand for another night, so the branches can come down. After that we put the lights on. The kids are so damn impatient, but they don't understand it's a process. Once it's finally decorated all four of us sit in the living room with the lights out and look at that tree all lit up.

Piper told me the other day that I always hated Christmas. I don't remember that. My memories are jumbled. Sometimes something comes right out at me crystal clear and I can remember the day Judy and I got married so sharp it brings tears to my eyes. Other times I can feel something tugging on my mind, but I can't put the pictures together in the right order. All I remember about Christmas is that tree. That tree in a dark room with a rainbow of lights.

Piper

Our routine was such that I had a lot of time spent lingering in a wide variety of waiting rooms for some time each day. I delivered my father to his specialist and then retreated to a vacant corner of the waiting room with my iPad to do research. Research on what I had done to cause my child's disability. The theories were abundant and almost one hundred percent faulted the mother in some way or another. If I hadn't chosen to have my child immunized, then it probably would have been the stress I was under during the second trimester that did it. If it wasn't the myriad of toxins in the plastics that polluted every aspect of his life, it was probably something hereditary that caused some simple switch to avoid flipping, some gene to mutate just enough to fuck up the whole package. I see now that my use of time was detrimental, but then I was stuck inside the dark cave of my child's diagnosis.

My sleep during this time was restless, my driving reckless. My mind, constantly churning through research studies and articles, both scholarly and otherwise, was rarely focused on what it was supposed to be focused on. I narrowly missed collisions on the ice-slicked streets multiple times. The worst of these was a red light I ran at a semibusy intersection returning home with my father from one of his appointments with the occupational therapist. I veered wildly through the path of several cars, causing the screeching of brakes and honking of horns. After I made it through undamaged, I pulled over to the side of the road and unclenched my hands from the steering wheel. I sat with my head in my hands, breathing rapidly.

"Driving is hard," my father said.

"Not really, Dad. I'm just distracted," I said. I tried to take deep breaths to calm myself and communicate with him composedly.

"No. I think it's really a hard thing to do. There are lots of different things happening at the same time. There are cars from that way," my father said, and pointed out his window. "But they're also coming from the other way too." He pointed out my window and then dropped his hand down into his lap. "I think you are a very good driver, Piper."

I laughed and shook my head. "No, you don't, Dad. You think I'm a horrible driver. You couldn't believe that anyone ever even gave me a driver's license. That's why you wouldn't let me drive your car. I could only drive Mom's car, when you weren't home."

"I have no problem believing that you are a

licensed driver, Piper," he said. "I think that you must have had to take a test and then you did well enough on it to get a license to operate a vehicle. I think I taught you to drive very well."

"Mom taught me to drive. You didn't want to get into a car with me. Then, when I backed into the mailbox one time, when I was seventeen, you said, 'Well, what did we all expect when your mother taught you to drive?'" I even adopted his gruff, condescending tone as I said it. After the words slipped from my mouth, I instantly felt ashamed. I waited for his reaction.

My father was quiet and studied his gloved hands in his lap, twisting his fingers around one another. "I said that?" he asked. He seemed genuinely confused; his face wore the wrinkled brow of regret.

I felt badly now for even bringing it up in the first place. "Yeah, Dad. You said that," I said, more quietly. I started to shift the gear back to drive, but my father put his hand over mine.

"Wait," he said. He paused and we sat there with his large hand covering mine. Finally, he said, "What did Judy say?"

I didn't know how to respond to my father in that moment. To have to remind my father of his past sins. I briefly considered telling him that Judy was fine, that Judy laughed it off and they hugged it out. I considered it, but after all these years, despite the shame that had just consumed me, the anger was greater. "She cried, Dad. Judy cried when you said that."

He took his hand off of mine and folded his hands in his lap again. I took that as the cue to continue our trip home. I was overflowing with a feeling I couldn't label. I had finally had an opportunity to make my father see how he had hurt my mother, hurt us, and all I could think about was how this meek creature beside me felt little like the monster I had grown up with.

My father turned on the radio; it was on the oldies station that he preferred. We had been listening to it a lot lately in the car; Fred especially enjoyed it and had memorized many of the lyrics to songs of my childhood. He and my father often sang along, both with their tuneless monotone voices.

It was an old song from the seventies that I recognized from the record collection that Curtiss and I used to listen to on my father's old record player when he was away on trips. I could picture the cover of the album: a moody, long-haired romantic in a turtleneck. My secret shame for my entire life had been my love of my parents' horrible seventies record collection. Just one verse of America or Bread took me back to the beanbags in the den, Curtiss and me singing into a hairbrush.

"Stronger than any mountain cathedral." My father began to sing along, eyes forward, pointer fingers tapping the beat on his sweatpants leg.

I joined him. "Truer than any tree ever grew."
We finished the verse together, and then I shifted
into drive and we drove the rest of the way home
without speaking, immersing ourselves in the
honeyed harmonies of the music of our past.

My research on the causes of autism yielded
many possibilities, but none were as painful as
the idea that fetuses exposed to antidepressants
in utero were more likely to become autistic.
This was when I fell apart. I had started taking
antidepressants in college when it finally dawned
on me that perhaps sobbing underneath my
desk, curled into a ball, wasn't normal behavior.
My depression was mostly managed for years,
and then I got pregnant with Fred. I decided
right away to wean myself off the medication,
sacrifice my feelings of calm and peace for the
health of my child. I was three months pregnant
when I had my first massive depressive episode.
For the first time in my life I contemplated the
possibility of ending it all. I ran through the
options in my head, the methods, the good-bye
letters. I envisioned driving my car off a bridge
and ending it all in a fiery crash. I got as close
as pinning down the method—handfuls of pills—
but I always ran into a significant hitch when I
pictured the creature swimming around inside of
me.

My depression hit rock bottom the day Isaac came home after work and found me holding my breath, underwater in the bathtub.

He pulled me up and shook me. "Piper, what the fuck do you think you're doing?"

"Nothing, nothing," I kept repeating. Isaac's raw panic had scared me and I suddenly realized the tip of the iceberg I had reached out my toe to touch. Isaac wisely didn't believe me when I said everything was fine.

I went back on my antidepressant and started feeling my normal but still slightly melancholy self again. Now I found that the choice I had made, the choice to live, had consequences too.

I had watched Fred as a newborn, fresh from my belly, for any of the signs of withdrawal I was told he might experience, but there were none. The effects of my damaged psyche lay in wait, coiled like a predator in a cave that will wait hours upon hours for the ideal moment to pounce. I had been watching Fred from the time he was a preschooler for signs of depression, flashes of an unexplainable sadness, but found none. His sadness always seemed to be connected to something he wanted and couldn't have, something he tried and failed at.

His temper tantrums often seemed rife with more frustration than anger. When he was two he became obsessed with shooting basketballs into the child-sized basketball hoop our neighbors passed down to us after their kids had outgrown it. He had become quite good at making baskets when he merely had to stand on his toes and sink the ball without a great deal of effort. His confidence was huge and remained so until the day he took his basketball to the local park and encountered his first full-sized basketball hoop.

"Fred!" I called repeatedly, trying desperately to call him away from the hoop and back toward me. He was on a mission, though. He reacted to his first several missed shots calmly, but the more his ball came up many feet too short, the more frustrated he became.

I came over to the hoop after watching him for some time. I wanted to give him the space to fail, but I could handle only so much failure. "Fred, let's go get some ice cream at the ice-cream shop. Come on, Freddy!" I tried to sound upbeat and like ice cream was a much better alternative than shooting hoops, but Fred wasn't buying it.

"Hoop!" he shouted mournfully, over and over, as each ball came up short. After five minutes, he exploded with emotion. He lay down on the pavement, clutching his ball to his chest, weeping. I tried to reason with him, snuggle him, anything to get him up off the ground.

Eventually I had had enough and so I reached down to grab him, and in his fit of frustrated passion he kicked me in the face.

"Fred!" I screamed. "You hurt me!" I was crying. It was finally enough to calm his storm, and he allowed me to lift him off the ground and we walked home. It was weeks before the black eye he gave me disappeared completely and months before I returned to that specific park with him.

Besides the depression I suffered from, there was also anxiety, which I saw in Fred from the time he was young, but I always felt that it was the lesser of the two-headed monster and figured we'd muddle through worrying together. My depression wouldn't reveal itself easily, though; it would shove forward a distant cousin in the family of mental health, a neurological relative whose presence was uninvited and unexpected, but staying put all the same.

After I had immersed myself in the mechanics, chemistry and consequences of autism all day, when Isaac came home from work my conversations with him were less than helpful. He could tell I was in a fragile state and instead of working until eight most nights, he came home at six, put Fred to bed at eight and then worked into the night. It was his best attempt at compassion. Isaac was more than compassionate; he treated me with the kindness and empathy one reserves for an elderly Alzheimer's patient who hasn't yet turned violent.

"So, Fred, tell me about your day, buddy," Isaac

said as we sat around the dinner table together, my father silent and staring at his plate.

"The hot lunch today was hamburgers and French fries but it didn't smell so good to me. Also, the meat was gray and the peaches that came with it were hot too, and I don't think that peaches should be hot unless they are inside a pie," Fred stated.

"You had hot lunch today, Fred? Good job trying something new!" Isaac almost shrieked.

"No, Dad. I didn't have hot lunch but seventeen kids in my class did and so I had a lot of hot lunches to observe." Fred would go on to describe how the insides of his worn sweatpants irritated his skin, and on and on.

Eventually when Fred tired of his monologues, Isaac would turn to me and gently ask about my day. I should have given him credit for trying, for asking, for making an effort, but all the times he didn't loomed so large in my memory that they easily smothered his small attempts to be supportive now.

"The same, Isaac. The same."

Fred went to bed each night, grinning, with Chuck Yeager warming his feet and his father lying stiffly beside him, still in his dress loafers and dress shirt. Sometimes Isaac would fall asleep and I would look in on them both. In the warm darkness, lit only by the airplane night-light near the foot of Fred's bed, it was sometimes difficult for me to tell the difference between them. Two lumps of man, one longer, wider, pin-striped shirtsleeves rolled up. And one smaller, slighter, clutching a worn stuffed hedgehog to his chest. They both could have been boys as they lay with mouths open, one arm strewn over each head, tousled heads of hair nestled into pillows. I didn't know if I should wake Isaac. I knew he wanted to work more, get more done, but part of me liked the fact that he couldn't. He couldn't be the superproductive hero to the people while he was lying there, mouth breathing. I could control that. I felt like much of my life was out of my control—my father's new state, my son's disability—and like a toddler I needed to grasp for power wherever I could find it.

Eventually, most nights, Isaac would wake on his own, and sometimes he wouldn't even go back to writing briefs or researching leads. Sometimes he would want to have a conversation.

He came up behind me while I stood at the kitchen sink and wrapped his arms around my waist. I flinched, not enough for him to notice. I told myself it was because he was touching my middle, which had grown chubby since my father's accident, my daily runs a casualty of the chaos. If I lamented their passing, Isaac was quick to remind me that my depression was better when I was getting exercise. I would flinch again.

"Piper, what are you thinking about?" he asked.

237

"I'm wondering if the school has made a decision about scheduling the IEP meeting."

"Honey, relax. It's going to be a long process and we can't sweat every step of the way." And he would nuzzle my neck and I would find no reason to relax.

"Everything I read says early intervention is the key, and since it's already so fucking late, I want to get something together, a plan, something to help Fred," I said.

Now Isaac would turn me around to face him, no matter that my hands were wet with tepid water and dish soap, flakes of soggy dinner stuck to my fingernails. "Piper, Fred is going to be just fine. You know that, right?"

This was the point when I would break down. "How do you know that, Isaac? He's got social-skills issues. He doesn't know how to have a normal conversation with another kid. He's got no friends. Kids are going to tease him, if they aren't already. It kills me, Isaac. Kids may be teasing him right now and he doesn't even know it."

"Piper," he said, as he clutched me hard to his chest, the buttons of his shirt pressing into my forehead. "Fred has lots of gifts. He's going to be fine. He's going to find his passion and be really, really good at it. Think about all the great things about Fred."

Now I sobbed. "I'm trying, Isaac. I'm trying,

but there's this other giant, awful thing standing in front of everything else. This label that means he's disabled."

Then the end, always the same, always less comforting than the time before: "Piper, he's still the same kid. He's still our Fred."

Piper

Isaac was indeed stepping up in ways that he hadn't before. I was certain it wasn't his job demands that had changed, or even his commitment to his family, which he always felt was sky-high. I think that Isaac saw in me a new level of anxiety, an additional layer of panic, and he was really worried about my sanity. There was a Monday in January, Martin Luther King Day, when Fred was off from school and my father had a daylong neurological test at the hospital to assess his brain's health, how far he had come since the "incident." I took secret umbrage at the description of my father's heart attack, subsequent dying and then living and now brain damage as an "incident." As if it had all happened in the blink of an eye, the weeks fraught with desperation and angst brushed away with one word. This was an important appointment, and a long one.

I had struggled with what to do with Fred, now that my mother was out of the picture and he had no friends eager for playdates. Isaac surprised me when he said he would take the day off from work and hang out with Fred. I could not remember the last time that Fred and his father had spent more than an hour together without my presence. I was only slightly concerned, less than I might have been months earlier. I had become fatigued, and with that fatigue my anxiety had waned. Isaac was thrilled with himself as a man and a father; stepping up like this gave him an ego boost that he never really needed. Now not only was he the hero of the people, but he was also the hero of his family.

That night he was tapping away on his laptop, on what I assumed was a brief, but when I walked past him I saw that he was reading Web sites about things to do with children in Madison.

"Are you looking for things to do with Fred?" I asked casually, secretly hoping that he would acknowledge my expertise in this area.

He snapped his laptop closed. "Nope, I got it, Piper. No need to worry about a thing." It wasn't worry that drove me to interfere, but the stubborn refusal to believe that anyone could do it better than I could.

The two of them lay in Fred's bed that night, whispering solemnly to each other, abruptly stopping when I peeked my head in the door. The next evening, they sat huddled on the couch around the slight glow of Isaac's laptop, studying maps and park details.

"What are you guys up to?" I asked, and sat down near them, hoping to be invited into their little tête-à-tête.

They glanced at each other and then back at me, shaking their heads with pity. "Man stuff," Fred said proudly.

I didn't like this idea, this new way Fred perceived himself. I was happy to keep him by my side as a boy for many more years.

Lance

My daughter told me that I didn't think she should get a driver's license when she was a girl. I don't remember why I would have said that; she seems like a very nice, responsible woman. This is what I remember about my daughter Piper:

Braids: two braids, one on each side, or sometimes one braid in the middle, shiny brown hair. Walking past her at the dining room table, tugging her braid, thick and silky in my hand.

Books: stacked up in her bedroom. She is lying on the couch on the weekend reading a book. I stand above her: "Get outside and get some exercise!" I yell, but I don't remember why. She moves fast with her book, away. Bedroom door closes.

The color blue: paintings and drawings with blue sky and sometimes blue water. Some are like a tiny child would make, but some take my breath from me because they are so nice. An art show, her painting in a very important place. We take lots of pictures and she smiles. Her smile.

Singing: she has a little tape player that has headphones and she is singing along to something on the tape that only she can hear. We are in the car and she is in the backseat with her brother singing about an eternal flame and it hurts my ears. I tell her so and she stops, but she cries and Judy sighs. Everyone is angry.

The doctor told me once that my memory would come back in pieces, but maybe not all of it. I hope the good parts come back last because I am still waiting.

Fred

Tomorrow is the day off of school and I am going to be supervised by Dad because Mom has to take Grandpa to the hospital for at least two tests and maybe three. Dad and I have been making a plan for our day together. He asked me what I wanted to do and I had to think very careful about what I would tell him. My dad is busy with his work that is saving people from jail. He is not around a lot because he has to save the people. Sometimes I think it is very good that my dad wants to save the people that didn't do the crimes. Sometimes I think that it is good to have a world where someone wants to save the people that didn't do the crimes. Sometimes I wonder how my dad knows for sure that they didn't do the crimes. When I ask him he says sometimes it is conflicting evidence or a witness that changed their story to the truth or it could be something new that just suddenly appeared like magic and means the person is not guilty. Dad says Fred do you want to be a lawyer too? You sound very interested in the mechanics of the justice system. I have to think about how to answer so I do not hurt his feelings. I say Dad I do not think I want to be a lawyer because I think that some people who do crimes are lying when they say that they did not do the crime and then I have to believe them and it is hard for me to believe lies. Dad says sometimes the truth has two sides. I say Dad truth is a word and it lies flat on the paper and cannot have two sides.

Sometimes I think it is very nice that my father wants to help the not-guilty guys because they have families and sometimes kids and maybe a wife. But then sometimes I think that I would rather just have a normal dad who believes the truth is just the truth and knows exactly what to do with me on a day off.

Piper

Martin Luther King Day dawned seasonally mild with light snow falling. Fred and his father had laid out all their warm-weather clothes the night before and rose earlier than usual to eat breakfast and dress. They were off in the Subaru as the sun rose, Fred wildly waving from his booster seat in the back. They had packs with lunches and snacks, a giant metal thermos with hot chocolate in it and a plan. They had told me nothing about where they were headed. My only clue came the night before as I put Fred to bed and Isaac worked at the dining room table late into the night to make up for not going in on Monday. I lay next to Fred, my feet awkwardly bent under the weight of a snoring Chuck Yeager, and I gently brushed the hair off his forehead as he regaled me with the details of the elaborate Lego scene he had created that day. He finally paused for breath and I said, "I hope you and Daddy have fun tomorrow."

"Oh, we won't have fun, Mom, not much. It's pretty serious business," Fred said as he stared up at the faded stars stuck to his ceiling.

"What's serious business, Fred?" I asked.

"Well, war is, Mom," he replied.

My father and I had to be at the hospital by nine, where they would attach a multitude of nodes to his head to read electrical impulses and signals and other things that, though I didn't understand, I could tell by the doctor's grave intonation were of the utmost importance. My father was, of course, ignorant of the significance of the tests. He sang along loudly and atonally to his oldies station in the car. His face showed little expression these days, the range of his emotions tiny, though before the "incident" he was capable of everything from rage to a jovial, almost sidesplitting glee in a split second's time, just long enough to turn away from his family toward the outside world.

"Dad, did you understand what the doctor told you about the tests today?" I asked.

"Sure, honey," he said, and nodded confidently.

"What did he say?"

He turned to me, studying my face before he answered. "He said there's electricity in my brain. Nothing to be worried about, nothing at all." He turned to look back out the window and hummed along to Gordon Lightfoot.

"Well, not exactly, Dad. They're going to measure the electrical impulses in your brain, in different areas in your brain, and then they'll have some idea how much your brain has healed and how much more it might heal. Does that make sense?"

He didn't answer me for a long time, just stared

out the window at the gray snowbanks and the naked trees. Finally, he said, "Nope."

I sighed. I had tried.

A cross-looking nurse smelling of cigarette smoke and mango body lotion led us to a chilly windowless cubicle. She roughly handed my father a worn gown with a raging pattern of pastel geometric shapes and wild squiggles parading across it. "Everything off but the briefs." I started to open the door to exit and let my father undress himself. He reached for my wrist and grasped it tightly.

"Don't go. I might . . . I might need help," he said.

I nodded and pulled the curtain around him, hiding myself from his nakedness until the last moment. I stood pressed against the door for longer than I thought the undressing should take and when I heard no sound of movement, I peeked through a small gap in the curtain to see my father still standing in the same place. He had set the gown down, but his hands were frozen on his sweatshirt hem.

"Dad, you need help?" I asked from behind the curtain.

When there was no answer, I peeked through the gap again to see my father's face reflected in the mirror. He had tears running down his cheeks. I pulled the curtain open and asked, "What's wrong?"

"Sometimes . . . sometimes my hands don't do what I tell them to do. I tell them to pull and they don't; they just stay there. Today I can't move them, Piper. They won't listen to me," he said, our eyes meeting in the mirror.

"Let me help you." I moved quickly before he could argue with me. I wrestled the hem of his shirt from his hands and pulled it over his head. He seemed surprised by my speed and brusqueness, but I had undressed and dressed Fred for years against his will and I had learned that the dresser had to move quickly and without consulting the dressee. I moved to pull down his pants.

"Stop, Piper. I don't want you to see, to see my . . . my . . ."

My patience was running thin. "Your what, Dad, your private parts, your underwear? What, Dad? I've seen it all before. I have a husband and a son." I stood, pushing the hair off my forehead, ready to forcibly remove his pants whether he liked it or not.

His reply was quiet, barely audible to me. "No. My socks. I don't want you to see my socks. One has a red stripe and one has a blue stripe. Around the top. They don't match."

"Dad, that doesn't matter. It's okay." I unfolded the gown and held it out to him.

"It does matter. It does. I want to look . . . nice. I want my socks to match. Things should match.

They are supposed to match. You like things to look right," he said. His bloodshot eyes began to fill with tears and I felt my impatience wane.

"I don't care about socks, Dad, really. Let's just get your gown on," I said. "The doctor is going to be coming in any minute to talk to you." He stood and let me dress him like I remembered Fred doing with snow clothes before he could dress himself. He wasn't resisting, but he wasn't aiding my efforts either. Just as I tied the second tie on his back there was a sharp rap at the door and it inched open.

Dr. Kamplow stuck his head in and, after I nodded, came in and shut the door behind him. Dr. Kamplow was the neurologist who would be in charge of the battery of tests that my dad would undergo, including another MRI, another PET scan and probably another test or two that I hadn't yet heard of. After a briefing from him, the surly nurse returned with a wheelchair and they wheeled my father off. His expression was vacant. His eyes were red veined and empty and his mouth a straight, unwavering line. I had read that depression was ubiquitous with victims of traumatic brain injuries, but this felt different to me. Besides the tears over things like one red-striped sock and one blue and forgetting the words to "American Pie," my father was generally emotionless rather than melancholic. I saw a terrifying lack of reaction to almost anything that he experienced, either happy or sad. When Chuck Yeager came to him and laid his head in his lap, giving his hand a few loving licks and looking up at him with worry, my father startled and then pulled his hand away with no recognition flickering on his face. When his beloved Green Bay Packers eked out a tight win in the fourth quarter of a playoff game, he sat motionless in the chair in the living room. Even Fred, who had never shown any interest in the few football games that Isaac watched, knew that jumping around and hooting and hollering were called for in a win against Minnesota.

On occasion, I heard the sounds of conversation from Fred's room after school when I thought my father was ensconced in my office, resting. I lingered outside the closed door, trying to pick up any snippets I could. Mostly, I heard the hum of Fred's trademark monologues on whatever he felt like talking about, with little interruption from my father. Once as I loitered outside I heard the undeniable sound of laughter. I threw the door open to try to catch them in the act of enjoying life, just to witness the possibility of it. My father was sunk down into Fred's denim beanbag chair on the floor, with his knees tucked up tight to his chest, and Fred was sprawled out on his bed with Chuck Yeager by his side.

"What are you guys doing?" I said, trying to sound cool and uninterested.

"Nothing, Mom," Fred replied.

I turned to my father. "What's so funny?" I asked, my voice light and curious.

He looked up at me blankly, as if just registering my appearance in his world. He shrugged.

"Just man stuff, Mom. You wouldn't understand it," Fred said, shrugging.

Later that night, after both Fred and my father were asleep, Isaac and I sat together with a glass of wine in front of the fireplace, an occurrence that because of its rarity felt artificial, like the serious conversation scene in a family drama.

"Piper, what does it matter? Can't you just be happy that your dad was laughing?" Isaac asked.

"It does matter. I want to know what happened to get any level of reaction out of him. He's like a walking coma patient most of the time."

"I'm surprised you care so much."

"What's that supposed to mean, Isaac?" I asked.

"Well, you made it pretty clear that you were only providing him with basic care, like on a survival level, when you told me he was coming to live here. I'm just surprised that you seem to be interested on an emotional level," he said with a shrug of his shoulders. Only Isaac could say something so completely true but hurtful with a shrug. It was just his job to remind me of the facts. He smiled at me and said, "Anyway, they were probably talking about farts or something."

Piper

While my father received his brain scans, I found myself parked in a coffee shop, my iPad lit up with possibilities once again as I waited for my father's tests to be completed. There was a new study that had just come out that talked about how stress during pregnancy could actually change the dynamics of a growing fetus's brain. The authors of the study gave examples of maternal stress that included drug addiction, abuse and homelessness. I had decided on my own that the stresses that I had undergone while pregnant with Fred, though not on the same grand scale as a dangerous meth habit or a violent spouse, could very possibly have changed the makeup of Fred's brain just enough to grow the autism.

My intense focus on finding the cause of Fred's diagnosis would not be deterred by anything, certainly not specifics. Even as a child I'd had to know why things were the way they were, asking for explanations for every decision from my parents, every assignment from teachers. My brain couldn't effectively move on to the next step until I had fully solved the problem of the first. I had contacted the principal of Fred's school almost immediately after the diagnosis to find out what we were supposed to do next. Though that was weeks ago, we still waited to hear.

I had been warned by Helen Suzuki that the school district might try to drag its feet; every new diagnosis that required evaluation by them meant more money lost from an already severely stretched budget. She had given me the name of the district's autism specialist to contact if I felt like we were in need of another advocate. I had not yet called, but I kept the business card with the number inked on it by Helen in the back pocket of my jeans, as if I would lose it if it were not in physical contact with my body. I was waiting, but I wasn't sure what I was waiting for. The autism specialist's name was Jack Butler and I often wondered what he looked like, who he was, what had drawn him to this job, which was surely short on benefits and recognition.

I was contemplating the mysterious Jack Butler again when my phone buzzed to alert me that I had received an e-mail. It was from the special education teacher at Fred's school and she was writing to set up the first team meeting to begin the process of evaluating Fred for an educational autism diagnosis. Though he already had a well-documented diagnosis for medical autism, the school district wanted to decide on its own if he was going to receive services from them. I replied, remembering to copy Isaac just before hitting send. I wasn't sure why I did what I did next; there was really no rational reason, just the feeling in my gut that I wouldn't regret it. I pulled the wrinkled business card from my pocket and forwarded the message to Jack Butler.

Much later that day, after the doctor had completed the tests and my father was resting in a hospital room, I was called in to Dr. Kamplow's office to discuss the preliminary results. He was adamant that he might have more to share after a few days, but he wanted to talk to me about a few things first.

"Piper, what is your feeling about your father's recovery?" he asked, leaning forward with his elbows wide on his desk and his hands creating a triangle shape—his listening posture, I guessed.

"My feeling? Like am I happy?" I asked.

"No, no. How do you feel it's going?" he asked.

"Oh. Well, okay, I guess. He doesn't seem very happy. He has a lot of memory issues. Physically he seems all right, mostly. He says his hands don't work sometimes. I don't know."

"Would you say he's depressed?"

"It's more like emotionless."

"Right. We're seeing a delay in recovery in the emotional-processing centers of the brain. It looks like they're recovering at a slower pace than other areas that direct intellectual processes. Is he violent or overly aggressive?"

I paused. "No. No, he's not." It struck me, not for the first time, that my father was another person, not one I knew well. "Pretty mild-mannered," I added.

"Is this what his personality was like pre-incident?" he asked.

"No."

Dr. Kamplow waited for me to add more information, but I sat waiting for him to go on. There was so much below the surface that I often refrained from rocking the boat even just a little for fear that the person asking would drown in my dysfunctional childhood. I'd spent so many years in therapy dredging up all the shit that sometimes it just seemed like too much work to unpack it all again. Besides, I'd found a general practitioner who would happily hand out prescriptions for antidepressants along with cholesterol screenings and pap smears.

"All right. Well, it's possible that he'll recover the emotional-processing abilities that are lagging, but it's also possible that his emotional faculties may be as restored as they're going to be. The same is true for memory. We know that people experience memory loss and then regain memories in unique ways and there's no logical sequence for recovery. Where would you say most of his memory loss is concentrated? Long term? Short term?"

"He seems to have different ideas about how he

got to where he is. He has a fuzzy recall of our past as a family but will suddenly be really clear on something," I answered.

"Could you give me an example?"

"Song lyrics. He seems to remember the lyrics to every song he hears, but he doesn't remember his dog, the dog he loved."

Dr. Kamplow nodded and made notations with a very expensive-looking pen on a tablet. He didn't seem surprised by anything about my father's case, which should have made me feel better but left me a little unsettled for reasons I didn't immediately understand. He continued to ask questions about my father, which I dutifully answered. He wanted my father to continue with the occupational therapist, despite my recalling their weekly battles over shoelaces. He also recommended yet again that my father start seeing a therapist who worked with traumatic brain injury victims. I nodded as if I was seriously considering the possibility, but I knew I didn't have the energy to fight my father on this issue when he was so firmly against it.

I stood up to leave when Dr. Kamplow cleared his throat and said, "Many caretakers find it helpful to have someone to talk to, a counselor or close friend or partner."

I stood looking at him, silent. How to explain that my story was too complicated for a counselor? Too painful for a casual cup of coffee with a close friend I didn't have anyway? Too tedious for a text exchange with my busy husband? He cleared his throat again and stood, obviously uncomfortable with my silence.

"You have someone, then?" he asked.

"I've got this," I said, and grabbed the sheaf of papers and walked out of his office to retrieve my father. I found him lying on a hospital bed fully clothed.

"Hi, Dad. Did you get yourself dressed?" I asked, ready to be overly complimentary.

"No," he replied without looking at me.

"Dad, who dressed you?" I started gathering up his jacket and other random possessions.

"The one who smelled like she put a cigarette in her smoothie," he said.

A sharp laugh burst from my chest, startling my father into looking at me. "That was a joke, Dad. It was funny," I said.

He studied me for a few seconds before a tight, awkward smile grew slowly on his face. He shook his head in mild disbelief. "A joke," he said. He rose from the bed and took his coat from me. "I said a joke." And we made our way out to the parking lot, where the late-afternoon sun was setting and you could feel the sharp edges of the cold winter air when you took a breath.

Fred

Maybe you didn't know that the Battle of the Bulge was in the wintertime in the woods in three different countries. Hitler and Germany planned a very secret attack on the good guys and they surprised them pretty hard. It was snowy and cloudy and pretty cold for those guys because they didn't have Polartec or Gore-Tex. The United States lost the most guys of any battle during the war, but the German guys used up so many of their resources that it wasn't one hundred percent good for them either.

When my dad asked me what I wanted to do on the day he was going to supervise me I said Dad I would really like to go to a battle reenactment. He looked surprised and then said that there weren't really any battle reenactments in the winter that he knew of. I said well that doesn't make sense because some of those tough battles did happen in the winter. I said specifically the Battle of the Bulge. He agreed with me that it did not make sense but he said that there might not be that many people that want to go see a battle reenactment when it is freezing out. I said then they are not really interested in the truth. He agreed with me on that too.

So we decided to plan our own reenactment in the woods of a park that was about an hour or seventy-two miles from my house. We did some research about where to go and made a packing list. Dad did not think that we should tell Mom because she doesn't really like wars and killing. We drove to the park called Kettle Moraine South in the early morning and we got to stop at the doughnut shop on the way and I got two doughnuts one that was a vanilla frosted and one that was a chocolate glazed and I ate both of them hurry-up fast.

When we got to the park we had to find the parking lot that was closest to the trailhead. There were no other cars there and that was good because I did not want to have any spectators for my first reenactment. The snow was a little crusty and some places on the trail were icy. We both had backpacks. Right before we set off Dad said wait Fred I want to give you something. And it was a knife. It was a very sharp knife that had a leather pocket that went around the silver blade and the handle was polished wood. I was quite a bit surprised but not unhappy. I said I don't think that Mom would want me to have a knife because I am only a kid. Dad said when I was a boy I had a knife that I took to the woods with me when my brother and I played. We cut up little branches and things. It was good to have. It was heavy in my hand. I said okay Dad and put it in the zip pocket of my coat.

When we decided to have a reenactment it was hard to decide who was going to be the bad guys and who was going to be the good guys. Even though the United States was the good guys they did not win the battle. The Germans were the bad guys, but they got to win. Dad said that he would be the bad guys, but I told him that I wanted to because I wanted to see what it feels like to win. My dad didn't expect me to say that but he said okay.

First we had to hike into the woods and then go off the trail so it was like the forest of the Battle of the Bulge. Then I was going to hide from my dad and ambush him when he came along. I did not ever ambush anyone before. Let me tell you how it feels. First it feels a little lonely because I had to wait in the brush for a very long time by myself and you can hear every little tiny sound of the forest around you and you can very much notice that you are alone. There is also a feeling of part nervous and part excited. You feel a little bit nervous because you have to do a very important and dangerous thing but you feel excited because you think if you do it good enough you might win the war.

I could hear Dad's feet crunching in the snow starting from far away. The crunching got louder when he got closer and also the sound of my heartbeat got louder until it was filling up my ears and hurting my head. A part of me wished that there was no ambush, that I was just at home with Grandpa talking about the Three Stooges. I was afraid. I decided that I was going to have to be brave because Hitler and all of Germany were counting on me to kill that good guy. I started to feel less afraid and I pictured all the important guys telling me that I did a good job and maybe I would get a shiny medal.

I put my hand into the pocket of my coat and I could feel that cold knife handle even through my gloves. I pulled it out as silently as I could because those crunching footsteps of the soldier were getting closer and closer. I was thinking that it must take a lot of hating to want to kill a person. I thought about how much those bad guys and good guys must have hated really fierce to kill so many of each other. I thought about being that German guy who was just a guy that came from a place that was in a war and I started to think about how much he hated that other guy who was just a different guy from a different place and I took the knife out of the leather pocket and held it in my hand. My breathing was fast, because the crunching feet were just over the little hill and I could see flashes of my dad's bright blue coat through the bare tree branches.

I took a deep gulp of cold air and then held my breath because my dad was maybe six or five feet away and then just when he was in front of me I jumped out with my knife and I raised it above my head. My dad yelled Fred no and I brought the knife down because I was a bad guy in a war and he was the other guy. He put his hand out in front of me and the knife sliced through his black glove. He pulled his hand back to his chest and looked down at it. I could see that there was some blood on the glove that must have come from his hand. The blood dripped three drops down onto the snow before my dad finally talked. He said very quietly Fred I think that we should go now.

Piper

My father and I returned home to find that Fred and Isaac were already there, Isaac working at the dining room table with his laptop and Fred, I presumed, building Lego structures in his room. The house was eerily silent, just the tinkling of Chuck Yeager's tags when he met us at the door, madly waving his tail and panting. Isaac's left hand was bandaged with thick white gauze.

"What happened?" I asked. I sat down at the table, looking him up and down for any other sign of injury. My mind went wild with possibilities: car accident, fireplace burn, burglar.

"Aw, Fred and I went out to the woods and tromped around and I cut myself with a little hatchet when we were trying to sharpen marsh-mallow roasting sticks for the campfire," he said, barely looking up from the brief he was reading. "Had to go to urgent care, got a couple of stitches, no big deal."

"That sounds exciting. Is Fred okay?" I asked.

"Of course Fred's okay. Why wouldn't he be?" he asked sharply, looking up at me from the brief.

"Oh, I just wondered if it scared him at all. You know, his father cutting himself with a hatchet might be a little traumatic," I said.

"No. He's fine. Just tired, I think. Big day." He turned back to his work very definitively, letting me know that he was done conversing.

I went to Fred's room, where I found him lying on his bed. He watched me come in and I detected a feeling of unease in him. "How are you doing, Freddy?" I asked, and I lay down beside him on his bed. I kissed his head and breathed in his smell.

"Okay. We went to the woods."

"I heard Dad got hurt trying to make marshmallow sticks. Bet that was kind of scary."

He was silent for a few beats before he answered, "Yes, Dad got hurt trying to make marshmallow sticks. Yes, it was scary."

Fred seemed distracted and worried. "Are you okay? You seem kind of worried."

More silence. "Do you think that Dad will ever want to supervise me again?"

"Of course he will, Fred. Why wouldn't he? It's not your fault that he cut himself. The fire and the marshmallows were probably his idea anyway, right? You don't even like your marshmallows toasted."

"Right. Not my fault," he said, and closed his eyes.

"I'll let you rest, love." I covered him with his old fuzzy blanket and headed for the door.

"Mom," he called after me.

I turned back. "Yes, Fred?"

"Dad believes that the truth has two sides sometimes. But I don't. I believe that there is one truth and it is flat."

I was puzzled. "Okay, Fred." It had been a strange interaction, but the strangest part of it hadn't been our conversation, but the sweet baby-shampoo smell of Fred's hair. He didn't smell like campfire at all.

Fred

I did not mean to cut my dad in the hand with my knife. I forgot a little bit that I wasn't the bad guy and he wasn't the good guy. He was mad. He said that he wasn't mad, but in the car all the way to the urgent care clinic he did not talk to me. I wanted to tell him lots of things like Dad I am so sorry and it was an accident and I didn't mean to hurt you but also other things like this is war and that means that people get hurt. I didn't say anything. At the urgent care clinic we had to wait in the stuffy waiting room for a long time and I was still wearing all my winter gear but my dad hadn't told me to take it off so I wasn't sure that was okay. After we followed a nurse in a teddy bear shirt and pants to a little room she said you can hang your coats on the back of the door and then I thought it was probably okay for me to take off my winter clothes because a grown-up said it was okay.

Dad told the nurse and the doctor that he cut his hand when he was trying to cut some wood with a very sharp knife in the woods for a campfire. I guess that everyone believed him because no one said hey it looks like someone cut you with this knife maybe it was your kid. My dad didn't tell anyone that I did it even by accident. I think that probably means that the thing that I did is very, very bad. My dad knows a lot about very bad things that people do because of his job and so I figured that he must know that I am basically a criminal now and he doesn't want me to go to jail. He never told me not to tell anyone about the real truth of what happened, but he told everyone a different truth so I guess the real truth is not good.

Dad did not ask me for the knife back, maybe he believed his own truth and so he forgot about me and that knife. I put it in the secret utility pocket in my backpack so that it could not hurt anyone there.

This has made me think about the truth more. I was thinking in the car when it was very silent that maybe different people have different truths. Like with those soldiers, the U.S.A. guys believed very strong that the German guys were bad and so it was okay for them to kill those guys. But the German guys believed that they were right really strong and so they believed that it was okay to kill the U.S.A. guys. How can both of those things be true? But they were to both those guys. The truth is a very twisty thing that can be on your side or on the other guy's side. I didn't know whose side the truth was on this time, me or Dad.

Piper

Fred retired himself early that night, which wasn't surprising. Since the age of six, when he had read everything he could find about the human body, he had been obsessed with getting enough sleep. I made the regrettable mistake of reading him a book about the importance of sleep to your health. While it may not sound like the event a parent goes on to lament for years down the road, the book included a chart entitled "How Much Sleep Do I Need?," which listed a person's age and the optimal amount of sleep they should get. He became fixated on the chart and quoted its wisdom often. "Mommy, I need ten hours of sleep every night because I'm a child under the age of ten." He would get into bed at eight and plan to be asleep at eight thirty so he could rise promptly at six thirty, having slept a restful ten hours. As soon as the clock struck 8:31, I would hear his voice call from upstairs, alerting me to the time and the fact that he was not yet asleep. These updates continued, working their way from mildly confused as to why he was still awake, through frustration, to whatever emotion is characterized by unending atonal wailing like an infant. Rage, perhaps? Nothing I said would placate him; he wanted only to sleep. I would try to explain that different people needed different amounts of sleep, but I was met with skepticism because the chart was the final word on the matter. Fred's sleeplessness made me thankful that I had not tried to restart my career when he started school as I had intended. I was often as sleep deprived as a new mother.

A child psychologist our pediatrician brought into an appointment as a consult had some advice. He was a kind-looking man with a graying mustache and a unibrow and he suggested to Fred that all he had to do was relax his entire body, part by part, and breathe deeply. But we were way past visualizing pillows made of clouds. He tried to convince Fred he didn't really need ten hours of sleep, but since he had no formally titled chart to back up his statement, his word meant nothing. He must have seen something in Fred because he recommended a second child psychologist, a woman whose office was in the dank basement of an almost windowless concrete-clad building on campus built during the brutalist period in the 1960s.

I hated visiting that office, but Fred never seemed to mind, telling me that he and Denise played games. I thanked my lucky stars that we had good health insurance and that my son playing Othello with a shaggy blond-haired golden retriever of a person wasn't on my dime.

After two months of every-other-week visits, she called me into her office and Fred waited on a damp, tweedy love seat right outside the door. I didn't like leaving him alone in the hall at only seven years old; I didn't think he was ready to wait alone anywhere. I reluctantly entered the cave of an office and noted that there were pieces of drawing paper and ratty crayons strewn about the low table. I guessed she must have had a breakthrough, a drawing of a monster that haunted Fred at night, a mysterious man that stood outside his window, some reason that he wouldn't or couldn't sleep. Instead she tossed her hair out of her face, squeezed her hands into the pockets of her well-worn jeans and said, "I just can't find anything. I can't find any reason for the anxiety, for the worry. I dig and dig and dig, but we just keep coming back to the fact that he can't fall asleep. He's anxious because he can't sleep. That's it." I didn't know whether to slap her or thank her. I wanted desperately for there to be a reason, a problem to fix, and she shook her head and shrugged.

Our next stop was a referral to the sleep clinic, where we were interviewed for over an hour by a young doctor with a short bob of red hair, patent leather high heels and a crisp gray pants suit. I guessed that sleep doctors rarely saw the guts or grime that most doctors did. She recommended a nightly supplement of melatonin for a period of six months and then weaning Fred off of it because it was only temporary and she was confident that by then the problem would be solved. For six blessed months Fred slept and I slept. I wondered if we really had to withdraw the supplement; it wasn't even a prescription. I ordered it online and anyone could take it. Isaac disagreed and believed that we should follow the doctor's orders. All was fine until one night well after the six months was up when Isaac was home in time to put Fred to bed. Fred, eight, innocently asked for his sleeping medicine, and our secret was out.

"Piper," Isaac said, marching downstairs, his voice straining to be calm, "we agreed that we would wean him off the melatonin after six months."

"I didn't agree to that, Isaac. You declared it and I didn't agree or not agree. He's finally sleeping. Why do we have to stop?" I faced him with my arms crossed; this was not a battle I was ready to lose. My child was finally sleeping.

"The doctor's orders were six months and then wean him off," Isaac restated.

"Isaac, you're hardly even here when Fred goes to bed. You don't have to deal with it; it's torture. He screams and cries like a newborn if he can't fall asleep."

"I've been here for that. I don't think it's nearly as bad as you make it seem," he said. This from the man who had slept through ninety-five percent of Fred's nighttime feedings and diaper changes. He continued. "I'm just looking out for his health, Piper. I don't want to drug our child just so we don't have to deal with tough stuff."

"It's not a drug, Isaac! It's a supplement. You can buy it at Whole Foods, for God's sake. It's not like Ritalin or Prozac. It's important that Fred get enough sleep so that he can function well at school the next day. You know what he's like if he's tired. I just want him to get the most out of his education." That was always the argument that won Isaac over. In the end, he agreed that we could reduce Fred's dosage (I never did) and wean him off when summer came (I never did). The joke was on me, though, because by the time Fred turned nine, the melatonin no longer worked. One night he was surprisingly unable to fall asleep, and then the next and then the next, until he was routinely falling asleep sobbing around eleven or twelve. We suffered the medical phenomenon known as "poop-out syndrome" and once again I was left to choose to spend my evenings drinking red wine on the couch, listening to my boy cry himself to sleep, or lying beside him as he tossed and turned and cried himself to sleep.

The morning after his failed outing with Isaac, Fred didn't want to go to school. This wasn't an unfamiliar scenario; Fred often declared that he wasn't interested in attending school, but through a well-rehearsed combination of quality reasoning and bribery, he eventually got on the school bus, very rarely in tears.

I climbed the stairs to wake him, singing my "Wake Up, Fred" song, the same song I'd sung to him since his birth. I pushed open his door, and though he was still in bed, head buried under the blankets, Chuck Yeager splayed out on his back, tongue lolling, the lump in the bed moved slightly so I knew Fred was awake.

"Freddy, time to get up, my love." My voice was full of fake cheerfulness; I was almost giddy with anticipation of his awakening.

"I don't want to, Mom," he said, muffled through the layers of fleece and dog.

"Sweetheart, you have to get up. You have to go to school." I opened the curtains, and though I imagined the sun streaming in, beckoning Fred to the day, I was met with a wall of gray fog instead.

"If I don't want to go to school, I shouldn't have to," he said. This was the point where our argument took its familiar route: the reasons Fred had to go to school, the length of time he would be at school. My overwhelming argument for school eventually wore him down with its rationality. Today, though, his response was different.

"Mom, I just feel like nothing is right in the world. I'm too sad for school," he said. My heart broke; I immediately feared that the depression that plagued me had finally found its way to my Fred. I pushed Chuck Yeager over, climbed into Fred's bed and clutched him. We lay there that way for almost thirty minutes before Fred said, "I feel better, Mom. I feel like the sadness is not so sharp."

We were running late by then, of course, and missed the bus, so I had to drive Fred to school. The doors were already locked, so we had to page the office and were buzzed in. I checked Fred in at the office and kissed him good-bye and watched him trod down the hall to his classroom. I started toward the door but then decided that as long as I was at school, I might as well take care of some other business as well. I turned back into the office.

"Excuse me. Could you tell me where I could find Jack Butler?" I asked the receptionist.

After the receptionist vaguely pointed out the direction of Jack Butler's office, finding it took me another five minutes of blindly wandering down halls and up and down half staircases that seemed to take me to the floor that I had just been on, despite the fact that I had climbed both up and down to get there. I walked past countless classrooms, busy with the sounds of morning routines, a blur of activity unrecognizable to those who weren't privy to the individuality of each classroom's routine. As I walked past the music room for the second time, I wondered how it was ever possible for a child to find the bathroom. I felt, strangely, as if I was in one of my recurrent dreams about my own elementary school, a large, unimpressive brick rectangle. In my dreams, however, it revealed hidden staircases and hallways, a labyrinth.

I found myself in front of Fred's locker and quietly opened it. I felt like a voyeur, an interloper in my child's private school life. It still amazed me that this child I bore and raised and gave my life for had his own life away from me. His locker was probably the same as all the others: musty boots sitting in a rapidly melting puddle of dirty slush, snow pants hanging by one strap, the bottom cuff dipping into the wet, his coat hanging, sleeves jammed full of hat and mittens. I adjusted the snow pants to keep them from the puddle. I stroked the sleeve of his jacket and zipped up a half-open pocket on his backpack. I gently closed the door again, overcome with a feeling of melancholy that can come only from the realization that the world moves without you pulling it along.

On Fred's locker, there was a magnetic picture frame; each child had one with his or her name slipped inside the pocket. From looking around the hall, it appeared that the child could have chosen to decorate it with markers and whatever level of artistic ability they possessed at age nine.

Fred's was a white background with the teacher's neat, studied script spelling his name in the center. No colors, no puppy dogs or rainbows, no family portraits. I traced the letters with my finger and felt the familiar tug of sadness that sometimes crept in when I felt like Fred's differences were on display. That tug could be tamped down in many situations, but as I stood in this empty hall, surrounded by all the cues of happy, healthy childhoods, it refused to sit down and be quiet.

I walked silently to the door of Fred's classroom, just a few feet down from his locker. I wondered if I would regret looking in on him, braced myself for what I would see. His classroom was a busy place; there were bodies moving around the room in some sort of purposed chaos, carrying folders or notebooks. I could see the leaded-glass cupboards that Fred had described to me and an empty fireplace hearth, now filled with pillows for reading. If I pressed myself up against one side of the doorway and stood on my toes and leaned just right, I could see Fred. He was at his table, writing in one of the notebooks we had picked out together back in August, just one of a pile of meticulously chosen school supplies. He was alternatively writing and looking up and studying something that wasn't visible to me. Then I saw a messy-haired blond girl lean in from the other side and point to something on Fred's paper. He looked down and looked back at her and said something and she replied. He nodded and handed her a red-colored pencil and then went back to his work. My heart leapt; I had observed a natural social exchange involving my son and a little girl who needed her hair combed. I stepped back from the door and continued down the hall, my step the smallest bit lighter.

The reason I had such difficulty finding Jack Butler's office was that it wasn't so much an office as a storage closet filled with office-type things. A large wood desk took up almost half the space, with wall-mounted bookshelves stretching to the ceiling, packed with lines of books and piles of books looking near collapse if the door slammed too hard. His chair was an old-fashioned wood office chair, the kind I imagined a newspaper editor leaning back in one hundred years ago, cigar hanging out of his mouth and smug expression on his face. There were a tiny child-sized table and two small wooden chairs, the kind you could pay a lot of money to get from Pottery Barn Kids, predistressed. I was standing in the doorway when I felt a hand on my shoulder.

"Can I help you?" a voice asked.

I turned around and was eye to eye with a man, Jack Butler, I presumed. "Jack Butler?"

"Sure. If that's who you want to see." He

smiled. "Come on in." He held his arm out to gesture me in, but the tight space made the gesture unnecessary and also physically awkward.

I stepped into his office but didn't know where to sit, guessing that the only adult-sized chair in the room belonged to him. He pulled it out a few inches for me, as far as he could in the tight space, to signify I should sit. I sat stiffly, finding my bulky winter coat took up a good portion of the room all on its own. He pulled out one of the small chairs and squatted down to sit on it, looking completely at home and terribly gigantic.

"How can I help you?" he asked, and smiled at me.

There was something about him that first meeting, something that drew me to him immediately. I felt like my eleven-year-old self on the first day of school, drawn in to the sparkling personality of Shannon Miller, a popular girl who would go on to make my sixth-grade year a nightmare. It might easily have been that most of the men I found myself dealing with throughout Fred's education were the same type of chinos- and tennis-shoe-wearing, balding, unassuming "men in a woman's world." They perfected kind of an almost apologetic half smile, completely bland and prudent. Mr. Butler was not that kind of man in a woman's world. He was younger than I expected and wore dark blue jeans, suede ankle boots, and a gray sweater-vest with a dress shirt underneath, with the sleeves rolled up a few inches on his forearms. He had a black scarf around his neck and had a small silver stud in his left ear. He started unwinding the scarf from his neck, the motion of his arms like helicopter blades in the small space.

"I'm Fred's mom," I said.

"Ah, yes. Fred," he replied. "I know Fred."

"I'm here about his recent diagnosis. I didn't think that you would already know about him. Or work with him or whatever." I was on edge. A swipe of panic charged through me when it seemed that maybe once again I was the last one to notice Fred's disability.

"I've been visiting with Fred since November. We have lunch together once a week. I run a social skills group for kids, well, *boys* who might be struggling with making friends. We eat lunch together on Thursdays."

I interrupted. "Here?" I couldn't wrap my head around the logistics of it, never mind process anything further.

"Oh no," he said, and chuckled. "We eat in the library."

I grimaced. "Is Fred okay with that?"

"Well, he told me right off the bat that food and library books don't mix, but he's gotten used to the idea, and as long as no one brings any books to the table, he's fine."

"How did this happen? I mean, why is Fred in

this group?" I shook my head. "Never mind. I know the answer. I mean, I had no idea he was getting this support from you. I thought that they had to clear that with me or something."

"Yes, a parent signed off on it." He pulled down a manila folder from the shelf above my head, leaning over me so that I caught a whiff of his deodorant, a heavily male scent. He opened the folder and pulled out a sheet of paper and handed it to me. I scanned to the bottom, looking for my signature, and found Isaac's. The date was November 2. He had signed it at the parent-teacher conference, after I had tuned out.

I handed it back to Jack and smiled reassuringly. "You're right. My husband signed it."

"So, what can I do for you, Mrs. . . . ?"

"Piper. You can just call me Piper. I sent an e-mail to the school about Fred's diagnosis, the autism diagnosis that we got from a neuropsych. The special ed teacher replied with, like, one sentence, and said that she'd get back to me, but she hasn't. I'm not quite sure what I'm supposed to do next."

"Ah. Yes." Jack nodded to himself. Then he seemed to shake himself out of it and continued. "Fred received a medical diagnosis of autism spectrum disorder, but he can't receive services until the school district gives him an educational diagnosis."

"Yes. I understand that, but I'm still a little confused. What's the difference?"

"Nothing, really. Same criteria, but the school district would like to decide whose differences require services. Same tests, same observational data, et cetera." He was twirling a ballpoint pen between his fingers and staring at the ceiling. He suddenly looked straight at me. "Nancy Edelstein is the special ed teacher here; she'll run the diagnosis process."

"Okay, then, sorry if this is rude, but why are you here? Aren't you the autism support person or something?"

He studied his pen and then looked up at me. "Good question. I'm a man, so I'm a minority." He grinned at me and continued. "I'm on the spectrum, so I'm like the superlative hire for the school district."

"On what spectrum?" I asked, my mind puzzling over which spectrum he could belong to.

"The autism spectrum." He opened his arms wide, almost touching the walls on either side of his office. "This is what autism looks like all grown-up," he said, and laughed.

I wasn't sure if this was something that I was supposed to laugh at too, or if it was like an ethnic stereotype joke that you couldn't laugh at unless you were the butt of the joke.

"I meant, what's your role in the educational diagnosis process?" I clarified.

"I know. I know. I'm just messing with you. I'll be there as a resource. I'll make sure the process is fair and unbiased. I'll probably offer observations on Fred because I know him."

He looked at his watch and jumped up. "Oh shit. I was due five minutes ago in a meeting." He reached out his hand to me and I stood and shook it. "It was great to meet you, Piper, and I'll be in touch real soon." He grabbed a folder off the desk and walked out of the office, leaving me standing there alone in a mild daze.

When I met Fred at the bus stop a few hours later, I planned to grill him about Jack Butler, this strange educational professional with the sharp blue eyes and wicked fashion sense. But Fred didn't seem to be in the mood to talk much.

"Mom, Jack Butler is another grown-up at my school. Schools are full of grown-ups that ask kids questions and want them to do their best work and make good choices." He walked the rest of the way home in silence.

Fred

Jack Butler is a grown-up at my school and Mom asked me about who he is today and I thought about that. He is a man and he is thirty-three years old. His birthday is September 18 and he doesn't have a wife, but he has an ex-wife and he has no children. Jack Butler has very light blue eyes and his hair is the color of tree bark, not the white kind, and he has his ear pierced like a pirate, but only with little dots, not big circles. We have lunch together at lunch bunch on Thursdays in the library but we don't read library books while we eat because food and library books don't mix. I bring a home lunch and Jack Butler brings a home lunch. He brings vegetarian sushi home lunch and I bring hummus and pretzel chips home lunch. He eats his home lunch with chopsticks and I eat my home lunch with my hands, unless there's applesauce and then I use a spoon. One time Mom forgot to give me a spoon and Jack Butler gave me a white plastic spoon that was in his desk drawer. It was a spoon but it had points on it and Jack Butler said Fred you have just been introduced to the miracle that is the spork.

Sometimes on Thursdays other guys eat lunch

with us too. Owen Parker is in third grade and he clears his throat in every word and one time I said Owen Parker it is hard to carry on a conversation with you because you clear your throat in every word and Jack Butler said Fred that is not polite and it makes Owen feel bad. I said I was just telling the truth and I didn't mean to make Owen feel bad. I told Owen that I was sorry and I liked the way he drew the Batman symbol on his notebook cover. Sometimes T. J. Brown eats lunch with us and he talks a lot and the times that T. J. Brown eats with us it is hard to carry on a conversation also because he makes himself in charge of the talking. One time when T. J. Brown was talking about the Packers from Green Bay, Jack Butler looked at me sneaky and winked. I guessed it meant that Jack Butler was not enjoying the conversation T. J. Brown was having with himself about football.

Mostly I like it best when it is just myself, Fred, and Jack Butler at lunch bunch because I get to be in charge of talking. Jack Butler said that we have to practice having a conversation because people don't like it when one person does all the talking. Jack Butler said Fred it took me a long time to learn how to carry on a conversation with another person. I was a grown-up man who didn't understand why no one wanted to talk to me until one day a guy said Jack you talk too much dude. Let someone else get a word in, man. Jack

Butler wants to help me learn how to carry on a conversation before I am a grown-up man.

I have figured something out. If I ask Jack Butler a question and wait for him to answer it politely and show that my face and body are interested in what he says, then it will be my turn to talk again and I can be in charge of the conversation. Here is an example of learning to carry on a conversation with Jack Butler. When Jack Butler is talking you have to use your eyes to look at him and point your body in his direction.

Him: How are you today, Fred?

Me: I am doing okay today, Jack Butler. How are you?

Him: Thanks for asking, Fred. I am feeling pretty good today.

Me: Jack Butler, did you know that World War I was called the war to end all wars but we still have wars in this world?

Him: Yes, I did, Fred. How about you ask me something about myself so that we can talk about something that we are both interested in?

Me: I do not think that I am interested in talking about you, but I will try.

Him: Thank you, Fred. I appreciate that.

Me: Jack Butler, which war do you think was the coolest one?

Him: Fred, that is not exactly what I meant.

Me: I will try again, Jack Butler. Why do you have an ex-wife but not a wife?

Him: That's a tricky question, Fred. I think I would rather talk about wars.

Piper

My meeting with Jack, packed inside his tiny office, unsettled me. I felt a vague sense of relief that autism would not end my child's life; he would go on to grow up. He could attend college and get a degree. He could work in a profession that required constant contact with people. He could go on to dress himself in dark-washed jeans and chukka boots. He might learn how to wear a scarf like a man. There was another feeling too, one that pressed up against the inside of my lungs and could suddenly take my breath away as I stood at the sink washing dishes or stood outside Fred's door listening to his sleep breathing, mixed with the snores of Chuck Yeager. It was the realization that this was not going away; this diagnosis was not something he would grow out of. He would not trade in autism for a fashionable wardrobe. All my research on the Internet, all the time spent learning everything I could about the disorder, could not prove this to me the same way that ten minutes in the presence of Jack Butler could.

The night after I met him, after Fred was soundly sleeping and my father was doing whatever he did in his room with the door closed, I googled "Jack Butler, Madison, Wisconsin" on a whim and to my surprise found a vast storehouse of information about him, straight from his own mouth. Jack was the author of a blog called, ironically, *Sweater-vests and Autism*, where he wrote about his own experience as a man "living on the spectrum." The blog was years old and well read, with thousands of followers. The archives were deep and I stayed up much too late reading his blog entries for the last three years. By the time I heard Isaac pull in the driveway and slammed my laptop shut, gulped down the last swallows of my red wine and looked at the clock, it was nearing midnight. I was certain I could pass off my Internet digging as an attempt to learn more about being an adult with autism and Isaac would gladly pat me on the back for finally accepting that everything would be fine and that would be the end of it. But it felt like more than that to me. I was embarrassed to say out loud that I felt like a child with a new friend, though I knew intimate details about his life and he knew me only in relation to my son. I was already picturing us chatting over coffee and bonding over Fred, something I hadn't done or even wanted to do with Isaac in years.

As I lay in bed, unable to sleep, waiting for my own generous dose of melatonin to kick in, I thought of nothing but Jack. I knew his marriage had failed because he had difficulty accessing his emotions and an annoying habit of walking out of the room while his ex-wife was still talking. I knew he had a brother that was "further on the spectrum" and was nonverbal and still lived with Jack's parents. I knew his favorite color was green and he was a sushi-loving vegetarian. I felt like he was my new best friend, someone I could talk to about Fred and my father and maybe my husband. I tried to push my brain back to Fred and how my knowledge about Jack could benefit or affect Fred. Yes, Jack was on the spectrum, but he led a full life, a quirky, sometimes difficult life because of his differences, but it was a life. He had a career and seemed happy, if maybe a little lonely, though he never used those words. I pictured myself as the one who could provide him companionship, understand him like no one else. We could be best friends like Shannon Miller and I never were. I could rescue him, I figured, but deep down I suspected it wasn't Jack who needed rescuing at all.

Lance

The night is a lonely time. I sleep by myself in my daughter's office. I used to be a pilot and I traveled a lot. I slept alone in a lot of hotels. Even though I was sleeping alone, I knew there was someone else at home sleeping alone too. Someone missing me and waiting for me to come home. Flying an airplane is lonely too, but in a different way. When you are up above the clouds you feel alone, even with a copilot next to you. When you are at the controls of that plane it's just you and the clouds. Nighttime was my favorite time to fly. I loved overnights because it was so quiet. It was soft voices and dimmed lights. It was quiet footsteps and coffee. We only spoke if we had to, like the nighttime demanded respect.

Flying an airplane at night is like a home at night—a home with a family sleeping and the hum of the dishwasher in the kitchen and maybe one lamp throwing low light across the living room. It is like the night-light in the bathroom and Fred's snoring. If I get up in the nighttime I go stand in the door of his room. He sleeps with the blinds wide-open and sometimes the moon is bright in his window and there is a beam of light that lights up his face. It is magical to me. It is the same feeling as flying at night.

I call her phone sometimes, Judy. She never answers it because it is the middle of the night and she has it turned off. I listen to her message and sometimes I talk to her. Her voice does not sound the way it does in my head. Her voice sounds cracked and soft. Her voice sounds like a person who is tired all the time. When I leave her messages I tell her about flying at night. I tell her about the silver clouds and the way the control panel lights up like tiny Christmas tree lights. I tell her about how I love to approach a city lit up at night. I love the sharp lines of light that draw out the edges of people's lives. People who are sleeping and don't know I am looking down at them. I tell her how every time I flew at night I must have missed her so much that it hurt. I tell her that I still love her and can't wait until she comes home.

She doesn't call me back.

Piper

Living with my father again had taken on a
rhythm—a rhythm that, while I would not say
I enjoyed it, I had become accustomed to. Besides
going to his appointments, we went for walks
together, as his therapists had told me physical
activity was crucial to his healing process and I
didn't trust him to walk alone. He continued to
puzzle me; though he could get lost less than a
block from my house, he could suddenly recall
very specific events from the past with a degree
of clarity that I found eerie.

One day we made our way through the achingly
cold February air to watch the ice fishermen on
Lake Wingra. I couldn't decide if I admired their
heartiness or was more confounded by the folly
of sitting outside in the arctic cold on an upside-
down bucket, hoping to catch a fish too small to
eat. My father asked, "Piper, did I cut Curtiss's
hair?"

"Yes, Dad. You did," I replied. I decided there
was no point in lying, though some might have
said it would cause undue pain for my father
to be reminded of his transgressions. I just so
strongly desired that he feel something, anything
at all, and the truth was that I was still unable to

completely forgive him for the man he once was, though there were days when I felt incrementally closer to a sort of passive forgiveness, a letting go of the past in wisps and crumbs.

He was silent for a long time as he stared out at the lake—time that I imagined his brain was chugging itself through the words he had just heard, processing the input and making a determination of its connotation and value. "He was in high school and he wouldn't cut his hair. It was long and greasy."

"I guess you could say that," I said, noticing how a small puff of air escaped my mouth with each word.

"I thought boys shouldn't have long hair. Boys shouldn't have long hair, Piper."

"Dad, anyone can have any kind of hair they want," I said, feeling the familiarity of this conversation. I had said some variation of those same words to Fred many times, each time he showed disdain at something that was different than he felt it should be.

He considered this point for a long time and then he said, "I guess that's true."

I pushed into new territory. "Maybe you should apologize to Curtiss. He might appreciate that." Though I had no trouble gently reminding my father of his offenses, this was the first time I'd offered the possibility that he take responsibility for them.

"I'll think about that, Piper."

Though we sometimes filled the daily silence with these meaningful conversations, if it was up to my father, most of our time together would have been silent. He no longer understood the intent of small talk and spent most of his time in his own head. I was finally able to coexist in a place with my father and not feel constantly on edge, unsure when his next blowup would be, uncertain which of our minor indiscretions would set him off. I didn't sit in his silence, wondering what I had done wrong anymore. Rather than a series of emotional mountains and valleys, a constantly changing landscape, with no clear path for safe travel, he was now a single plain. A straight line as far as the eye could see. My father was an emotional North Dakota.

This lack of emotional landscape shaped my days into a strange balance of silence and contact with people, just about always at opposites. When Fred left the house in the morning, my silent period began and then lasted until there was an appointment for my father or, less often, an appointment for myself. There could be entire days during which I spoke almost not at all from seventy thirty a.m. until three p.m. I don't know why this struck me as so odd; just months before this had been the normal pattern of my weekdays.

Before Fred was in school, there had been playgroups where Fred played alone and I eagerly soaked up conversation with other mothers. And of course, there had been Fred and his constant chatter. Although for years prior to my father's heart attack I had spent my days in silence, that silence took on a different weight when it was accompanied by the constant presence of another adult human. Though he said little, I could feel his constant physical presence wherever I was in the house. There were occasions when I thought I heard him speak or cry out for me, and I rushed to him, concerned that I had missed an important communication. I would often find him in his room or at the dining room table, where he would look up, surprised to see me suddenly by his side, confused that I was out of breath and demanding he want or need something from me.

During these months, I had almost no contact at all with my mother. Before my father's heart attack, we had often spoken on the phone several times a week and seen each other at least once a week; we met for lunch or coffee or a visit with Fred, maybe Sunday dinner if my father was flying. But she had disappeared from my life physically and, strangely, almost completely emotionally as well. My feelings about what my mother had done were complicated and were born of such a vast tangle of experiences and hurts that I didn't dare sit and untangle them. It became easier to just set them aside and promise to go back to them when life was easier.

Isaac tried to get me to talk about my mother and my feelings; he was more than happy to analyze my quiet on the subject as both unhealthy and dishonest.

"Piper, you must feel something about your mother leaving you with this, with him," he said, and gestured to the empty air around him, as if my father and his situation now took up every ounce of breathable air in our home.

I shrugged and went back to folding Fred's small superhero briefs into neat piles on the coffee table. "I don't know what you want me to say, Isaac," I said.

"Aren't you angry with her?"

"I don't know what I am with her. I know why she did it. I don't agree with it, but I understand. I can see the whole situation, all those years through her eyes, and . . . that's all I know about it right now," I said, and pulled out the underwear that was too small, to put away in one of the many rubber containers in the basement, where they waited with other stale clothes that Fred had outgrown, waited for someone to come along who didn't mind wearing used underwear.

"I mean, look at what she stuck you with, Piper. It's not really your responsibility. She's his wife. She should take care of him," Isaac said.

"I was the one who pulled him out of the nursing home, Isaac. That's on me. I guess I feel like she was done. She did all she could for him, gave enough of herself, and she just had nothing left. Honestly, I get it. I do," I said.

"What I don't get is how you're so Zen about this. This is a man you purported to hate for most of the time I knew you, and now you're not only letting him live in our house; you're taking care of him, like a child. It just doesn't make sense to me," Isaac said, matching up his argyle dress socks into neat piles.

"Do you want me to kick him out, Isaac?" I said. I was annoyed. I didn't understand why I couldn't just do the job. Why did I also have to understand why I was doing it? It had been put in front of me, placed there like a meal on a tray, and I was working my way through it, no matter if I liked beef stroganoff and canned peaches or not. "You have always been the one who said I didn't give my dad a fair chance, that I didn't forgive and forget or whatever. What do you think I should do? What do you think *we* should do?"

His answer always came back the same: of course we shouldn't kick him out; of course he would stay until he was fully healed and able to live on his own. He just wanted me to sift through my feelings about the whole thing, access the resentment and frustration, admit my displeasure with the whole thing. But I always wondered why. Why bring up the bile when there was nothing to do but swallow it back down?

I wasn't being one hundred percent honest with Isaac either. I was angry; I was disappointed and exhausted and frustrated. I spent the greater part of my days in quiet contemplation about my situation, imagining conversations with my mother and all the possible outcomes. I tried out the role of martyr and saint, the role of forgiver and aggressor, and found all of them wanting. My feelings about my mother and what she had done fell into a gray area, a place where they couldn't easily be labeled and sorted into baskets. It was preferable, however, to burrowing past the facade of my marriage. I visualized it as the earth itself, layers and layers, some older than time, with a hot molten center that you didn't dare touch.

It was an unusually warm February morning, the kind where you're either thanking God that all that rain isn't snow or wishing it was, the morning after one of these frequent and futile exchanges with Isaac, when the landline rang out in the midst of all the normal silence. We were in the long, drawn-out process of renouncing our landline in favor of cell phones only. Isaac had wanted to months, even years, ago, but I'd held on for reasons I was still unsure of. I wondered sometimes if the persistent quiet of my days was slowly getting to me and abandoning our telephone service gave me one less connection to the outside world.

I didn't recognize the number, but the area code looked familiar. "Hello?" I said.

"Oh, Piper. I didn't know if you'd be home." It was my aunt Jeanne, my mother's captor or her safe house, depending on your view.

"I'm here," I said coolly. I found my anger had an easier target with my aunt, as she had rarely experienced my father's abuse firsthand. She and I had exchanged only a few logistical e-mails over the last few months, and I wondered if I had missed one. I hadn't heard my aunt's voice since she had stood beside my mother at the hospital.

"I need to talk to you about something, Piper. I need to talk to you about your dad," she said, her tone making it clear that she was apprehensive about whatever it was she felt she needed to say.

"Go on," I said.

"Well, your dad . . . I don't suppose you know that he's calling your mother's phone?"

I said nothing, sat in the silence, as I was well practiced at doing.

"He's, um . . . well, he's calling her a lot, especially at night, and leaving messages for her."

"Do you think that maybe she should talk to him? It's pretty obvious that he wants to talk to her, Jeanne."

"Oh, Piper, I don't think she's ready for that. Could you just, maybe, speak to him? Or take the

302

phone away or something? It's upsetting to your mother."

The slow burn in my chest ignited and I found myself suddenly shaking with a physical anger I had kept quiet for months. I took a deep breath. "Jeanne, this whole thing is upsetting to everyone. He doesn't understand why she went away; he doesn't get it. He's not even the same person anymore. These things he did before? He's not like that now. I think my mom should talk to him. She would see that if she talked to him."

"Do you really believe that, Piper? Do you really believe people can change like that? He was horrible. Do you really think that's all just disappeared? I don't. I think it's still in there, and sometime when he's healed up, he'll be himself again. I'm sorry, Piper. I just don't buy it," Jeanne said. She had spoken aloud the nagging worry that sometimes woke me in the night: as much as I knew my father had changed, I wondered if there wasn't some minute chance it might all come rushing back someday.

"Fine. I'll talk to him, but I'm not taking the phone away. She's going to have to find a way to deal with this on her end. She can't just expect him to be okay with being cut off from her. He's like a child, Jeanne. He doesn't get it. And, Jeanne? Why didn't my mother call me herself? She couldn't talk to me about this?"

There was a brief silence. "She was afraid, Piper. Afraid of how you'd be. Afraid you would beg her to come home or take him back or tell her she was a bad person. She's not a bad person, you know."

I sighed. "I know." I hung up the phone, knowing that although I was hurt and angry and frustrated that my mother didn't call me herself, she was right.

I found my father lying on the pulled-out futon in the office. I stood in the doorway and took in his still body and my heart took a brief pause as I wondered if maybe he was dead. The feeling sat squarely in a no-man's region of morality. On one hand, I had wished my father dead before, many times over the preceding years, wished for a plane crash, colon cancer, or a run-of-the-mill car accident. If he was now lying in my office, dead, my hands would be washed of the whole situation, my days as caretaker done, my mother home again. Never again would I worry about his temper or judgment. On the other hand, the hand I had not previously known I even had, the thought of my dead father now produced a feeling of concern, regret, even grief. As I had told Jeanne on the phone, the man my mother had run from was no longer here. That man had died that day in the shower, replaced by an identical physical copy, with none of the same narcissistic, overly critical tendencies. This man had a tendency toward silence, toward sadness, toward simplicity.

His eyes were open and he stared at the ceiling, perhaps studying the same crack that Fred had once worried an unwelcome monster would ooze out of.

"Dad?" I asked.

First there was no response, but then he sighed the tiniest of sighs and turned to look at me. His crystal blue eyes, always capable of extreme anger or extreme joviality, were flat. "Yes, Piper?" he said, his voice cracking with disuse.

"I need to talk to you. I need to talk to you about Mom," I said, and I sat on the edge of the mattress, near him but not touching. My father and I had never had a very physical relationship, and though he had shown more tenderness in the last few weeks than he ever had before, I wasn't comfortable receiving it. "Jeanne called and said that you've been calling Mom and leaving messages for her on her cell phone."

"Yes," he said, nodding slightly, his eyes turned back to the crack, which spread from one wall across the expanse of the ceiling all the way to the opposite wall.

"Well, you have to stop, Dad."

"Why? Why do I have to stop? She's my wife. Judy is my wife," he said.

"Yes, but she isn't really ready to talk to you right now." I was struggling to find the words to explain this very adult matter to someone who now seemed to have the limited comprehension of a child. I felt the need to read Mr. Rogers's children's book on divorce, complete with glossy photos of dissolving families in bell-bottoms and turtleneck sweaters, suitcases packed. "Mom wants to be alone right now, I guess."

He was still for a moment, before turning his gaze to me. "But she's with Jeanne. That's not alone."

"Yeah. So, sometimes people want to be with some people and not other people. Like, they just need a break from a particular person." I felt like I was truly botching this exchange, tripping over my words like they were cobblestones.

He nodded again, soundless. "Okay."

"Okay? Are you sure, Dad?"

"I'll just wait until she doesn't want to be alone with Jeanne. I'll just wait until she wants to stop her break," he said. I didn't correct him; I couldn't tell him that there was no break, just forever. I couldn't lie to him about cutting Curtiss's hair and believing I was a bad driver, but I could lie about this. The only reason I could conclude for my sudden deception was fatigue. I was tired of hard truths.

I started to get up, but he grabbed my hand in his, the skin feeling as dry and thin as the wrinkled tissue-paper flowers Fred used to bring me from preschool.

"Dad, how did you know her phone number?"
I asked, since he had been particularly troubled
with his memory since the heart attack.

"Fred found it for me. I asked him to. Fred got
it from your phone book and he wrote it down."

"Oh. I see."

"Have you ever seen this crack, Piper?" He
pulled on my hand until I had no choice but to lie
down beside him. We looked up and analyzed the
crack together.

"It goes all the way across. All the way from
one wall to the other and back again," he said.

"It's an impressive crack, Dad."

"Is it very old?" he asked with a slight edge of
panic in his voice.

"Well, it's been here since we moved in ten
years ago, so it's at least that old, but probably
older. It seems like maybe it's grown, but it's not
something I really notice all that often."

"You should notice it, Piper. You should stop
and look at it. It's part of the house, but the house
doesn't fall down. It's cracked but it still works."

"I'm stopping and looking at it right now,
Dad," I said. We were quiet; I was beginning
to lose myself in the meandering of that crack.
I imagined it as a schism in the earth, a great
divide between light and dark, dropping down
to nothingness. If that crack opened up to
nothingness, what would happen if you fell in?
I had never spent so much time contemplating a

crack. I was getting ready to put my thoughts into words, share them with my father, our bonding experience over my home's mild structural damage, when he spoke.

"It looks like a road," he said, and he put his head on my shoulder. I felt that pause in my heart rhythm again, that missed beat, that uncomfortable sensation of sitting with the unknown.

"You're right, Dad. You're right; it does look like a road," I said, and I lay there next to him, my thoughts drifting, floating like the bubbles Fred used to love to blow: free and soft and light, until they landed on something and broke and Fred cried out in sorrow and rage.

Fred

When I got off of the bus and walked home 4.5 houses to our house, 2384 West Elm Avenue, Mom was waiting for me at the red front door. She was wearing a face like she needed to say some things to me. She was wearing a sad half smile and a wrinkled forehead that means worry. I walked up the concrete walk to our door and I counted every step and there were nineteen. I said Mom do you need to talk to me and she said yes Fred but it isn't a big deal. I said Mom you are wearing a big-deal face.

After I took off my mittens, hat, coat, snow pants and boots and Mom got me a snack of cheese and Triscuits, she sat at the table across from me and said Fred did you give your grandfather your grandma's phone number?

I said well yes I did. He needed to call her and she is his wife. I did not tell Mom that sometimes in the nighttime I dial the phone for Grandpa, if he is feeling extra sad and can't find the numbers. Mom sighed which is a grown-up way of saying you are right but it is still not okay. She said it's okay Fred, you did not know. I said what did I not know? And she said you did not know that Grandma is taking a break from

309

him right now and she doesn't want to talk to him.

I had to think about that because it did not make a lot of sense to me. I said are Grandma and Grandpa married? She said yes they are. I said don't married people like to talk to each other? She did not say anything for about seven seconds. Then she said sometimes people who are married are not happy and maybe they shouldn't even be married anymore, maybe they would be happier if they weren't married.

Mom are you happy? I said and she said right away of course I am happy Fred and then she ruffled my hair and stood up and turned away from me. Before she turned away I could see she was wearing a different face. It was an afraid face.

III *Spring*

Piper

Spring came unusually early, almost as a surprise; suddenly the white snow was gray, then black; then it was merely small islands of dirty ice with brown grass poking up in between. It was during this early spring that Chuck Yeager and I went from a cold avoidance to a detached ambivalence. We had accepted that our lives were now intertwined. It seemed that both of us had had enough of the rigid margins of the house, where we were safe from cold but sheltered from experiences. We had been shut in for so many months that the smell of stale closeness was evident only when you left the house and returned.

I wondered if I carried that smell of confinement with me when I ventured out into the world. I imagined that Chuck Yeager was ready to be done with the same rotation of scents finding their way to his nose: dirty boy, clean boy, crumbs, soup cooking, old man, me. Did he smell my discontent? Did he smell my unease with where my life had ended up, taking care of my father, waiting for my son to return home to me each day? Waiting for my husband to return home to me each night? I figured he must, given the fervor and single-mindedness with which he took in the smells of the outside world. Rather than run, we walked because he could not run and also take in all the olfactory stimulation he had missed all winter long. I was surprisingly fine with that, having reached a sort of comfortable companionship with my softer body. I let him lead me from fire hydrant to tree trunk to decorative boulder. I felt free, no longer the one making decisions. We were simply following our noses.

Chuck Yeager was the same in the yard. In the winter, I had simply let him out the back door and waited for him to silently pad back to me after doing his business quickly so he could return to his spot in front of the fireplace, where his belly would grow so warm to the touch I worried for his safety. Several times, I pulled him back away from the fire and he turned his gaze on me, unimpressed with my concern, and emitted a low growl. Now in the backyard I had trouble getting him to return, so I began standing outside with him and watching him sniff around at the detritus of winter, eat rabbit droppings and bark at the squirrels that were bravely endeavoring to retrieve black walnuts they had made the mistake of burying in our yard months before, before the arrival of this fierce canine protector.

Standing out there in the yard, under bare trees dripping with spring melt, between patches of ice and Chuck Yeager's own droppings, I had a lot of time to think, as if I couldn't have when I was inside. I spent a good amount of time considering my life and where I had been and the stunning fact that I had no idea where I was going. When I was in the midst of my career, I imagined myself on a trajectory that pointed only up, toward success. When Fred was born it was the same, a career of baby raising that led to child raising that led to the eventual victory of a young man capable of co-opting my responsibilities and then a young woman willing to fill in the gaps that Fred was unaware needed filling or uninterested in filling himself.

My plan had always been to continue my career where I left off when Fred went to school full-time, five years ago, but there was always something preventing me from taking the leap from theoretical to actual. Fred was a needy child, and though everyone who met Isaac would say he was anything but needy, I knew the truth. So much of what happened in our house was because of me. Isaac, this defender of the defenseless, this man who was "one of the good ones," would possibly starve and wander around in days-old underwear without me chopping root vegetables and standing in front of the washing machine daily.

I had gotten lost in these little tasks, these insignificant things that meant the world. Should

I now wish to return to my work, carve out a place in the world of watercolor illustration, use my office as the studio it was always meant to be, I couldn't. Now I had my father to raise, though there was no obvious end point in sight, no chance of him going off to college, meeting the right girl and becoming someone else's responsibility.

Deep down in the part of me that I reserved for hard truths and the acknowledgment of my own inner ugliness, I knew my father was not the real reason. I knew there were resources for people like me taking care of their parents. There were things like day care for the elderly that brought to mind projects involving macaroni necklaces and snacks of apple juice and Fig Newtons. There were transportation services that could shuttle my father around like a luxurious car service might in a parallel life. There were nursing homes. I had options, but I preferred to stand under those large oak trees, still bedecked with a few dried leaves that had refused to fall in the autumn, soon to be forced out by newness, and feel stuck. If I was trapped in this life I had not chosen, then it was irrelevant that I was afraid of all the possibilities that might be open to me. I encouraged flexibility in Fred, but I knew I needed the encouragement just as much as he did.

During these frequent walks, this everyday appointment with myself as psychologist since my old therapist had retired and just the idea of telling someone else my whole life story exhausted me, the idea of Jack Butler was just outside my thoughts, just on the periphery. I never considered an extramarital affair (I lacked the energy to invest in another person who needed things from me), but I was obsessed with Jack. My thoughts were neatly divided into pieces of pie, my brain one circle chopped into segments, and after Fred, my home, and my father, the next largest piece went to Jack. His piece of the pie was larger than even my husband's slice; after so many years of sameness and a distance that grew incrementally, Isaac was granted just the thinnest slice, the dieter's request. I forced myself to consider why this discrepancy existed. I rifled through my feelings, tried to look at the issue from all sides, examine its facets carefully. I could come up with only one reason, but I backed away from it often because of the potential it had to upheave my life. It was simple: Jack had not yet disappointed me.

So I pored over Jack's blog posts, friended him on Facebook and patiently waited for his acceptance, but only in the most casual of ways. I learned about every public aspect of his life and then found myself creating lengthy narratives about his private life, his relationship with his parents and disabled brother, his experience in community college and then as an older student at a generic state university in Minnesota, even his failed marriage. These were all scenes that polluted my head anytime it didn't have an immediate concern or mental chore.

I plunged deep into them all under the guise that it would help me understand Fred better, maybe not now, but someday. I reveled in our small contacts, our Fred-focused conversations. I e-mailed him with questions about the diagnosis process almost daily. "Just checking in . . . ," read the subject lines. He good-naturedly filled me in on the slow movement of Fred's case, encouraged patience, informed me when more information was needed. There were times when I thought if I looked carefully, overanalyzed just a bit, he had crossed the line from professional to personal, and I reveled in those small indiscretions. I wondered if perhaps he was home at night thinking of me, wondering, like I was, if our friendship might be destined to be.

On that early March day, my cell phone rang out to break my backyard philosophizing, and I am ashamed to admit that my heart vibrated when I saw it was Jack on the other end of the line.

"Hello, Mr. Butler," I said, unearthing a playfulness I had buried. I knew that I didn't sound professional or neutral, but after weeks of mentally preparing myself for just such a conversation, I felt confident, even cocky. A phone call out of the blue; my imagination could only point me in one direction: a cup of coffee? A matinee? A stroll through the arboretum?

"Piper? We've got a situation here. At school. With Fred." His voice was stilted, too staccato; there was none of the good-natured kindness I had imagined. The giddiness that I had experienced just seconds before transformed into humiliation—a deep, deep guilt that I felt would take gallons of scorching water and rough metal scouring pads to erase. My mind rushed directly to broken limbs and school shooters.

"What? What happened?" I asked.

"I just wanted to give you a heads-up. You're going to be getting a call from the principal. Fred is in the principal's office."

"What? Fred doesn't get in trouble. What happened?"

"Piper, he threatened another child. With a knife."

And the bottom fell out of my boat, the boat that I was using to float along on my unruffled sea of self-pity. I could feel myself going under.

Fred

It was just sort of something that happened. I did not plan to make it happen but I did not stop it either. It was just waiting in my backpack, in the extra utility pocket since the Battle of the Bulge with Dad and I could feel every day that my pack was just a tiny bit heavier than it should have been. I think probably I should have given it back to Dad a long time ago, after the accident where I cut him in the hand. I think it was a big mistake to keep it tucked into the Velcro pocket but I think it was a big mistake that Dad did not ask me for it back too. He is the grown-up and after all I am a kid who sees things differently.

Jackson started it. He was standing in the line at lunch with Wyatt Hicomb and a boy named Thomas that is not in our class and I have only ever seen throwing snowballs on the playground. I was waiting to get my French toast sticks because it was the first Wednesday of the month and that is the only time they serve French toast sticks with syrup to dip it in and that is the only item of hot lunch that I am interested in trying because you get your own cup of syrup and Mom cannot tell you it is too much. I was waiting there very patient and someone tapped me on my shoulder. I turned to look to say hey but there was no one there. I thought it was probably a mistake that someone thought I was a different kid and not Fred because Fred does not get many kids saying hello to him. Then there was another tap on my left shoulder and I turned again and there was no one there. I heard someone make a sound that was like a snort and laugh smushed together and I turned all the way around and it was Jackson and Wyatt and Thomas and they were covering their mouths with their hands like they thought they might tell a big secret.

Did you see who is the one who is tapping me on the shoulder? I asked them. They said no, no, we didn't see anything but they were laughing through their talking. I turned around again because they said that they did not see anything. Then I felt another tap on my shoulder and I whirled around as fast as I could and I saw Wyatt Hicomb pulling his hand away from my shoulder. Are you tapping me on my shoulder? I asked him but he said no. Then I turned around again but I tried to keep my eyes seeing behind me as long as I could and I felt a tap on the other shoulder and I turned around fast again and it was Thomas this time. Is it you guys? I asked them again. Jackson said no sorry Fred not us. I turned around again feeling very confused because I felt strongly that it was them, but they said it was not and that definitely counted as lying. Then they were laughing again and I turned around and might have shouted a little. What are you guys laughing at? Jackson said Fred in the dictionary next to the word "gullible" is your picture. Wyatt Hicomb and Thomas started laughing really hard and I could feel that my face was wearing a red color that meant embarrassed because I must have done something wrong.

It was finally time to get my French toast sticks and I did not sit by those guys. I know what the word "gullible" means and I know about dictionaries and there are very few dictionaries that have pictures in them just mainly ones for kids. I was about ninety-seven percent sure that my picture was not in the dictionary next to any words because I am just Fred. I was ninety-seven percent sure but I thought I should check anyway. When we got back to our classroom after lunch I sneaked over to the dictionary on the shelf under the second window and quick turned the book open to the *G*s. Then I heard someone laughing behind me. I whirled around again and of course it was Jackson. He said dude seriously? But he did not mean it like a question. He leaned in close to me and whispered in front of my face with his hot breath dude you are so lame.

I know what lame is and I do not think that I am that. There are some things that I do not like and some things that give me trouble but people tell me I am a good person. Jackson needed to know that I am not lame and I can have an adventure and be brave and be someone that makes people say hey that Fred kid is really cool and I want to know what he's about.

Piper

Fred's principal called just minutes after I got off the phone with Jack, shaken and overflowing with anxiety. He said little, just that there was an incident at school and I needed to come in immediately. I found my father reclined in the office, looking up at the crack in the ceiling again. "Dad?" I said.

He spoke without looking at me. "Yes." He sounded calm and sad.

"There's been a problem at the school and I need to go talk to someone."

"A problem with Fred?" He sat up quickly and turned to face me. His face wore an expression of genuine fear.

"It's okay, Dad. He's not hurt or anything. He's in trouble. I'm sure it's some kind of misunderstanding."

He nodded but did not lie down again. "I'll come with you. I can help. I can tell them Fred didn't mean it."

"It's okay, Dad. I was kind of thinking you could just stay here. It won't be very long and you just have to stay in the house," I said, trying to make it sound like no big deal because I wasn't sure what I would do with my father tagging along to the principal's office.

"Oh. Okay," he said. He looked disappointed, but I was sure he would quickly get over it.

We lived several miles from Fred's school and the drive was short. I parked and pressed the buzzer to be let in. The doors were unlocked only briefly now at the day's beginning and end. It was a safety measure, of course, but I had never been asked for identification; it seemed that any parent with a vendetta could still be granted entry and then do whatever damage the locked doors were supposed to be protecting children from.

A voice veiled in static came back to me. "You're here for?"

"I have to see Mr. DuPont. He called."

"Oh. I'll buzz you in, ma'am." The voice cut out and was followed by a long, high, static-laced tone. I grabbed the heavy handle and entered the school and rushed straight to the office.

The receptionist, Carla, clicked her tongue faintly and pointed to the open door of Mr. DuPont's office. Carla and I were merely acquaintances and I had had little business in the school office thus far. Her reaction to my presence was surprising, and it was perhaps the first moment I considered that perhaps Fred really was in trouble—not little-boy trouble, but real trouble.

• • •

I entered the principal's office and sat in one of the two leatherlike chairs that faced his large oak desk. I felt immediately that Mr. DuPont imagined himself a person serving well below his station. His office showed he had visions of downtown law firms or at least the district office. In my professional opinion the framed watercolor of sailboats at a regatta was so bad that I thought I might have trouble taking him seriously. The decor could almost have been considered opulent for an elementary school in a cash-strapped school district with broken desks and geography textbooks from before the fall of the Berlin Wall. In that split second I decided that this was a man who not only obviously had something against my son—who had never been in trouble before— but also had horrible taste in art and wasn't above pilfering the school budget for fake potted palm trees and the only air conditioner in the school. I hated him.

Mr. DuPont strode into the office and the first thing I noticed about him was how shiny his bur- gundy wing tips were. Given all I had taken in about him so far, I envisioned a shoe-shine station set up in the lunch room. He was followed in by Jack.

Mr. DuPont reached for my hand to shake. "Thank you for coming in, Mrs. Hart."

"Mrs. Whitman," I corrected.

He glanced down at the paper on his desk

and nodded slightly. "Oh, yes. Sorry," he said.

"Where's Fred?" I demanded.

Mr. DuPont put out his hand as if to slow me down. "No reason to panic, Mrs. Whitman. Fred is in Jack's office so we can talk privately."

He sat down in his wine-colored desk chair and began rocking slightly, tenting his fingers in front of his face in the spirit of a cartoon villain. It was a damn shame his sandy hair didn't form a sinister mustache for him to twist. Jack sat down next to me.

"Jack has just been filling me in on . . . Fred's situation," Mr. DuPont said.

"I'm sorry?" I said.

"His diagnosis, medical diagnosis. And, ah . . . where he is in the process of educational diagnosis."

I shook my head. "I'm sorry. I still don't know what happened."

"Fred threatened a classmate with a knife, Mrs. Whitman." He sat back in his chair and looked almost smug. I wondered if this was the kind of excitement he lived for as a principal, the kind of war story he could share with colleagues, the kind of anecdote he could unfold to show outsiders what it was really like in the trenches of public schools today.

"I don't understand."

"A knife. He threatened a boy in his class with a knife just a bit ago."

"Where did he get the knife? Was it from the lunchroom?" I asked.

He chuckled. "No, ma'am, we don't give out knives in the lunchroom."

"He doesn't own a knife; how would he get a knife?"

"He said he brought it to school in his backpack," Jack said.

My mind was flitting from possibility to possibility and my stomach lurched as I pictured Fred with a variety of weapons. I mentally scrolled through my kitchen to see if there were any missing knives this morning. A butcher knife? A fillet knife? Steak knife? Butter knife?

"Can I see it?" I asked.

Jack stood up and left the room briefly. I waited in a sort of fearful, ignorant silence. I wondered if I never saw the knife if it was possible that it had never happened.

Jack returned with what looked like an empty hand, until he unfolded his palm to reveal a pocketknife with a marbled wood handle and a shining silver blade.

"That's not his." I shook my head again, this time a firm no.

"He said it was given to him," Jack said quietly.

My mind instantaneously went to my father, the only person in Fred's life who I believed was mentally debilitated enough to give my child a knife.

Jack continued. "By his father."

Fred

I only showed it to Jackson. I only wanted him to peek at it so he could be impressed by me and learn what I am about. After math we go out into the hall to put on gym shoes if we aren't already wearing athletic shoes with no-slip bottoms. Jackson went out to his locker because he was wearing Crocs. I was wearing no-slip athletic shoes, but I followed him out there. He was sitting on the floor in front of his locker, changing his shoes. I opened my locker and reached into my backpack utility pocket and my hand closed around that knife like I was meant to hold it. I remembered when I was in the woods with my dad and I remembered that I was hiding and I was a Nazi and he was a good guy and I ambushed him and caused him bodily injury. I did not think there were that many kids that had a knife that they used to stab a person, even in the hand.

I put the knife in the pocket of my pants and I walked over to Jackson slow and quiet. He was finishing tying his shoes and I stood in front of him until he was done. He stood up and looked surprised to see me and said what do you want penis breath? I reached into my pocket and pulled out the knife and clicked it open. The blade was shining and it was still sharp and if I squinched my eyes real tiny and tight I thought I could see a drop of my dad's blood dried up on it. I held it up to his face which was wearing a face of what the heck. He said what the hell are you doing Fred? I said just showing you what I am about Jackson, that I am not a person who has bad-smelling breath. I said it real calm and not angry because even though Jackson wasn't a good friend to me and thought my breath smelled like private parts I thought if he understood me better he might think I was okay and not lame.

You're not supposed to have weapons at school Fred he said and I said that's why it was hiding and you can't tell. He kept looking toward the door of the classroom like he wanted to get out of there but I had one more thing to tell him so I got closer to him and our chests were almost touching and my knife was almost touching its tip to his chin. I whispered to Jackson I stabbed a good guy with this knife. I stabbed a guy in the woods. Jackson I was a Nazi and I ambushed a guy. Do you think that you would be interested in playing good guys and Nazis with me in the woods? I will let you be the good guy. I think you should play that with me Jackson. He pushed me away from him and ran into the classroom. I got a funny feeling in my head, kind of hot and swirly, and I got a tight feeling in my stomach.

Something didn't feel right about me and Jackson. His face kind of went from surprised and confused to very, very frightened. I didn't mean to make Jackson wear a frightened face. I just wanted him to wear an impressed face.

Then Mrs. Tieman came marching out of the room with a red, red, mad face and said very loud FRED!

Lance

The dog is crying at the back door and there is no one there to take the dog out and after I listen to him cry for a while I think maybe I should do it. I have seen my daughter take the dog to the backyard. First I have to find my boots. It is hard to find my boots so I wear my house shoes. I know that my daughter wears her coat outside so she can stand in the backyard and look at the trees. I find my coat and I even zipper the darn thing up. I think I might need mittens so I find some mittens and put them on. Then I think maybe I should have a hat because I'm not sure what the temperature is. I find my black wool hat on the shelf above the coatrack but I can't get it on because my hands are fat. I leave the hat inside. I open the door and the dog runs out to a tree like a bullet from a gun.

I walk outside to the center of the yard and stand in the spot where I usually see Piper stand. Her body is still and she tilts her head up to the sky. I try it. I see gray sky. I see clouds. I see the V shape of a bird very far away every once in a while. I see the bare branches of the trees crisscrossing the sky. I wonder what this means to her, my daughter. She is the person I am with all day, until Fred comes home and then much later my son-in-law, who I think is someone important. I do not see anything in the sky to make my forehead wrinkle. I do not see anything to make tears come down my cheeks. I do not see anything except the whole backyard.

I worry about Fred. He is a nice boy and a gentle boy but he likes to know things. I think it's good to know things. He told me that once I was stiff and frowned a lot. He told me that my daughter did not like me very much. He was sad to tell me. I want her to like me, so I stay quiet and make my face relax. I stand outside here so I can try to understand her. I see now that there are tiny buds on some of the branches. Spring.

The dog is done and is circling around my legs. He must want to go back in the house. I walk slowly back to the house and when I try to open the door it won't open. It is locked. I put my hand in the pocket of my coat and don't find the key there. I don't know what to do, so I decide that I will find Judy. I know that my house, mine and Judy's, is not very far. Mohawk Drive. I feel deep inside me that I have gone from there to here and here to there many times and I think that I can follow that feeling and find my house and Judy will know what to do.

"Dog, you wait here," I say, and I go out the gate to the sidewalk to find Mohawk Drive.

Piper

It took me a few moments to recover my composure, to mentally wrap myself around the idea that Isaac gave Fred this knife. I suddenly placed the event, the impetus for this whole sequence of misfortune: the hiking trip. Isaac said he cut himself on an ax, but it must have been this knife. I said a silent thank-you that it was not Fred who cut himself, seeing as the knife has been in his possession for months. My lifetime of suppressed anger at Isaac for his absence and lateness, his distracted nature, his small incompetencies, was nothing compared to the rage I felt reddening my cheeks and roiling my stomach.

I finally spoke, my voice almost echoing out in the wood-paneled office.

"Okay. His father did give him a pocketknife, for a hiking trip. Months ago. He must have accidently left it in his backpack. That's it."

"There's still the issue of the threat, Mrs. Whitman," Mr. DuPont said.

"I'm sorry. I know my son very well and he's not a violent person. He's not the type to threaten other kids."

"I'm afraid that's exactly what happened. The

boy was here in my office and told me everything that your son said to him. Would you like to hear it?" he asked.

"I guess I should," I said.

He began to read in a horribly monotone intonation, unnecessarily I felt, for the drama of it. " 'I know I am not supposed to have weapons at school so that is why I am hiding it. I stabbed a guy with this knife. I am a Nazi. You have to come to the woods and play Nazis with me and I will stab you.' "

I sat mute, unable to match these words up to the idea of Fred.

Mr. DuPont cleared his throat and then continued. "Mrs. Whitman, he also touched the knife to the boy's face."

A single cry escaped from my body, like a gasp but with the wet force of sadness and pain behind it. Jack put his hand on my shoulder.

"Now, we've got to decide what we're going to do about this," Mr. DuPont said with a degree of finality that signified that we three all agreed that a punishment was in order.

"Peter, what I was trying to express to you earlier is that this is a student with special needs; he's on the autism spectrum. We've got to give him some leeway here," Jack said.

"Has he got an IEP? An educational diagnosis?" the principal asked.

"Peter, you know he doesn't; we just talked

about this in my office. He's going through the process, which is long and, honestly, a shit ton of work," Jack said, and then turned to me and added, "Sorry," as if the fact that my son was causing him to use inappropriate language was embarrassing to him, or me, or all of us.

"I just don't see how we're going to treat him as anything other than a normal student if he doesn't have the educational diagnosis," Mr. DuPont said as he rocked his chair in tiny movements that gave the illusion that he was bouncing lightly.

I sat in the fake leather chair, gripping the wood arms with a strength I understood was unnecessary, but I felt the force of my emotions needed an outlet. Their argument, carried out in dignified urgency from Jack and an unnatural calm butting right up against arrogance from the principal, raged around me. I had always imagined myself as Fred's mother bear and expected that in a situation where my son was being threatened I would leap to his aid verbally or physically, whatever it took. Yet, as these two men discussed Fred's fate over my head, I was rendered voiceless in the face of this actual threat. I stood. "I want to see Fred."

Jack walked me down to his office. "We'll figure this out, Piper" was the only thing either of us said as our shoes clicked down the hall. I stopped in the doorway and saw Fred at Jack's paper-littered desk with his head buried in his arms. His body, which normally looked so small and boylike to me as I studied it while he ate and slept and read and bathed, looked suddenly grown. I refused to believe it was because he was not the little boy I forever wished him to be; I attributed it to an optical illusion caused by the tiny room overflowing with detritus.

"Fred," I said quietly.

He looked up at me, and his tear-drenched cheeks, his eyes red and puffy, and his nose leaking a small rivulet of snot broke my heart.

I ran the few steps to him and took him into my arms as best I could, kneeling down on the cold linoleum floor, wrapping him in the protection of me, placing him quickly and succinctly inside my bulletproof bubble of mother's love.

"Mom, I didn't mean to make him scared. I wanted him to see I wasn't lame. I wanted him to see I was an interesting person. I wanted him to see that I was normal," Fred stammered, each sentence punctuated by a heaving gasp of a sob. My baby was crying. Unlike my father, who was new to his emotional landscape, Fred was a longtime inhabitant of a monotone delivery and a relative lack of emotional response. I could remember very few times when he had cried over an injury that wasn't bodily but emotional, and I ached for him.

I smoothed his hair with my cheek, held his head tight into my breast and felt the tears soak into my shirt. I pulled him onto my lap and rocked him as he released gentle sobs and quiet words that seemed to be only for his own comfort and not my ears. We sat that way for what felt like forever, a level of physical closeness that he rarely afforded me but I could now see that I had been craving desperately. Eventually I looked up and saw Jack was still standing in the doorway, frozen. I straightened and wiped my own cheeks and returned his gaze.

"We will fix this, Piper. We will fix this for Fred," he said, and there was a tear in his eye, a vestige of his own boyhood pain, perhaps.

Mr. DuPont agreed to an out-of-school suspension while the discipline team tried to figure out what to do about my son's offense. Jack assured me that he would be working tirelessly on Fred's educational diagnosis and hoped to show we were far enough along in the process that a diagnosis was inevitable and so his supposed act of violence could be looked at with a more forgiving set of eyes. I nodded expertly, agreeing on the course of action, appearing to be all on board, but all I was thinking about was getting my boy out of there. We collected his things from his locker and made our way toward home, hand in hand.

Lance

Mohawk Drive is not so far from my new home; I have been counting the blocks. I always get stuck on what comes after twelve. I have stopped counting but I am still walking. I have not been in my house at Mohawk Drive since before the heart attack. They tell me I left the house early in the morning to go exercise and I haven't been back there since. My daughter has told me that Judy is in Saint Paul, but I believe that when I get to our house on Mohawk Drive she will be there instead. Saint Paul is not nearby and I don't know why she would be so far away. I know she is taking a break from me because I am hard to be with, but she didn't need to take a break from our home. We moved to our home when Curtiss was a baby. Piper was not born yet, but I knew that someday I would have a daughter. There are some things that I remember very strongly about my home, but some things are empty spaces. I can't remember what color the house is, but I remember that there is a large magnolia tree in the front yard that blooms pink and white in the spring and litters the yard with petals that smell so sweet they make me sneeze. I don't remember how many bathrooms there are, but I know that there is a laundry chute in the hallway upstairs and the kids used it to drop messages to each other down the metal shaft, and if you talk into the chute, your voice will echo all the way to the basement.

At Mohawk Drive I am happy. I don't know if I'm happy now. I feel other things that I don't know if I felt before. Restless. Peaceful. Tired. Alive.

Piper

Fred fell asleep during the short drive home; he was entirely drained from the outpouring of emotion he usually kept strapped down so tightly. He seemed the victim of a hurricane, wet, disheveled and in desperate need of a bed to lie in. Fred had never been the sort of child who fell asleep in the car and made long car trips a breeze if you drove through the night. He preferred to notice and comment on the passing scenery. I thought briefly of rousing him, but then more for my own selfish reasons than my concern for his waking, I decided to carry his sleeping body in to his bed. He was heavier than I'd imagined, but then, my last point of reference had been so many years before. I tried as gracefully as I could to wrestle his limp body from the booster seat that I insisted he still use. It was awkward work, but as a testament to his extreme fatigue, he slept on. I struggled with him to the front door and somehow managed to ring the bell with my knuckles.

There was no answer and no bark from Chuck Yeager announcing the arrival of a stranger, or someone who rang the bell. I waited a moment, then dug the key from my pocket without dropping my son in a feat of miraculous acrobatics I felt was akin to the average person lifting a car off an injured person in dire circumstances. The house was quiet, which wasn't much of a surprise, as my father made little noise. Chuck Yeager created more of a low din with his various whines, barks at passersby and snoring. I climbed the stairs deliberately, each step a small test I passed. I noticed at the top of the stairs that my father's door was shut and I assumed he was taking one of his many daily naps that were key to his brain healing and prescribed by his neurologist. I imagined I heard the quiet snores and rustlings of Chuck Yeager stretched out on the floor near my sleeping father.

I placed Fred on his bed, covered him with his fuzzy blanket and placed his worn hedgehog in the crook of his arm. I yearned to lie down beside him, curl my body around his and sleep off the residue of our horrible afternoon, but I had other things that I had to do. I kissed his sweaty sleeping head and he stirred. His voice was a hoarse whisper. "I just wanted to show him what I was about."

"I know, sweet boy. I know," I said. He was already asleep again when I closed his door and headed back downstairs.

I removed my wool coat and hung it on the back of a barstool. I took my phone out of the pocket and sat at the table. I took a deep breath and tried to calm myself, knowing that if I let emotion overtake me, my message would be a garbled mess and would only result in a confused return call from Isaac, and I wanted there to be no mistaking my meaning.

I knew I would have to leave a message, as Isaac was most certainly in court, in class, or in a meeting. I listened to his outgoing message, full of serious importance, and I felt my rage grow. "Isaac. You need to get home. Now. I don't care if you're in court or teaching or meeting with grad students. I do not fucking care. You need to come home now."

He would know my message carried grave consequence because I had long ago given up on asking him to come home in the face of illness or extreme need. I'd learned to deal with everything that came my way on my own. Fred sat watching hours of PBS as I suffered through the swine flu when he was four. When he was in kindergarten, my mother took me to three different obstetrician appointments that resulted in miscarriages and one particularly traumatic situation that involved the need for a D&C. After that I couldn't find the energy to go through it all again, so that was our last attempt at giving Fred a sibling.

When I came home from the hospital with Fred, Isaac took a week off but worked from home, taking conference calls as I endured nursing through mastitis. Isaac slept peacefully through a colicky baby with his days and nights mixed up. After he went back to work, for the first year he would return home by dinnertime and take Fred from my weary arms and quiet him with a loud shushing noise and a nonstop pattern of hearty slaps to the bottom, making it all look so easy. After struggling through some days, counterintuitively the last thing I wanted was for someone else to step into my role and make it look like a breeze. I wanted my partner to look at me and say, "You're right—this fucking sucks."

I stood at the kitchen window and looked out into the yard. The sky was a gray blue, the sun masked behind wispy clouds that seemed to want desperately to reveal it but hadn't the strength to part. There were buds coming out on the trees, a phenomenon that managed to surprise me every spring. One day the trees were bare, and the next time I took a moment to consider them, the buds had popped and spring had arrived again without fanfare. Through my limited field of vision out the small window, Chuck Yeager stalked into view, pacing back and forth. I was confused, as I thought for sure I'd heard him resting with my father. Had my father let him out and forgotten about him? It was entirely possible, as I did it several times a day, forgetting I shared a home with a dog at all until the mail carrier had the nerve to walk by our fence or I heard an anxious whine outside the back door and suddenly remembered it had been too long since I had seen or heard the dog. I opened the back door and called, "Chuck Yeager!" He stopped pacing and looked at me, panting. I believed this was a dog that would lecture and berate me nonstop, given the ability to talk; this was based on simply the level of vexation he conveyed with his eyes and whines alone. I often had to call him more than once because he would stand in the yard and calculate the costs and benefits of obeying me. Today, he ran over to the gate, sat down and barked a clipped, warning bark.

"What is it, Lassie? Has Timmy fallen in the well?" I shouted, and then muttered, "Fucking dog." I slammed the door. I don't know what happened in that second, if my sarcastic reference to Lassie unleashed a path of worry I had not previously considered, but a knot of unease formed quickly in my stomach and I bolted up the stairs to my father's room. I rapped on the door and heard nothing. I pushed the door open and found his room empty. I raced back down the stairs and out the back door. Chuck Yeager was prancing around me and yipping. I quickly reviewed the possibilities: my father knew no one else in the neighborhood, had never taken a city bus and moved slowly. Chuck Yeager continued to bark at the gate. I ran to the back door, reached inside and pulled his leash from its hook beside the doorframe. He happily let me hook it on his collar and pulled me back to the gate. I opened the gate and the dog tugged me outside and down the sidewalk.

I was not what you would call a dog person by any stretch of the phrase. Though I had dreamed for so many years of my own dog, all those years without a canine companion had distanced me from that dream. I tolerated his presence in my house because my son and father seemed to have some fondness for him. I could not forgive him for snacking on rabbit shit or the time he had decided to mark Fred's laundry hamper full of freshly laundered and folded clothes, making them all reek of urine. He was not a friend of mine. I did not peruse videos on the Internet of cute puppies or amazing dog feats. I had previously scoffed at the supposed intelligence of dogs, feeling that Chuck Yeager himself was ample proof that intelligence should be suspect.

In that moment, though, I let him lead me. In that exact place in time, I had no doubt that the dog would guide me to my father. I can't explain this sudden confidence in his canine instincts, which had previously involved rolling in deer shit and drinking from the toilet if Fred left the seat up. I followed him. I had not run in months; my will to exercise had been replaced with an uneasy acceptance of my soft muscles. I had forgotten the feeling of breathing hard and sucking in the cold air. I had forgotten the love/hate relationship

I had with the pain in my hamstrings as I began a run. We ran the entire mile to my parents' house on Mohawk Drive, which was exactly where Chuck Yeager was leading me. Now, in retrospect, I can't believe that I left the house without one thought about my sleeping son, but I can only shrug and explain that for the first time, my first thought rested on my father.

Lance

The magnolia tree is not in bloom yet. I am too early. I can see tight buds like flower teardrops hanging heavy in the low branches, but they are not blooming. There are no petals filling the air with their heavy scent and making me sneeze. I sit on the front stoop because it seems that Judy isn't here after all. I rang the bell many times and there is only a quiet house answering back. The secret spare key is gone. I thought it was tucked up on a little ledge by the light by the door but it's not there. I might have forgotten where it was hidden. Just in case I looked under the mat, too. Now I am waiting. I get up to start walking back, but I get dizzy and I suddenly can't remember which direction I came from. The houses to the right do not look familiar, but neither do the ones on the left.

I turn around and come back up the driveway, and now I am waiting again. The only phone I remember is too big to fit in my pocket and Piper told me it doesn't work outside anyway. If I look in the tall, skinny window beside the front door of my house on Mohawk Drive, I can see the phone on the wall of the kitchen. There isn't much I can see through that skinny space. I can see the doormat inside and a coat-tree that has a brown coat hanging from it that I remember I wore to church once. I can see the edge of the kitchen countertop off in the distance of my little window and I suddenly remember where the toaster is. If I turn my head far enough to the side, I can just see the arm of the navy blue leather recliner in the TV room.

I sit back down. I am not scared. I am lost but not scared. I am always lost now and being scared got to be too hard. I am lost now, but I can wait it out.

Piper

I found my father sitting on the front step of his house on Mohawk Drive. I panted with fatigue, my muscles already protesting the work-out. Chuck Yeager's body wiggled madly and he pulled me up to my father and began licking his face forcefully as his enthusiastic tail wags twisted his body back and forth. My father mildly pushed the dog off of him, but Chuck Yeager didn't take the hint and returned for more. I pulled him off again and he collapsed on the step next to my father with his head in his lap and his tongue hanging out of his mouth.

"What're you doing, Dad?" I managed through my gasps for breath.

"Waiting."

"What are you waiting for?" I asked. I thought when I found him I would yell. I thought I would be so angry with him for scaring me, but once I saw him, the anger dissolved into a relief and then a bottomless sadness that my grown father could wander off and become lost like a child. I sat down next to him, Chuck Yeager wiggling between us.

"I don't know, Piper," he said, and then turned to me. "I can't remember."

"Are you looking for Mom?"

"I don't know. I'm lost but not scared."

"You're not lost anymore, Dad. I'm here now," I said and I reached over and took his mittened hand. It felt cold in my own sweaty grip. I realized that I was suddenly cold, not wearing a jacket. I shivered a little.

"You're cold," he said.

"A little bit. But it's okay. I'm just glad we found you."

"Did I make you cold?"

"Kind of, I guess, but it's okay, Dad. It's not a big deal." I stood up and pulled him up too. He seemed shaky on his feet but stood next to me. He had always been taller than me, bigger all around like a father should be, but then I saw not only his mental frailness, but also a physical shrinking. A lessening of heft, of importance, of a physical place in the world.

"I'm sorry, Piper," he said.

I shook my head. "It's okay, Dad, really. Let's go home." I pulled on him again but he stood still.

"I think that I have a lot to be sorry about, but I've lost what those things are," he said, and his watery eyes looked into mine intently. "I want to say I'm sorry but I don't know for what."

"It's okay, Dad." I gave his hand a tug again and we made our way down the front path. Just before the sidewalk he stopped and looked back at his house again.

"There is one thing that I remember. One thing that I remember I am sorry about." He paused and then continued. "I'm sorry that we were too early for the magnolia blossoms."

I nodded and we continued home, me with my hand in my father's and Chuck Yeager prancing happily at the end of his leash.

We arrived home to find Isaac's car in the driveway. I was at first shocked, then remembered the intensity with which I had demanded that he return home and then cursed myself for leaving Fred alone, though it had been only about half an hour. We entered the house and found Isaac drinking coffee in the kitchen as he checked messages, no doubt piled up in the time it had taken him to drive the two miles home from his office. He looked up from his phone screen and stopped pacing when he saw my father and me.

"What the hell happened, Piper? I get this message from you and then I get here and no one is home?"

My father spoke up. "I got lost, Isaac, but Piper and the dog found me and brought me home."

At just that moment, Fred entered the kitchen, groggily rubbing his eyes, his hair a tangled mess. Chuck Yeager jumped up to lick his face. "Grandpa was lost?"

"Why is Fred home?" Isaac asked, and then quickly checked his watch. "Is he sick?"

"No, Dad, I'm not sick. I am home on an out-of-school suspension because of my violent behavior," Fred said.

"Dad? Fred? Would you please take Chuck Yeager into the family room? You can have some of your screen time, Fred. I need to talk to your father." As soon as I realized I had sent my son and father only several yards away from the kitchen, I said, "Isaac, we need to talk. Upstairs."

"You're damn right we need to talk. What the hell happened here today? I came home and Fred was wandering around the house, wondering where everyone was!" he said.

He followed me into our bedroom, where I closed the door. I went and sat on the edge of the bed and took a deep breath. "First of all, my father is fine. He walked home to Mohawk Drive and Chuck Yeager led me to him. Second, Fred is fine. He was hardly alone any time at all and he was probably asleep for most of it. But that's not what I want to talk to you about." I looked up at Isaac, who stood above me and reminded me of an angry father getting ready to lecture his naughty daughter, and my anger at him flared again.

"Sit down, Isaac." Now I stood in front of him. I rolled the kinks out of my neck and took a breath. "Where did our child get a knife?" I made each word carry the weight of my anger, so each word seemed to punch the stillness of our room.

"What do you mean, a knife? We have lots of knives in the kitchen," he said. He was turning his phone over and over in his hands, the modern equivalent of twirling a pen, and I took it from him because I wanted him to have no crutches, no little behaviors meant to calm.

"This was a pocketknife and he brought it to school. Another boy, Jackson, is saying that he threatened him with it. Where would he have gotten a knife like that, Isaac?" I asked.

He sat on the edge of our bed, mute.

"Could it have been from your day off together, Isaac?"

He still sat silently, his head bowed down so I couldn't see the expression on his face.

I jabbed him in the shoulder with my finger, surprising both him and myself. "Huh, Isaac?" I could feel the heaviness of my tone, the cruelty I never used with my husband or my son because I'd promised myself I would not repeat the sins of my father. I could not remember ever employing this level of nastiness to express myself outside of my own head. My tone carried the cruelty that had built up over the last nine years. The cruelty that had been nurtured just a tiny bit every time I had been left alone by my husband, every time he chose someone else over me or Fred, every time I had been let down by his nonpresence and sometimes even by his incompetent presence as well, those times he came through neatly forgotten.

He was silent, still.

"Isaac," I said sharply.

He looked up at me and said so quietly I had to strain to make out the words, "I gave it to him."

"You gave our child a knife?"

"He wasn't meant to keep it; it was just a pocketknife from our trip to the woods."

"But he did keep it, Isaac. He did. He kept it for months. Months. And you never considered that he might not be trusted with it?"

"I had a pocketknife when I was a boy, Piper." He was defending himself, but with no anger, no enthusiasm. His refusal to answer my cruelty with his own deflated my rage. I sat down beside him.

"But, Isaac, things are different now. Kids take weapons to school and people think they're going to kill everyone. You of all people should know this."

He was quiet again before he said, "I didn't mean for him to keep it. There was an accident and I forgot about it."

"What do you mean, there was an accident? On the trip?"

"Piper, Fred cut me with that knife, by accident, and I forgot to get it back from him in the chaos that came after."

I thought about what he said. "So, you didn't cut yourself making a marshmallow-roasting stick?"

He shook his head.

"Oh God." I gasped and hunched over until my head was almost in my lap. I felt sick to my stomach. "Fred stabbed you with the knife?"

I felt Isaac's hand on my back and wanted to shake it off but couldn't summon the physical energy. "It was an accident, Piper. We were doing a World War II reenactment and Fred was supposed to ambush me and he slashed the knife in my direction and I don't think he ever meant to make contact, but he did. It was awful. He felt awful."

"Why didn't you tell me? He must have felt so badly. Why did you lie about it?" I asked, and then it occurred to me. "Isaac, you asked Fred to lie about it? You asked our baby to lie to me?" The fire of my rage was so intense I shook. It was one thing for my husband to lie to me, but to put my child between us was inexcusable.

"No. No," he said, and shook his head vigorously. "No, I didn't ask him to lie. He heard what I said and I guess he thought he should."

"Of course he thought he should. If he hears his beloved father lie about something, of course he's going to lie about it too."

"I know that now, Piper, and I'm sorry."

"But why did you have to lie to me in the first place? Why didn't you just tell me what happened?" I asked.

"Because I know you, Piper. I knew what would

have happened if I had told you. You would have been irate; you would have been unreasonable. You never would have understood. You never would have forgiven me." His voice was calm and tinged with resignation, which served only to further inflame me.

I was angry. "You know what? That's not a good enough fucking reason. You fucked up; yeah, I would have been pissed. That's no reason to lie to me about my own child."

"It is, Piper; it is a reason, a really fucking good one. You don't understand how you are. You don't make mistakes and you don't tolerate mistakes in other people. You're just like your father."

I was stunned and confused. "Have you seen my father lately, Isaac? He's not thinking much about other people's mistakes."

"No, Piper, your old father. The father he used to be. The father that you hated with all your heart. He hated fuckups and so do you."

Now it was my turn to sit mutely. The sharp teeth of his words dug in and tore at my heart. Their attack was unexpected, but I felt in some deep, shameful part of me that Isaac was speaking words I had worried always rested on the edge of my consciousness but never wanted to unearth.

"I'm sorry, Piper. I'm so sorry this has happened. I did fuck up and I'm going to own that. But I'm not going to let you hold it over me. I will speak to his school and do whatever I can for Fred, but I will not continue to let you make me feel like shit about this. People make mistakes, Piper. Everyone does, and someday you will too."

He got up and walked out of our bedroom. I sat on the edge of the bed with the heavy ghost of his words beside me. I lay down on the end of the bed and my exhaustion consumed me and I fell asleep with tears streaming down my cheeks.

I woke up later, confused and headachy. The light from my bedroom window was dim and I figured I had probably missed dinner. I bolted out of bed and down the stairs. Halfway down I could hear laughter and voices. I slowed my pace and crept one step at a time until I could see into the dining room. Isaac, Fred and my father sat at the table together. There was no somber tone, only smiling faces. Fred tried out knock-knock jokes on the men and they laughed, one out of politeness and one out of confusion. I stepped down to the bottom step and Fred turned to see me.

"Mom. Dad made hot dogs on the grill for dinner and we had macaroni and cheese from the box and no vegetables whatsoever," Fred said. There was little trace of his earlier trauma, just faint circles under his eyes.

"It's late," I said.

Isaac sighed. "I did my best, Piper," he said quietly.

"No. I didn't mean that. I meant I can't believe I slept so long." I felt distrusted and misunderstood.

"Do you want a wiener, Piper?" my dad asked me. I couldn't help it—I laughed. I sat down on the floor and laughed until I cried. My father had been calling hot dogs "wieners" for my entire life, much to the embarrassment of my brother and me. The men at the table looked at me oddly. Finally Fred came over and crouched down beside me.

"Mom? Are you okay?" he asked, his arm around me.

All I could do was nod.

Later, after Isaac and I had put Fred to bed together, I stood outside in the backyard and looked up at the stars peeking through the newly budded branches of the trees as Chuck Yeager sniffed around the yard. Isaac came up beside me. "I spoke to the principal while you were sleeping. He told me what happened, or what he says happened. In the morning, I'd like to talk to Fred about it."

I was impressed. Isaac was behaving exactly as the concerned father that I had always wished for: handling things, taking care of what needed to be taken care of. I would have to admit that Isaac could provide assistance and comfort. He could perform the duties I wanted from him and maybe he had been trying harder than I thought all these years. I wasn't ready yet, though, not to hand over my mantle of complete responsibility for Fred.

"Can Fred go back to school?" I asked.

"Not tomorrow, but I'm confident that he will be able to soon. I think we've got a solid case here, Piper," he said. I felt the familiar slap of second place; I did not want this to become another crusade for Isaac, the defender of the defenseless. I just wanted him to be a father to Fred and a supportive partner to me.

"I'm sorry about what I said earlier, Piper. It was harsh. I do take responsibility for the knife incident. I should have taken it away from Fred right away."

I breathed in the moist, muddy air of the spring night before I spoke. "It was harsh, Isaac. But in truth it's given me a lot to think about. It's not something I ever wanted to even consider."

We stood in silence, taking in the night sounds. With a new appreciation I watched Chuck Yeager prowl around the edge of the yard, and Isaac stared up into the sky.

Finally, I spoke. "There's one thing I don't understand, Isaac. And I'm just trying to understand, really. I just want to understand what happened. If Fred cut you with the knife way back in January, why did he still have the knife now, months later?"

"Fred must have dropped it on the ground. I

was in shock, I think. He must have picked it up later. I guess I didn't consider that he might want it after what happened. Then I just forgot about it." His voice cracked and he continued through tears. "I'm so sorry I didn't pick it up myself. You'll never know how sorry I am."

Isaac and I stood on the deck together, side by side, arms crossed over our chests. Chuck Yeager came over and forced himself through the tunnel of my legs and stood there—feeling safe and protected, I guessed. He looked up at me with his anxious, pleading eyes, which never seemed to reflect a feeling of well-being, never showed a feeling of acceptance at the answers he received from the humans around him, and I understood his unease.

Fred

I can't go back to school tomorrow and I am going to pretend that it is a vacation day so that I don't remember that I am actually not allowed back at my school because of my violent behavior. I wonder if other guys who had to stand up for themselves and maybe defend themselves against the enemy got told they had violent behavior. When I sat in Principal DuPont's office on the first floor, to the right of the secretary's desk, he told me he was surprised I would threaten another student like that. He said he had always thought of me as a kind and gentle person. I said I am surprised you have ever thought of me as a person at all because I have never thought of you as any sort of person. He put on a frown face and didn't seem to like what I said.

I am having a hard time explaining to other people what I am about. I am not about violent behavior, but I am about being Fred. Dad does not understand why I don't just ignore people who call me penis breath because they are over-compensating for their own deficiencies anyway. Sometimes I think that Mom understands me but then I see out of the corner of my eye that she is looking at me in a sad way and I don't understand what about me is sad. Sometimes I think that Grandpa understands me but then I say something and instead of answering me he just looks out the window like he doesn't understand. Chuck Yeager seems like he might understand what I'm about as much as a dog can. He has kind eyes at me mostly, but sometimes I can tell he is annoyed that I am Fred.

Mostly Jack Butler understands me. When I was sitting in Mr. DuPont's office waiting and I was confused about what all the mad faces were about, Jack Butler came in and kneeled down in front of the chair. He said Fred I know that you are okay. I know that you are not a violent boy and you did not mean to hurt or scare Jackson. I said Jack Butler this is not what I am about. Jack Butler said I know Fred I know. We will tell them what you are about. We will tell them all together.

In two weeks I will be having a birthday and I will be ten years old. Grown-ups ask kids all the time what do they want for their birthday. I do not like telling people what I want for my birthday because you only get one every year. There is only one time in my whole life that I will turn ten years old and what if the thing that I ask for is a mistake? When I was having my sixth birthday I asked for a remote control helicopter that seemed like it was well constructed and had maximum playability based on the Amazon reviews that Mom read from the computer. When I got it for my birthday we put the six AA batteries into the helicopter and the four AAA batteries into the controller and then I flew it in the backyard with Dad. It was harder than I thought it would be and after five minutes it crashed into the trunk of a big tree in our backyard. The helicopter wouldn't work after that and I would not get another chance to get a birthday present until I turned seven.

This year when I blow out my ten birthday candles with one to grow on I won't wish for a helicopter because helicopters break. I won't wish for more World War II Lego bricks because the pieces can get lost or chewed up by Chuck Yeager. I will wish that I could find a way to show people what I am all about.

Piper

As I changed the sheets in my father's room the next day, while he sat in the desk chair and observed the crack in the ceiling from a different perspective, I found a wrinkled photograph under his pillow. I flipped it over and found a slightly out-of-focus picture of my mother and father with Fred on his first birthday. It was probably a castoff from the photo album, not quality enough to be included, but instead tucked into some desk drawer somewhere because I hadn't had the heart to throw away a photo of my infant son.

"Dad? Where did you get this?" I asked, and held the picture up. He sat on the desk chair and stared at a magazine I had gotten him at the bookstore. It was a sports magazine that my father had once read religiously, but now he had not gotten past the table of contents. "Dad?" I said again.

He looked up at me. "Piper?" he asked.

"Where did you find this picture?" I held it up again so he could see it. I expected a dull, distracted answer, maybe even just a shrug of the shoulders.

He leapt up from his chair as quickly as I had seen him move in months. He snatched the photo from my hand, clutched it to his chest and glared at me. "That's mine," he said.

I was shocked and had to take a moment to decide how to proceed. He was angry with me. He was experiencing a real, *strong* emotion. At the same time, he was being an asshole.

"You can have it, Dad. I don't want it. It was under your pillow and I just wondered where you found it," I said, and went back to stripping the bed.

"I can have it?" he asked.

"Yes, of course," I said.

The room was quiet and he sat still with the picture in his hands. I continued with my housework. Just as I finished putting a new case on his pillow, he spoke.

"That's Judy."

I sat on the edge of the mattress so our legs formed a small table. He set the photo down on his lap. I said, "Yup. That's Fred's birthday party."

"Fred," he said softly, and ran his large, rough thumb over the wrinkled image. "He was a baby."

"He just turned one." I remembered that party well. There were a few neighbors and the play-group moms, friends I had so long ago it felt like another lifetime. I could see one of them in the background of the photo holding her one-year-old daughter up in the air and grinning at her. Alice. Her daughter's name was Alice and her name was Krista. Our worlds had diverged when they moved to San Francisco. There were some e-mails and texts for a while and then just a Christmas card every year and now nothing.

My father's voice brought me back from my memory. "Judy is smiling. Fred is smiling too, a baby smile. Why am I not smiling? Wasn't it happy?"

"You didn't used to smile very much, Dad," I said.

"I wasn't happy at the party?"

"You were pretty much never happy." I paused. "Are you happy now?" I asked.

He stared at the photo and then looked up at me. "I don't know," he said. "Do I smile?"

I shook my head.

He looked down at the picture and then up at me with a blank look. Suddenly, his face contorted into a very exaggerated impression of a smile. I smiled back at him in the same way. He laughed at me, a quiet, slow chuckle, but the first I had earned on my own and not just overheard from another room. I laughed too.

He stopped. "Is Judy happy now?"

"I don't know, Dad. I don't know." I stood, patted him on the back and left the room. I went and lay down on my bed and tried to decide what to do. I had avoided all contact with my mother since her abandonment, relying on her copious notes on my father's care, which she had prepared while he recovered in the hospital and we all imagined that life would go back to its static state following his release. My reaction to her departure has always confused me. Isaac has stated and restated that I'm not angry enough and there are times when I agree with him wholeheartedly.

I carry my anger with my mother on my back, and until that day I carried it alongside my past anger with my father. My anger with him had raged hot for so many years I made it a permanent part of my identity. When I brought him here to live with me and my family, under my care, I still didn't imagine seeing him clearly, without the fog of my rage. But I realized now that my anger with my father had thawed and melted as he navigated his healing and approached the end of his recovery a different man. I had trouble drumming up my comfortable old level of fury when faced with a man who was unable to remember what it felt like to be happy.

I couldn't empty my deep well of anger completely because I still struggled with my feelings toward my mother, turning them over and over in my mind to make sense of them. My initial appreciation for her decision to leave my father after all her painful years beside him faded as I was faced each day with the man he had become. Sometimes as I sat waiting for him to shuffle out of an occupational therapist's office,

I let my mind wander and imagined what my mother was doing with her newfound freedom from his rule. I pictured her eating dinner in restaurants every night and ordering lobster as often as she desired. I pictured her sleeping late and lounging about all day with Jeanne trading paperback romances back and forth. I imagined her flirting with a kindly-looking older man who would no doubt appreciate her value. Rather than growing more accepting and forgiving over time, I had been stoking the fire daily, and after my father wandered away I felt that I was finally at my boiling point and I made the decision the next day to call my mother.

I had phoned my mother once, immediately after taking my father away from the nursing home I knew he could not stay in. I had left a message and she had returned my call with one word via text message: Sorry. I had not even tried to phone her again since; there had been only a handful of bland texts, mostly about the mundane aspects of their life that I had not been privy to: the name of Chuck Yeager's vet so we could refill his seizure medications; she had asked me a tax-related question in the winter. There were no niceties between us. She had not even asked about Fred, which had become her greatest act of cruelty in my mind, given the events of that time. I was unsure if she would answer when she saw my number appear on her screen, but then I decided that since I had not previously called her, she might infer that it was a crisis situation and answer out of fear of the worst, which gave me a slightly embarrassing feeling of pleasure.

"Hello?" Her voice was tentative.

"Mother?"

"Yes?"

"It's me, your daughter, Piper." I wanted to remind her of who I was and of the commitment she made to me the day I was born. "We need to talk."

"Is everything okay?" she asked.

"No. Not really. No. It's pretty shitty, actually. Fred is in trouble at school and Dad wandered away." I wanted more than anything for my mother to feel guilty for forcing me to deal with all this, though I also knew I didn't know what good that guilt would do me.

"Oh. I'm sorry, Piper. Do you want to talk about it, about Fred?"

"No, Mom, I don't. What I'd really like to talk about is Dad."

"Oh. I don't really want to talk about that."

"You know what, Mom? That's too bad, because I'm going to talk about him. He's not the same, Mom. He's like a shell of the person he was. Which is good, right? We wouldn't have wanted the old Dad back. Isn't that why you left him?"

She began, "Piper—"

"No. I'm not done," I interrupted. "He's like a child, Mom. He can't tie his own shoes, he wanders away and gets lost, he can't write his name. He talks like, thinks like a kid. He's sad all the time. He doesn't understand where you are and why you've left. He thinks it's because he left wet towels on the bathroom floor. He's changed."

"I see."

"You don't actually see, because you've had no contact with him, or me, for that matter. You have no idea what's going on. It's not fair to him because it's not him anymore."

"Piper, it's still him. I'm sorry that it's been difficult for you, but—"

"But what? But I chose this? I brought him here? I should have left him in that piss-smelling, concrete-walled cell? Did you even go and look at it? Did you even visit before you booked him a room for the rest of his life?" I asked. I was trying desperately to keep my voice down.

"Well, no, but it was supposed to be the best. It was supposed to be the best one. It wasn't supposed to be forever, just until he recovered enough to live on his own again."

"Where did you imagine that happening, Mom? He was just going to move back to Mohawk Drive and cook for himself? Play squash again with his buddies? Do you think even one of them has stopped by? Even good old Bob's been MIA. Dad can't tie his shoes. He can't drive. He walked to Mohawk Drive and couldn't find his way home again. He's like a giant, depressed preschooler. He's not going to live on his own. It's not going to fucking happen."

I stopped and there was silence from the other end. I waited it out.

Finally, my mother spoke, her voice shaking and quiet. "I'm sorry, Piper. I'm so sorry. I'm sorry for you and I'm sorry for him. I couldn't go back to him. I couldn't go back to that life. But I couldn't take care of him anymore either. I was done. I looked ahead at what I wanted out of the rest of my life and the thought of spending another day in that house with your father made me want to die. I couldn't do it. You don't know how depressing it was."

"You know, I do, actually. I do know how depressing it was because I lived there too. Curtiss lived there too. We were all in that fucking awful boat together and I'm the only one who didn't walk away."

"I'm proud of you, Piper. I'm proud of you for not walking away. You're a good person. I love you."

"A lot of fucking good that does me!" I shouted into the phone, and then threw it across the dining room, where it landed with an unsatisfying plunk in a basket of unfolded laundry. I knew

I had just assumed the mantle of martyr; I had painted myself as "poor little Piper, the perfect daughter." I had practically begged my mother to come to my pity party, but I didn't care. It felt so good to let that rage loose on her. I felt taller. My shoulders felt looser; my heartbeat slowed. I might have been a martyr, but I had learned from the best.

Piper

Late that afternoon there was a knock at the front door, shocking me out of a light nap on the couch. I was emotionally drained from my phone call to my mother and physically exhausted from another night of Fred fighting sleep. Fred was poring over a detailed encyclopedia of World War II vehicles and planes and offering me periodic descriptions of particular things that interested him. I learned over the years that he wasn't offering the information for me to discuss or comment on; he desired only a captive audience for his monologues, and if I gave an occasional grunt to signify my presence, I could lend minimum attention to his droning lists of trivial facts about any variety of subjects. Isaac found this rude and incredibly unparental, but in my defense, he had not spent the hours I had, pinned under my son's verbal assault of particulars.

Fred, though he was closer to the door, made no move to answer it, so I rose and went to the door; I peeked out the side window and found myself looking directly into the eyes of Jack Butler, who looked apologetic and awkward. I opened the door.

"Jack," I said. My first thought was about the state of my housekeeping and the cleanliness of my hair. I had not given up on trying to impress him.

"Hey. I just wanted to check in and see how Fred was doing and I have some paperwork for you to look over." His words were rushed and unsure.

"Oh, okay." I wondered immediately if I had missed a phone call or e-mail from him. I instinctively reached for my phone, which was in my back pocket.

"No. I didn't call or e-mail first. Shit," he stammered. "Sorry. Um, that was weird, wasn't it? I should have let you know I was coming?"

I waved him in. "No, it's fine. We're here. Obviously." Chuck Yeager came trotting down from upstairs, ears alert and eyes shining, ready to investigate the visitor. He went directly toward Jack and tried to nose his way through his legs. Jack stumbled and looked at me, embarrassed.

"Sorry. He likes to walk between people's legs. It's his weird thing," I apologized. Chuck Yeager continued to sniff Jack circumspectly, searching for some clue to his identity and life. I called into the living room, "Fred, look who's here."

Fred looked up and took in Jack's sudden appearance in our foyer with no recognizable emotion. He turned back to his encyclopedia and said, "Jack Butler, did you know that in World

375

War II there was a tank called the M4 Sherman and the infantry guys would walk next to it? Jack Butler, I think that doesn't seem like the safest place to walk."

"That's a good point, Fred. I think things were a lot different then, with war, and a lot of things I guess. I'm going to talk to your mom for a couple minutes and then I want to talk to you, Fred," he said.

I led Jack to the dining room table and sat. He claimed the chair next to me and pulled a manila folder out of his battered army green messenger bag. He started paging through sheets of paper, some sort of forms, but I had trouble concentrating. He was sharing observations and goals and expectations expressed in the form of percentages that confused me. He was incredibly focused on what he was saying and his words were a steady stream; his head was bowed down and he didn't once look up at me. I laughed quietly.

"What?" he asked, and then immediately seemed to know. "I'm too focused? Eye contact?"

"I'm sorry. I didn't mean to laugh. I just . . . Well, it's like having a conversation with Fred," I said. "But that's okay."

He closed the folder. "Basically, what I'm saying is that I'm finishing up the documentation. I've got all the reports and test results from the neuropsych. I have a questionnaire for you to fill

376

out. And your husband, if he wants. We're moving along. I have to schedule the first meeting to talk about our findings and our recommendations. I can't skip that step and the principal is dragging his feet a little. Not on purpose, I suppose, but he certainly isn't doing anything to help speed it along."

"Okay. Well, what does this mean about Fred? Going back to school?" I asked.

He took a deep breath. "Peter—Mr. DuPont—is saying that he's unsure that this was an act that's severity would be lessened by a diagnosis."

"What does that mean, Jack?"

"It means he wants to treat this like an offense by any other student. He wants to treat it like an act of violence and go to the district disciplinary committee about it." He paused, deliberately looked into my eyes and continued. "That means that expulsion isn't off the table."

I gasped. "They can't expel him. He didn't hurt anyone. He doesn't understand what he did; he's not violent." The tears welled up in my eyes and I grabbed Jack's hands. He didn't pull away immediately but sat with my hands in his large, warm hands. I felt such a profound connection to him in that moment. I understood how much it meant for him to engage in physical touch, because I knew how difficult it was for Fred to sustain any sort of physical intimacy for longer than a few seconds.

"What are we going to do? He doesn't deserve this; he isn't a bad kid. He's a good boy. He hates breaking rules, disappointing people. What are we going to do?" I rushed through my words, my thoughts leaving my body as they emerged in my brain. I was in panic mode. Jack reached out to me and took me into his arms. He was stiff, patting me on the back like a child, and I could feel the tension in his body.

"Jack Butler, why are you hugging my mom?" Fred's voice exploded from the doorway. "I think that hugging my mom is not your job," he said. His words relayed his puzzlement, but he seemed neither angry nor troubled, just mystified.

Jack let go of me and I went to Fred and tried to embrace him. He stood stiffly for a moment and then inched out of my needy arms. "You're crying, Mom. Your face is sad. Did something sad happen again? Is it because of my violent behavior?"

I knelt down to him and grabbed him by his shoulders, rougher than I meant to, but my love was harder to control than I expected. "You are not a violent boy. We are going to figure this out, Fred."

Jack walked over and put his hand on top of Fred's head. "Fred, I need to talk to you, too. I had a conversation with Mr. DuPont and I'd like to tell you what he said." He led Fred into the family room and they sat side by side on the couch. I felt distinctly and purposely not included in the exchange, but I moved closer so I could hear them. Jack was speaking very quietly and their heads were bowed together as if they were praying for an answer.

I heard Jack say, "Mr. DuPont would really appreciate it if you would apologize to Jackson and also to Mrs. Tieman and himself."

"Himself who?" Fred asked.

"Himself Mr. DuPont," Jack said. I noticed that Fred was twining his small fingers between Jack's larger fingers, almost without thought.

"I think I can understand why I have to apologize to Jackson; it's because I scared him, right?" Fred asked, and Jack nodded. "What is the apology for Mrs. Tieman for?"

"Well, I guess it's because you scared her too, Fred."

"What about himself, Mr. DuPont? Was he scared too?" Fred asked.

Jack thought for a second and then said, "I think that's more for inconveniencing him. For making his job more difficult."

"I have to be sorry that Mr. DuPont had a harder job to do?"

Jack shook his head. "I know, Fred, it doesn't make a lot of sense, but everyone would feel better if they could see and hear that you did not mean to scare or worry people," Jack said.

"Or make them have a harder time at their job," Fred added.

"Right. You would have to apologize and it would have to be genuine."

"How can I apologize genuine if I do not think I have to be sorry for making Mr. DuPont's job harder and making Mrs. Tieman scared?"

"Okay, Fred. You have to make it seem genuine. You have to act like you're sorry. Could you do that? Would you do that? I think that it would get you back to school sooner," Jack said.

Fred was quiet for what felt like a long time to me, and I was just about to move in and try to bring some clarity to Jack's request when he finally looked up into Jack's face and spoke. "What if I don't want to go back to school sooner?" I stifled another cry with my hand.

"Fred. You are good at school, remember? You learn new things and you can check books about World War II out of the library and—"

Fred interrupted. "The books at the Wendell Elementary School library about World War II are not a good reason to come back to school, Jack Butler."

"Work with me here, Fred. What about me? What about seeing me? Having lunch with me? What about Owen and T.J., your lunch buddies?"

"Owen is a throat clearer and T.J. only wants to talk about the Packers football team of Green Bay. I do not miss those guys yet. I do like to have lunch with you, Jack Butler, and carry on conversations."

"Will you apologize, then?" Jack asked.

"I will think about that, Jack Butler. I will think about it real hard," Fred said.

"I guess that's all I can ask," Jack said, and stood up.

I met him in the doorway and handed him his messenger bag. "I'll be in touch," he said, and let himself out. I stood watching the door close behind him.

Fred came up next to me. He looked confused. "Jack Butler said I have to apologize genuine. But I don't feel it genuine in my heart, Mom."

"Sometimes we must do things that we really don't want to do, Fred. It's part of life," I said. I reached down and grabbed his hand before he could pull it away.

"Like I don't want to hold hands right now but you are holding my hand anyway? Like that?" he asked as he wiggled his fingers inside my tight grasp.

"Yes, just like that," I said, but I didn't let go.

Fred

Jack Butler told me some things to think about. He told me that saying an apology to Jackson and Mrs. Tieman and Mr. DuPont is something that I should do. If you say an apology but you don't feel sorry in your heart does that count? I think that what Jack Butler is saying is that it does count if you are good enough at fooling people. This is what I have been thinking about apologizing to these three people:

Jackson: I guess that Jackson was scared. That wasn't what I meant for him to feel, but that is the way it turned out which sometimes happens. It is like when I told Owen at lunch bunch that he is hard to be by because he clears his throat so many times every minute and Jack Butler said that wasn't nice because it would hurt his feelings. I did not think that it would hurt his feelings because I was just trying to give him helpful advice on how he could be more successful with making friends. After that though I could understand that he might have felt sad, but I don't think he really did because I think he is pretty focused on clearing his throat. I think that Jack Butler was just using him as an example to me. So I can see that Jackson might have been scared. But here is the problem with Jackson. He called me penis breath and I don't think that he was trying to be helpful and give me tips to be more successful at friendships. I think that he was trying to make me feel bad about my own self. I think that he should have to do an apology to me too.

Mrs. Tieman: I know that Mrs. Tieman was worried because I saw that she had a worried face when she saw the knife. I think that if I can just explain to her what I was trying to do then she wouldn't have to be worried and I would not have to do a lying apology to her.

Mr. DuPont: I guess that Mr. DuPont thinks about me a lot. He said that. I do not think that I should have to apologize to him because his job was harder. If he just understood what I was about then this whole thing might go away. But then I remembered that when Oliver

Westowski in the fifth grade made the fire alarm sound very loud and made all the children and grown-ups go out of the school in an orderly fashion and stand on the sidewalk in the drizzle, he had to apologize to the whole school on the microphone in the office so that all the people in the school could hear it at once.

If I could use the microphone and talk in all the places in the whole school at once I would not want to waste it with a fake apology. I would tell people that they were wrong about Fred Whitman-Hart and then I would tell them the things that I am about, like petting my dog and reading detailed books about World War II and reenacting battles in the woods. I would tell them about my grandpa who had a heart attack and doesn't act like a one hundred percent live person anymore, but he used to fly planes. I would tell them that my mom is a painter and my dad saves people from getting punished for things they didn't do. I would tell them that I think Jack Butler is one of the cool guys and I love golden yellow cake with dark chocolate frosting for my birthday. I would tell them that sometimes I say things that hurt people or scare them, but I never mean to. The way that words can make a person feel is tricky because there are so many words in this world and how do you know if you picked a hurting, scaring one? I will try to use words that are kind and gentle. I know two words that I won't use for sure because they are hurting and not true: penis breath.

Piper

I imagined my father living a simple life after his heart attack, imagined that his brain was capable of simple operations and even simpler emotions. If I asked him how he was, initially he looked at me with a look of mild confusion as if the question itself was rife with secret codes; then he seemed to consider his answer and finally he said fine. He almost always said fine. It was strange to me at first, as if that one nugget of social nicety had withstood the damage to his brain. Then I contemplated the idea that maybe he was actually just fine all the time. Except on the day he had snatched his photo from me, I didn't see any of his old rage. I sometimes heard a light laugh or saw a small smile, but he was never overjoyed or full of passion. Just fine.

A few days later, on a sunny Saturday in May, when it seemed that spring's tug-of-war with winter had finally ended in spring's favor, I forced him outside to the backyard. I set him up in a patio chair with Chuck Yeager lying beside him, basking in the first gentle heat of the sun-warmed patio. Fred was busily digging for fossils in the back garden, which pleasantly surprised me. I wondered if we were finally moving past the horrors of World War II to delve into the horrors of mass extinction. At that point I would have readily traded Nazis for prehistoric carnivores in an instant.

My father remained uninvolved as I stretched his baseball cap over his head of greasy white hair. I had to remind him to shower every other day and realized as I lay in bed the night before that I had forgotten my caretaker's duty and now his head would take on the look and feel of Fred's unbathed hair, a state that had become more bothersome the older Fred got.

"Dad, I just need you to sit here and make sure Fred doesn't leave the yard, okay?" I said loudly to jolt him out of the light sleep he already seemed to be drifting toward. "Just keep an eye on him." Fred was more than reliable when it came to asking an adult before he left the yard, but one of the books I had been reading on how families deal with traumatic brain injury suggested finding suitable jobs for the injured to help repair self-esteem. I had never imagined in my previous life that I would have worried about patching up my father's self-esteem. I had always thought of him as unfailingly confident, veering directly toward arrogant.

"Okay, Piper," he said. He sat up a little straighter and turned to face Fred's hunched-over form directly. "He's digging."

"Yup. That's fine, Dad. Just make sure he doesn't leave the yard."

"What if he leaves the yard?" he asked.

"Well, before he opens the gate you can yell, 'Stop, Fred.' Okay?" I said.

He tried out the words, rolling them around in his mouth, maybe trying to summon up the confidence to bear the responsibility of them. "Stop. Fred."

I nodded, patted him on the back and went back into the house. Isaac was at a conference in Chicago, spending quality time with other do-gooders from the Midwest. I resented the fact that twelve hours a day, five days a week weren't enough time for him to improve the fate of the guiltless. The irony in my annoyance was that I really didn't need Isaac around; my life was pretty much the same whether he was home or not. But I wanted a partner. I wanted someone who was down in the trenches with me, dealing with all the shit and occasional magic of parenting. I wanted someone I could share an eye roll with or a glass of red wine with after Fred finally wailed himself to sleep. I wanted someone to share a laugh with over the crazy funny thing Fred had said. I wanted either a partner or a best friend.

I worried occasionally about what Isaac had said about my similarities to my father. If I dug beneath the surface of my life, I could uncomfortably pinpoint instances when I had reacted badly, when the ugly character of perfectionism had butted its way into a situation that was perfectly lovely. All these things I wanted from a partner, were they too many? Were they unrealistic? Was I unknowingly placing unfulfillable expectations on Isaac? Was I wrong to believe I deserved it all? It was a prickly place to wallow, my home for so many years; now, instead, the possibility that I had been wrong all along. It was something I tried to push out of my mind, but I found it creeping back in when I was performing mundane tasks.

I had decided that I would clean my father's room that day, as the onset of spring always made the distinct body smells of a winter house grate on me. I needed a distraction from the waiting. Waiting for word from Jack about Fred's diagnosis meeting. Waiting for word from Mr. DuPont about Fred's future at school.

I changed my father's sheets once a week and vacuumed every other, but I wanted to throw the window open and exorcise the sad haze that my father seemed to brew. I opened the window wide and I could see out to the backyard. I watched the three of them for a minute. Fred used my garden spade to poke holes in the unplanted garden, using it as a lever to overturn stepping-stones and occasionally tossing something I couldn't identify into a bucket beside him. My father faced Fred, but I could see only the back of his head; his silence might have been a peaceful relaxation or it might have been actual sleep. Chuck Yeager forcefully licked his genitals. I yelled out the window, "Chuck Yeager! Leave it!" His head popped up and he looked all around for the source of the command. I laughed, feeling a bit like the voice of God. My father didn't stir, but Fred turned around, and I hung my upper body out the window and waved to him, madly.

He waved back and then yelled to me, "Please don't fall out of the second-story window, Mom."

I gave him a thumbs-up and pulled myself back in. Spring had a way of dialing my attitude firmly to the jovial range whether I wanted it to or not; it always had. I married Isaac in spring. I gave birth to Fred in spring. Spring had always been my time for shaking myself out of whatever shape or size of funk winter had dragged me down into. I quickly stripped my father's bed and made it up again with new cotton sheets from the hall closet. I dusted the framed art and tidied up the desktop. I knelt down on the floor to capture any dust balls that might have resided under the bed and found a large sheaf of paper.

I recognized it as paper from an old sketch pad, about twenty-four inches wide and eighteen inches long. There was a stack almost an inch thick. I pulled the sheaf out and wondered where someone had found my old artwork. It wasn't mine, though. The first page was primarily blank, with a jagged pencil line crashing through it. It was interesting. The second was another jagged line, also made with pencil, but it seemed the artist had taken more care in its composition and the lines seemed to almost jump off the paper, the detail was so precise. I thumbed through and found that the whole stack was different representations of jagged lines. It occurred to me that the lines were quite similar to one another. I started from the beginning and studied the first carefully, so I might mentally compare it to the second and third and so on. The lines were nearly identical, and when they weren't, I wondered if it wasn't merely my eyes misleading me, since looking at them so carefully soon made my head hurt. I paged through them again, traced my finger over the deep grooves that the pencil made in some of the versions. In others, the pencil line was so faint that had I not known that line so well, I might have lost its course as it journeyed across the page. There was something beautiful about these lines to me, the way they stood out, lonely against the stark white paper. Or maybe the line was brave or proud. There was a raw power to those lines that I could not explain.

I started to imagine them with color, with various hues of blue or orange. I started to imagine what they would look like on canvas, on a rich black background. I felt animated in a way I had not for some time. I felt stimulated in a way that taking care of Fred and my father did not make me feel. Literature might contain tales of artistic awakenings, but I am confident that that day I had an artistic reawakening. I was born again into the artist's body and mind that I had abandoned years before. My fingers itched to pick up my brush again. I was already reimagining my portfolio, feeling briefly and foolishly that all that was necessary to restart my career was the desire to do so. I blindly saw no problem with getting my name back out in the world of illustrating. I saw no inconvenience to sending letter upon letter to publishers and agents showcasing my work. I imagined that the connections I had in that world had merely been paused, waiting for me to return triumphantly to paint illustrations of the human heart or depictions of the water cycle.

"Hello, Piper. Fred did not go out the gate." My father interrupted my artistic musings.

"What do you mean?" I asked.

"Fred isn't in the backyard but he didn't go out the gate," he said.

I stood, panicked. It was amazing how quickly my brain could leave behind its artistic ramblings and perform the role of mother. "Were you watching him, Dad? Like I asked you to?"

"I think I was mostly watching him, but then I think my eyes closed and when they opened there was no Fred," he said.

"What about Chuck Yeager? Did he take Chuck Yeager somewhere?" I asked.

My father looked perplexed. "Who is Chuck Yeager?" he asked.

"The dog, Dad, the dog." I jumped up and rushed to the open window. I could see that my father was right: the backyard was empty. I yelled for Fred. I yelled for Chuck Yeager. Within seconds both of them trotted around the corner of the house. I sighed; the tension melted off my shoulders immediately. Fred and Chuck Yeager had just moved around to the side of the house.

"There they are, Dad." I pulled him over to the window by the arm and pointed out Fred, who was waving from below. Chuck Yeager leapt around in circles and barked at us, no doubt trying to fathom how we had appeared in the sky. My father smiled and waved back to Fred.

"It's okay. Fred is in the backyard," he said.

"Hey, Dad, are these your pictures?" I asked, and I picked up one of them and held it out to him.

He studied the line and then nodded.

"Is it a river, Dad? It looks like a river to me, a winding river through the desert. Or a great gaping crack in the land."

He looked at me and then glanced up at the ceiling. I followed his gaze up.

"Oh. It's the crack. Just the crack in the ceiling," I said. I was disappointed. I wasn't sure why right away, but then after much more consideration I worked out the root of my disappointment. I wanted my father to have some sort of rich inner life. I wanted to believe that he was imagining rivers and chasms, not just staring at the ceiling.

"You just have to look, Piper. Remember? The house is old and it is cracked but it's not falling down," he said, and then looked at me with reverence.

"You did some really nice work with the pencil here." I pointed to a spot that had tiny wisps of detail. He nodded. Though I wouldn't have ever called my father an artist, I had faint memories of him drawing pictures for me that were remarkably well-done: a horse in a field, Mickey Mouse, an airplane. For him it had been a hobby, because no self-respecting person would expect to make a living from art.

"I didn't know that you could manage a writing tool so well, Dad," I said. I noticed then that something was missing. "Hey, you need to sign your name on these. Every artist needs to sign their work." I cleared off the rest of the papers from the desk and laid out one of the pages. I handed my father a pencil and led him to the chair. He sat gingerly and held the pencil in his hand. I waited for him to begin his signature, but he sat still and then finally looked up at me with his empty eyes.

"Go ahead, Dad. What comes first? *L*," I said. I picked up his hand and laid it on the page near the bottom right corner, where an artist's signature might appear. His hand just lay there, on that spot, a lump of flesh that didn't even know where to start.

Sunday evening, I got a message from Jack requesting I come in to school on Monday morning for the first meeting about the educational diagnosis that Fred's case seemed to hinge on. I listened to it and then set my phone down on the dining room table and unconsciously sighed. I think my initial worry was what to do with Fred; where at one time not that long ago I might have believed my father might be an acceptable caretaker for Fred for a short time, I was no longer confident in his abilities.

"What's up?" Isaac asked from his seat at the snack bar, reviewing briefs on his laptop.

I responded without thinking. "Nothing. Just a meeting."

"About Fred?" he asked.

I considered lying to him and telling him it was about my dad.

"Piper?" he asked.

"Oh, it's just a meeting to get caught up on where Fred's diagnosis is at," I said.

"Should I be there?" he asked, his eyes still

scanning his screen; only the question itself revealed his interest in the conversation.

I pictured Jack's tiny office. I pictured Jack and me, knee to knee on tiny chairs, one of his ever-present manila folders spread over our laps, heads together trying to disentangle the Fred situation. Then I pictured Isaac pulling up a chair and inserting himself into my area of expertise, into my friendship with Jack, into my little world, and my urge to lie to him overtook me. "No. It's not a big deal. I'll let you know when I need you there."

"What are you going to do with Fred?" he asked.

"I don't know. I don't think my father's up to it," I said.

"You know, Piper, you just have to ask and I'm happy to help out," he said.

The hot tangle of anger that had fermented over the last nine years began to boil deep in my gut. I took a breath and tried to calm myself. "I forget that you can help out, Isaac. You are so rarely available." I knew the sharp edge of my fury was palpable; it had been lying in wait for so long, crouching and ready to pounce. The fact that he had even asked if he needed to be there was galling to me, as well as being fortuitous. I wanted Fred's father to know instinctively that anything that had to do with Fred was of great magnitude. I wanted him to find a way to be there, but at the same time I knew I didn't want him anywhere near that meeting.

"Piper, I don't know what you need from me when you don't tell me," he said, snapping his laptop closed, signifying the beginning of a conversation that I was unable and unwilling to have calmly. "Do you need me to stay home with Fred? You never tell me what you need and then after the fact you act like I should have known and I have to tolerate your pissiness about the whole thing."

"I'm sorry? Did you say 'my pissiness'? Isaac, I gave up years ago asking for what I needed because you could never give it to me. Remember when Fred was born and I asked you for two weeks home with me? Remember that? I got three days before you started 'checking in' with work. How many times have I asked you to please not be home late because I was sick? Or Fred was sick? Or I was totally and completely fucking exhausted and needed a break?"

"Piper, you knew when I took this position with Innocence, I was going to have to put a lot of hours in and you never said boo about it. This is an important job, Piper. I don't think you understand how many people are relying on me. This has always been a sacrifice, for both of us. A sacrifice for the greater good."

"Oh, fuck you, Isaac," I said, and he looked stunned and then disappointed. "Your son doesn't

397

give a fuck about the greater good. He wants a father who's there for him. Who engages him. Nobody in this house gives a shit about how important you are except for you. Fred never signed up for this 'sacrifice,' Isaac."

"Now it all comes out? All your pent-up rage over my job? You couldn't have discussed this with me as the situations arose? You couldn't have acted like an adult and addressed these issues calmly? You had to internalize them for so long that you can't even see the fact that I'm trying?"

"Trying doesn't cut it. I need doing. I needed doing nine years ago, and one week of trying doesn't make up for Fred's entire childhood." Suddenly, I was exhausted. His comment about my similarities to my father bubbled up again and I felt an uncomfortable twitch of embarrassment. My anger had stolen my strength, and the authority that I had packed into my words unexpectedly liquefied, leaving me stranded in a pool of emotional fatigue. The argument was futile. After carrying my rage for so long and then finally releasing it to the world, I was shocked to find that the freedom I had imagined was nowhere to be found. In addition, I thought I would feel relief from yelling and cursing at my husband, but instead it took me back to so many instances of my childhood, standing in the hall listening to my father berate my mother. The shame overcame my pent-up anger and I became embarrassed.

"Isaac, I do need you to stay home with Fred in the morning. I do. I need to be at school at eight and Fred isn't allowed back yet." I got up, and started to walk away but stopped and turned back. "I'm sorry, Isaac," I said and then went up to bed. What was I sorry for? I was sorry for opening a long-sealed can of worms I had no intention of dealing with. And I was sorry for my delivery, too reminiscent of everything I hated.

I got to the top of the stairs and looked up to see Fred standing in the hall looking at me.

"Hey, baby. What are you doing out of bed?" I asked, uncertain if Fred had overheard his parents' conversation.

"You have to go to my school tomorrow?" he asked.

I took a breath, ready to explain away Mommy and Daddy's fight as nothing more than a misunderstanding and ready to hug away any worry over divorce or any marital unhappiness. "Yes," I said.

He brought a folded piece of paper out from behind his back and handed it to me. "Would you give this to Jack Butler, please?" he asked. I nodded and he turned and went back to his room.

"I love you, baby," I said, too quietly and too late. I carried the note into my bedroom, shut the door and sat on the edge of my bed, smoothing the paper in my hand. Finally, I unfolded it. It read, in Fred's perfectly childish handwriting:

Dear Jack Butler,

I want you to know that I am going to apologize to Mr. DuPont and Mrs. Tieman and Jackson if that is what you want me to do. I miss my school a little bit and I miss you a lot. Also I want to know if you will come to my birthday party at my house on Saturday May 16. My mom always says I can invite my friends to my party and you are my friend Jack Butler.

From,
Fred

Fred

There are lots of good reasons that a kid shouldn't get out of bed after their mom or dad puts them to bed and says good night Fred. Getting enough sleep every night is important so that you can grow and learn and all the other things Mom told me and I read about. Sometimes you can get scared if you are the only person in your house who is awake in the nighttime and you might worry about alien abduction or breaking and entering. Also, sometimes moms and dads say things to each other that are not meant for you to hear and then if you do hear them you can't go back to before you heard them and that can make the life of a kid confusing. All they tell you is they love you over and over and I love you Fred I love you Fred I love you Fred. But then they say words about you that don't say that and if you hear those words you might think that you are a problem. You might think that you are a problem and you should do an apology to them too, but you don't know what it was you did that made them talk that way to each other. It is best to stay in bed after bedtime. It's just best that way.

Lance

There is yelling in the evening, my daughter and her husband, and when it is quiet I get up and find Fred. When I hear the husband and the wife yelling, it makes my heart hurt, because I have a memory that comes to me very quickly and then blows away just as quickly. I can see me and I can see Judy and we are standing in the kitchen and my voice is very loud and my words are very angry, but I can't remember what the words are about. My face is hard and sharp. Judy's face is lined and drooping. I slam my hand onto the counter and then I stomp into the living room. I see two children sitting on the couch; they are huddled down like they are trying to protect themselves from a storm. They look up at me and their faces are scared and worried. I don't say anything but I stomp out of the house and get in the car and drive away. Then I lose the memory and I don't know what happens next. Do I go home and apologize? Do I go home and tuck my children into bed? I don't remember what I do next and I feel ashamed because I cannot ignore the memory. It is me. It is something I did.

I go into Fred's bedroom and he is lying very still in his bed, but I can see in the moonlight that his eyes are open. I lie down next to him and he doesn't stop me. So then I curl my body around him and smooth his hair. His cheeks are wet but his body and face are still. I am so sorry for him. I am so sorry that I yelled in the kitchen and scared the children and Judy. I smooth his hair until I can see that his eyes close and his breathing slows down. He is sleeping and I am so sorry.

Piper

I got to school just after the first bell rang
through the halls and most of the children
were already in their classrooms. I didn't want
to have to see Jackson or Mrs. Tieman so I sat
in the car and waited until I heard the bell and
then went in. There was a group of children
who were hanging up the flag on the flagpole
in front of the school; they looked older than
Fred, probably fifth graders. I was mesmerized
by them, two girls and two boys. The girls,
obviously approaching puberty long before the
boys, tried to maintain the utmost composure
and demonstrated a level of professionalism
that embarrassed me for them. The boys tried
desperately to make the girls laugh, several
times even using the American flag as a prop in
their jesting. It felt so normal, this relating to
one another, this back-and-forth dance between
social beings, and I lost it. I could never see Fred
standing there beside a girl who was dressed like
a demure prostitute, trying to get her to smile. I
wept. I had not let myself cry over Fred's current
situation, instead constantly reminding myself
that it was a mistake, an easily solved problem
that would soon be a memory. Now, for the first

time since the call came from the school, I felt the panic that this was going to be the way it was for my son. The way it was for my family. Never fitting in, never being understood. I let myself cry until the clock said I was five minutes late for my meeting with Jack and then I wiped my eyes and attempted to smooth myself out.

He was waiting for me in his tiny office and when I walked in he stood up. "Piper?" he said, a look of mild concern on his face. As soon as I saw him standing there with his look of bewildered concern, I fell into him, wrapping my arms around him. He put his arms around me and patted my back crisply as I wept into his gray sweater-vest. After a few seconds he pulled me away from him, held me at arm's length and looked straight at me. "Piper? Did something happen?" he asked quietly.

I sniffled and sighed. "No. Nothing. Everything. This whole shitty thing," I said. I sat down in one of the tiny chairs and said, "Fred says he will apologize, you know, to everyone you suggested. Will that help?"

"I sure hope so, Piper," he said, and sat down in the other chair, our knees touching. "Let me show you what I've got here and we'll set up the formal meeting for as soon as possible." He shuffled through computer-printed forms, which all looked identical to me, but as he read over each of them I saw that each one contained different nuggets of information about my son, different reasons he should be labeled disabled. I stifled a laugh. Months ago I had bristled at the mere suggestion that my son was "disabled," and now I was so hip to the idea, I was praying for it.

As Jack closed the folder on the last page and brought out his iPhone to look up his schedule for the week, I remembered my Facebook friend request, languishing in his in-box, probably forgotten.

"Oh, hey. Um, I friended you a while back, but you didn't reply . . . ," I said. I had planned to say more but his expression had changed from concerned professional to awkward teenager.

He opened his mouth to speak, closed it again, cleared his throat and finally said, "I don't really use Facebook so much. I just stick to e-mails with parents." He turned back to his phone.

I tried to copy his nonchalance and said, "Oh, that's cool." I felt a light flush spread across my cheekbones and a slight queasiness build in my stomach. I had pushed too far and suddenly I couldn't get out of that tiny room soon enough. I felt like a huge lump of a thing that ate up every kindness it was afforded and the exact opposite of everything that belonged in Jack's life. A nuisance. A problem to be solved. The furthest thing from a friend.

"I've got a message here from Mr. DuPont. He's got a meeting set up with the disciplinary committee for tomorrow. It says here that Fred's father will be there to present his case," he said.

"All right," I said. I stood up to leave and remembered the letter in my pocket from Fred. I pulled it out and handed it to him. "This is from Fred," I said, and I hurried out of the room. I didn't want to see the discomposure that Fred's birthday party invitation would cause Jack.

I got into the car and called Isaac. "You're presenting something to the disciplinary committee tomorrow?"

"Yes, I am. I'm presenting a case to defend Fred," Isaac said. I rolled my eyes.

"Well, what are we going to do with Fred?" I asked.

"I'm going to go alone, Piper. You're going to stay home with Fred this time," Isaac said.

"But I—I have to be there," I said.

"Why? You don't trust me?" Isaac spat. "You don't think I can defend my own son? You think I'll sabotage the whole thing?" The venom in his voice was tremendous and I recognized the tone immediately as the same one that had oozed from my own mouth the night before.

"No, Isaac. It's just what I do. Isaac, it's who I am."

"Not this time, I'm afraid," he said, and curtly said good-bye and hung up.

Isaac didn't understand. He had just brushed off my whole life's work as worthless. Standing up for Fred at the meeting was my job. It's mine. It's what I do. It's the only thing I do. It's all I've got.

The meeting was scheduled for three thirty p.m., after school, not that it mattered that much to us, because Fred wasn't in school. Our days since his suspension had taken on a cadence and included Fred doing chores, something that I hadn't previously required of him. I always knew I should require it, but when you have one child who is your full-time job, there are few things that are left undone. Now Fred had to make his bed in the morning, load his dirty dishes in the dishwasher, fold and put away his clothes and take the recycling bin out. He also asked if he might be in charge of walking Chuck Yeager. I knew there was no way I would let him do it by himself, so I suggested that we all—me, my father and Fred—walk Chuck Yeager together.

We waited to take our daily walk until late afternoon on that day, the day of the disciplinary committee's meeting. It had rained a warm, steady rain for much of the day, and although the precipitation had stopped, the sky remained overcast and thick with an almost viscous moisture. Chuck Yeager was hesitant to walk through the puddles on the sidewalk, one of his many canine quirks: he didn't like to get his feet wet but he loved to swim. It seemed strange to me that a creature who wouldn't hesitate to eat rabbit droppings or roll in a wide variety of rotting carcasses detested having wet paws. He had, in the last few weeks, endeared himself to me, though, and I patiently steered him around puddles.

I handed the leash over to Fred after Chuck Yeager had exhausted a small amount of his sniffing energy and seemed more ready to walk in a straight line at a steady pace. We circled the block before I asked Fred, "Do you want to go down toward the park?" Though the park was technically not a dog park, its large, wide-open real estate right on the shores of a small lake made it a prime spot for dog owners to allow their off-leash dogs to run at their full speed and chase down waterfowl and other dogs.

"I think that Chuck Yeager would like to visit the park, Mom. He really likes wading into the water and swimming after ducks and geese," Fred said. So we switched direction and waited patiently for the light to change and Fred to identify "the walking man," which meant it was safe for him to walk. My father trailed behind us several steps and took in the scenery with a solemn face. We arrived at the park and found that because it was still the workday and the recent rain had turned large swaths of the park into a bog, we were almost alone. There were no errant dogs roaming around, no small children out yet. Chuck Yeager had never shown aggression toward other dogs, just a tremendous intensity that scared me almost as much. When he saw a dog across the park, he dropped into a low crouch that reminded me of wildcats eyeing up their prey before they bounded away and tore their limbs off. He would slink along, crouched down and staring intently, hardly even blinking. There was an enormous amount of thought going on behind that stare, and that was what scared me the most. I could not predict what he would do next; mostly he seemed to reach a preordained distance from the dog and then bolt toward it as fast as he could; sometimes he reached that same distance and suddenly became disengaged and busied himself sniffing the grass instead. There were a few times when I saw something different in his eyes and snapped his leash back on in fear of what he might be capable of.

Fred asked Chuck Yeager to sit, and he took his time settling his bottom down onto the wet grass. When he was finally fully sitting I unsnapped his leash and said the word he was waiting for: "Okay." He sprinted toward the water's edge, and I looked up to see a flock of geese had settled themselves down at the banks of the lake. He made a beeline straight toward them and as soon as they saw him coming they flapped, honked and fluttered back into the water. Fred laughed with joy; it was entertaining to see one dog ruffle the feathers of a whole flock of geese. Chuck Yeager reached the water and stopped short. He looked out at the geese and barked. He looked back at us, walking toward him through the springy, wet soccer field, and whined as if to ask us to please get them back on the solid ground. Finally, he went for it and jumped into the lake. While he was a fast runner, he floundered in the water. He was capable of a sloppy dog paddle but never seemed very comfortable.

Fred cheered for Chuck Yeager and my father and I stood and watched his chaotic chase. The geese continued to honk as they swam in small huddles, all going in different directions, making it hard for the dog to decide which direction he should pursue. We stood and watched him for some time, madly swimming in one direction and then another, whining the whole time. I decided that he was out farther than I was comfortable with and I called him back.

"Chuck Yeager!" I yelled. "Come!" He did turn to look at me but quickly decided I wasn't worth his time and continued swimming. He was almost fifty feet from the shore now and I worried that he would drown from fatigue. I called him madly, whistled and used the most expressive tone I could muster. Fred had wandered off a few minutes before and was digging through the rocks on the shore near the boathouse with a long stick. He paid no attention to me yelling, lost in his own boy thoughts. My father stood next to me, silent. I clapped my hands and ran up and down the bank to get the dog's attention, but he ignored me, instead focused entirely on the geese, constantly getting close enough to one to convince himself he might actually catch it. I was frustrated and had run out of options when I remembered my father had once told me that if you walk away from a dog, you immediately become more alluring, so I turned to walk away.

"Dad, come on. Let's go; he'll see that we left and come running," I said over my shoulder. I felt like I was doling out the canine version of natural consequences, a discipline approach that I had long been told was the way to grow strong, conscientious kids. I knew I should let Fred fail and feel the natural consequences of losing his homework or forgetting his lunch, but when it came down to it, what I wanted most of all for Fred was a life free from pain, though every parenting expert told me I would one day regret it. I looked over to where Fred had been just minutes before and couldn't see his figure through the tall, dead grasses at the lake edge. My heartbeat increased, that familiar knot of parental dread retied itself swiftly and I now found myself shouting Fred's name over and over. I ran over to the place where I had last seen him and, as I ran, pictured his small body bobbing in the water, facedown, already dead. Fred could swim, but not very well, and every summer Isaac suggested swimming lessons and every summer Fred politely declined them.

"Fred!" I shouted again as I came around the last curve of the bank before the piers began lining up.

His head popped out from under a picnic table up the stone steps of the boathouse and my heart regained its proper rhythm and the knot in my gut unraveled as quickly as it had first knotted.

"What are you doing?" I yelled to him.

He untangled himself from the angles of the picnic table and awkwardly began running toward me with his hand cupped in front of him. When he reached me he proudly put his hand out to show me his discovery. "Worms," he said proudly, and grinned up at me. "Worms are the hardest-working creatures in nature, Mom." I kissed the top of his head and sighed.

"Where's Grandpa and Chuck Yeager?" he asked.

I had expected that my father had followed me over to look for Fred; it didn't occur to me that he might have other notions. I figured I had probably left him standing by the lake, staring dully at some imaginary spot in the distance. "He's over by the lake. Let's go get him."

As we approached the lakeshore once more, I spotted Chuck Yeager, swimming madly toward shore, a smoother, quicker swim than I had witnessed before. "Look, Fred. He's chasing a goose to the shore." As we got nearer the water, however, I could see that it wasn't a goose.

"That's Grandpa," said Fred, puzzled.

"Oh shit," I said, and took off again, running toward the water once more. My father was wading into the lake toward Chuck Yeager. All the geese had dispersed noisily and my father and the dog were the only creatures wading through the ice-cold water. "Dad!" I yelled over and over, but he didn't even turn his head in my direction, just walked farther out into the lake. Chuck Yeager swam fast, trying to reach my father, but he was still at least twenty feet away. I ran right up to the water's edge and shouted for my father. Finally, he turned to look at me, the water up nearly to his shoulders. As his eyes met mine, I felt a shiver run through my body. His eyes were dead. It hit me quick and hard. "Dad, what are you doing?" I screamed. His eyes were blank and he was frustratingly silent. "Dad, come back!"

"Grandpa! Come out of the water!" Fred yelled. Chuck Yeager was near my father and my father turned to him and suddenly seemed to register where he was. He turned back to face us and began the slow slog back out of the lake to the shore, with his dog swimming madly behind him. As he neared the edge, I ran into the water and put my arm around him; his clothes were soaked with cold water and he trembled. I helped him

414

out onto the shore and Chuck Yeager climbed out next to him and began his routine of shaking himself off and rolling in the grass. Fred ran to us and grabbed his grandfather by his icy hand.

"Grandpa, what were you doing?" he asked.

My father just looked down at him with tears in his eyes, the dead look gone and replaced by a look of cavernous sadness. He continued to study Fred but didn't answer.

"Were you trying to bring Chuck Yeager back, Grandpa?" Fred asked.

My father stared at Fred and a tear dripped down the bridge of his nose. He started to nod, very subtly at first.

"That's it, isn't it, Grandpa?" Fred asked, and began nodding as well. Soon they were both nodding in unison as we made our way away from the lake and toward home.

After we arrived home, I sat on the lid of the toilet and breathed in the steam from my father's shower. I had helped him undress and get into the shower and it had been at least ten minutes that I'd sat just feet from him and wondered desperately what he was thinking. I heard the front door open and Chuck Yeager bark. I went out into the hall and stood at the top of the steps while Isaac greeted Fred.

Fred asked, "Did you have my meeting at school, Dad?"

Isaac answered, "Yes, Fred. I think we should

have a family meeting and discuss how it went. Where's your mother?"

"She's upstairs watching Grandpa take a shower because he went swimming in the lake today to bring Chuck Yeager back," Fred said.

There was a brief silence before Isaac yelled, "Piper?"

I took a deep breath and headed down the stairs. Isaac stood at the bottom of the stairs, looking confused. "It was a rough afternoon," I said by way of explanation.

"I guess so," said Isaac, and he looked at me with a sudden depth of understanding that I hadn't felt from him in years. That look drew me to him, and our shared history flooded me with tenderness and need. I went to him and buried my head in his chest.

"Hey, Piper. It's okay now. Everyone's okay now," he soothed, holding me and rubbing smooth, rhythmic circles on my back with one hand while the other raked fingers through my hair.

I felt a release in that moment, a letting go of so much of my vitriol and resentment, and even now I couldn't say why. It might have been because he seemed to know the instant he looked at me that I was in pain. I was in pain and confused. I had come within minutes, I felt, of finding my father's dead body floating in the lake. It had affected me more deeply than I would have predicted and I sensed somehow that Isaac knew that and I was suddenly and profoundly thankful for him.

He continued to hold me as silent tears streamed from my eyes and Fred looked on curiously from around the doorjamb. I took a deep breath, not wanting to upset him any more than I already had.

"Piper, Fred," Isaac began as he gently pulled me away from him and held me at arm's length. "I have good news. Fred, come over here." Fred joined us in our family circle, a physical manifestation of togetherness that was unpracticed for us. "Fred, I spoke at the disciplinary committee today at your school, along with Mr. Butler. And after we presented your case, the committee has decided that you may return to school on Monday." Fred grinned and I felt my anxiety over the situation soften into relief and even a small amount of joy—joy that Fred wanted to go back to school. I had worried over his suspension that he might decide that being home with me was preferable to school and might never wish to return.

"Now," Isaac continued. "There are a few things that have to be done before you can return. You need to write a letter apologizing to Jackson and it has to be meaningful, Fred. Do you think that is something you can do? Write a real, true apology letter?" Isaac asked.

Fred thought for a moment and then nodded seriously. "Yes, but I might need some help because I don't feel a real, true apology all the way down in my soul."

I kissed Fred on the top of the head and said, "Of course, Fred. We'll help you." I was already mentally composing the letter.

After we put Fred to bed together and I checked and double-checked that my father was safe in his office bedroom, Isaac and I went out to sit on the deck. He carried two bottles of IPA by the neck, and as we sat on the damp wood of our deck, he handed me one of the condensation-covered bottles. As I took the bottle, he pulled my hand to his lips and softly kissed it. It was a small moment, only a second out of years and years of us, but it marked a recognition that our togetherness was a thing that could be tossed about by the rough waves of life.

"Tell me what happened, Piper," Isaac said.

I stroked Chuck Yeager, who was stretched out next to me, still exhausted by the excitement of almost capturing his prey earlier in the day. I found a calm in running my hand over his silky coat. I gave Isaac the entire account of our afternoon, from my father's general mood through our walk, and concluded with the expression of profound sorrow I saw on his face as he turned to face me from the lake.

"The look, it was so eerie. It was so empty

but seemed to be so full at the same time. There was a fear, but also a look of letting go," I said, trying in vain to explain what I saw. We sat in a companionable silence for several minutes, listening to the sounds of Chuck Yeager's panting, the crickets and the far-off sound of traffic, before he responded.

His voice was gentle. "Piper, you have a tendency to want to believe the worst; you're a pessimist. Don't you think it's possible that your father really thought he was helping the dog?"

As soon as he spoke the words "tendency" and "pessimist" I felt my hackles rise. I was ready to defend myself against his attack on my perspective, my personality, me. But then I took a breath and stepped away from my defensive position. Instead of jumping up to attack him, I breathed and sat with what he said. I had become used to sitting in silence and had learned that sometimes the answer can be found in that silence. Or the question itself loses its immediacy. Isaac was right; he was right about that. I was a pessimist. I was ready to pounce on the worst possibilities. Out of what, though? I wondered. Why did I so need to believe that the worst was always yet to come?

"I hope you're right, Isaac. I really hope that's what it was," I said, and I leaned into him and he put his arm around me and I remembered how well this fit, how it felt when he was in law school and I was in undergrad. It had taken him months of small talk at the coffee shop to ask me out on a date. I wasn't immediately convinced he was the one, but he won me over with his gentle kindness and the fire in his gut for justice. I was proud he chose me and I felt a warmth and respect that flowed back and forth between us like a current. I wondered, as we sipped our beer as the stars came out, if we could find our way back to that.

Fred

It will be my birthday party on Sunday. It will be my real birthday too. It does not always happen that way, sometimes you have a party but you did not really have a birthday yet and so when you celebrate it is not for real. Sometimes you have a birthday but then you can't have the party until the weekend and then that is not really for real either. But then, if you are lucky, you have your party and your actual birthday on the same day. I am going to have a theme for my birthday and it is going to be Searching for Dinosaurs. It is going to be a theme of paleontologists and archaeologists and searching for fossils and artifacts even though artifacts are not as cool as fossils. I am going to have all of the guests at my party help me look for fossils and artifacts in the backyard and I am going to bury some things in the dirt before the party so that my party guests can have a successful dig. My mom is going to get a cake from the bakery because she doesn't know how to make a cake that is shaped like a fossil or a brush or pick or piece of Native American pottery. I said that was okay this year because she is sad lately and I'm not sure it would be her best work anyway.

These are the guests for my party: Mom (coming), Dad (coming), Grandpa (coming), Chuck Yeager (coming unless he decides to take a nap), Grandma (not sure because she ran away to Saint Paul), Jack Butler (not sure but I hope so because he is my friend), Antonio Bortelli from next door (he is my neighborhood friend but he plays lots of soccer so Mom said he probably won't be able to come) and Owen Parker even though he clears his throat too much because Mom said I had to invite a friend from school that was not a grown-up if I wanted to also invite Jack Butler who is a friend from school but is also a grown-up. I do not know if Owen Parker will come to my house for my party because even though I told Mom that we are friends we are more like just two guys that know each other sometimes.

At my party we will dig for fossils and artifacts and play some other games that I made up and even one that is a huge board game on a piece of cardboard that has a path around it and Grandpa has been helping me color the spaces on it. I gave him the blue and yellow markers and he has to make a pattern with them while I do the tricky stuff. He can make a good pattern if he's not too sad.

Before my party can happen I have to write my apology letter to Jackson that is full of meaning or Mom said I can't have my party at all. I wrote my apology letter to Jackson because I already invited my guests and it is hard to cancel my party. Here is my letter to Jackson that Mom said was okay and Dad said was well supported. Chuck Yeager did not say anything when I read it to him but he licked my hand.

Dear Jackson,

I guess that you have had a hard time because of me and something that I did. I guess it's because I showed you the knife that my Dad gave to me because we were going to have some special Man Time. I did not know that you would feel so scared of my knife. I did not want to make you so scared. I was trying to tell you something, but I didn't know the words for it. Now that I have had lots of time to think at home and not at school because of suspension, I know what the words are. I wanted to say Jackson I am a nice person who is interested in cool things and I think that if you let me tell you about them you would see that I am a good guy and not a penis breath. I see now that showing you the knife and telling you about playing World War II with my dad gave you the wrong idea about me and in fact it scared you a lot. I am sorry that I did that to you. It does not feel good to be scared. I hope that you will forgive me and find lots of meaning in this letter because I put it in there.

Your classmate and maybe someday friend,
Fred Whitman-Hart

Lance

The memories are coming back to me in small pieces that I trip over and large pieces that paralyze me. I see pieces of my life all over when I am asleep and when I am awake. Yesterday I saw my son, Curtiss. I saw an angry, angry father and a teenage boy with long, greasy hair. I saw the man come at the boy with scissors. I saw the boy crying out and I could hear the boy's mother crying for the man to stop. The man didn't stop. He held the boy down on the plaid bedspread and pulled his hair tight and cut out chunks until the boy stopped struggling and lay mute on his bed. The mother cried and the daughter watched from the hallway but didn't cry, just watched with so much fear. When I wake up from the memory I am sitting at the desk in the office. My hands are gripping a pair of sharp silver scissors that I found in my daughter's desk drawer and the blade has made a thin cut in my palm and the blood is beading up like water.

This morning I saw the angry man again and he was a husband and he was standing over the scared wife and she was apologizing over and over. The angry man didn't care; he just kept shaking his head at her. He got tired of listening to her cry and apologize. He grabbed her shoulders and shook her. Then she was quiet. The man dropped down to the floor and he started to cry. He started to apologize and cry and she looked at him with hard eyes and turned and walked away. The angry man sat on the floor for a long time and wondered how to do better. I sit with this picture in my head for so long. I can't replace it with another because I don't have any memories of him doing better.

Today I see the angry man, dressed in navy blue. I see him walking away over and over again. I see him walking away from his wife. I see him walking away from his children. All I have is a picture in my mind of his back, broad and tight, never looking back. I try to shake the image loose, try to hit it out of my head, but it will not go. If I lie down on the bed, if I find the crack in the ceiling, I can find something to focus on. I can make the pictures fade away.

I am going to call Judy, even though I promised Piper that I wouldn't. I am going to call her and tell her now I remember what I did. I remember now that I hurt her. I understand why she wanted to run away from me. I am going to tell Judy that I understand that now. I am going to tell her it's okay.

I am going to call Curtiss too. I am going to apologize to him for cutting his hair. I am going to tell him that I didn't know and there were probably many times that I did the wrong thing. I am going to tell him that I am sorry and I understand why he doesn't come around. I understand why I am dead to him.

I am seeing so many things now, so many pictures in my head of things I wish would have stayed away. But I see flying too. I see the view from the cockpit, the blue sky and white clouds and sometimes the grids of cities below me. I see the whole world spread out in front of me and I am in control and I am good at it. I see the world around me and like God I am flying. I feel the peace of wide-open sky and the calm of being in control. If I remember flying before I fall asleep, I can fly in my dreams. I can fly anywhere, away from that man.

Piper

The morning of Fred's tenth birthday we woke to a gentle rain tapping at the windows, though the pompous weatherman had almost guaranteed unending sun. Fred wasn't disturbed in the least, though; he was adamant that digging for fossils and artifacts would be that much easier if the ground was soft. He told me that he was going to bury a collection of treasures for his partygoers to unearth, and I was desperate to see what he had amassed because of his predilection in toddlerhood of secreting things away. Isaac and I would madly search for every-thing from car keys to watches to remote controls and then find them stashed in the seat of Fred's ride-on fire truck or packed away in his tiny wheeled Thomas the Tank Engine suitcase. My mother thought it was adorable until he pilfered her pearl necklace on one visit to their house and my father warned that he might have a future as a pickpocket. I asked Fred to show me the treasures he planned to bury to allay my fears that anything truly important would be gone or anything embarrassing would be dug up by the lone child who would attend the party.

"If I show you the treasures, then they won't be a surprise to you, Mom," Fred insisted.

"What if I were to act as your assistant and not take part in the dig?" I asked.

Fred was thoughtful before he said, "Okay, you can be the lead paleontologist's assistant." Then he ran up to his room to locate the items to show me.

When he returned, he dumped out a Ziploc bag of fake gemstones and extra-shiny rocks, rusty Matchbox cars and a silver dollar. He also had several shards of what looked like one of our dining plates.

"What's that?" I asked.

"Pottery shards," he replied.

"From our cupboard?"

He looked away and took a deep breath. "Yes. I had to borrow one plate from our cupboard so there would be authentic pieces of pottery but I am sure that we can use superglue to fix it after the party."

I was about to lecture Fred on thinking through our choices, asking before taking and other parenting topics that seemed to readily apply to the situation but decided just before I drew breath that it could wait. It was his birthday and I could lecture him later. He set out to the flower beds in the backyard, mostly moist earth, rotting mulch, and dead leaves that had never been raked in the fall. There were a few spring bulbs popping their colorful heads up through the dirty brown, but I never knew their names, as they had been tenants here long before we had.

I was nervous about Fred's party, as I always was for him in social situations. I waited with dread for the day Fred figured out that his social life was lacking. I felt like each social situation I threw him into took him one baby step closer to this realization, but the end point just seemed to move a bit farther away with every social interaction that Fred didn't recognize as abnormal. This was the first year I required he invite someone from school, and the friend he chose, Owen, was not someone Fred had mentioned before. But then I had to remind myself that Fred rarely mentioned anyone from school but Jack Butler.

I had not heard from Jack if he was coming to the party today. I had mixed feelings either way. I knew that his presence would be enjoyable for Fred but I worried it would be awkward for the adult partygoers, mainly me. I e-mailed him after I delivered Fred's letter and before the disciplinary committee's meeting. I went out of my way to reassure him that although it would mean a lot to Fred if he came, we in no way expected that, since he was a busy man with a life outside of school, and so forth. He had never replied. There was an uneasy spot deep in the pit of me that wondered if my need for human contact had pushed Jack away, like the desperate teenager who will do anything to be noticed by the popular girls.

The first guest to arrive at the party (of the few who didn't already live there) was Owen with his harried-looking mother. They were ten minutes early and I was in the middle of putting together a multilayered Mexican dip that Fred would never touch; nevertheless, I made it in order to create a partylike ambience.

"Fred, can you get the door?" I yelled to him, as my hands were full of utensils smeared with refried beans and sour cream. He ran down the stairs and threw open the door.

"Hello, Owen. Welcome to my party. You can come in now and I want you to know that I would like it if you would get a drink if you feel like you have to clear your throat," I overheard Fred say from the front door.

"Oh shit," I mumbled, and wiped my hands on the closest dish towel I could find before rushing to the door to apologize for Fred's rude remark. I reached the door to find that Owen and his mother were standing awkwardly in the front hall. Owen was very blond and smaller than Fred and I remembered Fred telling me that he was a year younger. He was visibly uncomfortable and averted his eyes from my face even though I had put on my friendliest mom face.

"Welcome, welcome. Please come in. The party

is in the backyard. Fred, take Owen through to the backyard," I said. The boys disappeared immediately and I was standing alone with Owen's mother, whom I had never met. She was short and round and her blond hair was piled up on top of her head. She was wearing yoga pants and Nikes and was carrying a large orange handbag and a battered *Star Wars* gift bag that I assumed was for Fred.

"Hi, I'm Piper," I said, sticking out my hand, hoping that all remnants of dip had been wiped clean.

She shook my hand. "I'm Lauren," she said.

"Lauren, I am so sorry about what Fred said. About the throat clearing. Of course Owen can clear his throat whenever he needs to."

"My God, I hope he doesn't. I wouldn't wish that on my worst enemy. There are some days I think to myself if I have to hear that fucking sound one more time I'm going to run away for good. Then a minute later he does it again and I say the same thing. Then I have a glass of wine and another until the sound is just background noise. My therapist doesn't necessarily approve of self-medicating with alcohol, but she has given me permission to lock myself in the bathroom if it gets to be too much. It used to be snorting so I feel like throat clearing is something of an improvement. We take what we can get, right?" Lauren said.

I stood there and tried to figure out what to say.

"Sorry. Too much information, right? I have that tendency. I seem to tell everyone everything. It drives my mother-in-law crazy. She believes in practicing restraint above all other things. I prize sanity above all else, but rarely do I find it. You probably think I'm a horrible mother but if you lived with verbal tics you'd feel my pain. Maybe you do live with verbal tics?" She paused and I shook my head, genuinely sorry for some reason that I couldn't relate to her angst. "Anyway, it's nice to meet you," Lauren said. "Your house is great. Thanks for inviting Owen. We appreciate it."

"I'm just so glad that you could come. You're a bit early so I was still finishing up in the kitchen. Sorry," I said.

"No, I'm sorry. Owen's terrified of being late, hates it, so we get everywhere early. I can help you in the kitchen," Lauren said, and started walking toward the back of the house like she knew where she was going. "This way?" she said, and I nodded.

We swapped diagnosis stories over final party preparations in the kitchen and I found out that Owen had been "smacked with the label," as Lauren put it, at the end of kindergarten and struggled with sleep, food issues, and a litany of tics. I told Lauren the briefest version I could of our journey with Fred over fruit-plate prep, to which she replied, "Holy shit. You poor woman." Every once in a while, I glanced out the window and saw Fred and Owen side by side in the dirt, discussing something as animatedly as either of them could.

"What's Fred into?" Lauren asked.

"Now? Paleontology and fossils and stuff. We just came off a really long obsession with World War II, though. How about Owen?" I asked.

Lauren smiled at me as if she knew her answer to my question had the ability to change my life and then answered, "Dinosaurs." In that instant I felt a rush of something I had missed for so long: excitement, joy. I had walked the passageway of mothering my son alone for so long that the idea that I could walk in step with someone else thrilled me. I wanted to take Lauren into my arms and hug her. Let her know that it was possible that she'd saved my life. Saved my life by giving me the exact thing I never knew I needed.

The fossil-and-artifact dig in the backyard was a huge success, with Fred and Owen finding most of the treasures while my father carefully sifted through the dirt, avoiding any pickings, which pleased me because I felt like he really wanted Fred to find them. Either that or he honestly didn't see the items he passed over. As Isaac helped the boys scrub their treasures clean in a washtub with dish soap and Lauren reclined in a deck chair with her eyes closed, repeatedly running her fingers through Chuck Yeager's fluffy chest hair, the doorbell rang.

It was Jack Butler with a slim gift-wrapped package under his arm. There was a small flutter in my chest, but I wasn't sure if it was pleasant surprise or panic. He wore slim-fitting dark jeans and a fitted T-shirt with an old-fashioned newsboy's cap. He looked young and alive, with none of the fatigue that plagued Isaac. He also looked disappointed to see me open the door.

"Jack," I said. My heart raced a bit; suddenly I was nervous and felt as unsure as I had when I was thirteen.

"Oh. Hey. I was kind of hoping that no one would answer and I would just leave this on the front porch and leave," he said.

"Then why did you ring the bell?" I asked.

"Two reasons. One: it's customary. Two: to alert you to the package on your front porch," he said, and grinned.

I laughed. "Sorry I answered the door, then. Come on in." I gestured toward the party.

"I'm actually not supposed to be here, but I didn't want Fred to think I didn't care. I wanted to leave this for Fred," he said, and gestured to the gift.

"Thank you, from both of us."

"I also wanted to tell you something," he said uncertainly. "You're a really good mother. I mean, you are a good fit for Fred. Does that make sense? I'm not great with words sometimes."

"That was nice. Really nice," I said, and my hope for friendship briefly returned. Then he went on.

"I don't usually like to say things like that to parents. It's probably not that professional or what have you but you seem like you need to hear it," he said without a trace of malice or sarcasm, just a vague tinge of duty.

The excitement at the prospect of our future bonding dissipated immediately. My hibernating shame woke quickly and with a vengeance as I understood how he perceived me. I was as bad as I had been in sixth grade. Shannon Miller had pushed me down a greased bowling lane and now suddenly I understood why. I was desperately embarrassed and would not have complained a bit if a spot opened in the floor and I disappeared completely.

"Jack, I'm sorry if I was weird or inappropriate in any way. This has been a really difficult time for me and I haven't been quite myself. Thank you so much for everything you've done for Fred. Isaac said you did a phenomenal job at the meeting. Thanks for that and everything."

He visibly relaxed. "You're welcome. But your husband was the true hero there. If I'm ever wrongly accused of a crime and need to make an appeal, I hope your husband can do it," he said, but then paused. He continued. "Not that I've ever been wrongly accused of a crime or even committed a crime at all, with the exception of an underage-drinking ticket in college." He shook his head. "Sorry."

I held my hand out to him and grabbed his. "It's okay, Jack, really. I just want you to know how much I appreciate what you've done for Fred." I shook his hand.

He nodded and squeezed my hand. "Please let Fred know that I said 'happy birthday' and I'll see him tomorrow."

"Of course," I said, and closed the door as Jack walked back down the sidewalk.

Fred was thrilled with his party, pleased with his cake and nonplussed with his gifts. When he opened a stomp-rocket kit to use in the backyard from Owen, he looked it over and tossed it over his shoulder along with the wrinkled wrapping paper. I apologized to Lauren, embarrassed as always that Fred's social graces lacked grace. She waved her hand as if to dismiss my concerns as irrelevant and pointed at Owen, who had not even noticed Fred had opened his gift but instead meticulously studied the packaging on Fred's new Make Your Own Fossil kit. I relaxed; I had finally found company that I didn't have to constantly apologize to for my son's distinctive yet annoying behaviors. The same joyful calm I'd felt in the kitchen earlier flooded over me again,

437

and with it the tiniest feeling of peace and a whiff of emotional stillness I hadn't experienced for a long time.

Fred was delighted with his gift from Isaac and me: a large, glossy hardcover book on dinosaurs and fossils that was impeccably detailed and obviously meant for an adult audience. He delved in immediately, leaving Jack's gift of a thin stack of World War II comic books cast aside. I felt bad for Jack; in the time that Fred had been away from school, only days really, he had renounced World War II just as he had airplanes earlier in life. In the case of Fred, change didn't come slowly; it sometimes came overnight. He went to bed wondering aloud about the root causes of war and woke up pondering what the world was like before humans. I caught myself snared in what-ifs when I considered the idea that Fred could have been interested in fossils months ago, instead of now, and the whole trajectory of our family's life would have pointed toward another course. My pessimistic leanings were deep-seated and I had to push back against them rather than let them drag me down.

The party guests and I lounged out on the deck, soaking in the sun, while Fred and Owen pored over Fred's new book. Lauren and I sat together and alternated between silence and conversation, while Isaac, never able to sit still, raked the backyard and my father sat with his eyes closed and face tilted up to the sun. I studied his profile, the same profile I had been taking in since birth. The height of his forehead, the projection of his nose, his defined chin were all the same. His profile alone did not disclose the changes he had undergone, what he had endured. I was able to look at him, sunlit on that May afternoon, his silver hair shining, his proud features pointed skyward, and forget his sadness. I was able to look at him with something other than quiet resentment. I was able to look at him and feel a pull in my chest that I recognized as love, free from fear. Its unfamiliarity gave me pause; I was uncomfortable with the ease with which I labeled my feeling. Love for my father—real down-to-the-soul love—was something I had written off years and years before. Yet here I was, almost forty and understanding the depth with which a daughter can love her father.

Chuck Yeager's bark broke through our lazy spring afternoon. Chuck Yeager always barked when someone came to the house, anointing himself both doorman and security, but this was a different bark from the warning bark that usually greeted our guests. This was a bark that suggested familiarity, which said, "You! It's you!" This was someone the dog knew. Fred looked up from his book right away, as if he, too, recognized the discrepancy. I got up and walked through the house to the front door, where I found

Chuck Yeager pacing back and forth, whining and wagging his tail in winding loops around his backside.

"Mom?"

"Hello, Piper. I've brought a birthday gift for Fred," she said.

"Oh. I didn't know you were coming. I mean, I kind of assumed you weren't. The invitation was more habit than intention." I was cruel and I knew it. My newfound love for my father had blossomed without my mother's presence, and I felt the need to scramble to protect its newness by pushing her away.

"Can I come in?" she asked through the screen door. I had not opened the door and she and I had been interacting through a screened window panel in the storm door, as if I was a bank teller and she the customer asking to withdraw her savings.

I didn't know what to say. I didn't know what it would do to my father to see her at this point. He was clearly not in a good place, and her sudden appearance after all this time and all his wishing and hoping and confusion had the potential to throw him further down an abyss I didn't know whether I could pull him out of. I prepared to say no despite the overwhelming whines from the dog and the knowledge that Fred would be pleased to see her, if only just to receive another gift.

"Judy?" came my father's voice from behind me, frail and hoarse.

"Lance?" my mother said, confused. His voice held none of the same bravado it once had.

I turned to see my father standing in the hall, limp arms at his sides, hair mussed and skin cast with a gray-green color that I had not noticed as I gazed at him in the bright, exultant light of the afternoon sun.

"Lance," she said. "I got your message."

I turned back to my mother. "I don't know if this is a good idea. He's not in a very good place right now. Anything he said in a message isn't necessarily reliable or, you know, real."

My mother spoke quietly. "He apologized, Piper, for everything."

"Everything? Everything what?" I asked, bemused. I had not known that my father remembered much of anything based on what he said, and I was sure that his apology could have come only from a place of emotional disorientation.

"Can I just talk to him, please?" she asked me, though she gazed through the steel mesh at my father with a look I couldn't decipher. There was a tenderness to her voice, a kind of gentle sorrow.

I walked down the hall to where my father stood, expressionless. I put my hands on his shoulders. "Dad?"

He stood for a second and stared past me at

some invisible point in the distance, and then finally his eyes seemed to find me and he said, "Yes."

"You don't have to talk to her if you don't want to, Dad."

"Yes."

"I don't want you to think that this means anything. This doesn't mean that she's back or wants you back or . . . God, Dad. Shit, I don't know what this means," I said. I was rattled and uncertain I even had the right to tell him what to do or think about his wife.

"Yes."

"Yes what?" I asked.

"Yes, I want to talk to her," he said slowly. By now Chuck Yeager was beside himself, and when I opened the door to let my mother in, he leapt up and pawed at her, trying to lick her face. My anger with my mother mounted; I was angry at her for coming back now after all this time and offering my father what I was sure was a false sense of hope. I went back and forth on an almost daily basis; did I understand what she had done? Did I forgive her? Could I? As she walked by me and the dog leapt in circles around her, lapping at her, I said, "He just licked his own asshole with that tongue." And I slammed the door.

Lance

Judy comes and we sit on the couch in the living room. She sits next to me so our legs are just barely touching. She's older than I remember, but her skin is pink and she smells like lilies of the valley. It's the scent of Judy. The flowers look like tiny bells and when Piper was little she called them fairy's bells.

We sit on the couch and the dog is very happy to see her. The dog is trying to climb into her lap and she keeps pushing him off of her, but she is laughing too. There's a flash across my mind, in between all the images of anger and sad. It's a flash of Judy laughing at the altar of our wedding. I dropped the ring and she threw her head back and laughed her high, sweet laugh. I hold on tightly to this flash as it swims by.

She smiles at me and I am confused. She says she listened to my message and I tell her I am sorry that I called her again. I know I'm not supposed to call her. I tell her I had to call her because I remembered. She holds my hand and says that she is glad that I remembered, because it seems like it affected me. She says that in my message I sounded different, very, very sorry and sad. I tell her yes; those things are true. I tell her now I cry at night. I cry at night when I remember and that's what makes me so sorry. Her face is wet with her tears and I tell her that I don't want to make her cry anymore. She puts her arm around me and pulls me into her. Her body is soft. I thought I remembered that our bodies used to fit together so well, but now I am all angles and sharpness and I wonder if I was remembering wrong all along.

She says, "Lance, I want to ask you something," and I wait to hear what she wants to ask me. I have to focus on questions with all my energy or they slip through my mind without finding their answer. She says, "Lance, do you want to come home with me?"

I think for a very long time to make sure that I understand her question; I let it float around in my head, trying on answers, before I tell her, "Judy, I'm going to fly again. I can't come home."

Fred

My tenth birthday party was mostly a big success. I think that I have a new friend and if I try very hard to ignore his noises I can enjoy his company very much. There are some times when I get very distracted by his throat clearing and have to ask him very politely to stop. He says I'm sorry Fred I can't stop and he shrugs his shoulders and is not upset that I asked him to do that which is good because I don't think that it hurts his feelings after all even though all the grown-ups say it does. I had a good time digging for fossils and artifacts and Owen found a lot of them which is good because he was the guest and I wanted to be a good party thrower. I even got a cool kit where I can make my own fossils that Mom gave me but I am a little confused about how you can make fossils without dinosaurs but I think I will ask for help and it will turn out to be an okay gift.

Jack Butler did not come to my party but he did give me a present by magic. I wish that he knew that I am very interested in fossils and artifacts now and am pretty much an expert because I think he would have rethought his gift choice. I will still write him a real and true thank-you card because it was nice that he thought about my birthday even though he didn't think about it enough to come to my party. I will get to go back to school tomorrow and I will tell him that he missed a good time, but I don't want him to feel too bad about missing it so I will also tell him the cake was dry and crumby.

At the end of the party Chuck Yeager found someone at our door and even though Mom wouldn't let me go see who it was I knew in my heart that it was Grandma. I went around the side of the house and I left Owen with my big book of dinosaurs and I could peek in the window in the living room like a spy because I learned about that kind of stuff when I was an expert on World War II.

Grandma and Grandpa were sitting on the couch and they had stiff bodies and sad faces. Grandpa didn't say very much but he seemed like he was listening a lot. I wished that Mom had opened the windows up in the living room and I thought about going to tell her that the living room needed fresh air pronto but I was afraid I would miss something and besides she would catch me spying. Instead of hearing, I looked and I watched and I could see that when Grandpa finally talked, just a few words, like a little sentence, his sad face changed into a calm face and then I knew that Grandpa was on his way to happy.

Lance

The boy, my grandson, Fred, is ten now. The party is over and it is night. I am lying on the bed, watching the crack in the ceiling change with the changing light. Sometimes it seems to come alive and make its way across the ceiling in different directions. Sometimes it is perfectly still and I can watch it for hours and it doesn't move. There are times when it opens wide like a mouth yawning and there is a soft yellow light that seeps from the gap. A soft yellow light that I can see and feel and hear. I cannot hear its words; they are like a feather and a language I do not speak yet, but I feel their warmth and their promise. But sometimes the crack is angry and the lines run jagged and sharp. If I lie perfectly still, I can feel their razor teeth scratching across my wrists and neck. I can smell the blood and feel the biting pain. It is always there, a mirror I look up into. I can see myself up there, damaged.

My mind has come unlocked. The memories of my life come like a flood comes to a desert. The ground is so dry and hard there is nowhere for the water to go and it's dangerous for all the living things. When I sit they wash over me with their force, pushing me off my chair, causing aches

447

in my bones that creep into my deepest places. When I lie down they roll over me and cover my face; the breathing becomes difficult and tiring and I only wish I could stop struggling, but my body refuses to give up.

It becomes very dark in my room; the moonlight is dim and I can't see the stars from my window. I think if I can see the stars, their bright light can scare the flood of my memory, push back against the memories. So I get up and put on my slippers. I travel quietly through the dark house, down the steps and out the front door. I can see the stars but the edge of the park is calling me closer and I know that there are so many stars there that they can hold back the waters of remembering. I close the door gently and walk toward the park.

The street is quiet in the nighttime; the busy people rushing to work and rushing home again are sleeping. They do not have to push back, just move around in the world without weight. There are no streetlights in the park and the winding path trips me up. It is not where I think it should be and fools me into planting my foot in the soggy ground over and over. My slippers will be wet. I reach the dock at the lake, still and smooth, and the sky is open and infinite in front of me, above me, all around, and all the stars shine their light onto the flood and I can feel myself calm. I can feel the waters tire. I see one more thing. There is a baby, a baby boy, and it is Fred. My daughter is in the hospital and she has given birth to this fuzzy-haired boy, with a pink face and scrunched-together eyes. She holds him out to me and there is doubt in her eyes. I think about saying no but his warm body calls to me and I reach out and hold him to my chest.

I tip my head back and close my eyes. When I open them I am looking straight up into the night sky and I feel like I am flying again. I remember the feeling of flying at night, the comfortable aloneness, the warmth that can come from darkness, and the last of the waters slow to a stop. I can breathe again. But I know they will be back and I know that I will have to find the stars again, the night sky with its unending aloneness and its dark comfort.

I turn around and look toward the park again; the path is lit up by the stars overhead and seems to lead me directly back home. As I move down the path I imagine the runway, the anticipation of flying, the slow crawl that turns into tremendous speed and then flight. I am moving slowly down the runway, but I start to jog. I have not moved like this in so long. I have not found my tremendous speed in so long. My legs burn but I cannot take off until I have reached that speed, so I must run faster and harder; I must feel the burn travel through my blood and muscles and bones and nerves. I must burn all over to fly. I reach the end of the path and the sidewalk and then the street. I can push faster; I know I can. I can burn harder. My feet hit hard ground and I am so close. There is a bright light to my right and as I run I turn my head and look into it. It's the light of the brightest star. The star slams into my body and I fly. I fly and fly.

Piper

I woke up in the middle of the night, that time when the silence is so thick around you you're unsure that you've woken at all. It was a dream that woke me up, roused me and sent my hands searching for Isaac's body, naked beneath the thin blanket. I couldn't remember the specifics of the dream, only that I felt a ripe animal need that had to be satisfied and the subject of the dream itself was a mystery; I told myself it was Isaac. I reached around my husband's back and ran my fingers along his chest. I kissed his shoulder blades, though they were a little cold to the touch. I reached my hand downward and found my body doing things I had not done in so long, found myself exploring land I had decided months ago I would not travel to again. Isaac turned over and without speaking began to kiss me. Our kisses were hard and wet and he soon had my T-shirt up over my head and had found my breasts, nipples alert to his soft, teasing mouth. I pushed off my shorts with my foot and climbed astride him. My hair hung down and tickled his chest. I bent forward and our mouths found each other again as we came together and we were connected by some manifestation of our love, some reminder or hidden nugget recently unearthed, a new hope that we might be okay in the long run or at least for the time being. We moved in tandem and came together, panting, and I grinned down at him. I said, "I love you, Isaac."

He said, "I love you, too." I lay beside him and he ran his fingers through my hair. We didn't speak, though there was much to talk about, too much maybe. There were apologies at the tip of my tongue, mingling with truths that I still wanted to tell him. I was ready to face my faults, but I wanted badly for him to do the same. I still wasn't sure that I could get everything I wanted from Isaac, but for the first time in our relationship I wasn't assuming that I was the better spouse simply for wanting harder. As we lay there I heard the sirens wailing down the street. I heard their unending cry but thought nothing of it because when you live in proximity to a hospital you grow hardened to tragedy rushing by and announcing itself. It wasn't until the sirens stopped so close to our house that I wondered. I wondered for a split second where Fred was. Had he sleepwalked outside? I knew the answer was no, but Isaac took one look at the mild panic on my face and said, "I'll go check on him." He pulled on pajama pants and disappeared while I dressed myself and relaxed, certain my fears would soon be allayed.

It was only seconds later that he rushed back

into the room. "Piper. Your father. He's not in bed."

I jumped out of bed and we rushed around the house, opened and closed doors and searched every room, every closet. Chuck Yeager trailed us, whining. I yelled one time, "Dad." I called out for him only once, when I knew. I threw open the front door and bolted toward the park. On the street in front of the park entrance I could see an old sedan parked at an odd angle in the middle of the street. There were two fire trucks and an ambulance clustered around and a group of figures rushing around the nose of the car. I ran toward the scene and was met by a young police officer with a mustache who said, "Ma'am, I'm afraid you'll have to step back."

"But is it an old man? Like sixties? Is it my father?" I asked, and the officer looked back over his shoulder before turning back to face me.

"Would your father be out in the middle of the night, ma'am?" he asked.

"No, not usually, but he's not right. He suffered brain damage. He might have walked out in the middle of the night. He might have. I don't know. Can I please see if it's him?" I begged.

The officer turned away and went to ask an older woman a question. When he had stepped away, I could see the body lying on the concrete, twisted in an abstract form not common or comfortable for a human. I felt a hand on my shoulder and turned to see Isaac behind me. He was taller than me and I knew he had a better chance of seeing if it was my father. I looked up at him and he said, "Piper, I can't tell; there's a lot of blood on the person's face. Do you remember what he was wearing?"

I shook my head and the tears came. I did not know what my father was wearing. Like the mother of a missing child who can't remember the color of her child's jacket, I was useless. The throng of emergency personnel around the nose of the car hummed and still the young officer didn't return. The men and women were quiet, quieter than I expected. There was no yelling, no demanding voices; they were calm and moved like a machine. There was an electric buzz to their work, but little noise. I heard a sob rise in me and I released it into the quiet. The officer returned quickly and grasped my arm and led me to the grass terrace several feet away from the accident. "You'll have to wait here, ma'am. We're doing all we can right now."

I collapsed onto the dewy grass with Isaac falling down beside me and wrapping his arms around me. I closed my eyes tight and tried to recall what my father had been wearing when I said good night to him, when I last checked on him. It was a little after ten and he was lying on his bed, on top of the sheets and blanket, and staring up at the crack in the ceiling, though I wondered how he had seen it in the dark. I said, "Good night, Dad." I leaned over him and kissed his cheek.

He was quiet and I stood up and was just about to leave when he said, "Piper, do you see the light?"

I assumed he was talking about the visually deafening light the neighbor used when he worked on his motorcycle late into the night. I said, "I think that's Mr. Harris, Dad. He'll turn it off soon."

But my father didn't seem to hear me and said something so quietly I had to puzzle over the muffled words until I found a phrase that made sense. "Piper, you just have to look."

I opened my eyes again and I was returned to the scene, not having any better idea what my father was wearing, but I saw something in the street, about thirty feet from the melee. I saw a single charcoal gray men's slipper with red tartan lining and I knew.

My father was killed quickly; the car hit him and threw him into the air so far and high that when his head hit the ground it was over immediately. The driver was a young man heading home after a long shift tending bar. He was speeding, not expecting someone to run into the street at three forty-five in the morning. The Breathalyzer showed that he was just under the legal limit and he admitted he had had one beer with the busboys at the end of the shift. He was devastated, eyes red with crying, apologizing over and over once we were finally allowed near the body. He repeated numerous times that the man had just darted into the street from the park and he'd had no time to stop once he saw him.

I didn't know for a long time what happened to the young man after the police led him away and put him, sobbing, in the back of the police car. Later, one of the officers would phone me and tell me that the man had been given a speeding ticket and charged with reckless driving, but he pled out and received only probation. Several months after the accident, just when I felt calmer and the summer sun had made it impossible many days to lie about in my sorrow, I received a letter in the mail. I recognized the return address from the police report and didn't open it. I put it in my desk drawer and it still sits there, waiting for me to tear it open and unearth the man's apologies.

I don't bear anger toward the driver. I understand that it was an accident, something that might have happened to me or Isaac in some parallel universe. Even Fred holds no ill feelings toward the man and brings him up more than I am comfortable with, just wondering if he still feels bad. The anger came from another place. My anger, which I sat upon, tamped down and restrained, came from the futility of my father's last six months on earth. The futility of a man living a miserable life, beaten down by his disability, tortured by not remembering who he was, deserted by those he thought loved him. These were the things I found it difficult to swallow. Despite Isaac's best efforts and my new attempts at rejecting negativity, I still did not believe that my father went into the lake that spring to save his dog. I believed that I never really knew my father at all.

Piper

My father's funeral was the week after the accident, and the same cast of characters that had clogged up his room in the hospital months earlier telling Polish jokes and comparing golf scores reappeared through the doors of the funeral home, serious and sweating in suit coats. They had been absent for months, busy during the difficult times and now suddenly contrite. My mother stood next to me in the receiving line and I found it still difficult to face her. I had called Curtiss and expected him to come, but his flight from Chicago had been canceled and he was driving up with Daniel and would make the last half of the visitation. I had been unsure what to do about Fred, if he should be at either the visitation or the funeral or both. I asked him and he said that he would prefer to go to Owen's house for the visitation because he doesn't enjoy conversing with so many strangers and that he would come to the funeral because that's where you are quiet.

I stood in the receiving line and shook countless hands, some dry or slim, some pudgy or warm. I nodded as people reintroduced themselves and shared their memories of my father. Isaac stood next to me and took each hand after me, shook it again, received the introductions and memories anew without complaint. It felt like an interminable amount of time before Curtiss and Daniel finally arrived. Curtiss was dressed in a linen suit and looked young and fashionable, just barely on the edge of mourning. He approached me cautiously; our last conversation had been tight and fraught with harsh words and blame.

He opened his arms to me. "Piper," he said, and I reached for him and we embraced. He smoothed my hair and whispered in my ear, "I'm sorry, Piper. I'm sorry that you had to go through this."

I stayed, protected in my big brother's arms, for a long time. I finally pulled away from him to see I had left a wet spot on his previously pristine suit. "I'm sorry, Curtiss," I said as I vainly tried to wipe away the blemish.

He waved my concern away and took his place beside me in the line. Daniel started to step away, but Isaac reached out to him and stepped over, leaving him a place in the receiving line next to Curtiss.

We stood next to each other, shoulder to shoulder, and when the stream of mourners slowed I felt the need to share my new understanding of my feelings for my father. I said quietly, "Curtiss, he changed. He was a different man after his heart attack. He wasn't the same at all. I don't even think he remembered how he used to be."

"I know, Piper. He called me late at night. It must have been after you were asleep, just a few days ago. He apologized."

"For what?" I asked.

"For cutting my hair," he said.

I was shaken, stunned and saddened at the same time. I had not received an apology for anything. The line kept moving and the visitors didn't stop until the funeral director announced that the visitation was over.

That night we retrieved Fred from Owen's house and he regaled us with dinosaur facts that would have surprised a paleontologist. We tucked him into bed with his ragged hedgehog and Chuck Yeager, who didn't seem to be in mourning at all. Then Isaac and I sat on the deck and shared a bottle of red wine; though the humidity begged for a white, I needed the thick warmth of red blocking out the choke of sadness. I told Isaac about Curtiss, about my father's apology and their conversations about the past. I lamented to him my disappointment that my father had not atoned for his sins against me.

"Piper, maybe his whole last six months were his apology to you," Isaac said.

"That makes no sense, Isaac," I said, already starting to feel the warmth of the wine spread through my body and slow down my busy brain.

"Think about what a good friend he was to Fred. They were friends, Piper. Fred really needed a friend. Maybe that was your father's atonement: taking care of Fred in a way, loving him."

I let myself drift toward those moments I caught myself outside Fred's door, listening to the two of them together. Mostly, it was Fred's voice, but there were those few precious occasions when my father's rich baritone laugh broke through the sad haze of his existence. I considered the hours he had spent with Fred, listening to him orate, never judging him, never criticizing or snapping. There was one particular time that struck me suddenly as so much more meaningful than it had at the time. I stood outside Fred's door with a pile of folded towels in my arms. I had come upstairs and heard Fred ask a question.

"Grandpa, you are a grown-up man and I am a boy but someday I think I will be a grown-up man too. What is it about? Being a man." It must have been when he and Isaac were busy planning their day out, the day that would lead to so much heartache.

My father was silent for a while, but I stood there waiting, never doubting that he would answer Fred's question. Then he said, "Being a man is about taking care of people."

Fred said, "I am worried that I won't have anyone to take care of. I do not have a lot of people that want to be with me, Fred."

I bit my tongue; I longed to run into the room and take my son in my arms and kiss away his fears. I stopped myself, though, and I was glad I did.

"I want to be with you, Fred. You take care of me," my father said.

I thought about what Isaac said for a long time, until my head buzzed with alcohol and his words had lost their meaning. I looked up at the night sky. I found the North Star, Orion's belt and Jupiter. I decided I would accept my father's apology.

Fred

Today is the day of my grandpa's funeral. I have not been to a funeral before so I asked Mom what to expect and she told me all the things about it that I needed to know. I said Mom it sounds kind of like a sort of show on a stage with talking and music and then a party afterward except that instead of being happy at the party everyone is sad because the party is for someone who is dead. She said yes Fred that's basically it and then she hugged me and kissed me on the forehead and I let her. Mom said that people might want to say things at the funeral at a wooden box called a podium and we would listen politely and some of the things might be funny and some of them might be sad. She said they would be things people remembered about Grandpa or ways they felt about him.

I asked Mom if she was going to stand at the wooden box podium to talk about the ways she felt about Grandpa, because she has felt lots of different ways about him including very angry. She said that no she wasn't going to talk at the podium. She asked me if I wanted to talk at the podium but I think she was asking to be polite because she had a very surprised face when I said yes Mom I would like to speak at the podium with a microphone at the funeral about Grandpa. She said oh Fred. Well lots of people would be listening you know and I said yes you already told me that. I have some things that I would say about Grandpa into a microphone for people to hear. She wore her concerned face but she said okay Fred and then later I heard her ask Dad if he thought it was a good idea or possibly traumatic to my development as a person. He said no if Fred wants to do it then he should and then he hugged her and both of their faces were relaxed. That was nice because I am tired of tight mad faces and loose sad faces around here.

There are a lot of things that I would like to tell people about my grandpa:

My grandpa is a man named Lance Whitman who used to be a pilot but now he's dead. When I was little my grandpa wanted to teach me everything about airplanes because he knew a lot about them and had a lot to teach. Because I was just a kid I stopped getting interested in airplanes and got interested in some other stuff instead and then we didn't talk so much but we were still both Whitmans.

Then my grandpa had a heart attack and he had to go to the hospital and they thought he was going to die, but he didn't die and then he came to live with us because his brain was a little bit damaged. Even though his brain was damaged that is when my grandpa and I got to be friends. He brought along his dog Chuck Yeager and that dog and I really hit it off. At first my grandpa didn't want to talk much and he wore a sad, wrinkled face all the time. Lots of times we just sat together in my room with Chuck Yeager and I talked to him all about my life. After a while, Grandpa started to talk again and we could have a conversation instead of a speech by me, Fred. Do you know what my grandpa liked to talk about more than anything? He liked to talk about flying an airplane. When he talked about flying an airplane his eyes got more blue and his sad wrinkles smoothed out. He could look out the window at the sky and tell me all about what it was like to fly a plane. Lots of times he told me the same stuff about flying a plane over and over, but that was okay with me because he was wearing a peaceful face.

I had a dream the night my grandpa died that I was in a plane crash. It was a very bad one and there was lots of rubble and twisted metal all around and I could hear people crying out for help and the air was filled with dust and smoke and I was very scared in my dream because I am just a kid in real life and in dreams. But then someone came and took my hand and held it tight and it was my grandpa and he helped me up and we walked down the aisle of the crashed plane toward the place where there was a big hole, like the plane just got ripped in half and there was lots of bright light. And we got to the edge, right at the edge and there was bright light all around, almost too bright to see and my grandpa looked at me and said are you ready Fred and I said ready for what and he said ready to fly and I nodded and he held my hand tight and we jumped into the bright light and we flew.

One time I asked my grandpa how did a man act because it was something that I was thinking about a lot and when I think about things like that I need to have an answer before I can stop the thinking. He told me that you have to take care of people. My grandpa didn't always know how to take care of people, but he learned. I think I helped teach him.

Piper

After the funeral and Curtiss's short stay with us, my mother cleaned out the house on Mohawk Drive. She decided that she was building a kind of new beginning in Saint Paul and wanted to continue. At one time, I would have been devastated to lose her, but my relationship with her had changed. I had seen things about her I wished I hadn't. I had learned that the woman I held in my mind as strong and brave had a weakness I wasn't sure I could forgive her for. My feelings on the issue continued to evolve, changing frequently depending on my mood and memories. I found myself digging through the pile of what-ifs often. What if she hadn't left him? Would his life have ended the same way? Would his recovery have been different? These were, of course, futile games I played, for there were no answers. There were only the events that had transpired, now committed to history. There was the fact that on my best days I understood and forgave my mother, with a Zen-like peace. There was also the fact that on my worst I blamed her for everything that came after she walked out of the hospital on that cold December morning.

Before she left for Saint Paul again on a humid

June afternoon, right before the school year ended, she stopped by the house unannounced with a box. We sat on the deck with Chuck Yeager sunbathing at our feet and for a long time neither of us said anything. It was one of my better days and the fact that she was leaving brought up a sort of regretful sadness. Not regret that I could have done things differently, but regret over the whole mess life had handed us to wrestle into submission.

Finally, she spoke. "Piper, this is a box of your school things, papers and so forth."

"I thought you'd already given me all the boxes with my stuff like that."

"Well, I didn't know we had this one. I found it in the closet of your father's office. These are things he saved, things you did or made. I thought you might like to have them," she said. She pushed the box toward me and I took hold of it and pulled it onto my lap.

"Your father did love you, Piper. In his way, he did. Even if he never got up the courage to tell you so." I thought then of his kind words to Fred, his patience and understanding.

I nodded and bit the inside of my lip, unsure how to proceed, not in anger, but in a last-ditch attempt to understand. I still wanted to know, even this late in the game, even as the game, as it were, was over. I said, "When you came here, on the day of the party, the day before he died, didn't you see he wasn't right? Didn't you notice how sad he was?" The tears welled up in my eyes.

"Piper, I did see. I did notice. I asked him to come and live at the house again. I begged him. He said no. He didn't want to leave, Piper," she said, her voice rasping with the need to be heard.

She reached out for my hand and I looked down at it. Her hand was smaller than I remembered, the skin papery and dry. I imagined holding her hand as a child and the feeling of not only security but tranquility. I recalled reaching for her hand and inexplicably it always seemed to be there, reaching back. I took her hand in mine. We had both changed; I was no longer certain in my role as child. I had mothered my own father when his wife could not. I felt that the balance between us had shifted and our relationship would have to find a new course to travel if it were to thrive again.

My mother left with the promise that she would be back to visit in July, stay with us and spend time with Fred. After she left, I decided I was finally ready to tackle cleaning out my office, remove whatever was left of my father's paltry belongings and wipe the dust from the surfaces that had been ignored since before his death. I kept the door closed and out of habit I knocked lightly before I opened it. I expected, in some delusional and misguided way, to find my father lying on the futon, dressed in sweatpants and tube socks, staring at the ceiling, but when I opened the door it was only a musty smell and dust particles drifting through the sunlight.

The room stank, not of any dirt or grime, but of the profundity of one human's despair. Inside that room my father's sadness was palpable; it was like the ever-present humidity on an August afternoon. I could feel it sticking to the back of my neck and my forearms, making me itch to wash it away in the cool aqua water of the local swimming pool. I moved around the room, opening drawers that he had never really needed anyway, looking for some small token left behind. A token of what I didn't know, just something to prove to myself that he had been alive in this room. The drawers were mostly empty and in the closet I found a few lonely metal hangers clanking together. I got down on my hands and knees to look under the futon. There were dusty clumps of Chuck Yeager's fur and one worn sweat sock. As I reached into the dust and hair to pull out the sweat sock, I noticed that there was something else, a sheet of paper that seemed to be stuck between the wall and the futon mattress. I stood up again and fished my hand down into the tight area, scratching my knuckles on the sharp texture of the drywall. I pulled my hand back out and found one of my father's drawings. I sat down on the floor and studied the large piece of wrinkled sketch-pad paper, one edge ragged from being torn from its spiral binding. I fully expected to see another one of my father's renditions of the crack in the ceiling, but this was different.

Rather than one strong line with a definite path, this drawing was a collection of lines, bumps and rises that at first made no sense to me. It could have been a hilly moraine, covered with the short, rough pencil strokes of grassy fields. I closed my eyes and opened them again, willing myself to see the sketch differently this time. Now the lines came into focus and I could see a very close-up drawing of a hand, so large many of its fingertips went off the paper's edge. But the rises and valleys were the knuckles, the long, straight lines the fingers themselves, and the all-over texture seemed to be the tiny lines and patterns of the skin. His hand. No. I scrutinized it, feeling deep down that I was missing something. There, on two of the rises of the knuckles, there were two definite smooth areas, small ovals with no lines or textures. Scars.

I looked down at my own hands. There it was on my left hand—all that was left of a horrible spill I took in the third grade. I had scraped my knuckles down to the bone and sat in shock the entire bus ride, staring at my own bones, a part of myself I had never seen, always covered and protected. When I got home I calmly showed my mother, who wanted to take me to the emergency room, but my dad strode over and took my small hand in his large one and declared it a minor injury that would heal on its own. He clapped me on the back and went on his way. I couldn't believe I was supposed to walk around that way, with fresh air lapping at my bones, my insides wide-open for all to see. It did heal after a few weeks, leaving behind two small oval scars. They hadn't been as noticeable when I was a child, but now as my hands wrinkled and aged, those two spots of smooth pale skin stood out, a reminder that sometimes what's on the inside shows.

I thought of all the time I had spent with my father in the months that he lived with us, more than in my entire life previous to his heart attack. All that time I thought he was empty inside, a shell, a person-shaped container that held only what was necessary to physically function and none of what was needed to feel and love. But here I held proof that he was feeling something, noticing me. Not just me as a caretaker and domestic, but he was seeing me as an intricate collection of rises, valleys, hurts and healing.

I stood over the futon and saw a very faint but definite imprint of my father's body on the mattress. I lay down carefully in the imprint, not wanting to soften its edges for fear the last of his physical form would escape back into the ether. I lay where he lay, my head on his pillow, and the greasy-hair smell of a dirty pillowcase surrounding me. I closed my eyes and tried to imagine what it was like for him. Losing who you are, losing those you loved. I did not like the man my father was before his heart attack, but he was a man of purpose and conviction, a man with talents and beliefs and confidence, swagger even. Though his heart attack did not take his life, it had seemed to me that it took all the parts of him that were alive. But then I looked down at my left hand and those silver ovals of scar shone back at me and I wondered in that second if I had been wrong.

I opened my eyes, and they focused on the crack in the ceiling, the crack my father must have known intimately. I traced its origin and its journey from one wall to the other. I followed its meanderings and tributaries. I saw it so clearly in that instant; I saw both its power and its restraint. I closed my eyes again and saw my father's profile in the sun, the afternoon of Fred's party, the last day of his life. I thought about what he had told Fred about being a man, how I had at first reacted with contempt. What did he know about taking care of people? He had learned, though; he had learned to love and care. He had shown Fred such love. He had rushed into the lake to save his flailing dog, hadn't he?

I opened my eyes again and once again saw the jagged line of the crack. It had been there for years, maybe even longer than my father; I had no way of knowing for certain. In the end, though, the house still stood, despite it. Or perhaps, I mused, because of it.

I noticed it, Dad. I stopped and I looked and I understood it, and then I carried on.

Acknowledgments

Writing a book, fiction especially, with its lack of field experts and interviewees, can be a lonely endeavor. The fiction writer is trapped inside a world of her own creation, spending hours with imaginary people. When you set out to write a book, you cannot foresee the amount of time you will spend inside your own head, solving problems alone, puzzling through thickets of plot and character so dense you often wonder what the hell you've gotten yourself into. The bright light at the end of the tunnel is the finished manuscript, but there are bright lights along the way as well. The bright lights are those friends and family members, colleagues and critics, who will not allow you to tread down that tunnel without holding your hand, working out solutions over french fries and Diet Coke, reading and rereading with careful commentary each and every time, holding up thick-markered signs that read "You can do it!" and leading you right up to the bright light of a happy ending.

The bright lights along my tunnel have been many, as the tunnel has been long indeed. I never would have taken that first step without the wise guidance and sharp eye of Susanna Daniel at the

Madison Writers' Studio. I would easily have stopped walking and turned around completely in the early days of that journey without the companionship of the Septemberists: Curt Hanke, Rudy Koshar, Charity Eleson, William Lewis and Paul Waldhart. A special thank-you to Curt Hanke, who believed in this book so passionately that he was ready to add a publishing imprint to his advertising firm to publish it if no one else would. Your friendship and honest critiques throughout the entire process have been priceless.

I've been lucky for the past nine years of my writing life to have surrounded myself with readers and friends who will happily read whatever I lay down in front of them and provide support, solutions and stress relief when needed. My original writing partner and reader, Susan Gloss . . . how I've loved batting ideas back and forth with you over the past seven years; I literally wouldn't be here today without your help. My beta Amys: Amy Cartwright and Amy Fewel, who looked at me over pizza and said, "This is the one." A hug and a thank-you to the amazing spirit of Shelley Savage Caw, for her longtime support and friendship as well as for her creation of the greatest stress relief ever: Thursday Night Art Nite (love to the Art Nite Ladies—Shelley, Gretchen, Joy, Gina and Ruby—who keep me sane and let me swear up a storm when I burn myself over and over with a hot-glue gun). Discussing the writing process and life in general has been a wonderful perk of living across the street from Sally Jerney. Thank you for your cheerleading and friendship. Another thanks to my amazing coteachers at New Morning Nursery School, who have always supported my dream and made my "other" job so wonderful and fulfilling. They are truly a special bunch of women. And the best next-door neighbor, advocate, reader and friend a woman could ask for: Courtney Klaus, who will be signing acknowledgment pages in her newfound fame.

I'm not sure whether the right words even exist to express my supreme thanks and adoration for my agent, Christina Hogrebe of the Jane Rotrosen Agency, who rocked my world with one e-mail and set the wheels of my publishing dreams in motion. I admire her enthusiasm and persistence, along with her sense of humor and overwhelming kindness. I'm so glad you sat in the parking garage with my manuscript for hours on that April day; working with you is a true joy. Thanks also to Danielle Sickles, Global Rights Director at JRA, for giving this book wings to travel the world.

At Berkley, I have special thanks for the passionate and focused Kate Seaver, who is truly the editor that writers dream about. The first time we spoke on the phone, I knew immediately that you appreciated my little book and had the same big dreams for it that I did. Another thank-you to Christine Ball for her continued advocacy, from the early days right up to the finish line. It's a privilege to work with you.

A thank-you to my parents, Jan and Linda Brown, and my sister, Tiffany Horrigan, who have believed it would happen eventually for a very long time. Thanks for your patience. Wherever my grandma Lois is right now, I know she's smiling, because she predicted my success in grade three, when I created the pencil-and-crayon *The Leprechaun's Gold*. Much gratitude as well to my second family: Wes Anderson and the Busateris (special shout-out to Julia, who's getting a much earlier start than I did). I only wish Margaret were here to share in our joy and celebration.

Though writing is a lonely job, as I sit at my desk and type I'm often surrounded by people asking for crackers and homework help—my three children. Bode, Sawyer and Shepard, you are my heart, and I thank you for your patience and pride. You are all special young men destined for great things, and extra thanks for leaving me alone when I have important phone calls.

Last and by no means least, the love of my life, Tom. You have believed in me every step of this very long journey and have nurtured and helped to grow my dreams as if they were your own (even as I ran around slashing dreams left and right). You have held my hand with every step and infused the entire trip with light, warmth and love. I adore you.

Center Point Large Print
600 Brooks Road / PO Box 1
Thorndike, ME 04986-0001 USA

(207) 568-3717

US & Canada:
1 800 929-9108
www.centerpointlargeprint.com